MURDERS AT THE HARMONY HOLLOWS RESORT

A PRUNELLA PEARCE MYSTERY

BOOK FOUR

GINA KIRKHAM

Happy Reading! Gina x

BLOODHOUND
BOOKS

First published in 2024 by Bloodhound Books.

www.bloodhoundbooks.com

Print ISBN: 978-1-917214-75-9

To my wonderfully handsome and very debonair brother,
Andy Dawson

For 63 years of me coming second...
... and never getting the first slice of mum's strawberry shortcake!

PROLOGUE

JUNE 1998

The barre dug deep into Elodie Marshall's ribs, forcing a rush of air to unexpectedly expel from her lungs, and the arabesque that she had fought so hard to attain suddenly became an inelegant jumble of legs and arms. As if choreographing themselves to co-ordinate, the loud groan that escaped her lips was paired with an equally loud thud, as she hit the suspended floor of the dance studio, bottom first.

Giselle Moreau clapped her hands together, not in applause but to chastise the rest of the giggling students in her ballet class. Their laughter had barely ceased as she spoke. 'Mes chers, mirth at the expense of another's misfortune is not how we do things at Cragstone Manor Academy.' She waved her hand. 'Class dismissed!'

Giselle's French accent wrapped warmly around Elodie. She admired Giselle to the point of hero worshipping her. This woman was everything she aspired to be; she sometimes wondered if maybe she was just a little in love with her, too. She wasn't just her teacher; she was also her muse and protector.

'I'm okay...' Elodie quickly offered, keen to hide her embarrassment and the tears that now stung her eyes, as she vainly fought to keep hold of them whilst the only too familiar muffled sniggers echoed around the room. She knew the others thought of her as the class clown, the weirdo. She was the girl nobody would voluntarily choose to be friends with.

Elodie was the one student at Cragstone Manor who couldn't dance, couldn't act and, as the final nail in the coffin, couldn't sing. She was in fact devoid of any stage presence at all. Her only talent was a freakishly unnatural strength that belied her small stature, and one that had bestowed upon her the unflattering nickname of 'Pansy Potter' from the Beano comics. It was most certainly not the type of CV to showcase to the world when you had spent the best part of your childhood and teenage years in a theatre and arts school as the token 'famous name' pupil.

She was pretty sure her thespian parents didn't expect great things from her either, for her to follow in their footsteps by dipping her toes into the family talent pool. She knew she'd barely make a ripple; let alone the great waves they had done with their Golden Globes and Oscars. No. This place was just somewhere convenient and befitting of the family name to dump her as they travelled the world, whilst simultaneously distancing themselves from her, and hiding her from public view – because she hadn't quite turned out as they had hoped.

If Elodie was honest with herself, she wasn't actually good at anything. Something her parents were only too keen to impart to her with a regular monotony, combined with what they viewed as harmless teasing. Only it wasn't – harmless that is.

She utilised her towel to surreptitiously wipe away her tears under the guise of ridding herself of after-class sweat. Hastily packing her dance bag with her spare pointes and a half-drunk bottle of water, she listened to her classmate's inane chatter as they made their way out of the studio and down the stairs ahead of her. Their words hurt, they made her feel worthless, and their echoing laughter made her feel small.

'Dépêche-toi, Elodie.' Giselle ushered her out of the studio, her hand pressed against the small of Elodie's back, gently pushing her through the doors to join the others. They rattled firmly shut behind her, leaving her standing alone in the corridor, the lilting voice of Giselle echoing within the studio walls being the only sound that broke through the silence.

'Je désespère, I really do!' Giselle addressed the academy pianist, who mischievously tinkled the ivories of the grand piano in response to the teacher's frustration.

'Bleedin' hell, she's got two left feet that one, and she's definitely not quite right in the head...'

Elodie pressed her ear against the oak wood of the door and listened. She didn't recognise that voice at all; it was raw and quite common, but she was in no doubt the comment was about her. Hearing the short burst of laughter that followed the cruel jibe, her heart thudded painfully in her chest.

'Please say something, Miss, stick up for me...' The words were in her head, but her lips silently mimed them.

She held her breath, waiting for Giselle to defend her.

'If it wasn't for the fees her parents pay, plus having the kudos of their name associated with us, I'd be inclined to call it a day. I don't know how many more bloody hours I can waste teaching her, she's as clumsy as a cow on ruddy roller skates. Take it from me, a modern-day Margot Fonteyn she ain't...'

Elodie slumped heavily against the wall, pressing her free hand hard against her mouth to suppress the sob that bubbled up in her throat. There wasn't a trace of a foreign accent now, not French or language from any other exotic location for that matter, but there was no mistaking that it had come from the mouth of her idol.

She had just been brutally betrayed by the one person she trusted.

Giselle.

The rattle of the doors as they opened, accompanied by the hiss of the pneumatic closing system startled her. Desperate not to be seen, to be discovered eavesdropping, Elodie squeezed herself behind the bank of lockers. She held her breath fearing it would expose her, but this action just caused her frantic heartbeat to pulsate loudly in her ears.

Boom.

Boom.

Boom.

Her hands quickly covered her ears to halt what she feared was their speaker-like effect, as Giselle swept past her, oblivious to her hiding place. Elodie watched her glide effortlessly across the floor towards the stairs. She paused momentarily on the galleried landing of Cragstone Manor, its intricately carved oak rails casting playful shadows across the blue-grey carpet, backlit from the last of the afternoon sun that shone through the leaded light windows. Elodie watched the fine dust motes float haphazardly into the air in Giselle's wake, like lazy fireflies. Giselle leant over the rich wood, her hands caressing the banister rail as she looked down onto the entrance hall to the horde of chattering, giggling students below.

She dramatically rolled her eyes in annoyance. 'Mes chers, enough of the dilly and the dallying, make your way to the dining room, please!' She watched them intently. 'Vite, vite...'

The French accent that Elodie had so loved had returned, but it now grated on every nerve her body possessed, fuelling the burning sense of betrayal that gnawed at the pit of her stomach. She silently inched her way forward, hands outstretched, and just as Giselle had only moments before used her hands to gently persuade her charge to leave the studio, Elodie now reached out to guide Giselle to her own destination.

She felt the warmth of Giselle's skin arcing the short distance to bathe her palm as her muscles tensed ready. 'Au revoir, bitch...' Elodie whispered as she relished the power that surged along her arms and tingled out through her fingers. 'Let justice begin...'

Giselle heard the hushed goodbye just a fraction before she felt the powerful thump to the middle of her back, causing her breath to be momentarily caught and stilled, before the momentum pushed her over the banister. As the rail bit painfully into her stomach, jerking her forwards, her fingers frantically scrabbled for anything that would stop her fall. She caught and clutched one of the spindles, feeling the bite against the skin of her hand as she tipped over into the void.

'Please, no...' Giselle moaned, her eyes simultaneously holding fear and sadness as they briefly met Elodie's own hard, unyielding gaze. 'Please...'

Elodie watched as one by one Giselle's fingers lost their grip until she was left to face the inevitable. Giselle had no saviour and no amount of pleading would change her fate.

She was falling.

Falling, twisting and floating – just like the specks of dust she had left behind.

Down...

Down...

Down.

Miss Giselle Moreau, dancer, teacher, mentor and, most recently, traitor, lay in a crumpled heap on the black and white chequered tiles of Cragstone Manor like a grotesque rag doll, accompanied by an audience of those students who had stubbornly failed to obey her earlier instruction, and were now standing open-mouthed in horror. Too afraid to speak, too shocked to scream, mesmerised by the motionless body of their teacher.

Elodie looked down on her handiwork, a wry smile playing upon her lips as she took in the twisted, bent and broken legs of the once beautiful ballerina, a pool of crimson blood slowly fanning out from her golden tresses to become a halo.

A halo for a fallen angel.

'Oh gosh, it would appear my dear Miss Moreau is not as supple as I first thought!' she whispered as she giggled. A maniacal glint briefly touched her pale blue eyes before her mind, pushed to screaming, plunged into the darkness, finally allowing the madness to take her. Flinging her dance bag over her shoulder, Elodie Marshall grinned, then silently skipped across the atrium, opened a door that bore an elaborately decorated plate announcing the staircase to the turrets and disappeared...

'Stab the body and it heals but injure the heart and the wound lasts a lifetime...'

— Mineko Iwasaki

FRUGAL FINDS

PRESENT DAY

The little brass bell of Frugal Finds tinkled savagely as the door was exuberantly thrown open to allow the posse of ladies to spill in over its threshold. Miriam Howard, the proprietor of Winterbottom's newly opened second-hand shop, rubbed her hands together in glee. Pushing a stray curl of greying hair behind her ear, she stood tall and expectant at the highly polished glass counter, her notepad and pencil perfectly positioned and her vintage Victorian till ready and waiting for the pennies that would hopefully come her way.

'Morning, ladies!' she trilled.

'Morning, Mim, we've come to grab ourselves a bargain; our Pru said you've got some nice stuff in.' Clarissa Montgomery, stalwart member of the Winterbottom Women's Institute, eternal spinster, one quarter of the notorious Four Wrinkled Dears and an all-round mischief-maker, ushered her friend in ahead of her. 'Come along, Millie, you're causing a bottleneck. Poor Brenda is still wedged between Bob's delivery bike and the recycling bin outside!' She placed both hands on Millie Thomas's back and shoved her forwards. As Millie was inelegantly propelled into the display that housed several worn and crumpled leather handbags, the space she left behind produced the desired effect at the door. Poor Brenda Mortinsen's well rounded body shot through the gap like a champagne cork, closely followed by Ethel Tytherington and Kitty Hardcastle.

'Morning, everyone; it looks like I've arrived...' Brenda laughed as she picked herself up from the floor. She checked the knees of her stockings for damage and then vigorously brushed down her skirt. 'I'm hoping to find a nice summer frock, the warm weather is on its way and I need something cool and floaty.'

'You're in the wrong shop then, Brenda, you need Millington's Outdoor Pursuits in Chapperton Bliss; they do a nice line in tents...' Ethel sniggered, whilst admiring the ample curves that Brenda had cultivated through her love of bakery products.

'Ethel! That's quite enough,' barked Kitty. Although she was the past president of the Winterbottom WI, she still felt it was her role to chastise and keep her friends in check. Her legendary '*Ladies, please!*' when the gang became a little too exuberant for Kitty's liking was guaranteed to bring them all to heel.

Ethel snorted her dissatisfaction loudly at being chastised. 'I'm sixty-seven years old, Kitty, I'm not a child, you know!'

Clarissa quickly interrupted. 'Seventy-one...'

'Seventy-one what?' Ethel plonked a rather fetching straw hat on her head and turned to give her friends her best angle, the sunflower attached to the yellow band dropped down over her nose and swung from side to side like a metronome.

'You're seventy-one years old, Ethel. Knocking twelve months off, you can get away with, but four years? I don't think so.' Clarissa buttoned up the pale blue cardigan she had taken from a nearby rail and admired herself in the mirror.

Kitty shrugged off her outerwear and took the opportunity to disappear into the curtained-off cubicle to try on the sequinned blouse she had found on the bargain rail. She loved how the lighting bounced off the gloriously shiny discs, giving rise to a myriad of colours on the wall. It reminded her of the youth club discothèques of her teenage years.

Miriam watched the group of ladies excitedly searching through the rails whilst imparting local gossip and teasing each other mercilessly. She loved it when they descended upon her, and their collective friendship warmed her heart. She grabbed a spare coat hanger and began to follow them around the shop, prepared to tidy up in their wake.

Summer coats were tried on and then just as quickly discarded, draped over the chairs and counter. Cardigans were buttoned up, buttoned down and sleeves adjusted before being exchanged for a blouse, and feet were squeezed into shoes that were too small. It was chaos, but a lovely chaos all the same.

'Oh my goodness, I love it!' Ethel beamed with excitement as she checked out the rather fetching three-quarter sleeved navy-blue jacket that was draped over the end of the free-standing rail in the middle of the shop. Her fingers caressed the brass buttons and smoothed out the silk lining. She slipped her arms into the sleeves, shrugged the shoulders into place and stood at a jaunty angle. It fitted her to perfection. 'What do you think?'

Clarissa had to admit it did look rather smart on her friend. It was almost new and obviously a quality garment. 'It looks lovely on you, Eth, perfect. Are you going to get it?'

Ethel nodded excitedly. In the absence of a price ticket, she presented the jacket to Miriam, who, puzzled, checked her stock list. 'I don't know how I've managed to miss this one when I was pricing up...' She dropped her glasses to the end of her nose. 'Shall we say £5.00?'

Before anyone could say 'Jack Robinson', Ethel had whipped out a fiver and exchanged it for her bargain find that was now ensconced in a carrier bag that bore the logo of The Guilty

Grape off-licence. Clarissa had decided the cardigan wasn't quite to her taste and Brenda had tried but failed to squeeze into a rather fetching floral frock. Millie clutched a pair of white Clarks sandals under her arm as Miriam's till merrily rang out her takings from the ladies.

'Right, how about tea and a cake at Florrie's? My mouth's that dry I'm spitting feathers, and I've got some rather good suggestions for our WI days out to put to the vote.' Clarissa made her way to the door. 'Kitty dear...' she hollered back into the shop.

A muffled response came from behind the curtain. 'I won't be a minute.'

'Okay, we're just popping to the Twisted Currant Café; join us there if you fancy a brew.'

The brass bell tinkled a little less savagely this time. The ladies had sated their desire for bargains and were now able to leisurely amble along the High Street to Florrie's café. Miriam watched them chattering ten to the dozen as they passed by her window, her attention only broken by the vigorous swish of the metal curtain rings on the brass pole of the dressing room as Kitty emerged triumphant with her blouse.

'Wrap this for me, please, Miriam.' Kitty excitedly delved into her purse and slapped a note onto the counter before circling the shop. She checked the rails, then turned her attention to the chairs. As a last resort, she checked the floor.

'Miriam, dear, you haven't seen my navy-blue jacket, have you? It's three-quarter length with little brass buttons down the front...'

A WRINKLE IN TIME...

Prunella Pearce chased the last sultana from her morning muesli around the bowl with her spoon. When all efforts to capture it failed, she resorted to using her fingers. Popping it into her mouth with a touch of glee, she executed a lap of the kitchen table punching her fist wildly into the air, much like a footballer would after scoring a goal. She suddenly caught her reflection in the mirror.

Seriously, Pru... over a sultana? Girl, get a grip; you definitely need to get out more!

Picking at bits of squished dried fruit from her front teeth, she studied her reflection more closely. 'Dear Lord, when did they arrive?' She traced the creases at the side of her eye with her fingertip. 'Wrinkles! I've got bloody wrinkles, Binks!' She looked to her midnight-black cat who was hunched on the back of the sofa for some form of support and comfort. None was forthcoming. He gazed at her intently with his huge copper-coloured eyes before he lazily elongated his body and slid down onto the cushion. Scrunching her nose, she lifted first one eyebrow and then the other. When that failed to give the desired effect, she plumped for the finger and thumb solution, stretching the delicate skin of her lids, she pulled out and upwards and pursed her lips.

'I've got it in one, it's Cruella De Vil, isn't it?'

Startled, Pru knocked the floor lamp with her elbow. It wobbled slightly and then rattled back into its original resting place, leaving the shade askew. 'Jeez, Andy, have you got an insurance policy out on me?' She patted her chest to prove to him that his sudden appearance had surprised her. 'I've got wrinkles...' she wailed. 'We've been married barely eighteen months, and already I'm becoming Whistler's mother!' She sighed loudly as she plonked herself down on the sofa. 'Before you know it, it'll be rampant chin and nose hair!'

Andy grabbed a piece of toast from the plate on the table and checked that the thin layer of marmalade reached all four corners. 'Pull a nose one out and you'll know about it; it's bloody agony.'

'Really?' Pru grimaced, wondering how hairy his nostrils actually were and why she had never noticed them wafting in the breeze when she kissed him. 'How many have you actually pulled out to know that, then?'

'None of my own, but judging by the reaction of the guy asleep next to me on the bus, it seemed pretty painful!' Andy laughed loudly at his own joke and gave her his best flirty smile, hoping for one in return to lift her mood. 'Aww come on, my little turnip, just look on the bright side, I'm older than you, so although your looks are fading...' he bit into the toast and licked his lips, '...so is my eyesight! That works pretty well for both of us, wouldn't you say?' He waited with bated breath, struggling to find the next words that might safely leave his lips.

Pru's eyes widened, then just as quickly squinted. Her lips set in a thin line.

'I've just blown it, haven't I?' Andy hunched his shoulders up to his ears in contrition. 'Erm... what I meant was...'

Pru threw her hand up, palm facing him. 'Just leave it there, Andy, there's no point in digging that hole any deeper! Actually, changing the subject and talking about digging holes, have they said who is being seconded to the Brimstage murder case?' She secretly crossed her fingers in the hope that it wouldn't be him. Having a hubby who was a detective sergeant in the Winterbridge CID made for frequent trips to other forces to assist with major incidents. The only compensation for his absence if he was seconded was that it would give her the opportunity to not just paddle in the puddle of her beloved books and authors, but to dive headfirst and devote every waking moment to them. As the Winterbottom librarian at the little village library shop, this was her world when Andy wasn't around. Reading books, cataloguing books, sniffing pages, caressing covers, stroking spines and offering advice and suggestions to her regular customers, was her joy.

She did miss Andy terribly when he was away, but had quickly learnt to accept that this was part of being a police officer's wife, and she did have other strings to her bow to keep herself occupied in his absence on the days she wasn't needed at the library. Her best friend and fellow gin aficionado, Bree Richards, had encouraged her to set up The Curious Curator and Co Detective Agency. Their mutual love of mystery and mayhem had already given them a few narrow escapes with their part-time venture, but their enthusiasm was just as passionate now as it had been at the beginning.

Andy shrugged his arms into his jacket and adjusted his tie, patting it down so it sat neatly against his white shirt. 'Nope, we've not heard anything yet. It's a puzzling one for Nether Wallop, though. They still haven't recovered all the body parts; it looks like they've had a frenzied game of Whack-A-Mole at the scene; they've dug more holes than Hilda Jones has in her 80-denier stockings!'

Pru sniggered. Poor Hilda's winter hosiery had been the source of much amusement at the last Winterbottom Women's Institute meeting. Pru was their current president and had been called upon to restore order when Hilda had wandered in wearing faded tights that looked as though they'd been savaged by a cheese grater. 'Aww bless her, she just got a little confused, that's all. It did give everyone a bit of a giggle, though.'

Absent-mindedly searching for his car keys, Andy grunted his agreement. 'A little confused! Who on earth puts their underwear in a salad spinner with two capfuls of neat bleach?'

'She thought it was fabric conditioner...' Pru handed him the keys she had just found down the back of the sofa cushion. 'Not sure about the salad spinner, though.'

He gave her a mischievous look. 'Mmm... who knows what the senior members of Winterbottom village get up to behind closed doors, eh?' He wrapped his arms around her waist and planted a kiss on her nose. 'I know I say it every time, but please don't get up to any mischief with Bree today; that woman could lead a nun astray.'

Pru playfully punched him on the chin. 'Nothing so exciting, I'm afraid. Just some background checks for a family who think their eighty-nine-year-old granddad's twenty-seven-year-old fiancée might be after the family fortune.' She gave a wry smile. 'Although why they should think that beats me!'

RELATIVELY RETRO

'Oh for goodness' sake, slow, slow, quick, quick, slow. No, no, Macey – up on the toes and glide before the staccato!' Delphine 'Della' Claybourne, of the Wandering Waltz Dance Studio in Frampton Falls, clucked in frustration as she fussed around her star couple, clapping her hands in time to the beat. She waved dismissively to the pianist to encourage her to cease and desist with her version of the famous tango La Cumparisita.

Macey Griffiths and Tom Birks paused mid-backcross, Tom, opting to finish his sequence with his hands on his hips in mild annoyance, and Macey preferring to examine her fingernails. 'It's been a long day, Della, we're both tired. Don't you think we should call it for today?' Tom haughtily suggested.

Della's cheeks flushed pink, not from exertion, but from the bare-faced audacity of Tom questioning her teaching methods. 'Call it a day? I see, so do you want to call it a day for the Northern Ballroom Championships too? Easily done if you two can't put the effort in, it's no skin off my nose, and it would save me a fortune.'

Tom rolled his eyes. He knew Della would never consider

pulling out of a championship that would offer so much kudos to her dance studio if they were to win. 'The Northerns', as they fondly called it, attracted the crème de la crème of the ballroom dancing world, and the winning studio would be elevated to the legendary 'Glittery Halls of Fame' for all eternity and beyond. The winning name on the trophy was never scratched off or overwritten, nor was it tampered with on the highly polished brass boards at NBC headquarters; although there had been talk of bringing in a new engraver to correct the trophy and plaque that had hung for over fifty years above those revered boards. It still made Tom laugh that a highly intricate and ornate font had become the reason why his male counterparts actively avoided sequinned pants at the annual gala presentations. Being referred to as the next winner and holder of the 'Glittery Balls' trophy ensured they would be on the receiving end of every double entendre going during the weeks that followed.

Seeing no objections to her tart response, but nevertheless feeling a little guilty for her outburst, Della softened. 'Okay, pack up, but back here tomorrow, same time. We've still got a lot of work to put in if we're going to at the very least hope to place in the NBC, let alone win it!'

Macey wiped her forehead with the heel of her hand, brushing a damp curl of hair to one side. 'Have you ever been to this Harmony Hollows place before, Della? Is it really like they say?'

Busying herself with sheet music and files, Della didn't pay much heed, keeping her back to the couple. 'And what *do* they say, my dear?' She stacked the papers together and tamped them down on the desk, ensuring all edges met and were neat.

'That it's like a Butlins holiday camp, akin to something out of the 1960s, all bingo, dingy chalets, soggy chips and knobbly-knees competitions.' Macey waited for confirmation.

Della smiled to herself. That description had evoked so

many fond memories of her own time on the championship circuit. Her mind briefly wandered to her youthful hand holding the key to Chalet 10 at The Harmony Hollows Resort in Nettleton Shrub, a neat little one-bed holiday chalet amongst the row upon row of similarly styled units laid out in avenues. A strip of grass that ran the full length between each row showcased petals of pink, red and orange, the typical summer mix that was popular in the late 1960s, but still remained to this day. The gaiety and simplicity of those times had not been lost on the sixteen-year-old version of herself, nor had the first flush of freedom and, dare she say, decadence. A shudder ran down her spine remembering him, remembering how his steel-grey eyes would flirt with her as they danced to Creedence Clearwater Revival. She involuntarily closed her eyes, almost feeling his breath, hot and...

'Della!'

Startled, she dropped the papers, scattering them across the desk, a few sheets taking the opportunity to escape by wafting on a thermal. 'What, oh... yes, what where you saying?'

Macey gave Tom a conspiratorial smile before she returned her attention to Della. 'I said is it really like a Butlins holiday camp?'

'No, well er... yes, yes, I suppose it is a little. It's had some updating, but there's nothing wrong with places – or people for that matter – being a little bit retro. Now come on, I thought you two wanted to get home.' Della ushered them through the double doors of the studio. 'See you tomorrow, you too, Barbara...' She gave a little thumbs-up to her pianist before closing the doors behind them, leaving her alone in her sanctuary.

She stood in the middle of the room, arms out wide as she pirouetted, feeling the air rush between her fingers.

'Round and round I go, where shall I stop... nobody knows,'

she trilled to herself. Giddy and euphoric, Della staggered towards the small stage and took a bow. 'This is *my* domain...' she declared loudly. 'Everything I have worked for is here, isn't that right?'

She stopped suddenly, a sadness sweeping over her as she remembered that there was, as always, nobody there to answer her, nobody there to confirm or deny that it was her domain, nobody to encourage a conversation, and nobody to cheer on her achievements. If truth be known, there never had been and never would be anyone to share anything in her life. That had been her own prison sentence.

'Nobody...' she whispered as she flicked each light on the circuit board upwards. One by one, each strip light died, and the darkness fell in sections across the sprung wooden floorboards.

Clunk.

Clunk.

Clunk.

Until the blackness reached her.

And then she was gone.

EVERY LITTLE HELPS...

The heavy rain hit the windscreen of Pru's little Fiat 500, causing a curtain of water to roll down in an opaque haze that obscured her view. She shifted uncomfortably in the driver's seat and tried to stretch her legs whilst clenching the muscles in the right side of her bum. The familiar pins and needles that radiated into her thigh told her that it had inconsiderately gone to sleep. She side-eyed Bree, who had also conveniently nodded off, head lolling to one side and mouth gaping. Pru let out a snort of laughter.

'Whaat?' Bree's eyes jerked open. She quickly wiped away the drool from the corner of her mouth. 'What's the matter, has something happened?'

'I've just likened you to my right butt cheek...' Pru delved into her bag, discreetly pushing aside the unopened pregnancy testing kit, her fingers curled around the Twix bar that was nestled underneath it. Unwrapping the bar, she bit into it. Using it as a pointer towards Bree, she examined the rippled chocolate. 'They've shrunk, haven't they? They used to be quite big and chunky.'

'A bit like your right butt cheek, then?' Bree swiftly retorted.

She groaned as she followed the same routine that only minutes before Pru had executed. 'Jeez, my back's in bulk, the pitfalls of surveillance, hey? Is little Miss Gold Digger's visitor still in there?'

Pru allowed the wipers to briefly clear the windscreen. 'I can't use them too much, or it'll be obvious we're parked up and watching. We've got to be careful; if anyone sees us from the house, they might get suspicious, but, yep, he's still in there.'

'Christ on a bike, he must have some staying power then?' Bree grabbed the last Twix from the multi-buy packet. 'Can you imagine having someone in the bedroom department with that sort of athletic prowess to service your every need?'

Pru giggled. 'I have and I do!'

'You tart!' Bree snorted. 'Talking of which, any news on the baby front or are you two just enjoying the practice?'

Pru grinned, her hand subconsciously stroked her tummy as a natural warm glow washed over her. 'You'll be the second to know when there is!'

'You can't leave me hanging like that! You can be such an annoying mare at times, Mrs Barnes.'

Their laughter abated and a comfortable silence enveloped them, broken only by the crinkling of wrappers and muffled crunching from a handful of popcorn. Pru checked her watch. They had observed their target's house for over two hours now. 'Goldie', as they had named her for their notes, had greeted her young male visitor innocently enough at the front door, but had failed to take into account the darkening skies and poor weather, coupled with the sexy neon interior lighting of the front bedroom and a cheap roller blind. Their silhouettes had been lit up like a scene from *Home Alone* as clothing was flung into the air, and Bree's throw away comment that their target was clearly an animal lover judging by the position they were currently engaged in, had Pru choking on the mouthful of coffee she had just slugged back.

Pru yawned loudly. 'D'you know why your eyes water when you yawn?' She used the cuff of her jumper to wipe away the tear that had trickled down her cheek.

'Er... nope, why do your eyes water when you yawn?' Bree tried to sound more interested than she really was.

'It's not a bloody cracker joke, Bree. I don't know. That's why I'm asking you.'

Bree grunted. 'It's not really something I've thought about, to be honest. Look, we've got enough on her for now, how about we take the photographs we need when he leaves, and then we hit the Dog & Gun for a nice bag of crisps?'

A 'bag of crisps' was their codeword for a tipple or two when in the company of others. The last thing Pru needed was for her readers at the Winterbottom library to suddenly look upon her as the village lush each time Bree came bursting through the door, little bell tinkling, to drag her off for a G&T before the sun had gone over the yard arm. She checked her watch for the umpteenth time in as many minutes, a nice cold drink was looking rather favourable at this point in time. Andy wasn't going to be home until late, so it wasn't a hard decision to make.

'Here he comes...' Bree elbowed Pru. She quickly positioned herself with her mobile phone zoomed in on the front door to 12 Augustus Close, whilst Pru simultaneously enabled the windscreen wipers to give a clearer view. Their target and her visitor were locked in an embrace, and it was clear he was going in for the kill. Bree couldn't contain her excitement. 'Ooh it's going to be tongues! Come on, come on, give us a twirl, matey, say cheese...'

Swooooooosh...

Their excitement suddenly gave way to despair.

'You're having a laugh. I know every little helps, but not right now it flamin' doesn't!' Pru slammed her hands onto the steering wheel in frustration as the four tonne Iveco van emblazoned with 'TESCO Freshly clicked' painted along the side, parked in front of them, obstructing their view. As the minutes ticked by and their opportunity to grab the 'money shot' that would prove their case began to slip through their fingers, she grabbed the phone from Bree and jumped out of the car to brave the rain, only to come face to face with their target.

'Been a long day, ain't it, girls? Pity you missed the finale – it was rather tasty.' Goldie smirked and licked her lips. The muted navy-blue commuter umbrella shielding her peroxide locks and hot pink velour tracksuit from the rain, looked oddly out of place.

Pru knew her gaping mouth and startled expression was anything but professional, but she was so stunned to be confronted, she didn't have time to play a game face. She feigned ignorance. 'Sorry, I don't know what you mean?'

'You and her...' Goldie bent down and pointed a taloned finger at Bree who was hunched down in her seat looking out of the side window, desperately trying to appear innocent. 'They put you up to it, didn't they? Well, you can tell his tight-arsed family to wave goodbye to Papa's pennies, I ain't going nowhere!' And with that, Goldie turned heel and flounced back towards her house, pausing long enough to give a flirtatious smile to the Tesco delivery driver that had inadvertently saved the day for her.

Pru was crestfallen as she squeezed herself back into the car. Her mood was not comforted by Bree's uncontrollable laughter.

'Mrs Undercover Detective gets rumbled by Miss Under the Covers Floozy! That's hilarious.' Bree wiped her eyes with the sleeve of her sweatshirt. 'Come on, Dog & Gun it is for two large G&Ts, we need them!'

Pru switched up the heating to clear the windows. 'Make mine a lime and soda, don't think I'm in the mood for a gin...'

Bree gasped. 'Prunella Barnes, are you keeping something from me?'

A wry smile played on Pru's lips as she revved the engine and pulled out into the flow of traffic. 'Watch this space...' she teased.

A RECIPE FOR LOVE

Ethel Tytherington busied herself in her cosy cottage kitchen. Shaking out the damp tea towel, she tested the radiator with her finger and smiled as she hung the cheerfully coloured cloth over the warm metal. Albert, her husband of almost fifty years, hadn't yet checked the thermostat in the hallway, so much to her relief the central heating boiler was still pumping out plenty of heat to keep her fingers and toes toasty. His hatred of '*that infernal money-guzzling piece of tin*' hadn't waned in the slightest since its installation. She had secretly hoped he would have embraced its advantages by now, but all he saw was an extra bill that needed to be paid at the end of a quarter year. A sudden harrumphing and shuffling on the stairs gave her notice that she had perhaps spoken too soon.

'It's a ruddy 28 degrees, Ethel...' Albert, or Albie as she fondly called him, stood in the doorway between hall and kitchen, an aged thermometer declaring itself to be made in Switzerland because it had a little chalet and a few edelweiss flowers painted on it, pinched between his fingers. He flicked the strap on his braces against his crisp white shirt and waited for her response.

Tapping the wooden spoon back into the pan of porridge, she gave him her undivided attention. 'It's not 28 degrees, Albert, it's just a nice pleasant 19 degrees.' She placed two bowls onto the wooden chopping board.

'What does *this* say then?' The thermometer was gently laid onto the worktop for her to see. Albert's gnarled finger excitedly pointed at the red line paused in the glass tube and stood back in triumph. 'See, 28 degrees...'

'Love, it's been showing 28 degrees since 1976, mainly because we broke it in 1976, remember?' She looked at him with her head tilted in anticipation, waiting for the penny to drop, but on seeing his confusion, she felt an overwhelming sense of sadness. Quite often these days, when she could remember important times in their life together, it would appear that those memories had left him. She helped him. 'The heatwave of 1976, Albie...' She gave him a saucy wink. 'Remember?' She plopped out two dollops of the cooked oats into a bowl, sprinkled sugar on the top, added a little milk, and passed it to him.

'Oh, aye, now I do, you were a little tiger that afternoon, Eth... a little tiger!' He smiled at her and planted a kiss on her cheek.

A warmth spread through Ethel's heart. Although he could exasperate the life out of her at times, she loved him dearly, and she had no doubt that she had caused, and still did cause him unintentional strife on many occasions too. The summer of 1976 had been one of heady days, impossible heat, wine and... 'Rumpy-pumpy!' she said out loud, making herself blush.

Albert wiped his mouth with the napkin and allowed the spoon to rattle back into the bowl. 'We knocked it off the wall... and a couple of pictures too. You were mighty frisky that afternoon!'

Ethel closed her eyes, taking her thoughts back to the exact moment the damage had been done. In the midst of their mutual throes of passion, just at the point of no return, her back against the wall, the disapproving eyes of Albert's stern-faced mother had pierced her soul. Marjorie Tytherington had stared back at her from the portrait that had fallen from the wall onto the bedroom carpet, leaving Ethel under no illusion that the old trout would have been tutting loudly if she had been able to. Fortunately, they had buried her the month before, so any tutting Marjorie had felt compelled to do would have drifted only through the afterlife. Nevertheless, Albert had been fortunate enough to escape the mental image of his mother, but Ethel had been forced to endure flashbacks at the most inopportune moments from that day on. Mrs M. Tytherington Senior may have been dead and buried, but she had still acted as a pretty deft coitus interruptus for the remainder of the years Ethel and Albert had been actively 'active' in *that* department.

Ethel watched Albert polish off his porridge before he turned his attention to the round of wholemeal toast on his side plate. He carefully buttered it, just as he did every morning. Four small blobs, each meticulously scraped from the butter dish, would be secured in all four corners of the slice that had endured a No.3 browning on the toaster dial. No more and no less, so that it was toasted to his liking. The four blobs would then be spread crosswise from top to bottom and left to right before he would pause in the proceedings to locate his dentures. She winced ever so slightly. Dentures, like toilet ablutions, really should be a private matter behind the bathroom door, but Albie had lost all sense of socially acceptable behaviour a long time ago. He expertly secured his gnashers and took his first bite.

'You can't beat home-made bread, can you, Ethel? You can always tell the difference. I think this is definitely one of your better ones...' He smacked his lips together and patted her on the bottom as she sneaked past him.

'Of course, dear, only the best for you, my love...' she cooed whilst hastily utilising a clean tea towel to cover the shop bought loaf that was imprinted along the side with the word 'Hovis'. Happy her ten-year guilty secret was safe after a touch of arthritis had visited her fingers which made kneading a chore, she sat down opposite him at the faded pine table. She watched his contented smile and the way he gently comfort-tapped his fingers on the floral tablecloth as he devoured his toast. This felt like the right time. 'Albie...'

'Yes, dear...'

'I think it's about time we treated ourselves to a new bed, don't you?' She held her breath in anticipation. Albert was well known for his careful ways and replacing anything that hadn't broken, worn out or completely outlived its use, would remain in the Tytherington household literally until death did they part. She smiled warmly at him. It had taken years of practice to learn that having a sharp tongue didn't always get her what she wanted, so recently she had played to his soft side.

He looked at her in surprise. 'What's wrong with the one we've got? It's comfy, isn't it?'

Ethel shook her head and rose from the table. 'Albert Barnard Tytherington! How many times this week have we rolled over in bed and disappeared into that huge chasm in the middle of the mattress? You were embedded in my bosom for the best part of last night.' She tutted.

'It's not a chasm, it's a small dent!' Albert swiftly retorted. 'And it's a very nice bosom indeed, did you hear me complaining?' He gave her a saucy wink.

Grabbing the cast-iron frying pan, Ethel waved it at him. 'So, if I whacked you across the head with this...' She gave it a robust swing, forcing the air to make an impressive *swoosh* on the downward trajectory. '...Then in your world it would only make a small dent and not a chasm on your bonce?'

Laughing, Albert jumped to his feet and disarmed her.

Carefully placing the frying pan back on the stove, he grabbed Ethel around the waist and gleefully danced her around the little kitchen, singing to her a particularly cheeky little ditty he had just composed.

As he hit the punchline, Ethel gasped. 'Albert Barnard Tyther...' She was swept off her feet before she could finish her admonishment.

Giggling like teenagers, they continued their dance around the table and out into the hallway. It was a much slower tempo than it had been during that hot, heady summer of '76, but the years that had since passed had forged a love that encompassed friendship, laughter and a deep understanding.

A recipe for a perfect marriage.

HARMONY HOLLOWS RESORT

The darkening skies brought a sombre and heavy feel to the pretty spring flowers that were attempting to show their colourful heads in the neatly laid borders outside the chalet. Maggie Henshaw shuddered as the first fat drops of rain began to fall, causing a random pattern of spots on the light grey concrete path. She pulled her cardigan tightly around her and dropped the cuffs down to cover her hands, clutching the knitted fabric tightly between her fingers.

Harmony Hollows holiday camp was, in her opinion, a bipolar mix of happiness and deep depression depending on the weather. She had been here once before as an excited sixteen-year-old with hopes and dreams of becoming a world-famous dancer, but how times had changed. The start of this season had just begun, with the dribs and drabs of holidaymakers who were taking advantage of the cheap early-doors terms being offered. In reality they were guinea pigs. Management took great delight in testing new waters for the resort with the little groups that excitedly gathered in reception with their battered suitcases, knowing full well that few complaints would be forthcoming because, as the saying goes, 'You get what you pay for'. She hated that. It was taking advantage of those who could least afford anything nice in life.

She let the curtain drop, blocking out the dismal scene beyond her window, and turned her attention to her uniform that was hanging over the door of the single wardrobe. She sighed loudly and puffed out her cheeks. Butlins had Redcoats, Pontins had Bluecoats, even Hi-Di-Hi, the fictional television series had Yellowcoats, all very bright and gay. And then there was Harmony Hollows Resort with their miserable battleship grey polyester fabric. Granted they had given a small nod to cheerfulness by adding purple and lilac striped piping to the lapels, pockets and cuffs, but that did little to detract from the easily marked and pulled material. The slightest catch with a snagged fingernail would unravel a thread of nylon that was long enough to floss your teeth with.

Maggie was a reluctant Greycoat. Of all the things she could have been had her life taken a different turn, prancing around being manically cheerful on a daily basis draped in the most dismal colour imaginable, hadn't been on her agenda. Her low mood was suddenly interrupted by thundering footsteps along the walkway. The door to her small haven was flung open, blowing in a mix of a damp and bedraggled roommate and an empty crisp packet.

'Whoops, that was sudden!' Abigail 'Pinky' Perkins slammed the door shut behind her, and stamped her feet on the budget cord carpet. She bent down, picked up the bag between finger and thumb. 'Lunch, anyone?' She giggled.

'Even an empty crisp packet is better than what they're serving up in the staff canteen; have you seen it?' Maggie feigned gagging on her own two fingers. 'Cup of tea? There's a clean towel over there if you need to dry off.'

Grabbing a magazine from the small table, Pinky wrapped her hair in the towel, slumped down on her bed and adjusted the pillow behind her head. She watched Maggie execute her comical gait over the short distance to the little kitchenette. It definitely became more pronounced when she was tired or wasn't concentrating on disguising it. 'How's the leg?'

'Damp weather's a bugger, I always know when it's going to rain. My nan had arthritis too; we called her a witch because she could predict the weather, but now I know how she did it!' Maggie laughed as she slopped the milk into two mugs. 'I think I'm getting too old for this lark, to be honest.'

At fifty-six years young, Maggie was the oldest Harmony Hollows team member by a good decade, but in her book, she brought with her not just employment experience, but life experience too. She watched the teabags bob up and down in the two mugs, gradually darkening the mixture, and then helped them along with a vigorous stir of the spoon. Some of those experiences she would rather forget, but on balance, they had shaped her to become who she was today. As long as she kept them securely immured in her mind, with no means of escape, she could still lead a fairly normal life.

'Penny for them!' Pinky swung her legs into the air, deftly tapped her feet together in a rather ungainly ballet movement, and then dropped them down onto the shaggy rug between their beds. She squished her toes in the tufts. 'Did you see the notice pinned on the board giving us our roles for the new season?'

Maggie looked surprised. 'I didn't know it was out yet. What did you get?'

'The bloody "kids under 7" group...' Pinky rolled her eyes. 'I mean me and little ankle-biters, can you imagine it? At least I'm still doing the cabaret. I've been promoted to front of stage.'

Maggie smiled. 'Just don't be doing a Ruthie Lee, or they'll have you out quicker than they had Liz Truss out of Downing Street!' She handed Pinky her mug. Ruthie's high leg kick at the front of the stage during Cabaret Night was legendary. It had treated the grateful dads and horrified mums with hands covering their children's eyes, to a glimpse of her unfettered and unruly lady garden. A hasty costume change in the wings that hadn't gone according to plan, had left Ruthie totally devoid of knickers and the poor lighting tech with a size sixteen pair of cheap polyester fanny flossers hooked to his roving earpiece. Maggie smirked at the memory, then quickly prompted Pinky for her own seasonal role. 'Don't suppose you happened to see what I've got, did you?'

Pinky looked distinctly uncomfortable. Her eyes immediately settled on the swirling air bubbles in her mug, not daring to make direct eye contact with Maggie. She instantly regretted bringing the subject up.

Maggie wasn't letting it go. 'Well?' she queried.

'Er... bingo...' Taking a quick sip of her tea, Pinky waited.

Puzzled, Maggie pushed for a better explanation. 'Bingo what? Bingo, I've found my missing eyelash? Bingo, I've just remembered, unlike Ruthie Lee, to put my knickers on!'

Pinky looked mortified. 'Look, don't shoot the messenger – it's the nightly bingo. They've got you down as the caller!'

'*Bingo* caller! *Me?* You are joking!' Maggie's eyes widened as she looked at Pinky for any sign of humour. Just a tic or a twitch at the corner of her mouth would have been enough, but there was nothing.

At the grand age of fifty-six years, three months and four days, Margaret 'Maggie' Henshaw, with over thirty-five years' experience in the arts and entertainment industry, had been reduced to fondling balls and shouting numbers at a second-rate holiday camp.

EENY MEENY MINY MOE

The Major Incident Room at Winterbridge police station was a veritable hive of activity, not because they had a serious crime to solve, or an outstanding felon to catch, but because a revered piece of paper had finally been posted to the office noticeboard.

The expanse of green felt surrounded by a cheap pine frame on the wall was three bodies deep, as everyone stretched and strained their necks to see who had been rostered in the coming months. Amongst a tattered and torn flyer held on by a solitary drawing pin that announced a Christmas party from four years ago, and the results of the CID darts team challenge with Nether Wallop's finest arrow chuckers, was the holy grail of policing: the summer working shifts and allocated annual leave dates.

'*Gordon Bennett...*' Melvin Hibbert, the area Crime Scene Investigator grunted loudly and pushed his fingers through his hair in despair. 'My Norma is going to have kittens; I've missed out again!' He hastily pulled out his diary, opened it to the weeks that Norma had demanded from him, and ran his finger down the dates. 'Jack, you've got the weeks I need, any chance of a...'

Before he could finish, Jack Finnegan, the C team lead

detective sergeant, abruptly cut in. 'Not on your life or mine, mate! D'you think our Morag would welcome me with open arms if I told her the all-inclusive to Lanzarote I promised her was being swapped for your week in some run-down Butlins holiday camp? Can you imagine her watching numpties prance and twirl around a dance floor? She'd be more confused than Clarence the cross-eyed lion.'

Melvin was pretty sure Morag 'Cyclops' Finnegan would rather stick pins in her one remaining good eye than experience the joys of Harmony Hollows Resort and its knobbly-knees competitions. 'Not the holiday, just the dates. You can still have your sun, sea, sand and er... well, whatever you and Morag get up to in warmer climes, but just on the dates that I've got rather than the ones you've picked. Go on, free pints for six weeks? It'll get me out of the mire with Norma; you know how volatile she can be, I'll be a dead man walking by Monday if I don't sort this!'

At the prospect of topping up his already ample gut with a tempting bribe of Theakstons best bitter, his favourite tipple, Jack could almost taste the golden amber liquid. He smacked his tongue against the roof of his mouth. 'You're breaking my heart, Hibbs...' He clutched his chest to prove his empathy. 'I'm not promising anything, but I'll speak to her tonight. See if there's a bit of flexibility.' He took a slurp from his mug, swooshed the tepid tea through his teeth, and sat heavily in his chair. He knew with absolute certainty that his Morag had no flexibility whatsoever. He had no intention of asking her and subsequently suffering her wrath, but he would let Melvin down gently after what he considered would be a decent lapse of time to cover a supposed marital consultation. The fat file in front of him marked 'Nether Wallop Murder Enquiry' challenged him to make a decision. Detective Inspector Murdoch Holmes had given him a poison chalice, a cup that he was starting to feel he would rather drink from himself. The prospect of instigating the wrath of his team by selecting a DS and a DC to be farmed out for weeks on end to the back of beyond fell heavy on him. He ran his pen along the list, tapping at the two names that stood out for him. He turned his attention back to the room, scanning the faces of his team.

DC Tim Forshaw. Jack involuntarily shuddered. Tim was a nice young lad, keen but with very little lateral thinking experience and was prone to unfortunate outbursts of embarrassing empathy, as showcased the previous week when a victim's mother had been found comforting him with thirty-six sheets of aloe vera bog roll to wipe his eyes and blow his snotter with. He made a mental note not to utilise Tim for any future death messages.

DS Steve Bradshaw. He checked his diary. Steve was due on paternity leave at the end of the month if all went according to plan, so he was a non-starter. No point sending someone who would have to return before the investigation was wrapped up. The more Jack looked around the room, the more it became blatantly obvious that although he didn't want to lose Andy and Lucy from his team, his options were limited. He flopped the cover of the file over and took a deep breath. 'Andy...' He beckoned to his right-hand man.

Andy was working on a file with DC Lucy Harris, his partner in crime, as Pru called her. Lucy had grown up with Bree and had been part of the Winterbottom girls' crew in her teens. She was also now a very capable 'crew' member for Winterbridge CID, paired with Andy for maximum effect. They worked well together. Andy gave Lucy a knowing look, he was more than aware that their names had been top of the list for the Nether Wallop secondment.

'Am I right in assuming being summonsed has nothing to do with the empty biscuit tin, or the unfortunate dent to the offside front of the fiesta?' Andy gave Jack a wry smile whilst pointing an accusing finger at Lucy. 'Ask her where reverse gear is in a Ford!' He gave a gentle laugh, which encouraged Lucy to punch him hard on the arm.

'It could happen to anyone...' she chided, whilst simultaneously feeling the burn on her cheeks as she recalled her little accident. Slamming the CID car into what she thought was reverse gear in Winterbridge car park, she had enthusiastically revved the engine whilst looking over her left shoulder. No sooner had she released the clutch, the little Fiesta had lurched unexpectedly forwards. The ensuing crunch of metal as she hit the obstruction in front of her had forced her to proffer the immortal words of, *'Oh shit, where did that come from?'* whilst pointing animatedly at the brick wall that had stood its ground since 1932.

Andy gave his arm a swift rub. Between Pru and Lucy he was surprised he still had the use of both his arms, as their well-aimed playful punches frequently left his triceps for dead. 'We've got the Nether Wallop job, haven't we?'

Jack wished he didn't have to make eye contact with either of them, but they were the best they had and the ones with the least commitments for the foreseeable. He tried to justify his choice. 'I'm sorry, guys, neither of you have any court dates coming up, and all the cases assigned can easily be shared out amongst the team. And I hate to say it, Andy, but neither you nor Pru have little nippers to worry about, and, well, you're single, Luce, and pretty much in the same boat domestically.' He hoped that last comment didn't sound dismissive of her relationship status, but he had to consider the impact on the families and home lives of the members of his team. He pushed the folder towards Andy. 'Gill in Admin will arrange your accommodation, and anything else you need with regards to expenses. They're expecting you a week Monday; it should give you plenty of time to get yourselves sorted.'

Lucy followed Andy back to their respective desks and flopped down into her chair. She twirled it around aimlessly, stopping only when she started to feel sick. 'So, it's not our remarkable detective skills that sets us apart, then; it's me being a frigid spinster with no sex life and your Pru for not being up the duff!'

Andy laughed. 'Look on the bright side; you could have been chosen because of your driving skills!' He quickly shrugged his shoulder to evade the incoming fist from her direction. 'Come on, Stirling Moss, I'll race you to the Dog & Gun and you can showcase your parallel parking techniques in their car park instead.'

DIRTY GERTIE AND THE CUCKOO IN THE NEST

Life can nurture and then gift the most terrible tragedies to those who least expect them, something that Miss Sophie Hopkins of 28 Larton Lane, Little Kipling, was only too aware.

Sophie stared at the ceiling in her bedroom, tracing the cracks in the perished plaster. She always expected them, a mix of tragedies and disasters, they were never a surprise to her. She wondered if there was a stack of pretty pastel gift tags with her name on them somewhere. An exclusive batch, reserved just for her, and, if there was, would they say:

To Sophie 'failure' Hopkins
Wishing you the best of tragedies and disasters,
Lots of love
Life

She swung her legs over the side of the bed, rubbed her eyes, and reached for the little pill bottle. She popped the lid, took out the single white tablet, curled her fingers around the glass of water, and carefully read the label. Just as she did every single day.

Risperidone 6mg.

The tablet sat momentarily on her tongue, another one of her rituals. She often considered not taking it or leaving it longer than usual to see what would happen. Would the familiarity of the voices return to taunt her, telling her how worthless she was, how everyone was against her – or would they drive her to...

She involuntarily shuddered, not wanting to remember. She hastily took a large gulp of water to ensure her little lifesaver disappeared to begin its journey, a journey that would ensure she never returned to Waverley Park Sanitorium.

'Come on, Florence, time for breakfast.' She picked up the small tortoiseshell kitten, tickled her behind the ears, and kissed her little pink nose. 'It's tuna this morning, aren't you the lucky one.' Sliding her feet into a battered pair of lilac mules, Sophie made her way downstairs, pausing at the front door to pick up the post from the mat. Whilst Florence enjoyed her breakfast and the kettle rumbled and grumbled to reach boiling point, she searched through the post as though she were shuffling a deck of cards.

'Bin, bin, recycling, bin, bin... oh...' She paused holding the manilla envelope up to the sunlight that was shining through the kitchen window, in the hope she might get a sneak preview of its contents. 'Ooh, Florence! This could be it.' She excitedly gasped as she tore open the seal. Pulling at the folded contents, she opened it out and began to read, her trembling fingers making the paper dance.

Dear Sophie,

We are delighted to inform you that you have been successful in your application to become our resident photographer for Clampitt & Shoehorn Holidays.

The terms and conditions of employment are enclosed, along with your accommodation details. We can confirm that your first posting will be at The Harmony Hollows Resort in Nettleton Shrub for the forthcoming summer season...

Sophie didn't need to read any further; she had just been offered the perfect job that would allow her to go behind the scenes of her next project. The Open University foundation course in photography she had undertaken, when a change in her circumstances had dictated a different way of life for her, had not been a waste after all. For the first time in her life she had been good at something, and once she had discovered who she really was, reverting back to her birth name had given her a new start. Now the job of investigating her past could begin. She clutched the paperwork to her chest and watched Florence purring and preening; a full belly always made for a happy kitten. She felt sad to think that she would have to find a new home for her, she'd become very fond of her, and of course she had been good company to fill the void that her landlady had left. Miss Gertrude Timpson had been a bit of a shrew, always sniping and complaining, but her accommodation had been the best that Sophie could afford, so she had endured the constant put-downs and less than sanitary living conditions.

Until that fateful day.

It had been just one nasty remark too many. Dirty Gertie, as Sophie had nicknamed her, had spat the word 'useless' with a sneer when the toaster had caught fire, belching burnt toast fumes around the kitchen, and suddenly Sophie had snapped.

Well, it wasn't really Sophie, was it? It was that *other* girl. She had tilted her head.

Go on Sophie, do it! Do it now!

Miss Timpson had offered the perfect opportunity by turning away from Sophie, presenting the back of her head with its thinning grey curls held in a tight perm and her pink skin peeping through. Gertie had continued to witter away, sniping, grumbling and spitting venom – and before Sophie knew it, the veined marble rolling pin that she had so admired on baking days was in her hand. It was cool and heavy; she had liked how it felt against her skin. The muscles in her arm became taut as she swung it upwards into a graceful arc and with gathering impetus, brought it down again, and again, and again.

It was like beating a tune on a drum; it was music to her ears. She so wanted to dance to the rhythm, the sound deeply resonating in her chest as the blood-red spray peppered the walls, the ceiling and finally the floor...

Thump.

Thump.

Thump.

And she did dance, she danced and laughed and danced some more as Dirty Gertie, her glassy eyes reflecting Sophie's perfectly timed steps, lay slumped on the circular green coir mat.

And then it was over.

No grumbling.

No sniping.

No venom.

Just peace and quiet.

Miss Timpson had remained company for Sophie in the following days, propped up in the rocking chair, her rictus grin slowly distorting with each day that passed, until one morning Sophie made the decision that Gertie really was dirty – and just that little bit smelly – and as such should be put out with the trash. She had flung open the windows to air the rooms and then without guilt, kindness or respect, had hitched Gertie's feet under her armpits and dragged her body by the ankles across the floor like a drayhorse would pull its cart. It had been hard work. Several times she had paused to extricate a rug, two plastic plant pots, the previous week's edition of the *Kipling Gazette* and the cat bowl from under Gertie's large backside, that had been gathered by the slithering motion of her travels to the garden. Once the old witch had been interred and covered with a decent layer of soil, and after a nice cup of tea, Sophie had popped down to the animal rescue centre and offered Florence a loving home. It was a gift to herself for a job well done, along with a nice little yew tree sapling that she had unceremoniously dumped on top of the mound that was Miss Gertrude Timpson.

Sophie looked out of the kitchen window to admire her handiwork. It had been several months since that liberating day, and already the little tree had gifted her red berries against the lush deep green needles. A shiver ran down her spine. She didn't like to remember too much; it made her feel very melancholy...

...but not 'arf as melancholy as old Gertie must be feeling, seeing she's six feet under. She giggled at the thought, and then just as quickly drew a deep breath as she realised exactly why a hiatus in her medication would be a tragedy and a disaster...

But on this occasion, it had been a disaster for someone else.

THE VOTE

Florrie Patterson, the proprietor of the Twisted Currant Café, smoothed down her red spotted apron and adjusted the bow ties at the back, just as she did every single morning before eagerly flipping the sign to *open* on the shop door, ready to welcome the people of Winterbottom to her warm and cosy world.

Florrie took great pride not only in the tasty fancies, cakes and delicious sandwiches that she served to her customers, but in the ambience of her little café. Her fingertips gently touched the petals of the pretty pink tea rose that sat in a little glass vase on Table 3 before quickly smoothing down a crease in the floral tablecloth.

'Perfect...' She pursed her lips in pure joy and checked her watch. 'Mmm... not long now before I'm descended upon.' Gingerly grabbing the cake tongs, she tentatively tested them, another one of her morning rituals, whilst simultaneously checking out the bright blue sticking plaster on her other thumb. Just the mere memory of yesterday's little accident made her eyes water. She held the tongs up in front of her and watched the spooned ends with their sharp teeth clashing together. 'Ten years, and I still don't know how to operate these bloody things!' she grumbled. The bell above the café door suddenly tinkled loudly, heralding the arrival of her first customer.

'What on earth are you doing, Florrie? You can't catch flies like that, you know!' Hilda Jones bustled her way past Table 2, knocking it slightly with her hip. The little rose vase wobbled and teetered, first one way and then the next before settling back in its original place. She took up residence at their regular table and plonked her handbag down. 'Right...' her voice tapered off as she rummaged around in its depths, finally reappearing with a flourish of triumph, holding up a torn piece of paper. 'Here we go, shall I read it out or just give it to you, dear?'

Florrie smiled. She was more than familiar with what her regulars would have for their morning gathering, it was the same every single time, but she felt obliged to feign ignorance and allow Hilda to feel useful and in charge. Her fading memory left little for her to feel useful and in control of these days, although it was frequently a source of great amusement, something Hilda herself took advantage of on many occasions. She could certainly play to her audience over her faux pas when her sharp wit didn't desert her. Florrie could think of nothing worse than to lose one's marbles, but looking at Hilda now, content and mainly blissfully unaware of the state of the world, she secretly hoped that if her marbles went rolling under the sofa one day, never to be found again, she would be able to see the same benefits. She held her little notepad aloft, with pencil poised. 'You read it out, Hilda, that way mistakes can't be made.'

Hilda bristled with importance. 'So very true, Florrie.' She cleared her throat. 'Right, two packets of corn plasters, a hair net, pink mind, don't like those blue ones... oh, and some Gavin's Gone, please.' She gently patted her stomach.

Florrie stifled a smile. Quickly pinching her lips together, she composed herself. 'I think that list is for next door, love. You know Dylan's Pharmacy, and it's Gaviscon if it's for your tummy.'

'Well, that's a bit of a bugger, isn't it? I was quite looking forward to a bit of how's yer father from young Gavin before he left again!' Hilda laughed heartily as she rummaged in her bag for the second time in as many minutes. '*Voila*,' she said as she triumphantly pulled out another tattered piece of paper. 'This is it, but I think I'll just give it to you, dear.'

Florrie obliged. She stood behind the counter and watched as in turn, each of the little group arrived to start their morning meeting. Clarissa was next, followed closely by Millie Thomas and a few minutes later Ethel.

The famous, self-styled Four Wrinkled Dears were together again.

'Oh Florrie, could you add an extra few rounds of toast onto the order, please, I think Kitty might join us.' Clarissa hunkered down in anticipation of rapt attention from her friends. 'Right, girls, holiday season is almost upon us, and I've got these...' She spread out several pamphlets in front of her. '...I think I've found the perfect little getaway for us.' Her index finger, showing early signs of arthritis in the first knuckle, tapped on the glossy leaflet. 'Harmony Hollows Resort in Nettleton Shrub, for the Northern Ballroom Championships!' She sat back, smug in the knowledge that the latter would be a huge draw for the ladies who frequently fell into raptures of lust during *Strictly Come Dancing* every Saturday night, particularly when it was Argentine Tango week.

She was met with a respectful silence from her friends, one she was sure was nurtured by their mutual feelings of awe at her suggestion.

'Well?'

The seconds ticked by; the intermittent hiss of steam from Florrie's coffee maker being the only backdrop to the silence between them. Millie used the corner of her cotton handkerchief to surreptitiously rid the end of her nose of a small dewdrop.

'Blimey, don't all shout at once! Where's your sense of adventure? Knobbly-knees competitions, bingo every night, waltzers in the fairground, not to mention lots of nice young men cavorting their way across the dance floor. Come on, girls, it will be fabulous. Harmony Hollows is perfect for us, plus they've got early bird deals too!' Clarissa was determined to sell her idea; it was Harmony Hollows or bust as far as she was concerned.

Ethel was the first to speak. 'It's more like Harmony Horrors! Jeez 'Rissa, don't you remember that place made all the papers in the early 1980s? What was it? Hilda, you remember it; a double murder or something?'

'Bloody hell, Eth, Hilda can't remember what happened yesterday let alone something almost forty years ago!' Clarissa was quite peeved at their reaction; she had anticipated excitement and eagerness, not apathy and indifference. She took a slurp from her teacup and let it rattle back loudly into the saucer as a way of conveying her pique.

Hilda cleared her throat before she spoke. 'It was May 23rd, 1983. It was in all the papers. The poor girl was found strangled in one of the chalets, and if that wasn't bad enough, they found another body in the wardrobe, although how he managed to squeeze in there with a full-size industrial hoover was anybody's guess.' She spread a thick layer of marmalade on her toast and nibbled the corner. 'They reckoned it was one of those love oblong things.'

'With the hoover?' Millie looked at her in astonishment. 'And it's a triangle.'

'Ooh! didn't think of that; I always wondered what he was doing with it. Now we know!' Hilda gave a saucy grin. 'Mind you, the one that did it was never caught. It left a really eerie feel to the place afterwards, I can tell you.'

Ethel, Clarissa and Millie sat open-mouthed at her sudden ability for recall.

'Oh – and yesterday was Tuesday and I spent the whole day with my lovely Gavin.' Hilda waved a tattered paperback book at them, the glistening naked torso of a well-honed young man on the front glared back at them.

Eager to placate Clarissa, who, lips pursed to show her displeasure, was currently feigning interest in the aspidistra that was housed in Florrie's mum's old chamber pot next to their table, Ethel quickly intervened. 'Tell you what, why don't we bring it up at the next WI meeting and put it to the vote? I think it would actually be fun. Come on, ladies, what do you think?'

Millie finished munching on her crumpet and dabbed at the corners of her mouth with a napkin. 'Well, it's not like we're averse to a bit of murder and mystery, we *are* the fearless foursome after all. If we choose Harmony Hollows we could maybe do a bit of research before we go and see if we can implement our skills and solve... what do they call it?' She hesitated whilst she recalled the word she was looking for. 'Oh yes, that's it, a cold case! We could try and solve a cold case whilst we're there.'

Three excited heads nodded their approval, which would now allow for the rest of the morning's gossip to be divulged.

'So, what I really need to know...' Hilda hunched her shoulders to her ears and twitched her nose, becoming mouselike in her appearance as her tummy growled loudly. '... Does anyone know where my Gavin's gone? I'm a tad windy this morning.'

LOVE MEANS...

Pru banged the lid down on the kettle a lot harder than she had meant to. She knew she was being unreasonable. After all, wasn't this part of the job description – and it was hardly Andy's fault, he just did as he was told, obeyed orders. She shovelled the spaghetti from the strainer onto the plates, taking no care as to where it landed. Gone were the days when she would intricately weave a strand of pasta into a heart shape on the accompanying side plate and fill it in with rich red sauce. She examined the tangled mess and scrunched up her nose. A half-hearted attempt to shove the dangly bits back into place failed miserably, it just reminded her of her first ever attempt at knitting when she'd dropped more stitches than purled, much to her grandmother's exasperation.

'Here...' She put the plate in front of Andy and offered him a few meagre shavings of parmesan cheese from the bowl.

Andy sat, fork at the ready with an expectant grin, which soon faded when he saw Pru's face. He quickly stood up from the table, quietly cursing Jack for putting him in this position. 'Pru, I'm so sorry, but you had a gut feeling it was going to be me, didn't you?' He snaked his arm around her waist and pulled her into him, nuzzling her neck gently, feeling the warmth of her skin against his. He inhaled deeply, enjoying the scent of her favourite perfume: Hugo Boss Femme. 'I'll make it up to you, I promise, we *are* allowed a few days for a bit of home leave during the investigation.'

She broke away from him and grabbed the tea towel that was draped over the copper bar on the oven. 'I don't want you to make it up later...' The first tear welled up, plopped over the top of her lower lashes and rolled down her cheek. She savagely wiped it away with the waffle fabric of the tea towel.

Andy was perplexed. He knew Pru inside out, every emotion, every type of mood she could pull out of the bag to suit every occasion, her highs, her lows, her infectious laughter, her wicked sense of humour – everything! But this? This was just not like her at all. 'I don't know what to say...' He held his hands out submissively. 'Honestly, Pru, you've always known what my job entails, that this can happen. It's never bothered you this much before when I've had to work away.'

Pru jerked around to face him, her face flushed pink, the hot tears now making no attempt to restrain themselves as they poured down her cheeks. 'Well, I've never *not* been pregnant before at *exactly* the same time as being told I'm going to be on my own for months on end!' she sobbed. 'I thought I was this time, I really, really did. I felt different...' Her voice became small. '...But I'm not, it's just my body playing a horrible trick on me again. I'm running out of time, Andy.'

His natural instinct to protect her was suddenly overwhelmed; he was out of his depth. He could fight the enemy, he could stand in harm's way and take one for the team, he could even rush in when he knew he had no chance of survival if it meant protecting the one person he loved with all his heart, his Pru. But this was different, she didn't want saving, she just wanted him. He was at a loss. 'I... I... didn't know...' he stammered, and then just as quickly could have kicked himself. Was that the best he could come up with? He had completely lost track of the days and the weeks, focusing too much on work and not enough on their dream of starting a family.

Her sobs were now coming in heartbreaking staccato. 'I wanted to surprise you. I was so sure this time, Andy. I even bought these...' She reached into the little white gift bag on the breakfast bar and held out her hand.

'Booties?' He took them from her and marvelled at the delicate crochet work and the little white ribbons around the ankles, and his heart wanted to break for her and for the tiny symbol of life that he held in his hands.

'Maybe next time...' she sighed.

She nestled into him. No other words were needed as he held her tight, trying to chase the pain away.

'Maybe next time...' he whispered back.

RALPH

Ralph Fairbright repositioned his chair, bounced his bottom on the worn leather a few times before he settled himself down, and niftily executed one spin of the chrome base.

Wall...

Window...

Door...

...and back to where he had started.

He quickly jammed his hands out to grab the edge of his desk to stop the momentum. He placed his pencil in perfect alignment with his pen, side by side, which was aesthetically pleasing, flicked a biscuit crumb from his grey and lilac striped tie and stared for the umpteenth time that morning at the flickering curser on his blank laptop screen.

At fifty-eight years old, he was for the first time ever in his life at a complete loss as to what he wanted to do with what was left of his time on this mortal coil. His countdown to retirement had just been given a kick in the proverbial goolies, throwing his carefully laid plans into disarray. He was currently manager at

Briddleston Bay Resort in Grendel Scrags, and had been for the last ten years, a role that he would have been more than content to continue with right up until his team presented him with a half-deflated helium balloon in the Clampitt & Shoehorn colours of grey and purple, and a Happy Retirement card.

It was a far cry from his youth as a gaff lad on the waltzers at their flagship holiday camp in Nettleton Shrub almost forty years ago, but one he had worked hard for and had sacrificed so much. Skeletons that rattled loudly and with much frequency in his mental cupboard had kept him on the move and away from as many of those old bones as possible.

Until now.

He circled the Bluetooth mouse to enable the curser to dance across the screen. Finding his mark, he savagely clicked down with his finger, opening up the email.

'Bloody Harmony Hollows...' he whined. 'Just because some light-fingered asshole doesn't know how to cook the books properly!'

It was common knowledge that most, if not all managers at C&S, had their fingers in some sort of beneficial pie, syphoning off a few bob here and there from slot machines and cash purchases made at the on-site shops. Unfortunately for him, Bill Gibson at Harmony Hollows had managed to not only dip a finger in, but he had gone on to utilise his whole bloody hand. He'd been caught with his snout well and truly buried in the raspberry filling and had been fired for his criminal efforts. Now they were a resort manager down and Harmony Hollows was in dire need of direction with the up-and-coming Northern Ballroom Championships. This extravaganza of the 'tippy-toes troupes' promised to bring in hordes of eager fans that in turn would mean full chalets.

A tap on his door broke his train of thought. 'Enter...'

The door slowly squeaked open. 'Can we all come in,

Ralph?' Kim, his assistant, tentatively popped her head around it, the peeling cream paint stark against her tanned skin.

Ralph nodded. He knew he had probably been the last to know about his new posting; no doubt the whole camp and every member of his ruddy team had been talking about it for days over their breakfasts of rubbery scrambled egg and soggy cornflakes, laughing behind his back, making time to celebrate 'Rancid Ralph's' departure. That was something else he knew. He knew what they called him. He caught himself. Maybe he was being unfair on his staff and the Clampitt & Shoehorn confidentiality policy, and they really didn't know at all. Yes. That's what he was doing, he was being overly sensitive because of the circumstances in which he had left Harmony Hollows previously. He'd have to pick his words, let them down gently, tell them that they were losing him. Although having been given less than forty-eight hours to pack up and move on, there wasn't much time for etiquette and niceties.

Kim edged her way into the room, followed by the whole entertainments team behind her. Their dismal grey blazers added an extra touch of melancholy to the proceedings.

Ralph took a deep breath and exhaled. 'I hate to be the bearer of bad news but...'

Boink.

Boink.

Boink-boink...

The large silver and purple lettered balloon bounced, boinked and jerked above their heads, cheerily announcing their perceived misery at his imminent departure. Well, it actually said '*You're leaving – thank feck for that!*' but who was he to split hairs.

Kim looked sheepish. 'It was the only one in the shop at such short notice...' she apologetically whispered.

Ralph smiled and shook his head. 'Well, what more can I

say? Although I can see your obvious dismay at losing me...' He chuckled to himself. 'It's got to be bye bye, Briddleston Bay, and hello, Harmony Hollows Resort.'

WINTERBOTTOM WOMEN'S INSTITUTE

Kitty Hardcastle bristled with importance as she draped the Winterbottom Women's Institute cloth over the large pasteboard style table, ensuring their emblem, which had been so delicately embroidered in greens and reds, was dead centre and facing the front. She rummaged around in her holdall and produced a small vase and a bunch of artificial daffodils. Ramming them purposefully into the glass neck, she rearranged them carefully before standing back to admire her handiwork.

Winterbottom parish hall was filling up nicely for their WI meeting, the chattering voices of the ladies lifted up to the beams and just as quickly floated back down to warmly embrace them. She watched the members taking up residence in the same chairs they placed their bottoms on for every meeting. It amused her to think that the coveted pink velour seats at the front would only ever become available upon the sad passing of whichever member had 'bagsied' it all those years ago. Woe betides any newcomer who had the audacity to not notice and obey the strict protocols of 'derrière parking' at the Winterbottom Women's Institute.

'Ladies, ladies, your attention please!' Kitty briskly rang the little table bell to bring order to the gathered women. 'Ethel, if you can tinkle your fingers over the ivories for "Jerusalem" to open our meeting, that would be grand...'

Clarissa moved her shopping bag out of the way to allow Ethel free passage to the old church piano at the front. 'Think we'd much rather have a bit of the old Bee Gees, Kitty...' She pointed to Hilda who had barely settled herself into the chair before she had fallen asleep. 'A quick rendition of "Stayin' Alive" would suit this one down to the ground!' She laughed.

Hearing the collective giggles of the ladies, Hilda's head jerked up. 'I'm not asleep, I'm just resting my eyes...'

'Aye, if you say so, dear, but we all heard you snore!' Ethel tartly replied.

Hilda smirked. 'It wasn't a snore, it's me Gavin's Gone, it's working a treat for my wind...'

'Whoa, too much information there, Hilda!' Bree edged her way along the row and commandeered the chair next to Millie. 'Pru's running a bit late, girls, but I see it's giving Kitty the opportunity to relive her days as past president!' She jerked her head towards the table, with everyone's eyes on Kitty as she fussed and preened over the WI paperwork.

No sooner had the words left her lips, then the double doors swished open, spilling a flustered Pru through the threshold. They rattled shut behind her as she shrugged off her coat. 'Sorry, sorry, ladies...' She waved a hand in acknowledgement to her tardiness. 'I'm afraid I've got your Albert to blame.' She smiled warmly at Ethel who had become frozen over the ivory keys, her fingers splayed in anticipation of the first chord of their signature tune.

'Oh dear, what's he been up to now?' Ethel shook her head in exasperation.

Pru settled herself behind the table, edging Kitty to one side as politely as she could. 'He insisted on date-ordering the library copies of the *Winterbottom News*, all one hundred and twenty issues! I did tell him it was time to go home, but well, you know Albert; he's nothing if not methodical.'

Ethel grumbled. 'Pah, he's only dragging it out because he's not paying for your heating, he can be such a tight ar–'

'And did those feet in ancient time walk upon England's mountains green...' Hilda's strong melodic voice suddenly resonated around the room, completely drowning out Ethel's observation of her husband's ability to stay comfortably toasty without it hitting his pocket. Ethel quickly took her cue to accompany her as the rest of the ladies joined in.

After their opening number, the minutes of the last meeting were read, leaflets handed out for up-and-coming day trips, and offers of help for the Spring Fair cake stall were gratefully received. Then Pru came to the part that Clarissa had been virtually holding her breath for in anticipation.

'Right, our early summer break, well almost summer!' Pru crinkled the A4 sheet in her hands. 'Clarissa has come up with a super idea of a week or two in idyllic Nettleton Shrub at the Harmony Hollows Resort. It just so happens to coincide with the Northern Ballroom Championships, and I know we have a lot of *Strictly Come Dancing* fans amongst us–'

She was interrupted by a chorus of 'Ooh's' and 'Ah's' from the gathering, and a gentle hum of excitement.

'So, can I have a show of hands for those who would be interested in a ten-day stay? The dates are the 19th to 28th May, Friday to the following Sunday. Chalets can be shared in pairs, or there are single sleepers available, but keep in mind that if you do share it will keep the cost down.'

A flurry of activity caused the chairs to scrape noisily on the oak flooring as the ladies dug deep into their handbags for their diaries. This was quickly followed by a good show of hands. Pru counted them. 'Excellent, I'll send the booking form round, and once I've got the details of those that wish to go, I'll get it booked.' She handed the sheet of paper and a pen to Kitty, encouraging her to do the honours. 'Kitty, would you also be able to speak to Frank to see what deal he can do on the coach for us?'

Kitty blushed. It was common knowledge that Frank Atkins, the owner of Rubber Springs & Gaskets Coach Tours, was sweet on Kitty and she on him. Their affair was a secret that was most certainly not best kept. 'I will, but couldn't we consider somewhere else other than Harmony Hollows? It's not a very nice place. It's terribly run-down and, er... things have happened there.' Kitty felt sick at the thought of putting just one carefully manicured toe over the threshold of that resort.

Pru smiled. She knew Kitty was always one for the finer things in life, but not everyone had the means to afford up-market hotels or resorts. 'I think Harmony Hollows will be perfect for *all* of us, Kitty, and I know about the stories, but what happened was a long time ago.'

'Right, Harmony Hollows here we come!' Clarissa whooped loudly, elated that her suggestion had been so popular. 'Eth, you can bunk in with me, Millie, you and Hilda can share. This is going to be so much fun!'

Creeeerk...

The barn door to the kitchen slowly opened as Brenda's four plump fingers and a thumb made their regular appearance to wave wildly at them from the far side of the room. Each and every member held their breath in anticipation, hoping against hope it would be an apple and cinnamon delicacy or just a plain and simple Victoria sponge, rather than their nemesis and the cause of poor Mabel Allinson's unfortunate demise during Phyllis Watson's murderous spree.

Alas, it was not to be...

Brenda's flushed cheeks and cheery demeanour propelled her across the room as she excitedly announced the evening's refreshments.

'Tea and cake in five, ladies...' she wittered. 'We've got lemon drizzle and it's to die for!'

THE PERFECT STORM

All the elements were there.

The dark clouds gathering across the villages of Winterbottom, Frampton Falls, Grendel Scrags and Little Kipling were preparing to meet, to gather strength and momentum, before pushing their way towards Nettleton Shrub.

A perfect storm was brewing.

The resort stood quiet and still. The chalets with their stippled magnolia shells and grey shingled roofs sat stiff and regimented, their lines broken only by narrow paths that divided each perfect formation. The children's playground, deserted and bleak, played host to a ghostly merry-go-round as it squeaked and squealed in slow circles, pushed on by the wind. The long-ago abandoned fairground, its rusting skeleton bleak against the skies, lay dormant and unused in a far corner of the resort, hidden from the world.

Harmony Hollows was waiting.

The wheels had already been set in motion, by virtue of chance, and, if such a thing was to be believed, by divine intervention.

They were on their way – all of them.

In the months to come, Harmony Hollows would once again become the epicentre for dark deeds, its gruesome history in danger of repeating itself because they had inadvertently aligned themselves to the shadows of the past.

To become part of that perfect storm.

WITH A FRIEND LIKE YOU...

'Budge up a bit...' Pru plonked herself down next to Bree in their usual cosy snug at the Dog & Gun.

Bree reluctantly obliged. 'I'd just warmed that spot up and now you've pinched it – this bit's freezing!' She wriggled her bottom as if to prove her point and tipped her head towards Pru's double pink gin. The solitary half-strawberry fizzed and bobbed in the glass, challenging the mass of ice cubes for space. 'I'm sorry, truly I am.' She snaked her arm around Pru's shoulder to give her a hug.

Pru gently waved her hand, not to repel her best friend but to warn her. 'I can't do too much kindness just now, or I'll burst into tears again.' She gave a wry smile. 'I'll be okay, I was just so sure this time.'

Bree sipped her drink, deep in thought. 'How's Andy taking it?'

'He's hurting, but more for me than himself; he's more pragmatic than I am. His way of thinking is if it's meant to be, it will happen.' Pru shrugged. 'We've agreed to give it a bit of a rest for a while, see if that helps.'

'Oh my God, please don't tell me you're going for a "No sex please, we're British" time out in the bedroom!! How on earth will you manage with the Delectable Detective giving you spoons every night?' Bree was obviously flabbergasted that anyone could reject the delicious Andy when he was on form. 'Look, if you're not up for it, as your best mate I suppose I could always help out in the bedroom department – not for my pleasure, of course, but purely because of my devotion to you. I'm sure you'd do the same for me!' She took a sip of her drink and snorted more savagely than she expected, setting off a coughing fit.

Pru began to laugh. 'Oh yeah, with a friend's offer like that, who'd need enemies? Besides, you've been sharing your bed with Humphrey Hippo and a hot water bottle for the last two years.'

'Exactly! I'm desperate...'

They both began to laugh until the tears ran down their cheeks, a welcome distraction from Pru's original mood.

Bree checked her watch and indicated to Juicy Jason at the bar for another round of drinks. 'So, Harmony Hollows went to the vote and it's a goer. I take it we're sharing a chalet?'

Pru nodded. 'Of course, don't we always share?'

'Not when it comes to your bloody gorgeous husband, you don't...' Bree laughed.

'Actually, Clarissa was telling me a story about that place. Did you know there was a double murder there in the early 1980s, and an unsolved one at that?' Pru picked out the strawberry from her glass between thumb and forefinger and popped it into her mouth before rummaging around in her bag. She placed a photocopy of an old newspaper cutting onto the table and spread out the creases. 'It might be worth doing a bit of digging before we go, just out of interest. It might be fun to see where it happened; in fact, you never know, we could end up staying in the chalet where the dastardly deed took place. Now wouldn't that be fab?'

Bree side-eyed her. 'Uhm, not really. Jeez, you really are weird sometimes, Prunella Pearce.'

'Barnes, it's Prunella Barnes, and I just so happen to love my weirdness. Are you up for it? We can nip into town and visit Winterbridge library, have a look through their archives, it'll be like old times when we researched Phyllis's family home, Magdalen House.' She gave Bree a playful nudge with her arm. 'Go on, it'll be a welcome distraction for me.'

'You make it sound like a warm and cosy little outing; you almost got murdered twice during that escapade. I still can't believe that old Phyllis failed on both occasions, you must have a very stressed and alcoholic angel looking over you; it's the only way it could bloody cope!'

They sat in silence, mulling over the Magdalen case which had seen their old WI member, Phyllis Watson, orchestrating several grisly murders in and around Winterbottom, and one which had set them on the road to creating the Curious Curator & Co Detective Agency.

Bree plunged her hand into the packet of crisps that had sat untouched on the table. 'I suppose it could be fun, a real-life cold case. Can you imagine the kudos for our little business if we discovered a clue that could solve it after all these years?'

The gentle hum of conversation as the Dog & Gun began to fill with thirsty locals acted as a backdrop to their renewed silence whilst they stared at the newspaper cutting and weighed up the pros and cons of sticking their noses into someone else's business. The heavy oak stained-glass door opened suddenly, allowing a chill breeze to whirl its way across the stone floor to tickle their ankles. Pru shivered and craned her neck to see who had come into the pub. Her heart gave a little excited jump. 'Hello, Mr Barnes.'

'Nice to see I still have an effect on you!' Andy affectionately kissed the tip of Pru's nose before sitting down opposite her. 'Was that a shudder or a judder?'

'It was the wind...' She playfully flicked a beer mat at him.

Bree giggled. 'Now you're starting to sound like Hilda. That poor woman is such a martyr to her flatulence at the moment.'

Jason placed half a bitter shandy in front of Andy and waved a small blue bag at him. 'Nuts?'

'I'm good thanks, I've got these two!' Grinning, Andy pointed at his drinking companions.

'Andrew Barnes!' A second beer mat whirled its way towards Andy's head, this time courtesy of Bree. It missed and went sailing over the top of the carved oak snug divider.

'So, what have you two been up...?' He stopped mid-flow, catching sight of the A4 paper framing the yellowing snippet from the *Nettleton Shrub News* dated 1983. His lips set in a thin line as he turned the paper towards him. He raised an eyebrow, Roger Moore style. 'Dare I ask?'

Pru had the decency to look at least a little bit sheepish. She knew only too well Andy's views on them getting involved in anything other than the bread-and-butter stuff their agency took on, such as the more mundane infidelity cases, minor family thefts and tracing long-lost relatives. She tried to sound nonchalant. 'Oh, that? It's just the place we're going to with the WI posse for a dancing contest, it's pure coincidence that something happened there a long time ago.' She quickly sipped her drink to stop more words from leaving her lips; words that would probably get them both into Andy's bad books.

Bree bit down on her bottom lip and watched him intently. He sipped his pint and took longer than she thought he should to read the article. Finally he looked up.

'Double murder? Unsolved case? Please don't tell me you two are contemplating getting up to mischief – again?' His vibrant blue eyes darted from one to the other, searching their faces for any sign of a 'tell'.

'Don't look at me like that! You make me feel guilty even if I haven't done anything!' Pru gave him a cheeky smile, hoping to distract him, but the slight quiver to her top lip told him that she was hiding something from him. He actually found it quite cute, and any other time he would have kissed that gorgeous 'tell' until it disappeared, but right this minute, all he wanted to know was if he should be worried.

He turned his attention to Bree. 'Well?'

'Don't blame me, it's all *her* fault, *she* suggested it! Look, the photocopy is from the library... *her* library!' Bree turned away from his intense gaze and came face to face with Pru, her mouth wide open in astonishment.

'Jeez, throw me under the bus, why don't you? Fine friend you are! Look, it's nothing, we just said when we're next at Winterbridge library we'd have a look at their records, see what happened at Harmony Hollows. No biggie.'

'And then what?' Andy was trying very hard to stay mad at her, but he knew he was on a hiding to nothing. She had a steely determination coupled with a barely perceptible vulnerability, one that he couldn't help but admire, and one that also brought out his natural instinct to protect. He watched the sweep of her eyelashes fanning her cheeks as she looked down, considering his question.

'And then we go home and...' Pru winked at him, pursing her lips suggestively.

'Oh dear God, will you two get a room!' Bree slugged back her drink. 'I'm off home, Humphrey Hippo and my hot water bottle are waiting! See you tomorrow, missus.'

She flung the brightly coloured scarf around her neck. 'Don't do anything I wouldn't do!' The door clicked shut behind her, leaving Pru and Andy to contemplate their next move.

'Home it is then, my Loony Librarian…' He helped her on with her coat and took the opportunity to kiss the nape of her neck.

'Now that definitely was a judder not a shudder, my Delectable Detective…'

WAIT FOR ME...

The spring sunshine was favouring Albert Tytherington as he made his way along the cobbled path that curved and followed the edges of Winterbottom Pond. It dappled through the trees that were just starting to unfurl their buds, and then came to rest upon his olive-brown flat cap. It was one of his favourites, hand crafted from Harris tweed and an absolute bargain of a buy for £2.50 from Frugal Finds on the High Street.

Wearing it made him feel smart and gave a jaunty stride to his step. His shiny brown brogues with new laces kicked at the stray gravel, sending it scuttering into the water. He watched the little circles become bigger circles as the ripples spread out across the surface, stopping only when they reached the reeds and grasses.

'Albert! For goodness' sake slow down a little.' Ethel breathlessly caught up with him, her shopping bag still slapping against her thigh from the momentum caused by the little jog she had been forced to execute to reach him. 'What's got into you? It's like "here's your hat, what's your hurry?" this morning.'

'Time is marching away with all of us, my dear, no point in

wasting a second of it.' He gave her a warm smile and continued briskly on, leaving Ethel to follow in his wake. 'I'm already late for the library; poor Pru will be wondering what on earth has happened to me.'

Ethel's heart sank. This was the second time in as many weeks that Albert had got his days mixed up. 'It's not open today, Albie, it's Wednesday. The library doesn't open on a Wednesday, don't you remember?'

He stopped suddenly, his back still to her. She watched him as he looked out across the pond, lost in his own small world. She touched his arm gently to reassure him. Murmuring to himself, she strained to hear what he was saying, but it was a conversation that she was not to be privy to. 'Albie?'

He startled. 'Yes, my dear?'

'I think you said it would be nice to go and have a cup of tea and a scone at Florrie's, I'm sure that's where we said we were on our way to. Shall we?' She snaked her arm through the crook of his elbow and stood beside him. 'Maybe we could promenade there, just like we used to when we were courting. That would be nice, wouldn't it?'

For all her wit and sharp tongue, Ethel instantly knew that this was not the time to indulge it, but to offer comfort and distraction instead. She rested her head upon his shoulder, inhaling the scent of Old Spice aftershave that had clung to his scarf from his liberal splashing from the little white bottle. They walked on in silence, synchronising their pace, until they reached the halfway point of the pond, marked by a weatherworn wooden bench that had silvered with age. Albert stopped briefly to admire the sun sparkling on the calm water. His rheumy blue eyes, filling with tears from the cold, gave him a look of wonderment rather than sadness.

'Shall we rest here for a while, Ethel?' He gently lowered

himself on to the wooden slats, shuffling along slightly to allow room for Ethel to join him.

She nodded. 'Of course, love, we're not in any rush, are we? We have all the time in the world.' A gentle smile with a touch of melancholy brushed her lips as she read the tarnished brass plaque that had been thoughtfully placed in memory of a loved one on the back of the bench, its screws now rusted and standing proud.

No time to say goodbye,
Just a promise that you will wait for me.

Ethel inhaled deeply to keep the sudden rush of emotion in check. How poignant, but also how utterly heartbreaking. She couldn't begin to imagine how it must feel to not be able to say goodbye to someone you love. She gazed at Albert, her love of almost fifty years. They teased each other mercilessly at times, whilst exasperating and annoying each other in equal measure, but neither could be a whole without the other. If she went first she would wait for him for all eternity, no doubt about that. She felt him squeeze her hand.

'Penny for them...' Albert smiled.

'Oh, I was just thinking about the sentiment behind this plaque.' Her fingers reverently stroked the metal. 'It's so sad, isn't it? I'd wait for you.'

He gave a little chuckle. 'You'd have a bloody long wait, Eth, no way am I popping my clogs until I've had me money's worth out of the infernal bit of tin in the airing cupboard. And besides, if you're not here to keep me warm at night, I might even have to up the thermostat to keep me snug in my new bed – the one that I will have purchased after you've curled up your toes!'

'Albert Barnard Tytherington, you utter cad!' Ethel squealed.

'First thing tomorrow we're going for a new bed.' She held up her index finger to silence him. 'No arguments. If I'm going first, then I'm going attired in my best winceyette nightie on a memory foam mattress with pocket springs!'

Their heads touched with affection as their shoulders jiggled with laughter, and tears wet their cheeks to fondly evidence over fifty years of love, laughter, exasperation, happiness – and the promise of a new bed.

HAPPY BIRTHDAY TO YEW...

Sophie stood in the kitchen chewing the inside of her cheek. Her medication sat untouched by the kettle, which was merrily whistling away as it belched out copious amounts of steam. The rage was building within her again and would soon need an outlet. The unexpected appearance of Dirty Gertie's sister had well and truly thrown a spanner in the works, just as everything seemed to be going so well too.

You stupid, stupid woman. How on earth did you think you could get away with it? she mentally berated herself as she slammed the cupboard door shut and chucked a couple of teabags into the spotty teapot.

'Everything all right in there, dear?' The disembodied voice of Agatha Timpson drifted through from the morning room of 28 Larton Lane to add an extra layer of annoyance to Sophie's already fragile temperament.

She poured the boiling water into the pot and waited a few seconds before giving it a vigorous stir, all the while her brain was working ten to the dozen.

Two choices, Sophie, lie and keep lying or eradicate the problem...

'I'm good, thank you, Miss Timpson. Would you like some digestive biscuits, and I've got a lovely Victoria sponge cake too?' Sophie brightly trilled, desperately trying to drown out and keep the 'other her' in check until she knew how this would play out. She hoped the woman would simply accept Sophie's explanation for her sister's absence, drink her tea, eat the cake, and bugger off. Her fingers hovered over the pills, and then just as quickly pulled away. She would need that inner self if she were to choose option two; it was a selection she couldn't carry out on her own, so to suffocate it with medication would be a disaster.

'I don't mind if I do, it's been quite a journey to get here. I've been out of my mind with worry over Gertrude, I simply can't believe she didn't give me any consideration whatsoever, particularly when it's my birthday today...' Agatha wittered loudly. She happily accepted the cup and saucer from Sophie and finger-plucked a biscuit from the offered plate. She balanced it on the saucer. 'I've lost count of the messages I have left her, and the letters I sent – and what did I get in return? Nothing, absolutely nothing, and then I come here and you tell me she's had a late-life crisis and flown off to help out at a dog sanctuary in Thailand, leaving you to look after the place!'

Sophie found herself mesmerised by Agatha's tightly pursed mouth. The smoker's lines, furrowed deep around her lips, had enabled the bright red lipstick Agatha had smeared on to bleed outwards, reminding her of a grotesque marionette. 'It surprised me too, Miss Timpson, but I don't mind, although I will be leaving in a week or two to take up a new job.'

Agatha thought for a moment. 'Well, that settles it. I'll send for my things and I'll come and stay here, to take up the mantle, so to speak. This place could do with someone to show it a bit of love.' She swept her eyes around the dismal room. 'Our

Gertrude never was the best at keeping house. I'll have it shipshape for her return.' She placed her cup and saucer on the coffee table and eased herself up from the chair, making a steady pace to the window. 'Spring is upon us and this garden could do with a tidy up, and I know just the person to do it.' She swirled her fingers over the glass pane and checked the tips for dirt. 'That hideous tree in the middle can go for a start. Whatever possessed her to get a yew tree is beyond me; everyone knows it's a symbol of death.' She gave an exaggerated shudder.

Sophie stood rigid, her hand holding the cake knife that was poised over the moist sponge that she had just halved.

If only you knew how true that is, Agatha.

The last thing she needed was some geriatric Hyacinth Bucket poking her nose around and digging up something she would rather be left dead and buried – in the literal sense.

'A clematis would look nice against the shed too...' Agatha absent-mindedly straightened the lace runner on the sideboard, which caused one of the books that had sat regimented in the middle to fall over. She picked it up. A small burgundy red booklet displaying a golden crest on the front, dropped from its pages and lay stark against the cream material. Pinched between finger and thumb, she opened it, her lips moving in time to her whispered words. 'Gertrude Timpson, British Citizen...' Agnes's brow furrowed as she allowed her brain to process what she had just read. Sophie held her breath, waiting. Finally, Agnes spoke. 'How can she be in Thailand when her–'

Option two, Sophie, it's option two but how are you going to do it?

Sophie quickly flung her hands over her ears trying to block out the voice, a low moan escaped from her mouth. 'I don't know... I... I... but it's got to be quick!'

Still puzzled at what she had found, and surprised at

Sophie's outburst, Agatha turned to face her, Gertrude's passport in her hand. 'What has to be quick, dear?'

'This!'

Sophie lunged forward with a forceful upper thrust of her right hand. Agatha, her eyes wide, bulging with horror, fell against her, allowing barely an inch between them and Sophie's eyes.

Sophie twisted the knife before slowly withdrawing it.

'Why?' Agatha gasped. Her eyelids rapidly flickered and then set halfway between life and death, as the air that had once sustained her was ripped from her body.

Sophie watched her own reflection in the blue-green globes framed by sparse lashes, relishing the power, until the light within them was finally gone.

'*Because she can...*' the small voice replied.

A warm, scarlet wetness was shared momentarily between them, until Sophie let go of the now lifeless body of Miss Agatha Timpson, allowing it to slide slowly to the floor.

It had been a while...

The feeling was like an old friend returning.

Sophie dragged the corpulent corpse across the Axminster carpet and onto the chair that Agatha's sister had occupied at the time of her own demise, with the promise that she would at some point, once Sophie had finished with her presence, join Gertrude under the yew tree. She arranged Agatha's hands so they rested upon her lap and tilted her head to give her an air of interest, as though she could be privy to an overheard conversation.

'Well, I suppose it's better to have some company than none at all...' Sophie sighed as she dropped the bloodied cake knife into the kitchen sink, relishing its clatter against the stainless steel.

Throwing back her head, she laughed and laughed, until

exhausted, she stumbled into the morning room. Curling up on the sofa, she pressed her thumb between her lips, pulled the old patchwork throw over her shoulders and closed her eyes, sleep taking her almost as quickly as death had taken Miss Agatha Timpson.

NOT-SO-SKINNY DIPPING

Clarissa, Millie and Hilda sat with their backs ramrod straight, handbags on their knees and their best Sunday hats perched on top of their freshly coiffured hairdos, patiently waiting for Ethel to join them. Ethel, on the other hand, was blissfully unaware of their want, she was joyfully pumping her feet across the pedals of the aptly named Big Bertha, Winterbottom St Michael's billowing old church organ. Her fingers danced across the keys in a beautifully choreographed rendition of 'Love's Divine All Love's Excelling', as her head nodded and shook in time to the deep resonating sounds from the pipes.

Duuuuurrrr...

'Ooh, dearie me, our Ethel's just hit a duff note!' Clarissa cringed, bringing her shoulders up to her ears as though that action would muffle out the offending noise.

Hilda giggled. 'Aye, he is a bit of a rough old goat, but his sermons aren't too bad...' She gave Reverend Baggott a tight-lipped smirk as he wafted along the aisle, cassock billowing in his wake en route to the pulpit.

'Duff note, I said *duff note*!' Clarissa reiterated rather loudly.

'What's wrong with the cuff on my coat?' Puzzled, Millie examined the sleeve of her cream checked jacket.

'Dear God, don't you start, Millie!' Holding her hands in prayer, Clarissa looked up to the oak beams of the church, silently asking for forgiveness for taking the Lord's name in vain. She often wondered what she had done to deserve the frustrations of two wonderful friends who refused to even consider sharing a hearing aid between them, resulting in so many misheard conversations.

The last note of the organ melodically breathed through the pipes, until spent, silence enveloped the church. An awkward shuffling of feet on the stone floor followed as parishioners made themselves comfortable.

'Good morning and welcome to Winterbottom St Michael's. We are gathered here this fine spring morning...'

The Reverend Baggott's monotone voice droned on, becoming merely a backdrop to Ethel's antics as she made her way along the pew back to her seat. Clearly the Devil had bypassed the vicar's blessing and had come to Winterbottom in the form of her impish behaviour. Kitty was the first to suffer as Ethel deliberately swung her handbag that was hanging from the crook of her arm. It swiped Kitty's jaunty pink beret, knocking it from her head. As Kitty grappled to retrieve it from the pew in front, Brenda Mortinsen became the next to fall foul of Ethel's humour.

'Oops a daisy...' Ethel sniggered as she stumbled over the tapestry prayer cushion, landing awkwardly in Brenda's lap. 'Pity it's not December, or I could be asking what you're bringing me for Christmas!' Ethel's deft fingers animatedly pointed out the much talked about stray hair on Brenda's chin that was wafting in the current of warm air from the vented floor heating.

Brenda's plump hand immediately shot up to cover her mouth. 'Cheeky mare, *you* can talk; at least mine's just a wayward bristle. *Your* chin's got a twin!' Clarissa was quite impressed with Brenda's quick comeback. Normally one for cheerfulness and an easy-going demeanour within their little group, her regular offer of lemon drizzle cake was matched only by her peace-keeping abilities. To offer a sharp retort designed to sting was very unusual. Ethel plonked herself down on the worn wooden pew, squeezing herself between Clarissa and Millie. 'Ooh snappy!' She laughed loudly, giving the mentioned extra chin a little jiggle. 'Right, now we're all here, have a look at this...' She clicked open her handbag and rifled around, before furtively handing each of them a small glossy flyer. 'What do you think? Thought it might be handy to wobble our flesh and get a bit of practice in before we hit Harmony Hollows' outdoor pool. Apparently it's ruddy freezing all year round.'

Millie frowned. 'Aqua Aerobics and Wild Water Swimming? For *us* lot?'

As the Reverend Baggot's sermon continued, their excited whispering reached a crescendo, with Hilda's dulcet tones finally breaking through. 'The only thing that's wild about my water is the weekly free-for-all for an available toilet in Morrisons...' she squealed. 'It can get pretty rough in there when there's a few of us fighting for it. And that's another thing, I don't need a ruddy leaflet to tell me I've got a ladies' problem. Wild water women indeed!'

Several heads from the pews in front turned simultaneously to show their disapproval, with Kitty's stern face taking centre stage. 'Wild water swimming! She said *swimming*, Hilda, I heard that from here – and I really don't think we need to know about your little...'

'I'm sorry, ladies, did the middle of my sentence interrupt the beginning of yours?' Reverend Baggott, his large hands gripping the top of the oak wood pulpit, peered over his half-moon glasses and down onto the first three rows of his congregation. 'Well?'

An uncomfortable silence gripped three of the Four Wrinkled Dears and their friends, each casting their eyes downwards as if in prayer, but in truth it was more in contrition.

Hilda, nonplussed with the Reverend's chastisement, jutted out her chin. 'I was just saying, I've got a bladder the size of a peanut and... oof!' A dig in the ribs from Millie quickly put paid to her planned elucidation of her poor capacity waterworks and the benefits of cranberry juice.

Clarissa took charge under the watchful eye of the Reverend. 'We'll discuss this later at Florrie's, ladies...' She gave a simpering smile to the pulpit. 'Forgive them, Father, for they know not what they do,' she jokingly added under her breath.

'I heard that, Clarissa Montgomery! I might be a bit deaf, but I'm not bloody senile!' Hilda grunted in annoyance.

Ethel placed her arm warmly around Hilda's shoulders. 'I think the jury is still out on that one, dear.' She laughed.

A LITTLE BIT OF DIGGING

The regimented line of elm trees that sat in front of Winterbridge library still had remnants of their flower tassels hanging sparsely in places, the dusky pink now giving way to dark green oval leaves.

Pru and Bree stood at the entrance to the eighteenth-century building, the red brick façade as imposing as ever. Although the afternoon was warm for the time of the year, Pru shivered as her sightline took in the weatherworn headstones of the town's original graveyard. Standing like drunken soldiers, the moss-and-grime-covered stones lined the winding path to the sandstone chapel in the centre.

'Come on, Dilly Dolly Daydream...' Bree had been waiting patiently with one carved oak door held open for her.

The familiar smell of woodblock flooring, polish and musty books sneaked its way out through the opening to greet Pru's nostrils as she climbed the stone steps. 'It still reminds me of my old school. All that's needed is that sickly stench of boiled cabbage and the memory is complete!' She obediently followed Bree inside. 'Here we go, same place as last time, archives this way.' The now familiar backplate of polished wood with its gold-coloured hand and pointy finger, helpfully indicated the way.

Pru pushed hard against the wood, allowing a gentle hiss of air to be expelled from the door, the rubber draught seals parting company to allow them access to the revered section of the library. 'Oh my goodness, look! It's Cecily; she's still alive and kicking *and* still working here, she must be at least a hundred by now!'

Cecily Tucker, her name badge proudly displayed on her cardigan, looked over her glasses at the two women. 'Can I help you?'

Pru cleared her throat. 'Yes please, Cecily, we're looking for newspaper archives for May, June and July 1983, please...' She paused, a frown knitting her eyebrows together in thought. 'Actually, I think it would have to be the nationals, as the case we're looking for happened in Nettleton Shrub, so I doubt our local papers would have much on it.'

Cecily allowed her glasses to drop down and dangle on the ornately woven lanyard attached to each arm. 'Mmm... I see. It wouldn't be the Harmony Hollows unsolved double murder, would it?' She pulled an embroidered cotton handkerchief from her sleeve and dabbed at her nose.

'Yes, yes, it is! How on earth did you know that?' Pru tilted her head, waiting, she knew she hadn't given any hint of what she would be searching for, let alone mentioned Harmony Hollows.

'Because it's very unusual to have three enquiries made for Nettleton Shrub, from three different sources in as many days.' Cecily tapped her nose knowingly with her index finger.

'Who were the enquirers? Did they leave any details?' Bree was eager to know.

Cecily haughtily lifted her chin and pursed her lips. 'I'm sorry but I'm not at liberty to say; these things are strictly confidential.' She pointed the same mishappen arthritic finger that had directed them to the Magdalen House murder files the last time they had been at the library towards the appropriate reference section. 'Aisle 13c, search the year and it will give you the reel or plate code and the storage location. The readers are over there.'

Bree linked arms with Pru and hustled her forward to where Cecily had indicated. 'I'm sure they were the exact same words she used last time.'

'It was aisle 13b that time,' Pru hissed from the corner of her mouth.

Bree pulled away with a look of incredulity. 'How on earth can you remember that when you can't even remember to put the same colour socks on!'

Taking in the multi-coloured purple sock on one foot and the spotty green one on the other just peeping between trainer and sports leggings, Pru sighed. 'I was in a hurry and I didn't put the bedroom light on. Anyway, why didn't you tell me when you called to pick me up? I've walked right through town like this!'

'It's a sign of eccentricity; you'll fit in well with the locals.' Bree's fingers plucked at her bottom lip deep in thought. 'Who do you think has been snooping here, then?'

Pru sat down on the chair in front of the reader and screen. 'I'll take a wild guess that it's been Clarissa and friends for one of them. They think I don't know what they're up to when they get into their little mischief gaggle. As soon as Harmony Hollows was mentioned and its history, I saw their faces light up.' She pulled out her notebook from her jacket pocket. 'Right, your mission if you should choose to take it, is to find reel number M78453/83, which according to this should be...' she moved the mouse deftly over the computer screen and then looked behind her, '...located on that shelf over there.'

Huddled together, they spent the next few minutes slowly

scrolling through the reel, the pages sliding from right to left as their eyes scanned and skimmed each newspaper archive. February and March 1983 appeared and then just as quickly disappeared from view, to be replaced with another page of faded print and old grainy photographs.

'Here we go...' Pru's heart skipped a beat as the headlines screamed out to her from the 24th of May 1983 edition of the *Telegraph.*

HOLIDAY CAMP DOUBLE MURDER

Grisly discovery at Nettleton Shrub

A macabre scene greeted staff at the Harmony Hollows Resort in the sleepy village of Nettleton Shrub, with the discovery of the body of a female in one of the holiday camp chalets. The deceased, who has since been named by police as Deborah Anne Purkiss, a nineteen-year-old dancer from Bickerton Bay, is believed to have been at the resort for the Northern Ballroom Championships. A second body was later discovered during a search of the chalet. There have been no further details released at this time.

The silence between them was palpable, broken only by a breathless 'sheesh!' from Bree.

'It's not much more than the *Nettleton Shrub News* gave us. Quick. Scroll on. See if anything else was reported in the days following.' She elbowed Pru to jolt her into action.

The reader screen flickered as several pages were rapidly bypassed in favour of the 26th of May edition. That's it, there...' Bree's finger excitedly jabbed at the headline that informed them that the second body at Harmony Hollows had been identified.

IT TAKES TWO TO TANGO

23RD MAY 1983

'Faster, faster, make it go faster...'

Debbie Purkiss squealed with delight as the rough, but handsome gaff boy on the waltzer ride ferociously spun her brightly painted car. He gave her a wink and then with the agility of an acrobat, he jumped, his foot barely touching the undulating carousel floor before catching the next car in line to begin his routine once again.

Her head jerked back almost hitting the curved metal rim as her fingers turned white, gripped to the safety bar. She had never felt so alive, so exhilarated...

So free.

That's what she was, she was free. No cares, no worries, no orders to obey, just fun, pure and simple. She had left all her woes behind. It was all her mum's problem now, and as an added bonus, she was getting plenty of uninterrupted sleep – once she managed to find her way back to her chalet. She giggled. Several bottles of Babycham and a double vodka had somehow played havoc with her inner compass, not to mention her inhibitions too. She was still unsure that sharing her waltzer car with the holiday camp bad boy had been one of her better ideas, but he was rather gorgeous, so she could forgive herself just this once.

Larry Belfont was charismatic and dangerous in equal measure. Older, more experienced, but oh so desirable.

Her bleached blonde hair whipped across her face as the carousel's momentum quickened the rotation of the car, the deep beat of the music vibrated and boomed, further charging the electricity that was surging through her. His arm snaked around her waist, pulling her closer to him, the glint in his mesmerising grey eyes giving her a promise of what was to come as she slid along the seat. She inhaled the aroma of his leather jacket mixed with the heady musk of Brut aftershave.

'Maybe I will have an early night after all.' She gave him a sultry smile, and then just as quickly hoped her obvious admission of eagerness – or lascivity, as her mother would call it, wouldn't seem too forward. The ride came to a slow stop, their car swinging right to left until it settled, Larry took the opportunity to grab her hand, drawing her away from the fairground and onto the rigid paths leading to the chalets of Marigold Lawns in Harmony Hollows. She clutched the key to Chalet 13 in her hand, her decision made as he roughly pushed her against the wall, his lips meeting hers fleetingly. 'Not here…' she whispered. She dangled the key tantalisingly in front of him, caution thrown to the wind; this time she led him to where she wanted him to be.

Giggling, they fell inside the small room, slamming the door shut behind them, their heightened expectations of each other masking the danger that was lurking. Larry fiddled with the transistor radio until it picked up the strains of Barry White's 'Let's Get It On'. He grabbed Debbie tightly, pressing himself into her.

Creeeeerkkk…

'What was that?' Debbie pulled away from their embrace and jerked her head towards the small bathroom, listening intently. Larry

paid no heed, nuzzling further into her neck, his mind on other more important things. 'I'm serious, there's something in there.' She broke away from him, taking small steps towards the dark void, the weak bedside lamp barely reaching that side of the room, blocked by the large melamine wardrobe. Nonplussed that she was investigating alone, Larry threw himself down on the bed and sparked his Zippo lighter into action. The tip of the Silk Cut cigarette glowed in the dismal corner as it caught light. He inhaled deeply and exhaled with precision, allowing the smoke rings to pulsate towards the ceiling. 'Course there's something in there, two cheap bog rolls and your toothbrush…' he guffawed. 'Or maybe, just maybe, a Nettleton Shrub rat!'

Debbie felt along the rough wall of the bathroom for the light pull. Her fingers plucked at the cord's weighted end, but it bounced and swung out of her reach. Frustrated, she banged the bathroom door wider and stepped into the darkness, waving her hand in front of her, trying to catch it.

Thwump…

Thwump…

It bounced twice against the wall and then stopped. She stretched out her hand again. 'This bloody light…' Her words were suddenly cut short, replaced by a deep guttural gurgling sound. Before she could react, the thin cord she had been seeking was tightly wound around her neck, pinching and puckering her delicate skin. She flailed her arms, trying to strike whoever was doing this to her, but her need to fight her attacker was replaced with a more urgent need: the need to breathe. Her fingers frantically plucked at her neck, scraping and gouging her skin in a desperate attempt to pull the cord away, fear gripping at the pit of her stomach.

'Debbie?' Larry pushed himself up on his elbow and listened. 'Come on, Debs, you don't have to spend forever tarting yourself up in there. It's all here waiting for you; stop pratting around.' He made a show of gyrating his denim clad hips in time to the music, admiring

his own prowess, ignorant of her fight for life as he slugged back a good measure of Jack Daniels.

As Debbie's last breath ebbed away, a bleaker darkness took hold of her. It pulsated in time to her waning heartbeat; it grew with each passing second, pushing a blood-red backdrop to her eyes, lit by bursts of painful light.

Whump, whump, whump.

Until there was nothing.

Debbie was dropped silently to the bathroom floor as the shadow of her assailant elongated through the doorway, across the stippled walls, to curve and bend where the cheap cornice met the ceiling.

Waiting for the right moment.

If Larry had been less intent on practising his snake hips whilst filling his lungs with nicotine and his stomach with Tennessee whiskey that had thrown him into an alcohol-fuelled sleep, he might have noticed the intruder standing in the glow that the weak amber light had cast upon the floor. He might have jumped to his feet to fight, and he just might have won. Instead, he had to be content with one last snore and several skull-crushing blows to the head from a heavy metal doorstop in the shape of a marigold.

The intruder watched the last breath of Larry Peter Belfont and marvelled at the scarlet pattern that slowly spread and soaked the pillow before dragging his body into the wardrobe. Cleverly utilising the hosepipe of the hoover that was stored inside, Larry was wedged in the corner. In the hope that rigor mortis would soon set in, and he would be discovered in flagrante with the hoover nozzle, Larry's limbs were rearranged accordingly.

If death were not enough for Larry, then humiliation would be the perfect icing on the cake to make him pay.

THE LAST GOODBYE

As the early morning sun rose from behind the trees that bordered the small garden of Lavender Cottage, Ethel popped her pinny over her head and patted down the floral fabric. She had risen early to the promise of a warm breeze that would soon dry the weekly wash, so the sooner it was pegged to the line, the better. Her day was meticulously planned, once Albert had been fed and watered, she was meeting Clarissa and the girls at the Twisted Currant Café for tea, cake and a natter to discuss their findings on Harmony Hollows. Their foray to Winterbridge library the week before hadn't yielded much information for their cold-case investigations, but they had inadvertently fallen into the local White Lion pub for lunch and a few snifters of sweet sherry, before hitting Primark for their holiday clothes.

The cheerful chant of 'Harmony Hollows here we come!' had prompted them to spend more than they had anticipated, which said a lot when you were shopping in Primark. Clarissa had plumped for a rather fetching multi-coloured jacket that Ethel had disparagingly likened to Joseph's Technicolour Dreamcoat, and Hilda had chosen a pair of bright yellow harem pants with accompanying red and green tassels. No amount of dissuading her had worked, not even the threat of northerly winds to whistle up the legs and inflate her like a barrage balloon; her mind was set and she stubbornly refused to part with them. Ethel had eventually treated herself to a nice new pair of sandals in the vain hope that the weather would be fairly decent. Millie, on the other hand, had become rebellious, refusing to purchase anything from the store, but happily assisted the others by dragging the navy-blue shopping basket that resembled a Grimsby trawler net along the grey tiled floor.

Ethel smiled, she loved this time of the day; it had a special tranquillity that soothed her soul and helped her mind to drift, which it had just so easily done. Returning to the task in hand, she hooked the peg bag on her pinny pocket and picked up the laundry basket, simultaneously pushing the lower half of the barn door open with her hip. She stood momentarily on the porch, inhaling deeply whilst listening to the birdsong. As she made her way to the washing line, her slipper-clad foot kicked at the lavender that edged the cobbled path, the very plant that had given their home its name. It had been one of the first things they had loved about the place when they'd viewed it all those years ago, the front garden during July had been a veritable feast of differing shades of lilac and heady scents. She was pleased to see that there were signs of early flowering on the carefully planted row, which gave hope for a mild and warm May.

Ethel checked her watch. 'Ten more minutes, Albert Tytherington, and then it's up out of that bed, even if I have to turf you out myself!' she grumbled. She looked up at the bedroom window, the curtains still tightly closed. She had noticed him wearying after very little effort lately, and his afternoon snoozes had almost doubled in time, taking him up to four o'clock most days. She laughed to herself. 'Trying to get out of a trip into town for a new bed no doubt! Well I'm wise to your tricks, Albie...' She chuckled.

Laundry chores complete, Ethel filled up the kettle and settled the lid in place. Two cups, two saucers and, of course, porridge on the go. The slices of bread sat ready in the toaster, just waiting for her fingers to pop down the switch. She made her way into the hall, taking the time to straighten the edelweiss thermometer on its hook. She tapped the thermostat for the central heating and sighed. Eighteen degrees as set by the master of the house. She stood at the bottom of the stairs. 'Breakfast in five, Albie, your clean clothes are on the chair,' she shouted.

Returning to the kitchen, she shivered. It might have been pleasant outside, but the sandstone-built cottage didn't really warm up without assistance until at least the end of June, hence the need for a little bit of heating first thing in the morning. Her fingers touched the radiator, relieved to feel some warmth seeping into the metal. 'Albie...' she hollered again as she flicked the toaster down. 'Dearie me,' she chunnered away to herself as she made her way upstairs to wake him, '...not content with becoming Rip Van Winkle, your hearing is getting worse too!'

The latch on the door rattled loudly as she briskly entered their bedroom. 'Come on, lazy bones...' She skirted the edge of the bed and drew back the curtains to allow the sun to energise the room, and in turn, hopefully Albert too. 'Your porridge will be getting as lumpy as this bloody bed if you don't shift your bottom.' She prodded the sleeping form of Albert, his back facing her with the floral duvet tucked tightly around him. 'It's a beautiful day too, perfect for a stroll around The Green...' She positioned herself so she could see him, her hands on her hips and her lips set into a warm smile. He looked so peaceful she felt it would be a shame to wake him. She tenderly stroked his head and leant down to give him his usual early morning kiss on the cheek, but suddenly recoiled. With her breath savagely snatched away from her, she stood rigid with shock, a low moan escaping from her lips. 'Oh Albie, not now, my love, please not now...' she whimpered.

His promise to her had been broken.

He had gone first.

Her eyes brimmed with tears, the sob she so desperately needed to release caught in her throat. 'My darling, darling man...' She wept. Cradling him in her arms, she rocked him like a mother would a child, singing to him, wishing him well for his journey without her, then pleading with God to give him back. She wasn't ready, she hadn't been prepared, and all she wanted now was to have their time together all over again.

'What fun we had, what love we shared, Albie. What on earth am I going to do without you?' She sobbed, desperate for one last embrace with the man who had stolen her heart all those years ago, and who had now shattered that same heart into a thousand pieces by leaving her.

Ethel remained with him in the silence. For the first time in over fifty years the sound of her breath was not matched by the sound of his. She watched the sudden appearance of a singular grey cloud through the window, slowly pushing out the blue, making the small room darken by its unwanted presence. It was as though her loss was being felt by nature itself. She kissed him tenderly and closed her eyes. 'I will always love you, Albert Barnard Tytherington...'

As the words on the weatherworn bench had forewarned, there had been no time to say goodbye, but she knew deep down and with all of her broken heart that he would keep his promise to wait for her.

AN EMPTY CHAIR

In the days that followed the sudden passing of Albert, Winterbottom and its ladies rallied around and did what they always did best. They offered comfort and kindness to Ethel, along with the practicalities of small Tupperware bowls full of home-made soup, and decorated tins containing cake. This was mainly to encourage her to eat, but also as tokens of their desire to care for her, and more importantly, to have the chance to offer their time and a shoulder to cry on.

Pru sat behind her desk at the Winterbottom library shop, her chin propped by her hand, deep in thought. The high street shop that had been turned into a small community library after the main town library had closed, was usually her happy place. The loss of Albert was playing heavy on her heart. She couldn't imagine her own life without Andy, and they hadn't even notched up five years together, let alone fifty. She looked over to the empty chair where Albert should have been. The *Winterbottom News* was still neatly folded and untouched. She glanced towards her little tea-making cubby in the far corner. Albert's favourite mug sat cold and unused; the packet of digestives he favoured, still unwrapped. She missed him dreadfully; her little book haven just didn't feel right without him.

She swept her hand across the bound leather cover of the wedding album that lay in front of her, and reverently opened it. Her finger traced the outline of the photograph carefully fixed onto the first page. Albert's head was held high, his pride to have Pru on his arm was there for all to see. In the absence of her own father, Albert had been delighted to step into the breech to give her away. She turned to the pages that held snapshots of their reception. 'Aww look at this one…' she murmured to herself. Ethel, with her mouth full of cake was making Albert laugh, his eyes twinkling and crinkling at the edges. It was a moment of pure happiness and simple fun, captured for eternity.

Pru swallowed hard, desperately trying to push down the huge lump that had formed in her throat, but to no avail. The tears once again welled up and spilled over her lower lashes on to her cheeks. She covered her face with her hands and wept, feeling the loss of Albert as keenly as she had felt the loss of her father all those years ago.

The little brass bell above the shop door tinkled loudly, forcing Pru to quickly wipe her cheeks with the pulled down cuff of her jumper. She turned away and blinked rapidly, hoping that her eyes hadn't gone completely bloodshot, before turning back to see who it was.

'Oh, it's you…'

'Well, that's a nice greeting from my beloved, I must say!' Andy grinned. 'I've run across several counties to be with you in your hour of need, and all you can say is, "Oh it's you".' He wrapped his arms around her. She nestled her head into his chest, which gave him the opportunity to kiss the top of her head. 'Daft question I know, but are you okay?'

Pru pulled away from him and nodded.

He searched her eyes with his intense blue eyes. 'Really? So, is spidery veins with a touch of pink all the fashion for contact lenses this season, or have you been crying?'

She knew he had sought a twenty-four-hour compassionate leave from his out-of-force investigation, leaving Lucy to take up the slack, but his slight exaggeration of several counties being crossed to get to her, did make her smile. 'You're not Forrest Gump on a coast-to-coast marathon, Andy; it's two counties over and you came by car!' She loved that he never failed to lift her heart when she needed it most. 'How did you manage it, though?'

He flicked the kettle on and examined the unopened packet of biscuits, poking his finger into the side until he caught the cellophane wrapping. 'Er... I sort of made out that Albert was like a dad to you, so it went down as leave for a 'family bereavement'. It's only until tomorrow, but I guess we can cram in plenty of hugs, a bottle of wine or two, and an early night between now and when I have to leave.' He gave her a saucy wink.

'...And if *she* isn't up for it, Andy, I sure am! I mean, who wouldn't want a snog from the Delectable Detective?' Bree had somehow bypassed the bell and slipped unnoticed into the shop whilst they had been otherwise engaged. Rolling her eyes, she pointed a manicured nail at Pru. 'Only joking, you'd kill me!' She threw her hobo bag onto the reading table. It lay in a crumpled heap. 'I've just come from the undertakers with Ethel, we've got the date for Albert's funeral.'

Pru's heart jolted with the finality of Bree's words. 'When?'

Bree added an extra mug to the two that Andy had already set out, as the kettle reached its final rumble for the boiling point. 'Two weeks Tuesday. It's going to be a celebration of life, Ethel doesn't want it called a funeral, she wants everyone to know what a character her Albert was, and to remember him with fondness and laughter.' She sat down next to Pru and gave her a quick hug. 'I said we'd help.'

Andy placed the three mugs and a plate of biscuits on the table. 'Here we go...' he said as he offered them out. 'Whatever we can do, just say the word.'

The three friends sat huddled together, the rich mahogany of the shelves and reading desks adding warmth to the little shop, whilst the rigid spines of books in the collector's section fanned greens, golds and reds for interest. They simultaneously looked over to Albert's chair and raised their mugs in unison to the empty place.

'Forever missed, Mr Tytherington...' Pru whispered, as a gentle breeze pushed through the open door, drifted over to the reading desk and ruffled the edges of *The Winterbottom News*.

She dropped her eyes and smiled, a warmth replacing the chill she had previously harboured.

'For although there had been death, as the wind sighed his presence,
she closed her eyes and remembered...'
— The Author

SPECIAL REQUEST

'Well, hello again, Harmony Hollows. It's been quite some time...' Della Claybourne inhaled deeply as she watched the grey and purple flags either side of the entrance gates crack and flap in the wind. She wasn't sure if they were welcoming her or, like the last time she had been here, warning her. Mesmerised, she stood for too long reminiscing, until the wheels of the costume cases crunching on the crumbling tarmac behind her broke the spell.

'Where d'yer want these, Della?' Tom Birks, his patchy orange perma-tan and large pores giving him the look of a ravaged satsuma, swung the two large gold cases by their handles, performing a pretty nifty figure of eight with them.

Della checked her paperwork to tell him. Her eyes widened, it had to be a joke, surely. 'Oh no, Daffodil Lawns and Chalet 10!' she grunted.

'*What?*' Tom tipped his head and looked at her quizzically.

Flustered, she quickly turned on the poor boy. 'Nothing, nothing. For goodness' sake, just use your common-sense, Tom. Take them to your own chalets for now, I'll catch up with you and Macey in a minute.' She thrust their welcome packs at him. 'Your own chalet numbers are in there.'

As Tom trundled the cases through the gates with Macey in tow, Della read and re-read the welcome instructions. No amount of looking at the words would change what it said. She had been allocated Chalet 10, the very same chalet she had occupied on her previous visit, and it certainly wasn't something she welcomed. It was bad enough having to come back to Harmony for the championships, but to come back and relive that era all over again in such a personal space was asking too much of her. She crumpled the sheet of paper in her fist and marched with purpose to Harmony Hollows reception.

Although almost forty-years had gone by, it hadn't changed. Her fingers touched the large plastic banana tree that sat forlornly in a black and white striped ceramic pot. It had a look of desperation as it tried and failed to give the teak-clad reception desk an air of tropical elegance. The receptionist sat with her back to Della, the latest iPhone held to her ear by her scrunched up shoulder, whilst her free hands took advantage of a large patterned emery board.

'Excuse me...' Della waited, taking in the drab grey blazer and unattractive polyester skirt that had seen better days. Neither the blazer, the skirt, or the girl who was wearing them made even the slightest movement to acknowledge her. 'Hellooo! I need to speak to someone...' she tried again in a sing-song voice. Realising that her two previous attempts at being polite had gone unheeded, Della banged her hand down on the bulbous brass bell. It clanged loudly and skittered across the desk, disappearing over the side, landing with a clatter on the floor tiles.

The girl, her name tag introducing her as 'Stacey', quickly whispered into her phone. 'I've got to go, believe it or not, we've got someone *actually here* who wants something!' She dropped her phone and presented herself to Della. 'You rang, madam?'

Embarrassed at her unusual outburst, Della gave an apologetic smile to Stacey. 'I'm so sorry about that, I thought it was fixed to the top.'

'It *was*, madam...' Stacey had already retrieved the bell and was trying to stick it back into place.

'Gosh, I don't know my own strength at times!' Quickly changing the subject, Della pushed the welcome form towards her. 'Could I possibly have a change of chalet, please? This one is not suitable.'

Stacey examined the form and allowed a small *'tsssk'* to escape as she sucked her teeth. She took a clipboard from the hook on the wall and ran her pen down the list, checked the computer screen, and shook her head. 'I'm sorry, Miss Claybourne, we're full. It's the dance championships, you know, and this particular chalet was actually a special request by yourself!'

Della's heart thudded in her chest. 'No, no, absolutely no! I *didn't* request it; it's the *last* place I'd want to stay,' she emphatically stressed.

Stacey's expression gave an air of indifference. 'You have two others in your party, maybe they might exchange their chalet with you. I'm afraid that's all I can suggest.' She patted down the A4 sheets on her clipboard, popped it back on the hook, and began to rearrange her desk, a sign to Della that the conversation was over.

Della turned to leave, the key to Chalet 10 clutched in her hand. 'I was here in 1983, you know...'

Eliciting no reaction from the girl, defeated, Della gathered her belongings and began to leave. She stopped abruptly by the door, a cold chill suddenly creeping over her, almost touching her soul. It was as though the long dead were once again walking in the footsteps she was leaving behind her. She closed her eyes and shuddered.

Watching her, the shadow moved stealthily across the floor from one pillar to the next, keeping out of sight. Everything was coming together nicely and according to plan.

The game had at last begun.

EULOGY FOR A GOOD MAN

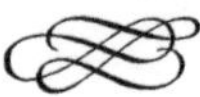

In the heavy silence of Lavender Cottage, Ethel sat on the end of the bed, her fingertips rubbing gentle circles in the quilted counterpane as a way of soothing the sadness in her heart. She looked around the room, taking in the things that had made her life as Mrs Tytherington complete.

A shared wardrobe and dresser, a silver frame of them both at the Shrigley Stiles summer fair in 1972, and Albert's unfinished edition of *The Magic Shop* by H. G. Wells, sitting on his bedside cabinet along with his spectacles, just as he had left them.

And their bed.

Only it wasn't *their* bed any more. It was just hers.

That was the reality she now had to accept. There was nothing in her life that was shared, Albert had gone, and it was just her. She eased herself up from the bed; the last few weeks having taken quite a toll on her. For the first time in a long time, she was actually feeling her age, and her quick wit had all but deserted her, which, in turn, made her feel ever so guilty. Clarissa, Hilda and Millie had virtually lived with her, sharing their friendship duties between them to ensure she was not alone or without soup, cake and even the odd bottle of sweet sherry. They above everyone else deserved to have the old Ethel back as soon as possible.

Reaching the bottom of the stairs, she stood for a while by the coat stand. Albert's grey macintosh hung limply from the curved mahogany peg. She tenderly stroked the fabric, bringing the sleeve up to rest on her cheek. She could still smell him, a faded mix of Old Spice and Pears soap. Her eyes settled on the edelweiss thermometer, still stuck at its legendary 28 degrees. Tracing the red line with her finger, she adjusted its position so it sat regimentally straight alongside the thermostat for the central heating boiler, its 18 degrees setting flashing in the digital window.

His 'infernal piece of tin'.

She chuckled at the memory of his regular lectures on heating and economy. It was so good to feel something other than sadness. For the first time since his passing, she had remembered him with a smile rather than tears. She hoped she was on the first rung of the grief-recovery ladder, ready to climb out of the bleak pit she had been living in. 'Well, that settles it, a Celebration of Life is what we are going to have, Albert, and I know just the thing to put a smile on their faces the way it just has on mine...'

She scurried into the kitchen, excitedly pulling open a drawer in the dresser. Laying out an A4 pad of lined paper and a pen, she popped the kettle on, made herself a nice brew of Yorkshire tea, and began her important task for the following day, her elegant handwriting spidering the page as she penned Albert's final goodbye.

A CELEBRATION OF LIFE

Albert Barnard Tytherington was not just my husband; he was my best friend, my soul mate, and my rock.

As you all know, Albie, as I affectionately called him, curled up his toes wedged in the deep chasm of our old mattress. And a chasm it most certainly was, not a small dent as he preferred to call it. I feel that I must add that the wear and tear on the springs from almost fifty years of marriage in no way contributed to his sudden passing, but it might have made it easier for the undertaker to extricate him if he had bought a new mattress like I'd asked him to.

Joking aside, there was nothing exciting or gossip inducing about his cause of death. As Albie used to say, if something wasn't broken, worn out, or had outlived its use, then it would remain in the Tytherington household until death did it part. My Albie got a little broken and a little worn out, and although he would never have outlived his use, his batteries just simply ran out.

Each day is a new day where I learn to live without his physical presence, whilst simultaneously living with all the beautiful memories that he gifted me during our years together. I miss him and his daily reminders that the 'infernal piece of tin' – our central heating boiler for those of you who don't know – is eating away at our pension. I miss his ability to turn a deaf ear to my nagging before he disappears to Winterbottom library for respite, and I miss pretending that I have baked his favourite wholemeal loaf for him, when in truth I've bought one every week from Florrie's café and shoved it in the baking tin once I got home.

Before we say our heartfelt goodbyes, I would like to leave you with a little ditty that Albie sang to me in our kitchen shortly before he shuffled from this world. I think this sums him and us up perfectly…

When the stars gave me Ethel,
I looked to the moon,
Not to give thanks
But to check for her broom…

Albie, you were a good man, a kind soul, and the laughter in my heart. Sleep peacefully, and don't forget to wait for me – there is still so much left for me to nag you about.

Your Ethel

She sat back in her chair, her teacup poised. It might need a bit more work, but the bones of it were pretty acceptable. There would be tears tomorrow, she knew that, but she also wanted laughter for a life well lived.

Ethel rose from her chair and pottered into the hallway, stopping once again by the two objects that had ruled Albert's daily routine. Smiling to herself, with a wistful twitch to the corners of her mouth that brought with it a feeling of mischief, her finger and thumb hovered over the round thermostat button. She quickly checked up to the heavens in case Albert was watching her – and with a flick of her wrist, she notched it up 10 degrees. Giggling, she sat down with a thump at the bottom of the stairs, the flashing 28 degrees now matching the broken thermometer.

'My dearest Albert, can you imagine, if you hadn't been such a good old soul, you could have gone to that *other* place…' she animatedly jabbed her index fingers downwards, '…just think of all the unlimited free heating you could have enjoyed if you had!'

MEMORIES

Kitty stood by her bedroom window. The large sycamores in the field behind Holly Cottage, that in autumn would shed their red, yellow and orange leaves like confetti over her pristine lawn, now swayed in the late spring sunshine, boasting new seedlings that offered the promise of warm days to come. It made her feel blue to think their boughs would forever shade the graves in Winterbottom St Michael's church that bordered her home. She hated the thought that, once gone, people were destined to be cold for all eternity. She had already made up her mind that when it was her time, she would be buried where the sun shone without risk of shadow.

Her pink Ted Baker Belle suitcase lay open but empty on her bed, her clothes and toiletries sat regimented next to it. Her 'to-do' list had been ticked, and Flo her ragdoll cat had been taken, scratching and yowling in her designer travel box, to *Pawsome Palace* cattery.

'Come on, holiday mood, hit me!' She stood in the middle of the room, her arms out wide, hoping to embrace the excitement and anticipation she needed for the trip to Harmony Hollows. Her objections had fallen on deaf ears, leaving her with two options: boycott the budget price for the ten days they'd opted for and remain at home on her own, or pack her bags, ignore the feelings of trepidation and anxiety, and just go with the flow.

She sat down on the bed, her fingers gently stroking the mohair cardigan that was neatly folded, the pearl buttons catching the sunlight that streamed through the window. Maybe it was time to bury her ghosts for good. She had tried many times over the years, but they always seemed to be floating around the next corner, waiting to jump out and ambush her. She picked up the cardigan and pressed it down into her suitcase, carefully placing a sheet of tissue paper over it before packing the rest of her clothes on top. She slipped a gold pair of sandals inside the mesh hood, along with her toiletries. Satisfied she had everything she needed, she zipped it closed and clicked the combination barrel lock into place.

'Okay, you win...' she whispered as she trundled her case out onto the landing.

It would remain to be seen how she would cope, but it was now or never. Harmony Hollows was the place that frequently invaded her dreams, it was her nemesis and had been for almost forty years.

'Well just look at me, Albie, don't I look like a right one, hey?' Ethel twirled around in front of the bedroom mirror; the lightweight fabric of her pale blue summer dress undulating with the gentle motion.

She picked up a cream handbag from the chair and hooked her arm through it. It didn't quite match her shoes, but nevertheless, she was still delighted with her bargain purchases from Frugal Finds. Her suitcase, which had been packed with her spoils since the previous evening, was propped up by the door, its one wonky wheel making it impossible for it to stand without support. 'I didn't buy the hat, Albie. It didn't look right, and I know you wouldn't have like it...' she warbled. 'Oh, and whilst I remember, you'll never guess what Florrie told me this morning...' She tipped her head and waited for the reply that she knew in her heart would never come.

She looked around the room, all the little reminders of him still there. His book unfinished, his glasses unworn, and the dent in his pillow that she had refused to change or to plump, and their 'love chasm' in the middle of the bed, testament to their almost fifty years of marriage. She so wanted to believe that he hadn't really left her.

But he had.

She had given him the most perfect send off, but in doing so, she had finally faced her loss and was now alone.

The sudden unexpected wave of grief that washed over her brutally pushed the air from her lungs, forcing her to sit down on the bed. She had heard people talk about the pain of loss, but until she had lost Albert, she had not realised that it was an actual physical pain they were talking about. That pain now tore at her heart and pushed into her throat, making it constrict as she fought the tears. Her fingers swept the counterpane until they touched his old gardening jumper. The one she now slept with every single night.

Rocking backwards and forwards, she hugged the aged woollen knit to her chest, burying her face into the rough fabric and wept. She could still smell him, and if she closed her eyes, she could pretend he was still here.

But he wasn't.

'I miss you so much, Albert Barnard Tytherington...' she whispered as she quickly unzipped her suitcase and pushed the jumper inside. 'There you go, my dear. See, we're never really apart, are we, Albie?'

AND THEY'RE OFF...

Clarissa carefully stacked her handbag on top of her suitcase. She checked the luggage label for the umpteenth time, and once satisfied that should her valise go astray between Winterbottom and Nettleton Shrub it would be swiftly reunited with her, she turned her attention to her friends.

'Is Hilda's bag packed and ready, Millie?' Clarissa's sandals tapped on the woodblock flooring before becoming muffled as she stepped on the burgundy-coloured rug that directed her towards the kitchen like an airport runway. 'Oh for goodness' sake!' Frustrated, she took a deep breath to quell the rising irritation she was feeling. 'Hilda Mary Jones, what on earth do you think you're doing?'

Hilda, nonplussed by her friend's sharpness, readjusted the cushion of the well-loved leather armchair she was sitting in and held out a bumper pack of ready salted crisps. 'Do you want one, 'Rissa? I'm just waiting for my holiday toes to dry before I put my shoes on.' She lifted her legs and wriggled ten white painted toes. 'Must say, I'm not much fussed on the colour, what made you get that shade?'

Clarissa checked her watch. 'Come on, we've got less than twenty minutes to get our well-padded backsides down to Florrie's to pick up the coach, and that's without a detour to collect Ethel...' She picked up the small bottle that Hilda had used. 'And this is enamel touch-up paint for the rust on my fridge, Hilda. You'll still be sporting those awful talons for the next five years, that's how long its guaranteed for!'

'I told her we didn't have time, but would she listen – no, no she wouldn't...' Millie wandered back into the kitchen and tutted as she tried to untuck the back of her dress from her knickers. 'Anyone else need a little tinkle before we go?'

Clarissa closed her eyes in exasperation. She loved her friends dearly, but a whole ten days with misheard conversations, confused wanderings, and trying to keep Ethel upbeat, was definitely going to be a challenge and a half. She just thanked her lucky stars that Hilda and Millie had been more than happy to share a chalet at Harmony Hollows. She had been surprised but very pleased that Ethel had made the decision to join them. In the aftermath of Albert's funeral, life had been very different for the foursome, their friendship had remained as tight as ever, but there had been a heaviness cast over them, or as Ethel had called it, a blanket of grief. They had each brought kindness, comfort and care to her table, but sometimes Clarissa wondered if it was enough – until one wet and rainy Wednesday morning at the Twisted Currant Café, when Ethel had made an announcement.

'It's time...' she had declared over a particularly delicious bath bun. 'Albie wouldn't have wanted me moping around, so Harmony Hollows here I come!' A ripple of applause from her friends had supported her very welcome decision.

Clarissa smiled at the memory. Her friend was on the road to what they called a 'life after', one that was best served by laughter and camaraderie. She watched Hilda with her newly enamelled toes and Millie with a section of frock still attached to the elastic of her knickers, skip along her path, suitcases rolling behind them. She closed her front door and double-checked its security by giving it a little push.

Life would be good again for them; it would level and lighten. She was very sure of that.

'Ladies, please, quick as you can. Find your seats... oh for goodness' sake, Brenda, move along so others can get on, it's not a cattle grid, you know; you can keep going!' Kitty Hardcastle waved her arms around to her invisible orchestra as the Winterbottom WI ladies boarded the Rubber Springs & Gaskets Coach Tours bus. Frank Atkins, owner and driver, gave himself momentary respite from stacking the suitcases through the cavernous opening in the side of his coach to give her a flirty wink, which made Kitty blush profusely.

Pru and Bree sat in the first two seats at the front, reluctantly allowing Kitty to take charge, watching her through the window. 'She's in full-on boss-bitch mode, isn't she?' Bree nudged Pru with her elbow. 'Bet you by the middle of the week Frank will be nipping between chalets offering her his annual service agreement, and she'll have a grin on her face as wide as the Mersey Tunnel.'

Pru giggled. Kitty's liaisons with Frank were the worst kept secret of Winterbottom village, although she was still oblivious to the gossip that went on behind her back. 'Look, here's Clarissa and the ladies. I'm so glad that Ethel changed her mind; it'll do her good to get away. Apparently, she's a champion bingo player, according to Hilda, so the evening entertainment at this place will be perfect for her.' Ethel's head suddenly appeared over the top of the safety rail that edged the steps, catching Pru off guard. 'Ethel! We were just saying we're over the moon you could make it,' she gushed, which made her inwardly cringe. Not wanting to sound as though she had been gossiping about her had made her sound insincere.

Ethel tilted her straw sun hat with her finger, cowboy style, and grinned. 'I wouldn't have missed this for the world. And do you think I'd let these three go without me? It would be chaos, I tell you, absolute chaos if I wasn't here to rein them in.' She pushed herself forward along the aisle. 'Come along, Millie. Get a move on. Actually, talking of bingo, you and Hilda are acting like two fat ladies, you're causing a bottleneck this end.'

'Cheeky, but I'm more legs eleven with my gorgeous pins!' Hilda hoiked a leg up high across the aisle, '...and I've got no-rust toenails too! Beat that, girls!' She chuckled.

Relieved at the banter, Pru chalked an imaginary one into the air. 'See, our old Ethel is back at last and in fine fettle too!' She paused, watching Millie struggle with the large gaily patterned canvas bag she had dragged with some difficulty, along the aisle. 'Dearie me, Millie, what have you brought? Everything but the kitchen sink?' Millie grinned as she squished it into the overhead rack. 'It's my knitting; when this lot were busy buying fancy clothes, I grabbed myself a bargain and got a bumper pack of double-knit wool in the shop next door. It'll keep me occupied if the weather's not so good.'

Pru gave Millie a helping hand, and then began to count heads and tick names on her list, until after fifteen minutes of pushing, shoving, giggling and squeezing, everyone was on board. Kitty was last to get on, giving Pru and Bree a look of disdain. For as long as she could remember, the front two seats had been hers and hers alone. Now no longer WI president, she had been consigned to the back amongst the riffraff. Kitty would have checked herself for that unkind thought, but was quickly distracted by Brenda waving animatedly from seat number twenty.

'Yes, Brenda dear, what's the matter?' Kitty stumbled slightly as Frank set the coach in motion, falling inelegantly into her seat, an explosion of silk blouse and white linen slacks. Brenda proudly displayed her large Tupperware box in the air. 'I've made a little something for the journey, ladies. Lemon drizzle cake, anyone? It's to die for!'

The collective groans of her fellow WI members were followed by a rousing rendition of 'Jerusalem' as the red and cream coach rattled and rolled out of Winterbottom, bound for much-needed good times at the Harmony Hollows Resort.

NELLIE

The early morning sun broke through the puffed white clouds that were lazily making their way across the sky, masking the fields that bordered Harmony Hollows Resort with dappled patches of fleeting darkness.

Nellie Girdlestone popped a dockered Embassy ciggie between her lips and sparked her cheap plastic lighter. The flame caught the stumped end of the cigarette and burnt with an orange glow. She closed her eyes and inhaled deeply. The nicotine rush hit her chest full throttle, which in turn set off a coughing fit. Her lungs rattled with the effort as she gave the offending item between her fingers a withering look, as though her poor health was solely the fault of Imperial Tobacco itself, and nothing to do with her own lifestyle choice. 'Bloody cheap crap...' she spat, picking a sliver of tobacco from her bottom lip between her nails. 'They still cost a ruddy fortune, though; it'd be cheaper to smoke my old man's sweaty socks!'

Not content with almost losing one lung, she took another drag; this time the effect was not as severe. She furtively inched her way along the pebble-dashed wall of the chalet block and peered around the corner to check that the coast was still clear.

Every time Nellie thought she had found the perfect place to indulge her habit, someone on the staff at Harmony Hollows would spot her, and either give her a dressing down there and then, or report her to management. It was only the start of the season, and she'd already had two warnings.

'Shit...' she grumbled as she spotted the group of Greycoats walking along the path towards her. She was in imminent danger of being caught again. Nellie quickly pulled back out of view and threw the cigarette into the plastic bucket at her feet, frantically fanning the air in front of her to disperse the tell-tale evidence. Grabbing the mop, she breezed out of her hiding place. The duster that had been tucked into her overall pocket was hastily whipped out and she began to clean the window nearest to her, paying great attention to the corners. No porthole cleaning for Nellie. She kept her back to the entourage as they strode towards her, playing out her role of resort domestic as they passed by, heads down, clipboards in hand, paying no heed to her.

In the centre of the group was the new resort manager, Ralph Fairbright. Nellie hadn't yet made up her mind as to what her opinion of Ralph Fairbright should be after all these years, but one bonus point she could give him was the upgrade in bog rolls for Harmony Hollows. He had decreed it would be 3ply quilted to replace the stingy, finger-through-the-sheet 2ply the chalets had been subjected to under the old regime. She had already acquired a pack of four rolls to take home, although how she envisaged smuggling them out, was anyone's guess, but she knew her Percy would be pleased to have such a special treat for his hairy backside.

Taking the master key from her pocket, she slipped the bronze shaft into the lock of the chalet and turned. The mortice gave way easily, allowing the door to swing open. Nellie checked the coast was clear and slipped silently through the threshold, the soft click of the lock as she pushed the door closed reassuring her that she was safely ensconced within the walls and out of sight.

She stood with her hands on her hips, surveying the room. It was relatively tidy and quite clean, not like the chalets on her list. Her allocated round was the one that was disparagingly known as the 'Harmony Hovels', the absolute pits of the resort. It housed a mixture of stag and hen groups, and those who liked to indulge in frisky weekends away, usually with a wife or husband that belonged to someone else. She pulled the sleeve down on her jumper to cover her hand and tentatively pulled open the drawer of the bedside cabinet.

'You've got to be kidding me!' she hissed under her breath as she pushed aside several pairs of large multi-coloured polyester bloomers. She picked one pair out and held them aloft. 'That's got to be one hippo-sized arse to fit into them...' she snorted. Suddenly hearing footsteps outside the chalet, she paused and held her breath. They grew softer as they passed, allowing her to at last exhale, forcing her chesty cough to put in another appearance. She knew she could always blag it and pretend she was just doing her job if she was caught, the perfect alibi being a cleaner, but she'd prefer not to be found with her hand in the till so to speak, especially in a chalet that wasn't on her list. She returned to the task at hand and rummaged around, her fingers like tentacles feeling towards the back of the drawer, the place all the golden oldies stuffed their treasures. It made her laugh to think the barrier of antiquated underwear they always arranged on top would be a deterrent. 'There we are! Come to Mummy, my shiny little trinket,' she cooed, as she held the gold brooch inset with sparkling green stones to the light. 'Beautiful...'

She slipped it into her pocket, smugly patting the fabric. It should fetch a few bob; tide her over until the next time. She wasn't greedy; her spasmodic pilfering of other people's possessions meant more often than not that their absence was attributed to forgetfulness and accidental loss rather than an actual crime. And that was just how she liked it.

Content with her haul, Nellie Girdlestone left the way she had entered.

Silently and unseen.

THE ARRIVAL

Frank steered his trusty coach through the wrought iron gates that announced their safe arrival at Harmony Hollows Resort by way of a large commercial sign. The circus style lights ran from corner to corner, framing the grey and purple lettering. Several bulbs were in dire need of replacing; they were either completely out or were flickering rhythmically.

Pru looked through the coach window and her heart sank. Even the two flags had given up the ghost and were hanging limply in the non-existent breeze. 'Oh jeez, it's like something out of the 1960s, it's so... so...' Her shoulders slumped as she let out a disappointed sigh, words failing her to describe her first impression.

Bree quickly helped her out. 'So run-down? Falling to bits? A poor man's Butlins?'

A commotion suddenly broke out at the back of the coach, which distracted them from their mutual feelings of disappointment. Pru turned just in time to see Hilda smack Brenda over the head with a rolled-up copy of the magazine she had been reading on the journey.

'Whoa, ladies! Ladies! What on earth is going on?' Pru jumped to her feet, making sure she kept hold of the handrails as she pushed forwards along the aisle towards the rumpus.

Hilda was beside herself with fury. 'She's just pinched my hat.' She animatedly pointed at the pink and white creation that now sat askew on Brenda's head, whilst trying to make a grab at the brim.

Brenda clung on to the hat for dear life, pulling the sides down over her ears. 'This is *my* hat, you silly old goat, I've had it for years; *you* don't have a hat!'

'Then why was it on my head? I saw it, it was reflected in the window!' Hilda was adamant. 'And then when I looked around, you're wearing it.'

'Because I'm sitting behind you, and it's my reflection! For goodness' sake, Clarissa, can you explain it to her?' Disgruntled, Brenda grabbed her handbag and pushed her way along the aisle, chunnering to herself.

Unfortunately Hilda wasn't finished. Grabbing the Tupperware box from seat number twenty, that in her haste to remove herself from Hilda's glossy magazine onslaught, Brenda had forgotten, Hilda popped open the lid and grabbed a slice of cake. Squeezing it between her fingers, she brought back her arm and delivered a throw that a Sunday cricketer would have been proud of. 'Take that, Brenda Mortinsen!' she hollered. The lemon creation sailed through the air, landing with a splat on Brenda's head. It clung momentarily to the brim of her hat before drooping over the edge and falling into Kitty's lap. Kitty screamed as she watched the sugared icing melt into her tailored white slacks.

'Look what you've done! You've dribbled on my Valentino Garavani's...' she squealed, turning several shades of pink as her blood pressure rose to new heights. 'These cost me almost eight hundred quid!'

'Pah!' Ethel scoffed to Clarissa from behind her hand. 'I'm sure that's not the only thing that's been dribbled on them before now...'

Bree quickly intervened. 'Ethel, that's quite enough!'

'What? I was only going to point out that Kitty is useless with a pair of chopsticks. Remember what she was like at the Dinky Dumplings Chinese restaurant? More went up the wall and over the tablecloth than down her gob at the WI Christmas party!'

Muffled sniggers ran along the nearby rows. The ladies within earshot were clearly enjoying themselves at poor Kitty's expense, with their reaction adding fuel to Ethel's rediscovered witty quips. 'And anyway, I know she got them from that posh second-hand clothes shop in town, she never paid anywhere near that much. There's been more bums in them trousers than I've had hot Sunday dinners!'

Pru desperately wanted to laugh too, but her role as president meant she would be expected to be peacemaker rather than participant. As Kitty scraped the offending cake from her lap, Pru quickly began to hand out the arrival packs to the ladies, happily distracting them from their brief encounter with Hilda and Brenda's little spat. That was something she would have to deal with later when everyone was settled.

'Right, if we all make our way into reception, Frank will offload your suitcases. They'll be stacked by the door for you, once you've been given your chalet keys and...' The gentle hiss of the coach doors followed by several pairs of sandals slapping down the aisle alerted Pru to the fact her captive audience were no longer captive. She watched them pouring down the steps, linking arms, giggling and almost skipping with excitement to the large poster outside reception, depicting the gigantic frame of the famous exhibition dancer, Troy Florentine. Arranging themselves either side of his toned and honed body, with their hands showcasing various parts of his anatomy, they struck a pose, allowing Frank to get the first photograph of their holiday together.

The insults fuelled by rolled-up magazines, lemon drizzle cake, hats, trousers and chopsticks, had been forgotten, to be replaced with laughter and the promise of fun.

The ladies of the Winterbottom Women's Institute had arrived.

RICH PICKINGS

Sophie hung her jacket on the back of the rickety chair in her chalet and then carefully removed the large manilla envelope from the desk drawer. Her fingers plucked at the contents, spreading the papers out across her bed.

Her small travel kettle clicked off, warning her that its contents were now ready for use. She poured the boiling water onto the teabag and stood mesmerised, watching the corner gently bob up and down as she plucked at the skin on her bottom lip. She plunged the teaspoon into the mug and stirred vigorously, taking pleasure in the mini whirlpool she had caused in the liquid, forcing the teabag to spin out of control.

Sometimes her life was like that. Spinning, spinning, spinning – with no end in sight. But right now, right this minute at Harmony Hollows, she was steady and very much in control.

She picked up the first sheet of paper and scanned the photocopied headline and news report.

HOLIDAY CAMP DOUBLE MURDER

Grisly discovery at Nettleton Shrub

Her lips moved in time to the words. She had read this edition so many times; she almost knew the text off by heart. It was something that both fascinated her and angered her in equal measure, and after a chance introduction at Waverley Park Sanatorium, she now knew which direction to take. A smaller envelope contained important documents. Her thumb peeled back the flap so she could retrieve them. She spread out two birth certificates, along with the death certificates for Deborah Anne Purkiss and Lawrence Peter Belfont. They were, of course, copies, but she hoped they would provide the links that she needed.

The next item to grace her hands was an edition of the *Little Kipling Gazette*. Sophie could feel the excitement rapidly rising as she read the first paragraph of their 'breaking news' section. The unexplained disappearance of elderly sisters. Two sisters, two counties miles apart, and two police forces involved in the investigation. The more she read, the more excited she became. House-to-house enquiries, press releases, house searches, and now they were considering forensic examination of both locations. A wry smile played on her lips. 'Forget the forensic experts, a gardener and a JCB would be more use!' she whispered as she giggled.

It was such a delicious feeling to know that she, and she alone, was responsible for the whole circus that was being played out.

Sophie had been good since her arrival at Harmony Hollows. She had been pretty tight with her medication; the last thing she needed was extra voices interfering with her cold-case investigation. The only one in her sights was the killer of Debbie Purkiss and Larry Belfont.

'But *you* are on my naughty list already.' She had wandered over to the window, her index finger pointing accusingly at the figure that was half-heartedly cleaning the windows of the chalet opposite. 'You are on a warning, dear, so be very, very careful as to what you get up to next,' she muttered to herself. Inadvertently or deliberately taking a life she could accept in her twisted world, but stealing? Well that really was the bottom of the barrel.

Sophie broke her gaze from the window and checked the time. 'Perfect... let the fun begin...' She grabbed her jacket and disappeared through the door.

Nellie Girdlestone, oblivious to her accuser, dropped the damp chamois leather into the red bucket and dried her hands on her overall. She watched the new arrivals excitedly trundling their suitcases along the gravel paths making their way to Marigold Lawns. She smiled, feeling an optimistic glow. They definitely had an air of rich pickings about them. This season was going to be a good one after all.

'Can I have the bed by the wall?' Ethel dropped her handbag onto the floral counterpane in Chalet 15 at Marigold Lawns, laying immediate claim to it should Clarissa decide she had a preference too.

Clarissa had barely shut the door behind them and was still busy manoeuvring her suitcase into the corner. She checked out Ethel's choice and then inspected the remaining bed. 'Whatever, I don't really see what the difference is, though; they're identical.'

Ethel plumped the pillows on her commandeered berth and sat down. 'Yours is closer to the door.'

'And?' Clarissa set her lips, wondering what on earth was going to come next.

'*And* you'll be the first one that gets kidnapped, murdered or haunted by the long dead of Harmony Hollows...' Ethel shuddered. 'They'll have to terrorise you first and it'll give me time to escape.'

Clarissa gave her best Elvis lip impression. 'You're such a thoughtful friend, Eth, it's nice to know I'm of some use. Right, let's get unpacked and then we can pop next door and see how Hilda and Millie are getting on. I think we're going to be referees this week, Hilda has become quite confrontational, hasn't she?'

Ethel nodded, feeling an overwhelming sadness wash over her. Albert's passing had given way to a realisation that nothing is for ever. Not life, not health, and not even your own mind, as proven by Hilda's mental fragility. Ethel had always clung to the belief that you should live each day as it comes, but now she found herself looking to what the future would hold, not just for her, but for her friends. For the first time in her life, she felt vulnerable.

She quickly checked herself, plastering a grin on her face to belie her thoughts. 'Hilda's just feisty; she'll be fine, we'll all be fine – as long as you remember to take one for the team by blocking *that* with your corpulent keister...' Ethel pointed to the door in question. '...then we should survive until the end of the week!' She laughed.

Clarissa checked her booty in the tarnished mirror of the wardrobe door. Ethel was right, not much would get past that, with or without her Spanx pants on. 'I'll have you know, I've spent years nurturing this shape, it doesn't come without hard work and sacrifice!'

'Well, you certainly haven't bloody sacrificed much in the food department then, that's for sure!' Ethel chuckled under her breath.

'You can talk...' Clarissa was just about to give a smart retort when a high-pitched scream seeped through the chalet walls, followed by frantic shouting. Ethel nearly fell off the bed, her handbag clattered to the floor, spilling its contents as she gripped her chest in panic.

'That's Hilda...' she gasped.

A CLOSE SHAVE

Ralph Fairbright adjusted his tie and patted down his blazer, ensuring the buttons aligned and the piped edging met cleanly. He straightened the name plate on his desk, proudly touched his antique brass darts trophy won from a fluke check-out double in 1989, and inhaled noisily, whistling through his teeth. His eyes took in the expanse of wall that held photographs of past and present employees and those that had gone on to make a name for themselves in the entertainment industry, their photographs showcasing theatre and television credits.

He brushed against the plastic fern in the corner trying to get a closer look, bending a frond out of shape in the process when it snagged on his trousers. There was one particular photograph that haunted him. He didn't want to look at it again, but he was compelled to.

The black-and-white print with its chipped brown frame looked stark amongst the others. He knew that it shouldn't stand out, but it did. His finger traced the tarnished plaque underneath.

Harmony Hollows Staff 1982–1983 Season

'The dream team...' he grunted. Each face celebrated its youth, every pose displayed either a devil-may-care attitude, or just plain mischief and fun. His gaze settled upon the young lad at the back, dark hair curling slightly where it touched the shoulders, not quite a mullet, but still cool enough for the job. Ralph could almost feel the soft leather jacket he was wearing, his fingers involuntarily rubbing together, evoking memories of times long past. His eyes scanned each figure. Nellie Girdlestone stood out from the centre row, with her wide Colgate-toothpaste grin and blurred hand that had been waving at the time the camera shutter had blinked. She had been a drinks hostess in the Marina Lounge and quite a pretty one at that, but very much the little vixen. She was still here at Harmony Hollows, one of the longest serving members of staff, but now she was old and a cleaner to boot. He hadn't even had the good grace to acknowledge her when he had arrived, and neither had she to him. Then again, maybe she didn't remember him. He patted his thinning locks across his head, sucked his stomach in, and checked the photograph again. Deflated, he didn't have to wonder why Nellie wouldn't recognise him; the young lad in the leather jacket was long gone.

He was just a memory.

He continued with his search until there she was, his 'little dancer', standing at the edge of the group, showcased on the front row. He remembered how he had begged the camp photographer to allow her to be included. She hadn't been part of the team, but he desperately needed something to remember her by.

He touched her face, his finger leaving a print on the glass. 'Debbie...' he whispered as the pain, anger and guilt once again welled up inside him.

A loud knock on the door to his office broke the moment. He coughed to clear his throat before answering, afraid that its vibrato would give him away. 'Come in...'

A very flustered Stacey bowled through the threshold, pink-faced and breathless. 'Mr Fairbright, sir, there's been an incident at Marigold Lawns – it's Chalet 13!'

At Chalet 13, the commotion had attracted several other guests. who were now all milling around outside, desperate to discover the reason behind the high-pitched screams.

Whilst Clarissa embraced Hilda, pulling her close and patting her on the back to calm her, Millie, nonplussed about the evolving situation, rummaged in her holdall. 'I've got just the thing, hang fire.'

Pulling out a large brown paper bag, she tipped it upside down and shook out its contents. Several pairs of 80 denier tights, a packet of crisps, and a Mars bar dropped to the floor. 'Here, wrap that around her lips and tell her to breathe slowly.'

Shocked at Millie's sudden turn of leadership, Clarissa obliged. She clenched her hand around the neck of the bag and poked her fingers in it to make a decent opening before offering it to Hilda. 'That's it, deep breaths, Hilda, dear, deep breaths...' She watched the bag inflate and deflate.

Hilda's screams had brought Pru and Bree running from their chalet next door to assist, having abandoned their first glass of wine of the day on the bedside cabinet.

'What on earth's happened?' quizzed Pru.

Still comforting Hilda, Clarissa pointed behind her. 'It would appear that Hilda was having a little snooze and someone came out of the wardrobe over there.'

Pru knelt down to be on a level with her. Hilda's small grey eyes, pupils dilated with fear, blinked rapidly. 'Did you see who it was, Hilda? Any description of them?'

Hilda shook her head vigorously. 'No, no, they were just all in black with...' She made a motion over her head, indicating they were wearing a cap. 'It gave me such a fright when they burst out through the doors, I can tell you. I wouldn't have minded if it had been that Henry Gazelle fella using my wardrobe to change into his Superman underpants, but I wasn't that lucky!'

Pru smiled. 'Cavill, his name is Henry Cavill.' She turned her attention to Millie. 'Did you see anything?'

'No, nothing. I was having a little tinkle in the bathroom, and the first thing I knew was Hilda screaming at the top of her lungs... I've never pulled my Alan Whickers up so fast in all my life.' Millie paused to think. 'The front door was wide open when I came out, though, and I found this on the carpet.' She handed Pru a small earring. 'It's not mine and Hilda doesn't have pierced ears.'

'I don't think Henry Gazelle does either...' Hilda snuffled into a paper tissue.

Pru examined the plain silver earring, aware that it could just as easily have been left by the previous occupant of the chalet and missed in the cleaning process as belonging to the intruder. Not wishing to alarm any of the ladies further, she decided to play the incident down, and judging by the looks she was getting from everyone, including Millie, the odds were getting higher by the minute that this whole incident was either a figment of Hilda's imagination or a vivid dream. 'I'll let management know what has happened, but I think it could be a case of a mistaken chalet, someone has got a little lost and wandered in to the wrong one – or, you never know, maybe in the absence of a telephone kiosk, it really was Henry changing into his undies in your wardrobe!' She tried to keep her voice light and added a little chuckle at the end of the sentence. 'I really don't think it's anything to worry about.'

Bree filled two small glasses with a medicinal dose of sweet sherry and gave one each to Millie and Hilda. 'Well, girls, I can't believe we've only been here less than two hours, and already we've made our mark and terrified half the guests at Harmony Hollows. I do hope your antics aren't going to turn into another Montgomery Hall or Rookery Grange fiasco.'

Pru was inclined to agree that a cake fight and now another wardrobe intruder alert was about par for the course with the WI entourage. She just hoped that the rest of their holiday would be enjoyed without further incident, but looking over and catching the glint in the eyes of Ethel and Clarissa, she knew she was on a hiding to nothing.

LEGS ELEVEN

Maggie Henshaw's soft sneakers squeaked loudly on the polished floorboards of the stage. It still amazed her that anyone would think it was acceptable to wax and shine where the feet of dancers, comedians and singers would tread. She pulled the heavy deep red brocade curtains together, blanking out the vibrantly painted panto scenery on the back wall of the stage, before adjusting the height of the microphone. She coughed loudly.

'Testing, testing. One, two, three...' She lifted her hand to shield her eyes from the spotlight. 'Did you get that, Mark? Any feedback?'

'It's good to go, Maggie, although it might need a slight adjustment for the bingo tonight. They've got the preliminary dance-offs this afternoon, so no doubt some numpty will fiddle with the settings.' Perched behind the sound deck, Mark Joynson, the resort's electrician, sound man, mechanic and all-round handyman, gave her the thumbs-up. 'I'm on a shift at the pool now, so d'you need anything else before I feck off and save lives?'

Maggie smiled. 'Save lives? Mate, we'd be lucky to get

anyone in that pool; it's bloody freezing. When was the last time you saw anyone swimming in it?'

Mark grinned. 'August 1994, I think. It's that new broom in the management team, Mr Fairbright. He's authorised upping the water temp, so we're expecting a full house this afternoon...' He lifted his arm and flexed his bicep. 'Time for "Mighty Marko", lifeguard and superhero, to show his skills – my kiss of life is to die for!' He gave Maggie a flirty wink.

'That defeats the object just a bit, don't you think? Your drowning victims are supposed to live, not die!' Not expecting a response from him, Maggie turned her attention to the bingo barrel, still despondent that her entertainment career had fallen to the new lows of juggling balls and shouting out numbers to the eager, the desperate, and the just plain bored. She arranged the multi-coloured balls in order, checking each number needed for a game was present, and then stacked the cards. Marker pens, or dabbers and dobbers as the regulars called them, were available to purchase, but many brought their own. Some even had lucky ones. 'Is that a lucky golden dobber in your pocket, or are you just pleased to see me?' She giggled. Plonking herself down heavily on the upholstered stool, she stretched out her left leg. The pain streaked agonisingly along its length, finishing by her hip. Mon Dieu, qu'ai je fait pour mériter ça?

'What?' Mark had barely left the Marina Lounge when he heard her shout out.

Maggie could have kicked herself with her one remaining good leg. A split-second lapse of concentration and she had forgotten who she was supposed to be. 'Oh nothing; just me mumbling away to myself counting balls,' she quickly lied.

'Can't tell you how relieved I am, I thought you were hexing me with some sort of dark incantation.' He cocked an index finger towards her and laughed.

'Believe me, buddy, there are plenty of others at the front of the queue before you!' she quipped. 'Now go and save some lives in the warm chlorinated waters of Harmony Hollows.'

Nellie puffed away heavily on what she considered to be her lifesaver, when in truth every cigarette puff she inhaled into her lungs was actually shortening her life by eleven minutes. She'd read that in a magazine once, and it had scared her for as long as it had taken her to light up the next ciggie. As far as she was concerned, everyone had to cark it at some point. Her sister, who had been one sandwich short of a picnic, had curled up her toes in some god-forbidden mental institution, so at least Nellie would be meeting the grim reaper doing something she enjoyed.

She inspected her nicotine-stained fingers and split nails. That had just been one of the closest calls she had ever had. She'd been at Harmony Hollows in various roles and guises for over forty years, and had never once been caught pilfering from the guests. She pulled out the single silver earring from her pocket. 'Fat lot of bloody use this is now...' she huffed to herself. She still couldn't believe how stupid she had been, or why she had taken the risk in the first place. Nellie hadn't anticipated the pair of them coming back from their little wander around the gardens so soon, catching her in the act and forcing her to hide in the wardrobe.

Unfortunately, the old dear having the snooze had been more daft then deaf. That had been mistake number one. Mistake number two was not waiting it out longer in the wardrobe to make her escape. Instead she had taken the chance and gone for it, making a bit of a commotion in the process. The old girl had woken, and, much to Nellie's surprise, had a good set of lungs on her, which had quickly summonsed her friend.

She had waddled in from the bathroom with her cotton fineries around her ankles, trying desperately to pull them up without falling over. That one action had given Nellie the chance to make it to the door without being seen for a second time. By the time the elastic trim was around the companion's waist and her nether regions had been respectfully covered, Nellie was long gone.

She took a final drag of her fondly named 'coffin nail' and dropped it into the bucket; the soft hiss as it hit the water and was extinguished made her shiver. There was something definitely missing in her mundane life these days, if almost being caught on the job gave her that much fear and excitement in equal measure. In her youth she had been a force to be reckoned with. These days, with a blend of age and lowly employment status in this dump of a holiday resort, she was virtually invisible to everyone – apart from the old dear in Chalet 13 and Maggie Henshaw when she was trying to catch her having a crafty fag.

If only they knew...

She shivered again, the smell from inside that wardrobe still stuck in her nostrils, evoking so many lost or best-forgotten memories. It had been the same wardrobe that had held the industrial vacuum cleaner and the body of Larry Belfont in 1983.

She smirked at that memory.

Oh what a delicious season that had been.

BINGO

'It's bright pink! I've never worn bright pink lipstick in my life...' Bree smacked her lips together and checked her reflection in the mirror. 'What do you think?'

Pru pulled the white T-shirt over her head and flicked out her hair. 'It's bingo, not a speed-dating night; there won't be much on offer for you to pull – not unless you fancy Ralphie, the camp commandant!'

Bree wrinkled her nose and stuck out her tongue. 'I'm not that desperate, thanks.' She gave her hair one last brush before turning to look at Pru. 'Do you think it was just a funny turn Hilda had? I didn't like to say anything, but you do know what chalet they've got, don't you? Maybe it had something to do with that?'

Pru knew only too well. As soon as she had read the accommodation packs with the allocated chalet numbers, she had double-checked the newspaper reports. Only one, *The Nettleton Shrub News*, had revealed the actual scene of the murders in its article, penned by their local roving reporter: Chalet 13, Marigold Lawns.

'That's just superstition and coincidence. Granted it's a bit creepy to know you're staying in a room where two people met a horrible end, but honestly, after forty years do you really think some long-ago murderer is going to come jumping out of the wardrobe to frighten two genteel ladies half to death?'

'*Genteel?*' Bree sniggered. 'Hilda and Millie are hardly genteel, and when you throw Clarissa and Ethel into the mix, well, they'd make any murderer run for the hills.'

'Joking aside, it's best not to mention it to any of the ladies, or imaginations will run riot. Look what happened at Montgomery Hall! Hilda had men jumping out of wardrobes there, too…' Pru pursed her lips together and rolled her eyes.

Bree opened the door, the slight evening breeze pushing its way in. 'That's the trouble, though – she was right. There *was* a man in her wardrobe, and we didn't believe her that time either.'

Clarissa had confidently shoulder-barged her way to the best tables in the Marina Lounge, arms laden, and had deftly draped coats, handbags and anything else she had been given onto the chairs to reserve them for the WI ladies. She stood back in triumph as Ethel, Millie and Hilda sank their bottoms onto the velour pads, ready to join the others for bingo night. In her day, Clarissa had been the sun-lounger queen of Torremolinos; the speed with which she could whip out a towel at 5am to bagsy a sunbed whilst still under the influence of half a gallon of sangria from the night before, was legendary.

'Ooh Clarissa, Clarissa dear…' Kitty, tottering on high heels, clattered her way across the dance floor, desperately trying to retain her pink gin and tonic in the glass. 'Has it started yet?'

Clarissa delved into her handbag, pulling out a chunky blue dobber, bingo cards, and a packet of peanuts. 'They're just setting up, but you missed the cabaret; it was wonderful.'

Ethel harrumphed. 'Wonderful – if you're chuffed about having several unclad foo-foos shoved in your face during the can-can! Where's the decorum when you need it?' She laughed.

Kitty looked mortified. 'Strippers! They've got strippers at Harmony Hollows! This will never do; it's supposed to be family friendly entertainment...' She slugged back her gin to calm her nerves.

'They weren't strippers; they were perfectly respectable trained dancers, and you couldn't see their foo-foos, Ethel; they were ostrich-feather hems.' Clarissa laid out the bingo cards so they had one each. 'It's apparently a good jackpot tonight: £50. So get your dobbers dobbing, ladies!'

As the Four Wrinkled Dears and friends rearranged their chairs, drinks and cards, relishing the atmospheric hum from a full room, Maggie Henshaw stood backstage watching the happy campers through the peephole at the side of the wings.

'Break a leg, Maggie!' Pinky skipped along the stage crossover, shedding feathers and glitter from her costume as she went. 'They're a hard audience tonight; you're going to need all the balls you've got to keep them happy.' She laughed.

Maggie couldn't have felt more deflated, defeated or despondent. She straightened her jacket and tucked a stray strand of hair behind her ear. Pushing out a vibrant red lipstick from its gold case, she slicked on a final coat and smacked her lips together. 'Right, let's get this show on the road...' She parted the heavy curtains and slipped out into the spotlight; microphone clutched in her hand.

'Ladies, gentlemen, boys and girls, welcome to Harmony Hollows Bingo Bonanza...' Maggie stood, arms out wide with the most welcoming and happy smile she could muster, but inside she was dying a thousand deaths. Her hand wavered over the turning handle of the huge drum that contained the balls.

'Let the spinning begin!' She gave four rigorous cranks of the handle.

The game was on, the first ball dropping down into the opening. She plucked it out between finger and thumb and held it up.

'First out, Dirty Gertie, number thirty...'

She paused.

'Fifty-two, Danny La Rue...'

Next up.

'Two fat ladies, Sixty-six...'

Hilda was on high alert and before Clarissa could stop her, she was on her feet. 'It's clickity-click for sixty-six. Two fat ladies is eighty-eight. If you're going to do the job, at least get it right!' she hollered.

If the arse could have fallen out of Maggie's world any further to completely destroy her day, then at that point, it just did. 'Maybe it's just two slightly overweight ladies with big bottoms, fat thighs, and a flat chest,' she bristled.

Hilda's own bottom hit the chair with some force, helped on its way by Clarissa tugging the back of her jacket, pulling her down. 'For goodness' sake, Hilda, sit down and leave the poor woman alone.'

Grabbing the next ball, Maggie continued. 'Forty-two, Winnie the Pooh...'

She watched a wash of lilac-rinsed heads bob up and down, dobbers frantically smashing out numbers on the cards until finally...

'Number eight, Garden Gate...'

'House! Wahoo, I've won!'

Shielding her eyes once again from the spotlight, Maggie looked out into the audience to see the card, held high in the air, zig-zagging between the tables towards the stage, attached to the hand of a rather exuberant woman in her late forties. The static from her lilac shell suit crackled and rustled as she ran across the dance floor. Maggie took the card from her and carefully checked the numbers.

'We have a winner! Can we all give a round of applause for Mary from Daffodil Lawns...' Maggie handed the envelope containing five crisp ten-pound notes to Mary, who promptly snatched it out of her hand and stuffed it down the front of her tracksuit bottoms.

A weak ripple of hand-clapping followed Mary back to her seat.

Ethel downed her sherry and held out her glass, ready for it to be replenished. 'Well, that was a bit rubbish, wasn't it? I didn't even get chance to make a line on that one. Honestly, talk about this place being pretentious; it's like trying to make a silk purse out of a sow's ear. Daffodil *Lawns,* I ask you! It's a strip of bloody grass between the rows of chalets, not the centre court at Wimbledon!' She popped a peanut into her mouth. 'I do hope this place gets a bit more exciting, don't you?'

A flash of light caught them in that moment, not giving the ladies time to smile, before their images were caught and their retinas saturated and blinded by dots and spots, impairing their vision.

'I'd be very careful what you wish for, ladies...' the disembodied voice behind the camera promised them.

THERE'S NO PLACE LIKE HOME...

Mary Beaney staggered along the path, the weak lights that perched above each chalet door guiding her towards what she hoped would be her comfy bed. She'd lost track of how many paths she had taken ages ago, and was now just relying on intuition.

Two steps forward, three steps back...

She was very much regretting her decision to spend most of her bingo winnings on several pints of Diamond White cider in the bar. She belched loudly, leaning on the pebble-dashed wall trying to get her bearings. It felt like she had been wandering around for hours trying to find her way back from the Marina Lounge. Every sectioned block of chalets looked the same. She checked her key fob again and squinted.

'Flower...' she spluttered to herself. 'Nope, nope daffodil, definitely a daffodil...' She checked the large wooden sign that had been hammered into the grass strip between the avenue of buildings. Scrunching up her nose, she held the fob up to the sign and came to the conclusion that the pictures matched. 'Huh, Midvale School for the Gifted...' She chuckled before putting a bit more effort into moving her legs.

That was the thing about being drunk. You had to rely on autopilot, which was fine if the cabin crew, aka her legs, would do their bit to make the journey possible. Mary stumbled, and the ground suddenly rose up to meet her. She fell to her knees, giggling.

'Here, let me give you a hand...'

Mary dropped sideways onto her bottom and looked up trying to make out who her potential saviour could be. The damp from the tarmac was beginning to seep through the thin material of her shell suit. She shivered. Not through the chill air she was suddenly feeling, but from the aura the figure in front of her was radiating. Being from the Irish side of the Beaney family with their regular appearances at fairgrounds and circus tents as fortune tellers and dubious clairvoyants, her gypsy second sight had kicked in, giving her a heightened uneasiness and a huge dollop of suspicion. Her fingers probed the inside of her pocket, reassuringly touching the remaining £10 that was scrunched and folded inside.

The lighting behind the figure formed a halo around their head, which made her laugh out loud. 'Well, you're no bloody angel, are you?' she nervously spluttered.

'Shall we make this a game?' The voice was strained, as though it was being disguised.

The warm, comforting drunkenness she had been harbouring was now rapidly deserting her, bringing a startling clarity to her thoughts with an unnatural fear creeping into her soul. 'Just leave me alone; go away or I'll... I'll scream...'

'No need to get hissy, missy. I see you're ready for a bit of a workout, nice tracksuit by the way. Tell you what, I'll give you a five-minute head start...'

Frantic, Mary scrambled to her feet, not waiting to hear any more, and began to run. Her Adidas trainers scrunched on the gravel as she attempted to navigate the corner, one leg splaying out to the side as she stumbled, landing awkwardly. The palms of her hands stung painfully as they hit the ground. She pushed on, veering across the grass and over the flowerbed. Her heart was pounding so fiercely she thought it would explode. She opened her mouth to scream, but only a rasping croak wheezed and whistled over her vocal cords.

Run, Mary, run... don't stop, whatever you do, don't stop...

She hadn't intended to stop. That was the last thing she wanted to do, but the ligature around her neck yanked her backwards, not giving her time to realise what was happening. She struggled, she punched, she flailed her arms and kicked.

'Surprise, surprise – I lied. Five minutes was far too long...'

The cord tightened, nipping the skin on her neck. Mary writhed and fought, desperately, trying to claw with her fingers, but all she reached was air. Tighter and tighter it squeezed, until she thought her neck would snap and the skin on her cheeks would burst with the pressure. The pulse beat harder and faster in her ears.

Thwump, thwump, thwump.

If she had been the possessor of another breath, she could have used it to laugh at the mental vision she suddenly had of her own demise, her neck resembling that of the Scarecrow from the *Wizard of Oz*, hessian skin, all puckered, wrinkled and pinched by aging rope.

Her body spasmed violently in her final throes of life as a low gurgle escaped from her lips.

Mary Beaney, forty-eight years of age and not destined to see forty-nine, merry divorcee of Wallingford Wells, lover of shell suits and Adidas trainers, slowly saw her life flash before her eyes. She felt it was quite ironic that her memories of a life not yet lived to its full three score years and ten, were doing anything but flash. In reality it was a cumbersome, slow movie reel, flickering and stuttering.

Until finally the fight had gone and the light had been extinguished – just like Mary.

The last impression for the eyes of Mary Jane Beaney to feast upon had been her own limp hand, holding the key fob for what should have been her safe haven, and the place she couldn't find:

Chalet 8.

MIRROR, MIRROR...

Della Claybourne yawned and rubbed the sleep from her eyes and arched her back. The bed she was currently lying on in Chalet 10 groaned its displeasure. She ached in places she didn't know existed, and had just endured the worst night's sleep that she could remember. Not content to have the same chalet as forty years ago, she was pretty sure, judging by her level of discomfort, it was the same bed and mattress. The icing on the cake had been the thumping and banging from the chalet next door that had awoken her at some ridiculous hour of the night.

She swung her legs over the edge of the bed, her feet dancing on the rug as they felt for her flip-flops. She pottered over to the desk and checked her schedule for the day. Tom and Macey had made it through the first round, not with the best scores possible, but enough to keep them clear of being eliminated. There had been a pretty poor audience attendance too, the majority of the happy campers preferring the newly opened swimming pool or the two-for-one drinks at the bar. She had expected more, considering it was the championships. She wondered how her dancing duo had fared themselves overnight, she was pretty sure that Macey had overindulged on the Babycham at the nightly bingo, judging by her inability to put one leg in front of the other on the way back to her chalet. Fortunately, being the gentleman he was, Tom had escorted her safely to her bed. Della had decided not to bother them with the upheaval of exchanging chalets. By the time she had caught up with them on their first day, they had both unpacked and settled into their respective abodes and, to be honest, it wouldn't matter which chalet she had been housed in, the memories would still be stuck in her head. Every corner at Harmony Hollows held a moment in time for her.

Whilst she waited for the kettle to boil, she slipped into her leggings and sweatshirt and tied her hair into a high ponytail. Catching sight of herself in the mirror, she sighed loudly. 'Dear God, it's the same mirror too...' Her finger traced the starburst of de-silvering that had turned black at the edges. What wasn't the same was the reflection. She stared for longer than she really wanted to, taking in the lines and creases in her skin, the hooded folds of her lids, the age halo around her once blue eyes. She looked away briefly, preparing to wallow in self-pity, but the pull of nostalgia forced her to return her gaze. For a brief moment, she thought the younger Della was looking back at her, but it was just wishful thinking and a trick of the light. Tears pricked and stung as she fought the poignancy of the moment.

'Would you have loved me now, Larry?' she whispered.

She knew in her heart that Larry Belfont had loved only himself. He had been a user and an abuser of women, particularly young naïve girls like she had been back then. She had been just one of many. They had all been made to feel special by him, only to be discarded when the next batch of holidaymakers arrived. Her fingers curled into the palm of her hand, her nails painfully scraping the skin. She tipped her head and pursed her lips. 'You deserved everything you got, Larry – including the hoover!'

As the anger and guilt at the memories returned, she sought an escape for them. Grabbing her chalet keys, she yanked open the door and slammed it shut behind her. Whoever was in Chalet 8 was going to be that outlet, and it was a pretty big piece of her mind that she was going to be sharing with them, whether they liked it or not. She knew she should have politely knocked, or even just tapped lightly on the window, but that action would have belied her true feelings. Instead, she banged her fist heavily on the bright yellow door.

She waited.

Then tried again, this time more forcefully. The door popped open just by the sheer impact of Della clumsily heralding her arrival. Her fingers tentatively pushed it further.

'Hello, it's only me from next door... we really need to talk about your nocturnal antics; they kept me awake half the night, you know.' Della knew that was a bit of an exaggeration, but whoever was staying here wouldn't know that. She waited a few minutes more and then stepped inside.

It was hard to make anything out at first, the closed curtains bringing a grim blanket of darkness to the small room, but the early morning sun was inching its way through the open door, casting a mellow shaft of light across the grey rug. Della peered into the gloom, and as she tentatively crept further inside, she allowed the daylight to swallow up the darkness, illuminating two lilac-clad legs and a pair of white Adidas trainers sprawled across the floor.

The scream slowly built in Della's chest as her throat tightened, making her gasp for the next breath.

'No, no, no...' she wailed as she staggered back through the open door.

The body of Mary Beaney hung limply at the end of the bed

like a giant rag doll, the cord from her tracksuit top had been hooked over the wooden end-post of the bedframe before being strung tightly around her neck.

Her eyes, bulbous and unseeing, still radiated the terror that the realisation of an inevitable death had so tragically brought her.

CAN YOU KEEP A SECRET?

The bustle and hum of the resort restaurant and its diners, accompanied by the melodious strains of 'Food Glorious Food' over the tannoy system, rankled Ethel. She flicked a rubbery blob of scrambled egg around her plate.

'Glorious!! I think not. I've seen Albie blow better from his left nostril...' She chortled. Taking a bite from the corner of the toast, she looked to her companions for their reaction. She wasn't disappointed.

Clarissa's nose crinkled and her face took on a slightly green hue. 'Really, Ethel, isn't that something best left unsaid, particularly whilst everyone is eating. It's akin to discussing your...'

'Bowels...' Hilda absent-mindedly offered.

Ethel, Clarissa and Millie did a double take. 'That's not what I was going to say,' Clarissa prompted.

Unperturbed, Hilda continued. 'I quite fancy playing a game this afternoon if anyone is up for it. They've got quite a nice crown green here, and you can hire the shoes, you know.'

Ethel gave a sigh of relief that they weren't about to be subjected to Hilda's bathroom activities and was just preparing to correct her, when Clarissa nudged her in the ribs, jerking her head towards the small entourage that had just entered the restaurant, weaving their way through the tables. 'That's her there.' She indicated to Della being supported by Tom and Macey. 'She's the one that found the body.'

The morning had been a hive of activity with police, ambulance and finally what the ladies knew to be the coroner's van, all converging on Daffodil Lawns at Harmony Hollows. Their collective attempts to nonchalantly 'promenade' along the path near the scene to get a better look and the lowdown on what had occurred, had been thwarted by the Greycoats staff and a grim bunting of police tape that fluttered in the breeze.

It had taken Ethel less than five minutes and a bit of flattery with the camp domestic, to find out what was going on. 'It was the woman in that ghastly boil-in-the-bag tracksuit from the other night, the one that won the bingo.'

'What a waste…' Millie offered by way of sympathy.

'Not 'arf.' Ethel mused. 'That fifty quid could have got us quite a few sweet sherries from the bar.'

'Ethel!' Clarissa couldn't help but laugh, as irreverent and unsympathetic as Ethel was being, it was a quick and funny retort.

'She told me they're treating it as an accident, but obviously there's going to be a post-mortem. Which means…' Ethel sipped daintily from her teacup, a complete contrast to her egg-flicking action from only moments earlier.

The Four Wrinkled Dears huddled closer together, excitement building and anticipation almost taking their breath away as they waited for Ethel to continue.

'…It means we have time to do a bit of digging of our own!' She sat back, a contented grin highlighting the laughter lines around her eyes.

Millie wasn't sure. 'Isn't it a bit dangerous, Eth? I mean they still haven't caught the murderer from 1983. What if they've come back and it wasn't an accident after all, or what if Hilda's wardrobe intruder is the culprit?'

'Exactly. How exciting would that be? We could help solve an historic murder and a new one, too. Come on, don't let our bit of research before we came here go to waste.' For the first time since Albert's passing, Ethel was alive again with a purpose.

Clarissa nodded in agreement. 'We do this on one condition. We don't let Pru, Bree or anyone else know what we're up to. Are you okay with that, Hilda? Can you keep this a secret?'

Hilda clucked and chuckled to herself. 'What secret? Look, I've got bloody Alzheimer's, so what do you think?' She laughed.

ROGUES' GALLERY

Sophie, bathed in the red glow of the makeshift dark room, used the bamboo tongs to carefully lift the papers from the trays, and pegged three prints onto the line. She worked digitally most of the time, but still preferred the old methods. She loved the creative process, the waiting, the anticipation and then the reveal. She was lucky that Harmony Hollow still had the old equipment. It had taken a good few hours to get it up and running again after such a prolonged period of disuse, but it had been worth it. Discovering the old sub-station bunker on the abandoned fairground site had been an added bonus too. It was hidden from prying eyes and would serve her well for her final performance.

She stood back to admire her handiwork, a tense feeling gnawing at the pit of her stomach as she searched each face, not one of her subjects aware that she had captured their image.

Della.

'Was it you?' she whispered.

Ralph.

'Or you, Mr Fairbright?'

Nellie.

'What did you see, Nellie Girdlestone?'

Three people that changed the course of a life.

Her fingers probed her rucksack until she found what she was looking for. As a matter of habit, she rattled the small pills in the brown bottle before popping the lid. She held a tablet up in front of her. Against the backdrop of red, it became the moon. Sophie laughed. She could easily live on the moon if she had the chance, away from everybody and everything. She wouldn't have to take her little pills as she wouldn't be a danger to anyone; she could be whatever she wanted to be.

On the moon.

Pulling her notebook towards her, she opened it at the page she had been working on. Each name had a brief bio beneath it, apart from Maggie Henshaw, the bingo caller. Sophie could almost see the wispy tentacles of a memory in her mind's eye for Maggie, but it remained out of reach. Maggie had been at Harmony Hollows in 1983, but her life had undergone a hiatus. She could find nothing on her from the age of eighteen. It was as though she had existed one day and then poof, gone, only to reappear twenty years later. Sophie had been like that, dragged kicking and screaming to Waverley Park Sanitorium, only to emerge years later with more than half her life erased. Maybe Maggie was a lunatic too, just like she was. Could that be why she was so familiar?

She marked each entry with a number, leaving Maggie as a possible. Satisfied her book was in order, Sophie sat and waited until the photographs were ready to be cut and pasted, keeping everything perfect, just as she liked.

Ralph Fairbright ran his fingers through his hair in a combination of frustration and angst. He slammed his pen down on the desk and roughly loosened his tie. He felt as though he was suffocating.

'This is all I bloody need, barely two months into running this place, and some oven-ready turkey in a lilac shell suit has decided to top herself! Wasn't the fifty quid enough to keep her happy until she got home? Why do it *here*?'

Stacey looked at him with utter contempt. What she really wanted to say was sitting on the tip of her tongue, but as dreadful as this place was, she still valued being in gainful employment. 'We don't know if it was suicide, Mr Fairbright. It could have been a very tragic accident; by all reports, Mary Beaney was extremely drunk when she left the Marina Lounge.'

Ralph riled again. 'Exactly! Can you see the headlines? "Happy Holiday Camper gets drunk on bingo winnings and accidentally garrottes herself with a ten-quid shell suit from Primark." It'll still be our ruddy fault, because we funded her getting rat-arsed on cheap cider.' He sat down heavily on his swivel chair. 'Have the police finished with the chalet yet? I've got it booked out as from tomorrow, so if they have, get the domestics in to clean it up.'

'Yes, Mr Fairbright, sir.' Stacey picked up a file from his desk and muttered under her breath, 'Gosh you're all heart, sir!'

'And while you're at it, tell Maggie to up the bingo bonus to a hundred smackers tonight. I hope it'll give them something to smile about. This episode is the talk of the resort.' Ralph dismissed her with a wave of his hand. He opened the first page of the *Nettleton Shrub News* and read the headline, groaning loudly as he did so. It was no longer confined to camp; it was now out there for all to see.

TRAGEDY AT THE HARMONY HOLLOWS RESORT

Bingo jackpot win precedes unexplained death...

A DREAM IS A WISH YOUR HEART MAKES...

Pru made herself comfy on the bed, plumping the pillow up behind her head. She pressed her mobile phone to her ear and closed her eyes, listening to the comforting *brrrrr, brrrrr* tone, and waited for Andy to answer. He was a little slow today; he didn't pick up until at least the fifth ring.

'Yellow...'

Puzzled at the Americanised accent, she paused. 'Er... pink...'

'I stink! Well, Mrs Barnes, that's a fine way to greet your husband.' Andy laughed.

She loved their stupid opening conversations; he never failed to come up with something that would make her smile. 'I thought we were creating rainbows, my Delectable Detective,' she teased.

'Believe me, my Loony Librarian, it's not rainbows I'm thinking of creating with you; just you wait until I get home!'

Pru could hear rustling in the background as he spoke, imagining stacks of files and his head barely emerging over the top of them. 'Are you still working?' Andy had been giving her generalised updates by text on how the Brimstage investigation was going at his end, and how he filled his hours being away from home, but she still worried about him. 'And are you eating properly?'

'You heard the fish and chip paper rustling, didn't you?' He licked his lips loudly so she could hear. 'I've just heard this afternoon that we're being moved over to Little Kipling for another investigation.'

Surprised, Pru sat up, readjusting the pillow behind her. 'Why? I thought the Nether Wallop job was all hands on, what with it being such a high-profile murder case.'

She heard Andy sigh. 'It is, and remains so, but *too* many hands at times if I'm honest, and that's not just the body parts that are turning up. It's getting a little overcrowded in the incident room here, so they can spare us. As the out-of-force detectives, we're the easiest to move over to another investigation. It's a Misper case: two elderly sisters. Well, it *was* a Misper case; they've finally found them. The search team at the scene came up trumps with their trusty spades. Unfortunately the victims were acting as human fertiliser to a particularly fine specimen of yew tree in the back garden of the house in Little Kipling. So now it's a murder enquiry.'

'Oh God, how awful! Any leads?' Pru knew he was unlikely to name names, but he was well aware that her curiosity always got the better of her, so fingers crossed, he might throw her a snippet to keep her satisfied.

'Nothing as yet. There was apparently a female lodger, according to the neighbours, but we've got nothing on her. The place was clean, in fact too clean, so I've requested a second sweep by forensics. Anyway, enough of the dismal stuff I get paid to deal with. How's the WI holiday going?' He stifled a snort, knowing full well there would be some disaster or calamity to report with the ladies.

Pru huffed. 'Well, first we had Hilda with an intruder in her wardrobe; Ethel's done nothing but complain about the quality of the food and not winning the bingo; Clarissa has perfected the seat-saving challenge; and Millie is – well, just Millie.' She paused trying to think of what else she could regale him with. 'Oh, yep. Kitty is clearly getting serviced by Frank, judging by the grin on her face at breakfast and... oh I almost forgot, there was a dead body in one of the chalets this morning.' She felt throwing that in as an aside would make it sound like a normal, run-of-the-mill event.

'Pru! Please tell me you're not getting involved in something you shouldn't. How many times have I warned you, and how many times have I had to come racing to the rescue? Please, please don't poke your nose, however cute it is, in whatever is happening there.'

Pru pondered his impassioned plea. 'Don't worry; apparently it was either an accident or suicide. Well, that's the word on the streets.'

'Word on the streets! Come on! What are you – Columbo?' As funny as her comment was, he was secretly relieved it was nothing that would spark her amateur detective skills into action. 'Anyway, as much as it pains me to leave you, I've got to finish up and drag my massive backpack downstairs. Lucy is waiting with the engine revving. I'll call you when I get to Nether Wallop.' He smacked his lips together and blew her a kiss, which disappointingly sounded more like a duck in a phone box than a loving gesture.

'I hope that massive backpack is not a euphemism for your lovely bum, Mr Barnes. I'd hate to see it dragged anywhere but into our bed...' She giggled. 'Love you...'

'Ditto...'

Pru pressed the red circle and dropped her phone onto the bedside cabinet. She missed him dreadfully and would have given anything to be with him right now, but all she could do was count down the days until he had a long weekend off.

She would definitely make it a weekend to remember, however, without the added pressure of baby-making. She felt a small lump form in her throat and a dull ache pull at her heart. Quickly pushing the feeling back, she ran her hand over her tummy. It would all be down to nature and chance from now on: no more planning, no more tears, no more anxious waits...

...and no more dreams that didn't come true.

WINDS OF CHANGE

'Have you got it?' Clarissa zipped up her windbreaker and patted her pockets.

'Yes, sir.' Hilda threw a salute whilst waving the torch with the other hand. 'And I've got us some snacks too, just in case it's a long stake out.' She presented two KitKats, a packet of crisps, and a screwed-up bag of mint imperials for inspection.

Ethel grimaced. 'Those aren't the same mint imperials from Rookery Grange, are they? If my memory serves me right, you'd sucked every one of those before sticking them back in the bag!'

Hilda looked sheepish, quickly shoving the bag into her multi-coloured nylon holdall. 'I might have tested one or two, but you'll easily know which ones, they're a bit smaller than the others...'

Clarissa took the opportunity to intervene. 'Hilda, dear, it's not that we're not grateful for your little treats, but it's not going to be a stake out. We're just going to have a little wander around the camp after tonight's bingo session, see if there's anything out of place, and maybe try and find the chalet that was the scene of that double murder.'

Millie was busy tweaking her hair in the mirror, wildly

wielding a can of Insette hairspray as though she was spraying bugs and not her own greying tresses. 'I still can't see the point; it's not like we're going to find anything exciting or even useful. The most we've got out of our little bit of research was what everybody else has been privy to from newspapers.' She popped the cap back on the aerosol and examined the result. 'And that Mary woman was an accident.' Surprised at Millie actually voicing an opinion, Clarissa and Ethel were temporarily lost for words.

Eventually Ethel spoke. 'It's for fun, Millie. We don't actually expect anything, but I must say my spider senses are tingling at Mary's sudden demise; it just doesn't sit right with me, and I'm sure the police will find out something in due course. So in the meantime, there's nothing stopping us entertaining ourselves by doing a bit of snooping. Come on, it'll be just like Montgomery and Rookery, all over again.' She shrugged the bag strap onto her shoulder. 'That was such good fun, wasn't it?' Ethel's enthusiasm was met with silence. She addressed each friend in turn. 'Clarissa? Millie? Hilda?'

Clarissa was aghast at how quickly Ethel seemed to have forgotten the trauma. 'Oh yes, we had great fun at the last one. Remind me what was fun about being hog-tied in the basement of an old people's home waiting to die?!'

'But that's the point, we *didn't* die. We lived to tell the tale, and it was exciting, exhilarating, and made us feel alive. You've got to admit it, just because we're getting older, for once we weren't invisible. We were *important*.' Ethel stood triumphantly with her hands on her hips.

Tired of arguing, Clarissa acquiesced to her enthusiasm. 'Okay, whatever you say, dear. Right. Is everyone ready? It's a £100 bingo bonanza tonight. Now that will definitely keep us in copious amounts of sweet sherry until the end of the week if one of us hits the jackpot!'

The wheels were in motion. Truth and justice had lain dormant for almost forty years, but the winds of fate were finally blowing true.

The next stage of the Perfect Storm had begun.

It was a rare treat for Harmony Hollows to incite such interest and excitement within its bleak walls. The neglected buildings still held host to dark secrets and desperate dreams in equal measure.

It thrived on them.

The needy, the vain, the lonely, and the despairing were perfect to maintain its foundations. They were the bricks of its soul. But the sudden influx of another want, in the guise of curiosity, had now surged through Harmony Hollows, bringing it alive once more with its messengers.

The seeker of truth...

The detectives...

The boomers...

The heart of Harmony Hollows, Chalet 13, held its secrets close.

But for how long?

DUCKING AND DIVING

The evening had been a roaring success for the WI ladies. Although the winning jackpot number of 'Duck and Dive 25', hadn't been on any of their bingo cards, some, including Ethel, had won a ten-quid line. That stroke of luck had stopped her grumbling for all of half an hour, whilst she downed the double brandy she had treated herself to with her winnings. Hilda had already made several trips to the bar for schooners of sherry and a couple of bags of crisps. She had played the 'forgetful old lady' card to perfection and, through empathy from the bar staff, had appropriated at least four of those drinks on the house.

Although Pru was starting to feel the effects of too many pink G&Ts, she had still done her duty, ensuring that after the last ball had been juggled and called, all the ladies had made their way safely back to their respective chalets before she had returned to the lounge to join Bree for a nightcap. She had a feeling that the nightcap had been the drink that had finished her off; she was feeling rather queasy. Almost tripping over the threshold of the Marina Lounge as the fresh air hit her, she stumbled into a large puddle that had been left as a result of the 6pm grass sprinkler system. She giggled. 'Oops, nearly…'

Bree grabbed her by the arm. 'D'you know what? I've come to the conclusion I must be getting desperate for male company, I actually started fancying Troy Florentine when he was shaking his maracas in that demonstration dance number,' she sighed.

Releasing a loud burp, Pru paused to adjust the lace on her high-top sneaker that was digging into her ankle, disappointed at how wet they were. 'A decent pair of budgie smugglers would have prevented that!' She snorted. 'Honestly, Bree, believe me, you'll never be that desperate, he's wearing a toupée – and half that tan would end up on the bedsheets.'

The late evening air had a chill to it, forcing Bree to pull up the collar of her jacket as they made their way along the dimly lit path towards their chalet. 'Have you told the girls about Millie and Hilda's chalet yet?'

Pru shook her head. 'No, and I'm not going to. If we did, can you imagine the furore we'd have? They'd never spend another night in there, and goodness knows what Hilda would have coming out of the wardrobe then…'

Here and there, the orange glow behind curtained windows revealed the occupied chalets, giving the park a less dismal feel. Pru peered into the distance and squinted, she could just make out three, no, maybe four figures, keeping to the shadows up ahead. She shook Bree's arm. 'Correct me if I'm wrong, but who do those ahead look like to you?' She pointed towards the paths that traversed between the chalets.

Bree followed her finger. 'Well smack me over the head with a wet copy of the *Yorkshire Gazette!* If I didn't know better, I'd say it was our intrepid foursome. Now what on earth are they doing out of bed?'

Seeing them had quite a sobering effect on Pru. Shoving her

hands into her jacket, she marched ahead. 'I don't know, but we're going to find out!'

Clarissa stopped abruptly as she reached the end of Marigold Lawns. She darted her arm out sideways in an attempt to halt the progression of Hilda, Millie and Ethel, but momentum had got the better of them and they rear-ended each other, forcing Clarissa to stumble forwards. 'When you've quite finished, Millie, you may extricate your chin from under my right armpit!' She checked the number of the last chalet in the row: number 20. 'Okay, ladies, to the left, and then we'll be on Daffodil, and then we need to make our way to Mary's chalet.'

They set off at a steady pace, keeping close to the walls and as far away from any security lighting that would reveal them. 'Ooh this is so exciting...' Millie whooped in a failed stage whisper, the sherry she had enjoyed giving her both confidence and a warm glow. She was met with a collective 'shush' from her friends.

For the second time in as many minutes, Clarissa slammed on the anchor. This time she had to contend with Hilda's chin under one armpit and Ethel's nose under the other. 'Listen...'

The four of them stood in silence.

Squelch... squelch... squelch...

It stopped as suddenly as it had started. They stood huddled together, inhaling the cold air, a welcome intake after holding their breath. When silence reigned once more, it encouraged them to continue in their quest. They bumbled on along the dark path, the chalet lighting ahead guiding them to their destination.

Squelch... squelch... squelch...

Panic got the better of Millie. 'Clarissa, Clarissa, it's the

Harmony Hollows murderer come back to get us, and I'm the fatty at the back,' she squealed. 'Ethel told me they always pick the fatty off at the back – and that's me!'

'It's the monster from the marsh!' Ethel squealed. 'We're doomed, I tell you; we're all doomed...' Her humorous impersonation of a Scottish accent didn't alleviate the sudden alarm that cloaked them.

Whoever was following them was getting closer.

Squish, squish, squish...

'Quick...' Clarissa pulled her friends into the brick bin store. 'Get down, hide...'

Crouched in the most inelegant and uncomfortable positions possible, crushed between plastic industrial waste bins and discarded cardboard boxes, The Four Wrinkled Dears closed their eyes and held each other close.

Squish... and then silence.

The seconds ticked by. Clarissa was considering fronting it out. Ethel had other ideas; she would rush whoever it was and ding them over the head with her handbag. Millie was promising that she would go on a diet so that she would never again have to be the fatty at the back, and Hilda was totally unfazed as she didn't have a clue as to why she was out after dark.

'And what, may I ask, are you four doing sitting amongst the garbage of Harmony Hollows Resort?' Four pairs of startled eyes glared back at Pru, caught in the weak beam of her pocket torch. 'Come on, out you get...' She offered a helping hand and ushered the ladies back onto the path, lining them up. She was aware that Bree was trying her hardest not to laugh, but like children the frisky foursome didn't need any further encouragement with their antics.

'We got lost and couldn't find our chalets,' Ethel was quick to offer. 'And then we thought whoever was following us might be the murderer from 1983!'

Pru smiled. 'Ah, I see. So you being on Daffodil Lawns has absolutely nothing whatsoever to do with the recent passing of Mary Beaney, then?'

'No...' was the abrupt answer from Clarissa. 'Whatever makes you think that?'

Defeated, Pru decided to let things lie for the moment, but promised the ladies that tomorrow would be a different matter. Tomorrow they would be having a little chat about the dangers of poking large noses into where they weren't wanted or needed... which was quite ironic considering the advice that Andy had given Pru herself earlier that evening.

As the posse of Winterbottom ladies made their way back to their respective chalets, huddled together and chattering ten to the dozen, they remained blissfully unaware they were being watched.

Squelch, squelch, squelch...

FINAL DESTINATION

Trevor Pickford made himself comfortable in the small chair that had been provided in his chalet. He took a swig from the bottle of Peroni lager and wiped his mouth with the back of his hand.

'One hundred smackers, you absolute beauties,' he growled. He kissed the crisp twenty-pound notes and set them down on the coffee table. His love affair with bingo had started when he'd taken his old mum to the Mecca Bingo hall in Blackpool on their annual summer holiday in 1989. Granted, he would have preferred to be sitting in the local pub downing a couple of pints of Carlsberg, but Cora Pickford wasn't one to be left alone; the amount of mischief that woman could get up to in five minutes was nobody's business.

One year he'd left her sitting with enough bingo cards to last the afternoon along with half a bitter shandy, whilst he'd taken the opportunity to nip off to Wetherspoon's for a decent pint. Barely an hour had passed before she'd been arrested for theft by the local plod, after being located in a nearby café trying to flog ten pairs of cerise pink Ethel Austin thongs to unsuspecting victims, whilst picking the sultanas out of an Eccles cake and flicking them at the poor waitress. As a consequence of Cora's magpie-like existence and her inability to pay for brightly coloured items, Trevor had been forced to endure full bingo sessions to accompany her and, in turn, keep her out of HMP Styal. Years of small wins and the anticipation of a sum that would change his life, had eventually indoctrinated him into the bingo family, and he was addicted.

He cocked an ear and listened. Her buzz saw snoring from the next room told him she was well and truly in the land of nod. At ninety-seven years old she was still as sharp as a tack, slower on her feet, obviously, but could still whip him into shape with her vicious tongue. He took another swig from the bottle, the tiniest feeling of guilt gnawing at him. The bingo win had been hers, really, the winning number was on her card, but a quick sleight of hand when she wasn't looking, and the card had become his.

'C'mon, Ma, what would you have done with a hundred quid, eh?' He wasn't really addressing her; he was just thinking out loud, trying to justify his deceit. 'I deserve it…' he blustered. '…and I'll treat yer to something nice to make up for it.'

Pulling himself up out of the chair, he took the opportunity to give his armpit a good scratch before lumbering over to where he was keeping his hidden stash of Peroni bottles. The wardrobe door creaked on its hinges, momentarily masking a similar creak from his chalet door as it slowly opened. The soft click as it closed again, alerted him.

'What the hell…?' But poor Trevor didn't have the opportunity to finish his sentence. From nowhere the figure flew at him with more strength than he had anticipated, knocking him against the wall. Every ounce of breath he possessed, which wasn't a lot considering his ample beer gut and reduced lung capacity from smoking forty Benson & Hedges a day, was expelled in a grotesque wheeze.

He desperately fought to regain his balance, but the numerous bottles of beer throughout the night had left him as weak as a kitten. His head was roughly twisted around, his attacker's hand tightly curled into a fist gripping his long hair.

'Trevor Pickford you scruffy devil, get that bloody hair cut...' Cora had nagged him time and time again. *'But I'm a rocker, Ma...'* Strumming an imaginary guitar, he'd danced around her. *'... rockers don't have short back and sides!'*

He wasn't sure why, when fighting for his life, he should remember that conversation, but right now he wished with all his heart that he'd taken her advice, as he saw the corner of the dressing table looming up towards him. He squeezed his eyes tightly shut hoping that if he couldn't see the inevitable, he wouldn't feel it.

He was wrong.

Trevor's uninvited guest slammed his head with such force into the hard wood, he imagined the dresser as well as his skull, shattering into a thousand tiny pieces. Sparks and lights danced behind his eyes, the blackness acting as a perfect backdrop to showcase their brightness. He felt a warm gush of liquid wash over his cheek and tasted the tang of blood in his mouth as he was dropped roughly to the floor.

His voice was weak. 'Ma, help me...' He grunted as a second blow rained down on him, bringing with it a complete and final darkness.

In the distance he could hear the whistle of an old steam train floating in and out of his subconsciousness, its melodic softness becoming louder the closer it became. Trevor stood with his feet firmly planted on the platform, the steam blocking his view of the track. He looked down at his hand, his trembling fingers holding a ticket. He mouthed the solitary word written upon it.

'Nowhere.'

Without hesitation, he stepped onto the running board of the *Judgement Express*.

The journey to his final destination had begun.

THE DISCOVERY

The sun rose slowly over the trees that for centuries had spread their roots in the fields surrounding Harmony Hollows. A tiny wren, perched on a pink flowering hawthorn branch, sang to its heart's content, heralding what promised to be a beautiful day.

Sophie tipped her head to one side, trying to get a better look at it through the blossom, her camera at the ready. For those that were superstitious, she knew the wren was the harbinger of determination and change, or things to come. That made her smile. Well, she certainly had the determination, and if her past was anything to go by, that particular trait would definitely work towards the 'things to come' part of the portend.

'Morning, Sophie.'

The unexpected voice made Sophie jump. She hated that feeling, the feeling of being scared; of not being in control, even if it was only fleeting. She quickly turned, shielding her eyes from the sun with her hand. 'Oh, hello, Maggie, are you an early riser too?'

She was secretly pleased to be this close to one of her potential subjects, particularly one that gave her such an uncomfortable feeling of familiarity. Her eyes took in the faded scar that had silvered with age, the one thing that punctuated the otherwise perfect complexion of Maggie Henshaw's face. Her nose was slightly off centre too, and a further scar spidered from it to her top lip.

Maggie laughed. 'Not really, I just happen to be sharing a chalet with a lovely, but very noisy snorer! Pinky, bless her, does seem to have a problem with her sinuses, so I thought a bit of fresh air would liven me up before work.'

'Me too, well not the snoring bit, I just didn't do too well last night, either...' Sophie was not going to impart that the real reason for her lack of beauty sleep was because of her nocturnal wanderings around the camp.

Maggie studied the young woman, but in a way that she hoped wouldn't make her feel under the microscope. 'I know you're the photographer here, but have we met before? I just get this feeling we have. I used to be a–'

A scream suddenly shattered the early morning stillness. It was pitiful, a howl like an injured animal. Maggie, confused, desperately looked around, trying to locate where it had originated from. Within seconds, doors were opening from neighbouring chalets, spilling out holidaymakers in pyjamas and dressing gowns on to the paths of Bluebell Lawns.

'Over there...' Sophie pointed to the doorway of the two-bedroomed chalet.

Cora Pickford stood in her blood-soaked nightdress on the threshold of Chalet 25, her hands as red as the geraniums in the nearby flowerbed. 'My son...' she wailed. 'My son is dead!'

Cora's legs gave way and she crumpled into Maggie's arms, revealing the scene behind her. Maggie felt sick, a cold sweat working its way along her back. She wanted to look away, but couldn't; it was a macabre attraction to something she had only ever seen in films. 'It's not good, Sophie,' she whispered, fearful that any over-reaction would generate hysteria amongst the crowd that had gathered. She handed her two-way radio to Sophie. 'Call it in, tell them there's been another accident and it's serious.'

Maggie knew the score. She knew what would follow now, and whilst she remained as professional as she could be under the circumstances, her heart broke for the frail old lady in her arms. The elderly go first, that's the order of life. At least that's what her mum had told her, that no parent should have to bury their children, but Cora would. She looked at Sophie for reassurance and to break her away from her dark thoughts.

If ever a look could chill her to the bone, it was Sophie's expression and demeanour. She appeared to be enjoying what she saw, literally savouring every single piece of the horrifying scene.

How very, very strange...

A new circus was about to begin at Harmony Hollows Resort, one that was guaranteed to give Ralph Fairbright something more than a mild headache, and for Maggie to have more than a little cause for concern.

THE MISSION

Unusually subdued, Clarissa, Millie and Hilda sat with their breakfasts untouched. Ethel, on the other hand, was bursting with excitement. She bit into the piece of toast she had just lavished with best butter and strawberry jam. 'Well I never! This must have happened whilst we were investigating last night,' she cheerily offered to her companions. 'What fun!'

Aghast, Clarissa shook her head. 'I don't think it was fun for that poor soul, or his mother, do you? And we weren't investigating, we were just having a wander, if anyone asks.'

Ethel shrugged. 'Well, they say accidents do happen, that it's part of life, but I'm not convinced.'

A short silence followed Ethel's observation, giving Millie time to pour out the pot of Yorkshire tea into their respective cups. There had been no official confirmation that the rise in body count from one to two was anything other than an accident. It had just been assumed by those in the know that Trevor had slipped and fallen, banging his head on the dressing table after consuming far too many alcoholic beverages. The smashed bottle of Peroni next to his battered bonce and the large stash of six for a tenner bulk-buy packs in the wardrobe had added to that assumption.

'I'll tell you what, I wouldn't want to win the jackpot now, not for all the coffee in China!' Hilda blew on her tea to cool it. 'That's two happy campers over two nights that haven't lived long enough to enjoy their winnings.'

A second silence fell over the Four Wrinkled Dears as they digested that snippet of information. Each mulling over the probabilities, each coming to a different conclusion.

'Just coincidence...' Clarissa announced.

'Maybe it was to steal their winnings...' Millie hunched her shoulders up to her ears and gave a side-eyed glance to see if anyone outside their circle was listening.

Ethel bristled with confidence that her conclusion would be the correct one. 'Well I don't think either of them are bloody happy now, do you? As I said before, I don't believe in coincidences. It's definitely murder; I'll stake my life on it!'

Three astonished faces stared back at her.

'Shush,' Clarissa hissed. 'If we do have a rampaging murderer in our midst, the last thing we need is you offering yourself up as their next victim. Honestly, Eth, what's got into you?' Clarissa had noticed subtle changes in her good friend since Albert had died, a cynicism that hadn't been part of her personality before losing him, and a daredevil attitude to things that would have normally made her think twice.

'I'm just saying, that's all. I'm not actually putting my name down for an early shove into the next realm to join Albie, but how many fatal accidents can you have in less than a week in a run-down holiday camp?' Ethel pursed her lips and tilted her head, waiting for a response from her friends.

Clarissa had to begrudgingly concede that she did have a point. 'For now, we look on them as accidents and concentrate on our original plan: the 1983 double murder. There's less risk with that one, it's so old it's almost stagnant! We still haven't identified the scene, so…' She pulled out her notepad. 'Ethel, you seem to have a rapport with the cleaning staff so your challenge, if you so wish to take it, is to see if you can find out which chalet it happened in.'

Ethel nodded, pleased that she had been given such an important task.

'Millie, I need you to see if you can discover if any of the current staff at Harmony Hollows were employed at the time of the 1983 murders.' Ticking off that task with her pencil, Clarissa looked at Millie for confirmation that she had understood. 'Hilda, can you go with Millie and make up a chatty duo between you, as though you're just curious golden oldies? Lay on the vulnerability a bit. You could make out that you're worried about what happened; they're bound to open up to reassure you.'

With all their tasks allocated, the friends grabbed their belongings and made their way out of the resort restaurant, chattering ten to the dozen. They were fuelled with excited anticipation and a touch of devilment, as they went their separate ways, eager to be part of a cold-case adventure.

Ethel had already spotted the cleaner she had previously spoken to ambling towards Bluebell Lawns, swinging a bucket and mop from arms that a primate would have been proud of. She gave a wry smile. Who better to know the ins, outs and goings-on of Harmony Hollows than a cleaner, particularly one that looked as though she had been here since the first foundation brick had been laid. She pulled down her summer hat and quickly followed her.

Now was as good a time as any.

IT'S A MURDER!

LITTLE KIPLING

The desk they had given Andy as the out-of-force DS, was squeezed into the corner of the Little Kipling CID incident room with an expectation that he would share it with Lucy. His fingers massaged his temples as he read through the update they had given him.

He had been quietly pleased that his request for a second sweep by forensics had discovered a single bloodied fingerprint on a plastic plant pot behind the pantry door. The print hadn't matched either of the victims, but the DNA from the blood had been confirmed as a match for Gertrude Timpson. The cellophane wrapping that was still partially attached to the pot indicated it was a relatively new acquisition to the Timpson household. All they needed now to progress the investigation was a positive ident for the print itself. Whoever it belonged to had definitely been at the scene at the time of the first murder.

A red flashing 'urgent' marker pulsated at the top of his computer. He clicked on the tab and expanded the screen, his heart suddenly beating just that little bit faster.

'Luce, quick, we've got it, we've a match for the fingerprint...' He sat back in his chair and finally allowed the breath he had been holding to expel from his lungs. Lucy scooted her chair over to him, stopping abruptly in the small amount of space he had left for her between his own chair and the wall.

She leant in, squinting at the screen as she read the report, silently mouthing the words to herself.

Elodie Marshall, date of birth 22nd March 1983
Attempted Murder June 1998
Deemed not fit to plead. Guilt determined by jury on a trial of facts.
RESULT: Committed to Waverley Park Sanitorium
under hospital order 18th August 1998

'Sheesh, that's some CV for a young one.' Lucy scribbled the case number and Elodie's details in her notebook. 'I'll get the ball rolling, see what else we've got on her, and where she is now. We've got to assume that she's out if her print was left at the scene, and it's odds on she's the favourite for the lodger the neighbours told us about. Are you going to inform the DI?'

Andy nodded. 'Once she's updated, I'll bring up the old case file for Marshall.' He sat staring at his screen for longer than was necessary; for all his years in the job, juvenile offenders for serious offences still made him question the future of humanity. All he had to do now was once Lucy had collated all the intelligence held on Elodie, figure out what her involvement was in the Timpson murder case and why her bloodied fingerprint had been found at the scene.

Robert Limpett MRCS, MB, BS, LRCIP, better known (but only behind his back) as 'Barnacle Bob', peeled off his blue gloves. The satisfying *thwack* from the latex gave him his usual feeling of a job well done. He kicked down on the clinical waste bin pedal and dropped them in.

'What have we got, Bob? An accident?' Optimistically hopeful as always, Detective Sergeant Ezra Maynard waited patiently in the viewing gallery; the body of Trevor Pickford neatly sewn back together was a stark contrast to the stainless steel of the autopsy table.

Bob sighed as he made an entry on the large whiteboard on the wall. 'It's no accident, Ezra, not unless Mr Pickford here managed to perform the second coming of Christ, arise from his unconscious state, and smash his own head in for the second time in as many minutes.' He popped the top back on the marker pen. 'My report will be more detailed, but the injury to the front of his head is consistent with it making a forceful impact on the corner of the dressing table, however here...' He turned Trevor's head. 'This is a second site of trauma, and the one that did the damage. He was hit, probably when already unconscious, with a heavy blunt object causing death.'

Ezra's analytical brain rapidly began processing the information. 'The Mary Beaney death, has that been listed yet?'

'She was slipped down the list when this one came in...' Bob flicked over the sheet on his clipboard and checked the names. 'She's listed for tomorrow; it would have been this afternoon, but we've got a bit of a backlog – two females from a house in Little Kipling. Now that will be a challenge; one is a bit fresher than the other, but they've both been feeding the worms for some time.'

Ezra was aware of the Timpson case. Back at his office, some had voiced their relief that they hadn't been rostered to work it, and one or two, mainly the eager and young in service, had put their names down as reserve, just for the experience.

A loud voice boomed in the background. 'Ezra Maynard! What brings you to the delights of Uncle Bob's emporium?'

Ezra grinned. He would recognise that voice anywhere. 'Andy Barnes, you old rogue, what gives?' They warmly shook hands.

'The Timpson case. I've been seconded over from the Nether Wallop Brimstage body parts job to lead on this one. And you?' Andy was delighted to see his old study buddy from years back. They had both been on a six-week CID residential course many moons ago, and had forged a good friendship over pints of Theakston Old Peculier and the PEACE interview guide.

'A just confirmed suspicious death from a local holiday camp. Initially, it came in as an accident underpinned by excess alcohol, but Bob's just put the dampeners on it being a "stamp it, file it and go" job.' Ezra checked his watch. 'I'm just going to phone this in to the DI, and then do you fancy a coffee before your slot with Bob?'

Andy felt his heart sink. 'Which holiday camp?'

'Harmony Hollows in Nettleton Shrub. Why? Do you fancy a week there? Didn't have you down as a *Hi-De-Hi* type of guy, Andy!' Ezra laughed.

'Mate, if you knew my wife, you'd know why I'm worried – that's where she is now, along with a good portion of the Winterbottom Women's Institute.' Andy ran his fingers through his hair, resigned to what would come. 'When you get a quartet of Miss Marples and a duo of Agatha Raisins running amok where a murder has just been confirmed, there is definitely going to be trouble ahead!'

FOUR WOMEN, NO CRY...

The morning had been fairly fruitful for two of the Four Wrinkled Dears.

Ethel had been unsuccessful in her attempt to accost the cleaner. She had followed her diligently at a safe distance until she had turned a corner in Bluebell Lawns, and by the time Ethel had caught up with her, she had disappeared. Ethel was amazed at how fleet of foot she had been, considering she was overloaded with buckets, mops and cleaning products.

Millie and Hilda had been more fortunate, having garnered enough information on the resort staff to know who was still in residence and treading the entertainment boards since that fateful day in 1983.

Hilda was also very excited to impart something else she had discovered on their travels. Through the fronds of the plastic kentia palm in the reception area, she had spotted the tall poster advertising the evening's entertainment. 'You'll never guess what, they're holding this evening: a Rasta Night! How exciting is that? I love me a bit of Bob Marley, don't you, Clarissa?'

Clarissa held the bottle of sherry to the light, the dark liquid showing a satisfying, almost full line before she poured out their favourite tipple into plastic cups. 'I'm more a mix between Abba and Mickey Bubbles, but I must admit *Jamming* was quite iconic.' She slowly gyrated her hips and bounced on the balls of her feet as she hummed the tune, taking care not to spill a drop of sherry.

They had split into their usual pairs, taking a bed each in Clarissa and Ethel's chalet. The weather had turned rather blustery with rain forecast, so they had broken out the first bottle from the secret stash they had brought with them for such an occasion. 'Right, what have we got?' Clarissa held her notebook and pen, keen to get on with the proceedings.

'Well, as far as I can tell, it'll be music and dancing and... oh I know! Why don't we dress up, and get in the mood? It'll be such fun. I bet you there'll be others getting dressed up, too; that's what they do at these type of holiday resorts.' Hilda had completely gone off track.

Ethel smiled; it did sound like fun, but Clarissa was frustrated. 'What I meant is, have we got anything from you poking around today, Hilda? Did you find anything worthwhile about the staff?'

Millie quickly intervened. 'We've found three members of staff who were here when the murders took place in 1983. Some moved on, but, strangely enough, have recently come back to Harmony Hollows. Quite a coincidence, methinks.' She pulled out her own notebook. 'Right, first up: the camp commandant, Ralph Fairbright. He worked here during the summer season that year, on the waltzers. He was apparently quite a jovial lad, one for the young ladies, bit of a roving eye.' Millie winked and tapped the side of her nose. 'He left not long after the murders, but stayed with the company and worked his way up to manager at various resorts. He's just been transferred back here from Grendel Scraggs.'

Hilda joined in, reading from her own notebook. 'Then there's Nellie Girdlestone, née Nell Collins. She was a barmaid at the time, but now she's one of the domestics. She's that big woman we see mooching around; always hides behind the bin store with a ciggie dangling from her mouth.'

Millie tutted and scrunched up her nose. 'Finally, there's Maggie Henshaw, our nightly bingo caller. We only found out about her being here because she's been reminiscing with the receptionist. Maggie was a competitor in the dancing competition that was being held at Harmony Hollows in 1983; she was only young then, we think about sixteen, but now she's back here as a member of staff. She's apparently done quite a few seasons during the last ten years. She's got arthritis in one of her legs that ended her dancing career, and she had some sort of accident...' She pointed to her face, indicating the scars that Maggie's face held. 'How that happened, we don't know.' Millie snapped her notebook shut. 'That's it, nothing too exciting – and unbelievably no gossip, either.'

The four of them sat in silence, mulling over their progress.

Clarissa topped up their cups. 'Okay, good work, girls. We shall mobilise again tomorrow morning, but in the meantime...' and with a devilish grin, she jumped up and flung open the wardrobe. 'I'm definitely up for it, are you?' She held the multi-coloured jacket she had purchased in town, against her. 'Bob Marley, eat your heart out!' She danced around the small room, singing to herself.

Hilda clapped her hands in glee, the warming liquid she had just gulped from her cup adding to the feeling of wild abandonment. 'I've got my yellow harem pants, they'll be perfect!' she squealed.

Millie watched her friends come alive; their enthusiasm infectious. 'I know, why don't we make ourselves some dreadlocks? We'll certainly wow them when we walk in tonight

– I bet you nobody else will think of having them!' She slid off the bed, grabbing hold of the chair to ease herself up. 'I've got all that coloured wool I brought with me; I knew it would come in handy. Clarissa, dear, crack open another bottle; ladies, get your crocheting fingers at the ready, I'll be back...'

HIDE-AND-SEEK

The water cooler in the corner of the Little Kipling Incident Room gurgled loudly as Andy finished filling his cup. He took a sip of the ice-cold water, amused to think that every single police station in the country probably had a water cooler that gurgled. He wondered if it was a prerequisite when the estates department ordered them, that they all had to sound like DS Jack Finnigan's stomach after six pints of best bitter and a curry. He made his way back to his desk and flopped down onto his chair. It juddered and dropped down a couple of inches.

'Christ on a bike, lads, if you're going to sit on my chair, at least take the settings back to what they were before your arses covered it!' His hand wiped his tie over the water he had spilled; it beaded and then flicked across his desk, forcing him to utilise the sleeve of his jacket to mop it up from the red cobra file in front of him. He spotted Lucy weaving her way through the randomly dotted desks. He waved her over. 'Please cheer my morning up; what have you got?'

'Don't get too excited. It's been a struggle, like wading through mud.' Lucy took a sip from her mug. 'Right, here's the biggie. Elodie Marshall is the daughter of Clare Mayer-Marshall, better known by her stage name of Clare Simmons, and Richard Mayer-Marshall.' She waited for a reaction.

Andy shrugged. 'And that's supposed to mean something?'

'Duh, *Deadly Disclosure*, *A Perfect Death*, *Fears of the Few* ... need I go on?' Lucy was appalled that Andy even had to ask. She'd just given him three of many blockbuster Oscar-nominated films they had appeared in, and the blank look on his face told her that he still didn't have a clue. 'Don't you go to the cinema or watch TV in your spare time? They're Hollywood's golden couple – well, they were many moons ago.'

He at least had the decency to flush a nice shade of pink whilst squirming in his chair. 'I might watch them, but I'm not that bothered as to who appeared in them. So, what you're telling me is Elodie had famous parents?'

'Yep, hence her being at the Cragstone Manor Academy. I've tried to contact Clare and Richard; they're filming in the Australian outback – some sort of budget remake or sequel to *Cocoon*.' She frowned and bit the inside of her lip, deep in thought. 'Well, I suppose they're in the right age bracket for it now. Anyway, I've spoken to their agent and told them it's imperative that we speak to them urgently.' She swirled the mouse on the mat and opened up the screen on the PC. 'Elodie was released from Waverley Park Sanitorium; the dates are all there...' She used the curser to guide Andy to the relevant information. 'She has regular medication and was deemed fit to be released into the community. I requested the medical records.'

Andy didn't want to sound ungrateful for the work she had put in, but apart from circulating an all-forces-wanted/missing and updating the Police National Computer, there wasn't much more to be done until Elodie Marshall was located and brought in for questioning. 'What type of release order or licence did she have, Luce?' He tapped the mouse, bringing it to life. 'Straight cough, I can give you chapter and verse on prison release conditions, but my knowledge is a bit thin when it comes to mental health facilities. Was it signed off by the Courts as part of the sentencing?'

Lucy turned her monitor to face him. 'It's all there. I've got uniform doing house-to-house again, and the last photograph we have of Elodie is this one...' She flicked her notebook open. 'We've got one witness who didn't speak to the woman staying with Gertrude Timpson but saw her a couple of times in the front garden. His description isn't too far out for Elodie, but it's not a positive ID. I think we also need a road trip to Cragstone Manor Academy.'

Andy doodled on the scrap pad next to him. 'Right, update the board with what we've got; we'll keep Elodie Marshall as our main person of interest.' He pinched the bridge of his nose and sighed loudly. 'But there's also another way of looking at it, just to put the cat amongst the pigeons.'

Lucy bit down on her bottom lip. She knew only too well how Andy's mind worked. 'Go on...'

'Considering we already have two victims from the house, Elodie could easily be another one, sandwiched between Gertrude and Agatha, and that's why we haven't found her!'

THAT'S AMORE

The raucous laughter emanating from the reception area of the Marina Lounge gave promise of an evening to remember for the Four Wrinkled Dears. Clarissa, Millie and Hilda stood huddled together on the grey and purple swirled carpet, waiting for Ethel, who had quickly diverted to the ladies' loo upon their arrival. The short walk from their chalets to the venue had clearly been a little taxing on her waterworks after too many glasses of wine during the afternoon.

Clarissa smiled to herself. They had indulged in such fun after Millie had dragged her faithful tattered wool bag into their chalet, and over the following few hours, whilst enjoying a particularly nice nutty sherry and several glasses of red wine, their needles and hooks had worked tirelessly to create costumes and dreadlocks that promised to be the envy of everyone attending the Rasta party. She was so looking forward to a night of fun and laughter, and maybe a little bit of devilment, too.

'Ta-daa…' Ethel bounced out of the powder room, trailing a multi-coloured chiffon jacket in her wake. She flicked the vibrant wool strands that had been attached to her own hair with a couple of kirby grips. Courtesy of an old necklace, she had also incorporated colourful beads at the ends of each dreadlocked tress and had then passed the rest on to Millie.

Her friends clapped their hands in admiration. Millie giggled loudly. 'Ooh, you do look wonderful, Eth! We *are* going to be the talk of Harmony Hollows Resort tonight.'

'What do you think of my harem pants, then?' Hilda gave a twirl to show her best angle, the slight breeze picking up the fabric and making them billow out like a balloon.

Ethel, her sharp wit having returned after so many weeks of sadness, had her response ready and waiting. 'Like you've gone overboard on the sprouts and your Gaviscon has failed you, Hilda my dear...' She laughed.

Not to be outdone, Millie joined in, flinging her head around in wild abandonment, thoroughly relishing the sound the beads at the end of her hair made, as they rattled and clacked together. As it had been her wool they had used, she had taken the opportunity to ensure her dreadlocks were longer and more vibrant than anyone else's. They whirled out like helicopter blades, swirling around her head. 'Ooh look at me...' she jauntily trilled as the momentum carried her across the carpet.

'Millie, watch out!' Clarissa tried to make a grab for her, but her reactions were a little too late. Millie's colourful strands made one last bid for freedom before hooking themselves around the ornate light fitting on the wall. Her head jerked sideways as she stumbled backwards.

'Don't move, dear, I'm coming...' Hilda and her pants billowed their way across the expanse that Millie's exuberant dance had left between them, desperate to assist her friend. 'Oh my goodness, just look at you!' she exclaimed.

Millie grunted. 'I would if I bloody could, but I'm just a little preoccupied at the moment.' Her fingers grasped at the strands that had come adrift from her head.

The doors to the Marina Lounge suddenly swung open, spilling out several holidaymakers, the deep bass beat of the music momentarily filling the reception area before being swallowed up when the doors slowly hissed shut again.

Clarissa had just enough time to spot Pru, Bree and the rest of the Winterbottom Ladies at their regular tables before the doors sealed themselves. She adjusted her lime green and orange beret that had, up until 2pm that afternoon, been the spare tea cosy that she took everywhere with her, just in case. A few little stitches to close up the spout and handle holes, and she had a titfer that Bob Marley himself would have been proud of. She clapped her hands loudly. 'Come on, ladies, enough of the hanging around. I've just spotted our friends and we've got some dancing to do!'

Millie, ably assisted in her escape from the curved brass arm of the wall fitting by Hilda, straightened her remaining locks and pulled her felt hat down over her ears.

'Now you look like Benny Hill...' Ethel offered, by way of a backhanded compliment. 'Right, girls, are we ready? Okay, just like we practised this afternoon; plenty of *joie de vivre*. We've got to let them know we've arrived. No invisibility cloak for us, ladies, we're on fire...' She blew on her fingers to prove the vibrancy and energy they needed to display.

Together they linked arms and burst through the double doors into the Marina Lounge, whooping and hollering loudly. Delighted to see that their excitable entrance had very quickly stilled the other party goers, they cranked up their exuberant performance a notch or two, with Ethel and Hilda arms in the air, managing a pretty nifty bit of pelvic gyration.

'Blimey, if I didn't need a new hip before, I will after this...' Ethel laughed as she danced in circles waving her hands.

The other guests had stopped their own celebrations, glasses raised to lips, forks mid-mouthful, heads tilted and hands covering eyes. Their astonished and amused faces were a picture, which only prompted the four to play up to the crowd.

This was exactly what they had hoped for: the grandest of entrances.

Hilda played air guitar on her handbag, whilst Millie made another attempt at dreadlock swinging, but as far away as possible from anything that could leave her dangling like a novelty car air-freshener again. Ethel and Clarissa took the limelight with their jerky dance moves, shrugged shoulders and bouncy toes, which completed the ensemble.

Ethel broke away from the group to take a bow. 'Ladies and gentlemen, I give you *Slob Parsley and the Inhalers...*' She laughed, fit to burst, as she watched her friends, fuelled by too much alcohol, give it their all. She waved enthusiastically at Pru and the WI ladies, beckoning them to join their fun.

Pru stood with her mouth open. 'Dear God, Slob Parsley and the Inhalers!! Please tell me I'm dreaming...' She grabbed Bree's arm, unsure if it was to attract her attention or to stop herself from falling over.

Kitty flopped down into her chair, the embarrassment of a full house feasting upon the antics of *her* WI ladies, ripping her breath away. 'Ladies, ladies, please...!' she whimpered, desperately wishing the highly polished floor would open up and swallow her whole.

'It's a Rasta party! Come on, give it some welly, folks...' Millie rattled her dreadlocks with more gusto than she really should have done, and the impetus propelled the beads along the shafts of coloured wool, popped off the ends and scattered them across the floor. They rolled and skittered under tables and chairs.

Clarissa, suddenly sensing something was amiss, went from four beats to two and then to a complete stop in her dance routine. She looked around at the sensibly dressed party goers as it dawned on her that Dean Martin singing 'That's Amore' was definitely not something Bob Marley, with or without his Wailers, would have sung.

She slowly took in her surroundings: the buffet tables with crisp white linen cloths strategically placed at the side of the dance floor, with their green, white and red paper runners stretching from one end to the other, laden with culinary delights. She read the little cards that had been placed in front of each bowl, her lips moving silently as she mouthed the words:

Curly pasta in tomato sauce

Pasta bake

Penne pasta in a creamy sauce

Tuna pasta

Spicy pasta

Chicken pasta...

She marvelled at the colourful Italian flag bunting, riding high above the tables and the little mini flags on sticks that Brenda, Miriam, and her friends were now half-heartedly waving. 'Oh dear...' Clarissa gasped. 'This is *not* the Rasta Night we thought it was, is it, Pru?'

Pru choked back her laughter and shook her head. 'I'm afraid not...' She pointed to the large roll-up banner behind her, which announced a cultural evening of music and food.

Clarissa quickly removed her tea cosy and ran her fingers through her hair. She swept aside the single frond from the kentia palm that had partially obscured the advertising stand.

Harmony Hollows
PASTA NIGHT
with
music, dancing and great food

Her shoulders slumped and her cheeks popped like a hamster as she watched Millie and Hilda, still oblivious, giving their audience the full experience of a non-existent Rasta Night, and for the first time in her well-lived life, she used the word she had been saving for such an unfortunate occasion.

'Bollocks...!'

LISTENING IN

Nellie Girdlestone kicked the red plastic bucket out of the way and plunged her mop into the swirling murky water, giving it a good soaking. Slapping the wet fibrous strands down onto the doorstep tiles of Chalet 17 in Marigold Lawns, she gave one vigorous wipe before being distracted by raised voices from the chalet next door.

'I've never been so embarrassed in my entire life! We are most definitely the talk of Harmony Hollows now; how could I have been so remiss as to not check what Hilda had told us!' The first voice was full of annoyance and regret.

Nellie patted her overall pocket to check that her cigarettes were still safely ensconced in its depths before allowing a smirk to touch her lips. She ran her finger down the chalet list that confirmed the occupation of Clarissa Montgomery and Ethel Tytherington in number 15.

'Not 'arf! You can say *that* again...' Nellie chunnered under her breath as she made another attempt to mop a particularly tough pigeon deposit from the ceramic tile. Everyone, and by that she really did mean *everyone,* was talking about the four old dears and their slight misunderstanding the previous evening.

'Slight misunderstanding? My arse! I'd say, in my humble opinion, it was more like a bloody big embarrassing feck up!' Nellie sniggered, as she moved in closer to listen.

The two voices continued to debate their faux pas loudly, making Nellie feel like she was listening to a 1950s soap opera on the radio. She wished she could peep through the window and make it a TV show instead, but being caught spying on guests would probably get her into as much trouble as being caught with an Embassy ciggie dangling from her bottom lip. The voices continued, but this time the second voice held a more composed approach.

'Clarissa, dear, please calm down. It gave everyone a good laugh; we still had a super time – and look at this way, it's not like anyone died, is it?'

Nellie stopped what she was doing, her heart skipping a beat. She was right, nobody had died last night. Considering Harmony Hollows' track record the previous two evenings, apart from the antics of Miss Montgomery and her friends, nothing out of the ordinary had happened.

She totted up the losses that Harmony had endured over the years, the very thought of them exciting her. Marigold Lawns had produced its most famous double murder deaths in 1983, the odd smattering of lifestyle heart attacks had followed over the years that had added to the total. She couldn't think of anything worse than curling up your toes wearing your best string vest and Y-fronts in a run-down holiday resort with a tattered copy of *Men Only* on the bedside cabinet. She shuddered as her fingers absent-mindedly tapped the cardboard carton of the cigarette packet. And then, of course, most recently, there was Daffodil and Bluebell Lawns with Mary Beaney and Trevor Pickford. She thought it quite funny to think that the guests from Primrose, Cornflower and Snowdrop Lawns could be quaking in their boots, wondering if their little haven would be next to suffer a tragic loss or a grisly murder.

'Bet that creepy old bugger would charge them extra for the gruesome entertainment...' Nellie chuckled. It was funny how she could no longer see the young, carefree Ralph Fairbright of their yesteryears, who was such a hit with the young girls as he swung them around on the waltzers, offering his charms to any that would succumb. He had been replaced by the overweight, oily vision he now presented around Harmony Hollows. His nickname of *Rancid Ralph* had followed him from Briddleston Bay, and it really suited him. She hadn't let on to him, but then again, it wasn't like he'd acknowledge her, either. She looked down at her pendulous bosoms, ample hips and rugby player thighs and sighed. Yep, she herself was a far cry from the slender blonde of 1983, with pert norks that were housed in a rather fancy *Miss Mary of Sweden* bra, so she supposed it worked both ways, really.

She dropped her mop into the bucket, quickly checked the coast was clear, and took the opportunity to sneak off to the bin store for a ciggie break and to contemplate the potential implications, financial rewards, and pleasure of another suspicious death at Harmony Hollows.

DS Ezra Maynard held the phone to his ear by his shoulder, utilising his free hands to grab for a pen and a scrap of paper from his desk. He pushed several files to one side until he found what he was looking for. 'Go on, Bob, what have you got for me?'

As soon as Bob Limpett had announced himself, Ezra knew that a call from the Home Office forensic pathologist would be news he wouldn't want to hear. 'Can you send over the post-mortem report, Bob? I take it she's had a mortuary ident and the family are aware?' He listened intently. 'Yep, I'll apprise the DI; he may link and get the senior investigating officer from the Pickford case on this one, too.' Multi-tasking, he beckoned over one of his team before returning to his conversation with the pathologist. 'Any forensic recovery from the body?' Ezra's shoulders slumped, as though an extra weight had been placed upon them. He finished the call and swirled the mouse to wake the monitor screen.

Angie Denham, one of his longest serving detective constables and his most trusted right hand, stood with her arms folded around a thick investigation file. 'Bad news?'

Ezra opened up the Pickford case, the cursor moving quickly around the screen. 'Afraid so. Mary Beaney wasn't an accident or suicide. Barnacle Bob has just confirmed it as a murder: she had perimortem injuries...' His fingers tapped across the keyboard. 'She fought for her life; that poor woman didn't want to die. The skin under her fingernails was hers, she clawed at her own throat, Angie.' He shook his head.

'Echoes of 1983, Sarge?' Angie chewed at her bottom lip, more than aware that Ezra had already read through the cold-case files from the Purkiss and Belfont double murder.

'I can't dismiss it because that one remains unsolved, with not even one suspect, but these are two totally unrelated victims as far as we know, two scenes, and nothing to link Beaney and Pickford other than they were staying at the same resort.' Ezra gathered his notebook and files, preparing to knock on the DI's door. His mind was racing ahead, desperately trying to slot everything he had into neat little files inside his brain, keeping them at the front so they could be easily opened when needed. He had visions of this case, *his* case, being another '1983': an unsolved double murder that would tarnish his career for all eternity and beyond, just like it had for old Dennis Skelhorn, the DI in charge of the original Purkiss and Belmont job. Dennis had retired a broken man, the one case he hadn't been able to bring home and he had died never knowing.

Ezra closed down his screen and sighed, aware that all eyes would now be on him. 'It looks like the curse of Harmony Horrors has struck again...'

A COLLECTION OF MEMORIES

The news that Mary Beaney's death had not been an accident spread like wildfire through Harmony Hollows, causing a mixture of concern, fear and good old-fashioned gossip. Although the sun shone brightly on the shingled rooftops of the chalets and bathed the colourful flowers in the border displays, the grey underbelly of death furtively skimmed along paths and through alleyways, until it found its way into the bones of those who had felt its icy touch in 1983.

Della Claybourne's fingers pulled at the curtain on her chalet window. She shivered. It felt as though the fabric itself held the memories that she had tried so hard to forget. She mentally berated herself. How on earth could a bit of cloth hold anything but dust? Although Harmony Hollows was stuck solidly in the past with its dated chalets and buildings, the owners had at least had the decency to decorate with fairly new soft furnishings. Her finger traced the daffodil pattern of the fabric. Closing her eyes, she conjured up how it had been the last time she had stayed here. She could see the pale grey and lilac stripes that had once adorned the window, the chalk-painted walls marked and blistered in places, the muted glow from the table lamp that sat awkwardly on the bedside cabinet, its grubby shade casting a shadowed glow across his face as he lay on her bed.

Sweet sixteen and never been kissed...

Until *he* had come into her life.

A single tear tracked its way down her cheek as she remembered. She recalled how he made her feel special; she remembered his words; and she remembered his promise. The knot tightened in her stomach, and she fought back the feeling of betrayal as it once again paid her an unwanted visit. 'You didn't keep that promise though, did you?' She angrily swept the wetness from her cheek with the heel of her hand.

She looked around the room that had finally held her safe that fateful night when she had fled and sought its sanctuary, remembering how its walls had closed in, making her world smaller and so much sadder, until finally the pain of betrayal had turned to rage.

'A promise is meant to make something, but instead you broke it, and in turn you broke me,' she quietly sobbed.

'You got exactly what you deserved, Larry Belfont...'

Ralph Fairbright slumped down into his chair, the ice cubes in the crystal glass that held a double measure of Glenfiddich single malt Scotch rattling against the sides with the momentum of his sudden drop. He slugged back more of the amber liquid than expected, which set off a coughing fit. He eventually caught his breath and wiped his chin with the sleeve of his jacket.

'Two bloody murders, what *is* it with this place?' he grunted. As he was addressing an empty room he didn't expect a reply, but it felt good to vocalise his thoughts. He got up and stretched his legs on a short jaunt to the drinks cabinet on the far side of the room. Pouring another measure of Scotch, he held the glass to the light to check the level, and decided that the occasion warranted an extra dash. As he tipped the glass to drink, his eyes drifted to the print on the wall, his *Harmony Hollows Staff 1982–1983 Season* photograph.

He didn't want to think about it, but as they always did, his memories had a knack of creeping into his soul, whenever and wherever they wanted to. He had no control. They were brutal and selfish memories, designed to taunt him and tear his heart into a thousand pieces. The tip of his finger gently traced the outline of his 'little dancer' through the glass of the frame. Things could have been so very different for him if she had reciprocated his feelings and accepted his promise to forsake all others for her. He wouldn't have been a fly-by-night like Larry; he would have loved and cared for her for all eternity. He had made his declaration of love for her, but she had cut him down in such a cruel and public way. She had laughed and humiliated him in front of everyone, and had then chosen Larry over him.

He refilled his glass, now totally oblivious to how much he had drunk. He didn't care that the clock on his wall read 11.03am; he didn't care that at any moment Stacey could come bowling in with letters for him to sign and complaints to answer.

He didn't care one iota for anything anymore.

This was what returning to Harmony Hollows had done to him; it was slowly eating his soul whilst simultaneously crushing his heart. A sudden, sharp pain radiated along his left arm making him gasp, before slowly releasing its grip and allowing him to breathe again.

It was reminiscent of that fateful night when he had fled from Chalet 13 on Marigold Lawns, his heart pounding fit to burst, the sweat soaking his skin as his leather jacket stuck to him like clingfilm. He had carried on running until his thighs cramped and his throat was raw. Hunkering down behind the industrial bins, his sanctuary, he had wept as the terror and guilt in equal measure flooded through his veins to become part of him. He had brutally beat himself around the head with his own hands, rocking backwards and forwards, trying desperately to destroy what was now seared into his brain like a freakish horror movie, the image playing and replaying with no end in sight...

...of the bloodied head of Larry Belfont and the lifeless body of his little dancer.

Maggie Henshaw carefully tapped the bingo cards down onto the table and patted the sides together to ensure they were straight. She adjusted the old-fashioned microphone stand and kicked the cable to one side, allowing a clear space on the stage. 'Jeez, talk about an accident waiting to happen!' She pinned the cable back and clipped down the cover. She couldn't believe how lax and untidy the Northern Dance organisers were. They had been in for rehearsals in the morning and left the Marina Lounge looking like a bomb site. She checked her watch. A full house was expected for the afternoon qualifiers, and she was determined to set up her bit for the bingo evening and disappear before the dancers descended. She bent down and picked up a cold, rubbery dollop of pasta that had evaded the cleaner's broom, flinging it into a nearby bin. It slapped against the side, momentarily juddered, and dropped to the depths of the black plastic bin-liner.

She stood in the middle of the dance floor and looked up at the stage. This was where it had all begun for her, where her hopes and aspirations had grown from small seeds of passion for the discipline of dance to a career in entertainment and teaching that had spanned almost four decades. She preferred to remember the happy times at Harmony Hollows that season, not the brutal end. She closed her eyes to shut out the image of Larry Belfont, and instead quickly replaced it with the brightly coloured ballroom gowns, sequins and bouffant hairstyles of 1983. She hadn't been placed at all that year in the championships, but she had been bitten by the dancing bug, and the flouncy gowns had given way to tutus and ballet shoes as she had progressed with her training. She still remembered her first pair of pointe shoes that had made her feel as though she was floating on air when she danced. A smile touched her lips as she looked around the dance floor, the gossamer ghosts of the past still twirling around her. This was where it had all begun.

As if on cue to spoil her happy memories, a violent spasm of pain shot through her leg. Her nose screwed up tightly as she breathed through it. 'Damn it...' she grunted through clenched teeth. She hobbled over to the cushioned booth and slumped down onto the velour fabric, catching sight of her reflection in the mirrored backdrop. The light caught her profile, casting a harsh reflection across her skin. Her finger traced the scars, awakening the moment of regret that always came with the memory. 'Je ne méritais pas ça!' She wished with all her heart that she could turn back time.

Her childhood had been humble, but she had been happy, until the shame of those beginnings had burnt fiercely on her young cheeks. Realising she could no longer live within her own skin, she had shed the old Maggie and emerged like a butterfly from its chrysalis. She had spread her new wings and reinvented herself, and had at last been accepted into a world that had previously looked down upon her. But in doing so, she, too, had looked down upon another, an action that had eventually brought about the tragic consequence of its own.

Maggie allowed the mixture of sorrow, guilt and anger to wash over her.

What a terrible decision that had been.

She was now Maggie again, but a new Maggie, not the Maggie she had left behind. She was now the one with scars the world could see and legs that had suffered such trauma they would never again carry her to float on air or pirouette across a stage.

'Oh what a tangled web we weave...' she whispered.

'The worst of all deceptions is self-deception...'
— Plato

LOOSE LIPS

Pru bounced down onto her bed, her mobile phone clutched firmly in her hand. She checked the screen and sighed. 'I think Andy has forgotten about me!' she huffed.

Tightening the pink hair scrunchie, Bree flicked her ponytail and gave it another once over with the hairbrush. 'Why? Just because he hasn't sent you a text in over two hours! Blimey, Pru, we're holidaying and he's working; give the lad a break! I've only spoken to Nathan once since we got here.' Nathan, Bree's sixteen-year-old son was currently staying with his dad, Bree's ex, Martin, at his caravan in North Wales.

'I'm missing him, that's all.' Pru jerked her legs over the side of the bed and sat up. 'I just wondered if he'd heard anything about what's going on here. You've got to admit the days are pretty boring, so a bit of juicy gossip from the horse's mouth so to speak...'

'Just the days?' Bree laughed. 'I can't really sugarcoat the night-time entertainment much either, but then again, the ladies seem to be enjoying themselves. Mind you, not one of them appears to be interested in the dance championship or bothered that it's being held here, even though that's why they came.

They're just content to have had a photo with Troy Florentine's poster, and the chance that they might bump into him in person at some point. The girls have actually gathered up their swimming costumes and towels and are hitting the swimming pool today, so Ethel tells me.'

Pru pulled a face and wrinkled up her nose. 'God help the lifeguard then!'

'I think that's why they're going; apparently he's quite a dish for an older guy – not that I'm interested in the slightest...' Bree carried on packing what looked like a child's plimsol bag from a PE class.

'Not interested? In the slightest? Not even a little bit?' Pru's fingers deftly plunged into the bag and pulled out a polka-dot bikini top. 'What's this, then?'

Bree gave a smug smile. 'I'm only going to make sure they don't get up to mischief. You know what they're like. It's kindergarten for the golden oldies when they go on the rampage! Jeez, Pru, you know I kissed Martin and ended up with a bloody frog, do you think I'd risk snogging a lifeguard? God knows what he'd turn into, probably a tasselled wobbegong, knowing my luck!' She grabbed the top from Pru and shoved it back into the bag. 'So which double murders are you wanting to poke your nose into, then? The 1983 one as we planned, or the current ones?'

'We can do both, can't we? We're women; we can multitask!'

Bree snorted her distaste. 'I think that dated observation was reserved for the kitchen in the 1950s, like sieving cauliflower whilst feeding the baby and agitating the dolly-tub.'

Pru's hand snaked out and grabbed the KitKat that Bree had left within her reach. She ripped off the red wrapper and snapped it in half, offering her the two chocolate-covered fingers. 'Women through the decades have been the champions that make us what we are today, so don't knock it!' She executed a revolutionary punch into the air. 'Okay, I've been thinking, so hear me out on this one. We haven't got anywhere at all on the 1983 murders, probably because far too much time has elapsed, but, and I know it's a big but, we have more chance in finding something out about the recent ones as everyone is talking about them, and, as we know, loose lips sink ships. Look, I've made notes.'

Bree gave her a wry smile and shook her head. 'It's not World War Two, and we're not American. Blimey, the only thing nautical round here is that battered old rowing boat by reception, filled with pansies and empty lager cans!'

'It's just an idiom. What I meant was that we can pick up a lot of info if we're prepared to keep our ears to the ground and our wits about us. It's the talk of the resort; we're bound to find something out.'

The expression on Bree's face was one of doubt. 'If you say so. I'm just amazed they haven't sent us all home and closed the place down.'

Pru rubbed her fingers together. 'Money, the dance championships, and logistics. Ralph Fairbright would fight closure all the way. Look, whilst you're having a swim with the ladies, I'm going to take a stroll around Daffodil and Bluebell Lawns and see what I can find out. Apparently, forensics are back at Mary Beaney's chalet. Kitty was saying the new guest was moved out pretty pronto once they'd confirmed it was another murder; it's cordoned off and they're in there now with all their equipment.'

'It'll be compromised though, surely?' Bree bit into the wafer and licked the chocolate from her bottom lip.

'That's why I want to speak to Andy. He said he'd bumped into the DS that's working on the case – Ezra something or other. You'd be amazed what I can wheedle out of my husband.' Pru laughed.

Bree pushed her hairbrush into the bag, pulled the drawcord, and slung it over her shoulder. She watched Pru as she excitedly popped the notebook and pen into her slouch bag and slipped her feet into the white Nike Air Max trainers whilst chattering ten to the dozen. She had had plenty of experience with Pru and her 'investigations' over the years, and the more she worried about her, the gut-churning pull at her stomach got stronger and stronger. She opened the chalet door and stepped out into the sunshine. 'Please don't do anything I wouldn't do; just think before you dive headlong into this.'

Pru had already slipped past her and set off at a jaunty pace across the grass. She turned and skipped backwards, whilst simultaneously doffing a jaunty salute to Bree.

'I won't, just so long as *you* promise not to get up to anything naughty with the Luscious Lifeguard!'

A NEED FOR JUSTICE

Sophie stood in reception. nervously nipping at the skin on her thumb with her teeth. Her eyes furtively darted between the reception desk and the newspaper stand that stood rigid next to the potted plastic banana plant. Several newspapers were folded behind Perspex slots, but one in particular, the *Nettleton Shrub News* had been placed in full view. In large bold letters the headlines screamed at her. She felt sick, excited and important, in equal measure.

LITTLE KIPLING DOUBLE MURDER
Detectives appeal to victim's lodger to come forward and assist in their investigation

She wanted to get closer, to read the actual article, but at the same time her anxiety pulled her back. Ever since the bodies had been found she had expected a neighbour to point a finger at her during the house-to-house enquiries the police had carried out, but she had been clever and had kept herself to herself whilst she had lived there. They didn't even know her name. There would be nothing on her – or so she hoped. She had since changed the colour and style of her hair and now wore make-up. Even her clothes were different: flamboyant and bright.

She was different.

Nothing like the meek, mousey Sophie of 28 Larton Lane, Little Kipling. She was now strong, focused and driven.

Suddenly her anxiety cranked up another notch, a fleeting panic fluttering through her veins.

What if they had circulated a photograph of her…?

Don't be ridiculous, when was the last time you had your photograph taken?

What if they've found something that has my name on it…?

But you made sure there was nothing left behind – didn't you?

Her brow furrowed in thought. Had she? She couldn't remember. She was so sure she had been absolutely meticulous in her clear out of Gertrude's house, but her suddenly fuddled mind was making her doubt the courage of her convictions. She nervously gulped down the lump in her throat. The air that was forced along her windpipe produced a painful bubble in her chest.

She could almost see her meticulous plans for the truth dissolving before her eyes. All the years of heartache, searching for answers and justice, were in danger of being lost. She grabbed the newspaper and furtively shoved it into her bag. She tilted her head to listen to the 'other' Sophie as her peripheral awareness melted away.

'Of course it's all prepared; it's perfect. Nobody will find it…' she muttered under her breath. 'It's on track, I just need to think…'

Stacey, her head barely visible over the top of the reception counter, watched the strange woman pacing up and down, talking to herself. From day one she had been wary of Sophie;

she had set her spider senses tingling with her odd ways and vacant eyes. It astounded her that a photographer, and a professional one at that, could be so devoid of the warmth and personality that would be needed to produce fun snapshots of holiday camp life. 'Are you okay, Miss Hopkins?' Stacey wished she didn't have to ask, but Ralph had told her that being new to Harmony Hollows she should keep an eye on her, make sure she was settling in all right.

Sophie's gaze bore right through Stacey. 'Of course I am, why shouldn't I be?' Her head tilted the opposite way, a quizzical look passing over her face.

Taken aback, Stacey rambled. 'Oh, I just thought maybe, you know... umm... maybe you wanted something?'

Sophie smiled. It was a smile that failed to cause kind crinkles at the corner of her eyes or to bunch up her cheeks in joviality. It fixed, rictus and cold on her face, totally devoid of any feeling. 'Oh, only justice, Stacey, just a little bit of justice...' she eerily replied.

It was not just any old justice that Sophie craved – it was going to be *her* justice and *her* justice alone.

TELLING TALES

Pru did her best to look as nonchalant as possible as she bounced along the paths of Daffodil Lawns in her whiter than white trainers. Every time a foot strode out in front of her, she cringed, wishing she'd at least had the forethought to rub a bit of grime or grass on them. Nothing screamed fitness-fail than a pristine pair of plimsolls. She had hoped that her guise as an early morning jogger would allow her to access all areas without question.

She turned the corner and stopped, hands on hips and bending forwards, as though catching her breath. She actually wanted to laugh; she'd barely worked up a sweat as she'd walked most of the way, only breaking into a run when she reached the path leading to No 8, Mary Beaney's chalet. As expected, there was plenty of activity outside the fluttering tape cordon. Two officers in white paper suits, one carrying a large case, were deep in conversation. Getting as close as she could without arousing suspicion, she leant against the wall of the neighbouring chalet, pretending to stretch her hamstrings whilst she listened in.

'I'm sorry, Ezra, there's very little to go on, Chalet 8 is a compromised scene. The resort cleaner did a fair job with the

Domestos bleach, and since the incident there's been another guest staying in it. We've done elimination prints from them, but other than a fibre strand wedged in a crack at the end of the bed where the body was hanging, we've got nothing.' He clicked the lock on his case, pulled out a clear evidence bag and held it up.

Pru couldn't believe her ears. This *had* to be Ezra, the old friend that Andy had told her about. What were the chances that she'd be in the right place at the right time whilst he was here? She *had* to find some way of speaking to him.

Ezra peered at the grubby grey string curled inside the bag. 'Is your guess the same as mine, Phil?'

Phil Diamond, Nettleton Shrub's CSI, raised one eyebrow. 'Well I don't think she was flossing her teeth with it; my guess is it'll be a match for the cord that was around her neck. You can see why this place is called "Camp Cadaver"; I'd definitely think twice before booking a holiday here!'

Casting a quizzical look, Ezra checked his notes. 'Two in 1983, and then these two this week... It's hardly the actions of a serial killer, Phil...' He snapped his notebook shut. 'Though granted it's not ideal having two dead on my watch.'

Phil gave him a respectful half-salute and shrugged the strap of his camera case onto his shoulder. 'I suggest you take a look at the regular calls here for sudden deaths over the years. Far too many guests don't check out the same way they checked in. Heart attacks, strokes, aneurisms and accidents, Harmony Hollows has a pretty poor track record. You can't even blame the food.' He laughed.

'Maybe they opted for the all-inclusive range of medical issues as standard,' Ezra quipped.

Ezra's riposte made Phil smile. 'What's their slogan? "Come as a guest, leave as a friend". In my humble opinion it needs updating to "Come as a guest, leave in a casket!" On that note,

I'll bid you good day, I'll have the report for you as soon as possible.'

The next part of their conversation was mumbled, forcing Pru to move a little closer, hoping their words would carry towards her. Frustrated, she took the decision to be proactive. She stopped stretching and jogged on the spot before setting off again, angling herself so that her elbow nudged Ezra as she went past. She made a dramatic show of pausing in her exercise regime to apologise to him.

'Oh my goodness, I'm so sorry...' she gushed. 'I get so engrossed in this jogging lark I sometimes lose my spatial awareness.'

Ezra, caught off guard, smiled at her. 'No worries, no damage done...' He laughed as he rubbed his bicep, feigning injury. 'But they do say jogging is bad for you, you know!'

Pru pressed her index finger to her bottom lip and squinted her eyes in thought. 'I know you, don't I?'

Ezra looked at her the way a detective would look at a suspect. 'That's the one question every police officer dreads in a social situation. Please don't tell me I've arrested you at some point?'

Pru flashed him one of her best disarming smiles and took a deep breath. Blagging a mate was one thing, but a police officer was on an entirely different level. This could work, or it could go badly wrong for her. She knew detectives always had a photograph taken receiving their certificates at the end of a training course, so that could do the trick. 'Got it! You know my husband, Andy. Andy Barnes from Winterbridge CID, I've seen you in a photo together.'

His demeanour softened. 'I certainly do, I hope it was my best side,' he joked, 'and just so you know, he's told me all about you!'

'All good, I hope... for his sake.' At any other time, Pru would have punched the air in triumph; she now had an 'in' for her snooping. 'Are you here for the two murders? It must be early days for your investigation.'

It was now Ezra's turn to smile. 'And *that* was one of the things he did tell me about you…' He paused and looked around to see if anyone else was accompanying Pru. '…and your friends. Now what did he call you?' His eyes shifted to the left, a sure sign of recall.

Pru's shoulders slumped. '"A quartet of Miss Marples and a duo of Agatha Raisins" by any chance?'

His wide grin told her all she needed to know. Andy had beat her to it and had tipped Ezra off. She would deal with his traitorous ways when she next saw him, death by tickling or a smelly sock under his nose would be punishment enough, but for now she would have to rely on the little snippet she had been fortunate enough to garner from Ezra's conversation.

Just how she could find data on all the deaths at Harmony Hollows was anyone's guess, but The Curious Curator & Co always had their ways and their means.

HEAVEN'S GATE

The musical backdrop of 'The Sun Will Come Out Tomorrow' circled its way around the Marina Lounge.

Maggie checked the stage curtains, kicked one of the footlights back into place, and repositioned the microphone. She held her hand over her eyes and squinted into the seating area towards the lighting and tech booth. 'Mark, can you get them to open the doors before the Bingo Babes burst them open?' That expression made her smile. Seventy per cent of her audience were what was fondly referred to as the 'Golden Gamblers', their age not hampering them in the slightest. Their keen eyes, sharp-as-a-tack mind, and rugby player abilities to tackle anyone in the ruck that attempted to steal their regular seat on Bingo Bonanza Night, was a sight to behold. She'd spotted many an 80-denier clad leg from Bluebell Lawns strike out and foul a fellow player from Daffodil Lawns, lurching them headlong onto the dance floor because they had dared to place their handbag on a reserved chair. Such was their fierce competition for the best seats in the house.

She looked at the throng, their noses squashed against the

glass panels, waiting. It reminded her of greyhounds in their traps, eagerly preparing for the gates to be lifted. Mark's hand hovered over the large metal plate at the side. He took a deep breath, smacked it hard, and quickly stood to one side as the click of the mechanism alerted the waiting horde. Experience had taught him that you didn't stand in the way of eager bingo players.

'Annnnnnd they're off...' Maggie's voice boomed out from the strategically placed speakers as the doors burst open. She watched them pour along the aisles until they found their preferred tables and sat down. Coats were hung over chairs, bingo cards shuffled and handed out, and finally the drinks were served. She checked her itinerary. First up was an appearance by Troy Florentine. Maggie knew he would do a quick circle of the dance floor to show the ladies a glimpse of his bronzed torso through the gaping cutaway at the front of his silk shirt and flex his muscles with a solo Argentinian tango. Once he had revelled in the *oohs* and *ahs*, he would do a rapid vanishing act back to his chalet for his nightly liaison with whichever poor girl, either guest or employee as he wasn't fussy, had fallen under his spell.

The lights turned down low and a hush fell over the audience. She took her place behind the microphone.

'Ladies and gentlemen, please put your hands together for the one and only – Mr Troy Florentine...'

The atmospheric lights burst into action, facilitated by Mark in the tech booth using the crib sheet Troy had insisted upon for his entrance. She was grateful for her respite in the wings, which gave her time to roll her eyes and pretend to shove two fingers down her throat and retch as Troy burst through the curtain, flinging his arms above his head. She saw Pinky watching her and grinned. 'He's such a creep, isn't he?' Pinky laughed and nodded her agreement.

Troy stood in the centre of the dance floor, his chin jutted out and his head held high. As the 4/4 beat of the music filled the Marina Lounge, he began his famous exhibition dance, relishing the applause when he executed a particularly impressive sequence of boleos. He skimmed the three edges of the audience, inviting them to feast their eyes upon his honed body and to enjoy his craft.

'Blimey, look at his teeth…!' Ethel squealed as a beam of ultraviolet light lit up Troy's gnashers, making them glow. 'Even Shergar couldn't boast a set like that!'

Hilda was already up on her feet, the passion of the music energising her soul. 'It's not his teeth I'm interested in!' she hollered back as she made a grab for Troy. 'Just look at his–'

'Hilda! For goodness' sake, sit down…' Kitty grabbed Hilda's arm and dragged her back to her seat, giving Troy time to make his finale and take his fluorescent donkey teeth back to the dressing room without being accosted further.

Disappointed, Hilda chugged back her sherry. 'I was enjoying that.'

Pru laughed. 'We know!'

Maggie reappeared through the curtains, relieved to be out of Troy's reach as he was currently giving anyone backstage who would listen, chapter and verse on the appalling lighting effects of Harmony Hollows dance floor, and the old dear who almost ripped his carefully manicured chest hair from his Miami bronzed pectorals. She smirked as she adjusted the head mic she was now wearing. 'Right, my lovelies, whilst Troy gets his breath back, get your dabbers and dobbers at the ready and let's roll for the £150 bonus that our resort manager, Mr Fairbright, has sanctioned for tonight's game of Bingo Bonanza.'

A roar of appreciation went up from the audience.

Pinky watched from the wings, an overwhelming sadness for Maggie touching her heart. She knew how much this role was crucifying her friend, but every night she still came out and gave it her best. She was a professional through and through. She listened as the numbers were called, lines were won, and the jackpot number was finally claimed.

Maggie held the ball aloft. 'Number twenty-seven, the Gateway to Heaven...'

A loud squeal from the back of the room gave promise of a worthy winner. Once again Maggie watched as the bingo card held aloft jiggled and bounced between tables and aisles until the holder reached the stage. Maggie checked the numbers and offered the coveted envelope.

'Ladies and gentlemen, we have a winner, take a bow Hester Blakemore of Primrose Lawns. Well done, Hester!' Maggie shook her hand and watched her do a happy dance back to her table.

Clarissa was unimpressed. 'What's wrong with us at Marigold getting a look in, hey?' She jammed the lid back on her dobber and dropped it into her handbag.

Hilda was engrossed with her pencil and notebook, eagerly scribbling on the pale blue lines. Once satisfied she had everything she needed, she closed the cover. 'We've got plenty of time, 'Rissa, we could easily make the jackpot, and if they keep putting the prize money up, who knows, we could be millionaires by the end of the week!'

'Highly unlikely,' Ethel offered. 'But a nice idea all the same. To us!' She held her sherry glass aloft.

The Four Wrinkled Dears, poorer for not having won but richer for their friendship, raised their glasses to toast Hilda's pie-in-the-sky dream of a decent bingo win and a nod to their sisterhood.

BATHROOM VANITY

Troy Florentine slammed the door to his chalet in a temper. He kicked off his shoes and looked longingly at his bed: the pristine sheets had been folded back ready, with two elegant long-stemmed glasses sat waiting on the bedside cabinet, and his mini fridge, which he had insisted upon as part of his booking at Harmony Hollows, holding a bottle of La Gioiosa Prosecco that had been chilling nicely since earlier in the day.

His hands bunched into fists as the realisation hit him that his carefully procured seduction package was now about as much use as a chocolate teapot.

He wandered into the bathroom and turned the bath taps on. Testing the water as it splattered loudly onto the bottom of the ancient cast iron, he rammed the plug in, putting all his angst into that one action as he thumped it to make it fit. He knew he needed to calm down and a nice, deep hot bath would, he hoped, do the trick. Grabbing the bottle of *Trojan's Tickle* bubble bath, he squeezed a copious amount of the blue liquid and swirled it around the water until it complied with his savage agitation and began to produce bubbles.

Now naked, he took the opportunity to admire himself in the full-length mirror on the door of the wardrobe, but this time, instead of a haughty pride, he felt an unusual sense of desperation. Time was marching on for him; he wasn't getting any younger. His body ached in places that ten years ago he didn't know existed, and the cost and effort in the upkeep of his physical self was starting to grind him down.

His fingers plucked at the front of his hairline as he gingerly peeled away the glue, enabling him to remove in one easy movement the coiffured rug that had been specially dyed in seductive sable to match his eyebrows. He dropped it onto the bed where it lay like a dead guinea pig. He didn't have to remove his chest hair – that had already been done by the excitable old dear halfway through his exhibition dance. He'd barely made it back to the dressing room before it had peeled itself away from his skin, slid down his silk shirt and dropped to the floor – at the feet of his intended conquest for the night, the rather luscious hoofer, Candy Cane. Candy's response had been to hysterically scream 'Rat!' before promptly kicking it several feet into the air with the toe of her tap shoe.

'Trust me to pick a woman with a bloody rodent phobia...' he sighed as he poured himself a drink and chugged it back, not even bothering to savour its fruity-floral aroma. Candy had then point-blank refused to accommodate his invitation to spend the night with him, and the laughter from the rest of the dancers as he frantically tried to retrieve his figwig that was still swinging from the lighting gantry, had ensured he went back to his chalet alone and suitably embarrassed.

He lowered himself into the mass of bubbles, being careful not to spill one precious drop of his second glass of Prosecco. With the warm water enveloping him, he sunk himself down into its depths, hoping to wash away his foul mood rather than his fake tan. With his arm hanging over the curved edge of the bath holding the glass, he submerged his head and held his breath, relishing the gentle *thud, thud, thud* from his heartbeat as it echoed in his ears, accompanied by a low swooshing sound. It reminded him of the sea lapping the sands on his childhood holidays, when life had been so much simpler and sweeter. His little feet had paddled and kicked the foam, but panic had set in when the advancing waves had reached his Scooby-Doo swimming trunks...

The sudden memory of that awful day forced Troy to surface from his bathwater more rapidly than he would have wished. The water drained over his bald head as his glass jerked, throwing Prosecco over the tiled floor. He used his free hand to rub his eyes, clearing his vision. He blinked several times, his brain trying to compute what was now standing above him.

The dark silhouette loomed menacingly as it shuffled to the end of the bath and held up a hand to stay him.

'What the fu...' Troy didn't get a chance to finish his expletive, or to ask why a total stranger dressed in black was in his bathroom.

Two strong hands firmly wrapped themselves around his ankles and savagely yanked his legs up into the air. No longer caring about his precious glass of liquid, he relinquished it. The glass dropped, shattering on the tiles as he frantically tried to grip the sides of the bath, but it was in vain. His body slammed backwards, smacking his head painfully on the curved cast iron, sending shooting stars behind his eyes, as he was forcefully pulled under the water.

Troy thrashed and struggled, sending water surging over the edge of the tub, but still his assailant kept a firm grip on his legs. Panic and fear seized him, just like it had on that day at the beach when the waves had taken him, the salt water burning his throat – only that time he had been rescued, his tiny limp body brought ashore and his life had been saved.

Who the hell are you? Why are you doing this to me? Why?

Questions, so many of them, were invading his brain as he struggled with every ounce of strength he had left. He was getting weary; the control over his muscles was ebbing away, leaving only the dispiriting futility of fight. It was very clear to Troy that this time there would be no saviour to rescue him. He was going to die, and in doing so, the world of dance would be a much poorer place without his Argentinian tango, his Miami bronze tan, and his curly chest hair.

He gave one last painful convulsive thrust of his body as what seemed like several gallons of *Trojan's Tickle* filled his lungs, a poor substitution for the life-sustaining air he so desperately needed. Troy spasmed twice, and then reluctantly relaxed into death, accepting his fate without further question, his eyes open and hauntingly mesmerising through the rippled water.

The shadow watched, relishing the moment an air bubble burst from Troy's mouth, popping as it reached the surface of the water.

The last breath.

There was something quite special and incredibly exhilarating about that precise moment. It was a privilege to see and share it, and an honour to know that one had facilitated it. And then, without pomp or ceremony, Troy's toupée was dropped from above, landing like a moth-eaten sporran to cover his rather disappointing wedding tackle.

With dignity in death fulfilled and a job well done, the shadow left as they had arrived at 27 Primrose Lawns... silently.

DARK DEEDS

The dark room was just that: dark. It was also bleak, cold and uninviting. Sophie flicked the light switch on, and a low buzz gave life to the single red bulb hanging from the ceiling. It glowed rhythmically as it bathed the room and chased away the blackness.

She stood in the centre and stretched out her arms, willing her fingers to touch the rough brick of the walls, to allow her to feel something. Anything. Her heart and her conscience felt nothing, no guilt at what she had done, or trepidation as to what she was about to do. If her soul couldn't feel, then she needed her physical self to perceive by touch to keep her grounded. She tried again, until the muscles in her arms began to burn with the effort. She knew it was a futile action, the walls were just too far away from her, but in her mind her arms were pliant, almost rubbery. She watched them undulate and wobble as they stretched, further and further away from her. She was hallucinating, something she had experienced before, just after she had despatched Gertrude Timpson. It was the unfortunate result of not taking her medication. She had needed strength and her inner voice to guide her for the tasks at hand; she didn't need it subduing with her little white pills.

And the voice hadn't disappointed her.

She tipped her head as it spoke to her again.

You are the clouds that gather,
You are the winds that destroy,
You are the lightning that will strike,
You ARE the perfect storm...

'I like that...' she whispered. 'Yes, I am the perfect storm, and when I've finished there'll be so much destruction and devastation left behind they may even name it Storm Sophie.' She giggled uncontrollably, envisaging the headlines in the *Nettleton Shrub News*. Mind you, what she had planned would most certainly make the nationals, much more than the little village press for Miss Sophie Hopkins and her dark deeds.

And there was so much more to come.

Sophie looked around the room, her unrestrained imagination showing her pictures of how it should be set out. Once content that the layout would work, she set about her task. The ambient red glow of the room was exchanged for bright LED floor spotlights that were strategically placed to highlight the four chairs that sat side by side in the centre of the room. She ensured there was a foot's gap between each one. Next, she hung several white sheets she had borrowed from the laundry room onto the wall behind the chairs. It gave a nice, clean backdrop for her production. She unravelled the washing line she had found in the cleaner's cupboard on Bluebell Lawns, looped one end, and hooked it over the curved wrought iron wall attachment. Stretching it across the room, she looped the other end and tied it to a shelf bracket.

Next came the photographs. She pegged each one carefully onto the line.

Ralph Fairbright above the first chair.

Della Claybourne above the second chair.

Nellie Girdlestone above the fourth chair.

And the third chair remained unallocated – for now.

She dragged the purple office partition wall from the corner and set it alongside the chairs.

Sophie stood back to admire her handiwork. It tickled her pink that her organisational skills had produced a set up that resembled an episode of *Blind Date*, only this time each of them were already well acquainted. The only one they wouldn't know would be her...

'And I'll be the one asking the questions!'

She knew one of them was guilty, but in their own individual ways they all had been part of it, and when the time was right, she would reveal all.

MURDER HE SAID

As if things couldn't get any worse for Ralph Fairbright. The day had begun on a dismal, and quite frankly, inconvenient note. He sat with his head in his hands, wondering what he had done to deserve not only a run-down, pathetic resort as his last management position before retirement, but also a new world record for the number of dead bodies a place could rack up in such a short space of time.

Stacey pushed the mug of coffee towards her boss, along with a sheet of A4 paper that would give him the run down on how many guests were currently waiting to register a premature check-out. She swallowed hard and carefully picked her words. 'These are just the ones that are bothering to check-out, Mr Fairbright. Security have reported at least one family of five that just legged it through the camp gates at breakfast when the news broke.' She scrunched her nose, waiting for his reaction.

'Bugger the lot of them; let them go! They won't be getting a refund.' Ralph took a loud slurp of his coffee. 'At least we've still got the tippy-toes lot; they spend a decent amount at the bar and will, I hope, keep the rest of the punters happy.'

Stacey shifted uncomfortably in the chair. 'The NBC

organisers are threatening to pull the plug. They're worried that this will jinx the whole championship, but the police are now stopping anyone from leaving.' She unclipped a card from her file. 'You've got to ring them on this number, but before that, DS Maynard is waiting to speak to you. He asked that you meet him at Troy's chalet.'

Ralph sighed, and quickly dismissed her with a wave of his hand. As the door clicked shut, he opened the cupboard in his desk and searched the shelf, annoyed that his carefully laid out mini bar appeared to have been tampered with. He'd have words with Stacey later. Small bottles clinked together until he found what he was looking for. Forgoing the miniature bottle of whisky that was now positioned at the front, he grabbed the brandy that had been shoved to the back. Pouring a good slug into his coffee he chugged the warm mixture in one large gulp. Feeling its burning sensation he relaxed back in his chair, glad of the raw discomfort that would take his mind off his current situation.

Promising himself a couple more jiggers of the amber nectar before he faced Ezra Maynard, Ralph closed his eyes and wished with all his heart that he was a million miles away from Harmony Hollows.

The exact same wish he had made in 1983.

Ezra watched Phil Diamond meticulously work his way around the body in the bath. The mood was sombre. The floating toupée had provided a small respite with a moment of dark humour that had lightened the mood, albeit briefly, but it was quickly back to business. 'What have we got, Phil?'

'A dead body...' he quipped as he took a sample of the water and held it up to the light. 'I'll know more once the PM's been done, but I think you need to let Bob Limpett and the coroner know before the body is moved that this isn't accidental.'

Although Ezra suspected as much, he gave a low groan of despondency. 'Early indications?'

'Bruising to the ankles and calves in a finger pattern and further bruising on the shoulders, and with the amount of water on the floor I'm pretty certain Mr Florentine didn't dance the fandango in the bath of his own accord to cause this mess.' Phil took a step back. 'I'd say he was held by the ankles and pulled down into the water. See here...' He pointed to the marks that were now vivid on the skin. 'It's virtually impossible for anyone to pull themselves back up when the legs are suspended; the head remains under water. Depending on the strength of the assailant, it can take minimum effort to maximise a death.'

'Who found him?' Ezra hated being so sharp and short with his questions, but he needed progress.

Phil checked his notebook. 'A Miss Candy Cane – and, no, that's not her real name. It's a stage name, apparently. She rejected him last night after an incident at the Marina Lounge, but had a change of heart, fancied a bit of Prosecco, and came looking for him. She's a mess, bordering on hysterics.'

Ezra raised an eyebrow. 'I've heard it called some things in my time but...'

'Nope, it's genuine. He had a temptation package in the mini bar, which included a fairly decent bottle of Prosecco, although according to resort gossip, Candy wasn't the first to quaff from his champagne flute, so to speak!' Phil grinned.

'Right, I'll let you get on. I'll speak to Ralph Fairbright and get one of the team to follow up on every conquest our *milonguero* here has had since his arrival at Harmony Hollows.' Ezra was pretty impressed with his knowledge of Argentinian address for the dancer, although where he had first heard it, was anyone's guess. It was just one of those useless bits of subconsciously stored information.

He made his way to the door, ripping off the forensic overshoes and placing them in an evidence bag. He dated and initialled it and handed it to the exhibits officer before stepping outside into the sunshine, his thoughts vying for position in his mental filing cabinet.

Three murders in less than a week, and not one suspect.

So far there had been no links between each victim, no forensics of note, and no background on any of them that would indicate a purpose behind the murders. The means and opportunity were there for all to see, but the important part of the investigative M.O.M principle, the final 'M', was still eluding them.

Motive.

Ezra was suddenly aware of movement behind him. Turning quickly, he saw a dishevelled Ralph Fairbright standing behind the fluttering scene tape. He jerked his head in acknowledgement. 'Mr Fairbright...' Before he could finish his sentence, Ralph, face florid and sweaty, launched at him, index finger pointing wildly.

'Have you any idea what this will do to me having you lot snooping around my resort? People are wanting to leave, they've got coaches booked, jobs to go back to, they've even got bloody dog sitters they've got to get home for and I've got new arrivals descending tomorrow!' Spittle flew from Ralph's lips, forcing Ezra to take a step back to avoid being drenched. 'And you've commandeered my private suite for your investigation, along with my parking space for your bloody vehicles.' Ralph could only mourn the loss of his 65-inch flat screen TV which was now fixed blank and dormant on the wall of his suite that had been turned over to several uniformed officers by Head Office.

Ezra sighed loudly. 'I need you to calm down, Mr Fairbright.

This was a decision taken by the senior investigating officer; nobody leaves until we have verified each and every person here, be it guest, competitor or sneaked-in unpaid and unregistered stowaway in the boot of someone's car, and more importantly, until we have interviewed any witnesses.'

Ralph was not going to be appeased. 'What about the arrivals?'

'No arrivals, Ralph. Your HQ has been more than understanding and are contacting them on our behalf, plus they're sending additional night-time security patrols. Look on the bright side, you've only got three small no-go cordons in place for each scene – the whole place could just as easily have been shut down.' Ezra watched Ralph's eyes widen with the realisation that his little empire was at risk. 'The only reason it wasn't is because it was deemed to be a logistical nightmare to scatter potential witnesses and suspects to the four winds.'

Ezra didn't wait for Ralph to reply; he quickly dipped under the yellow tape and strode purposefully along the path and out of sight. He had more important things on his mind than the histrionics of a budding Basil Fawlty.

THE RIVALS

If Ethel's legs could have carried her any faster, she was sure she would have qualified for the next Olympics. She cursed as her sandals slapped and skidded along the paths of Marigold Lawns, wishing she had been sensible that morning and chosen her Mary Janes instead. They at least had a solid rubber sole and more staying power for a decent geriatric sprint.

Reaching her chalet, she burst through the door. ''Rissa, 'Rissa, there's been another one!' She panted whilst wildly waving her arms, the excitement in breaking the news completely destroying all chance of ladylike decorum.

Clarissa's head popped around the door frame of the bathroom, a toothbrush still firmly wedged in her mouth. She quickly removed it and spat a splodge of Colgate toothpaste into the sink. Dearie me, calm down! For goodness' sake, Eth, you'll give yourself a heart attack! Now slowly, what's happened?'

Ethel slumped down onto her bed, patting her chest to quell her heart's pounding beat and assist the flow of words that were at risk of choking her. 'I went to get us a pint of milk from the camp shop, and they're all talking about it. There's been *another* murder at Harmony Hollows... and you'll never guess who it is!'

'Was it the camp commandant, old Riveting Ralph? Now *he* definitely wouldn't be missed, the miserable old sod.' Clarissa chuckled, determined to lighten the mood. 'Or how about that horrible woman on the scrambled egg at breakfast; you know, the one that dollops it on the plate like its wallpaper paste? She's flicked more down my cleavage than I've dropped down there myself! I wouldn't be surprised in the least if someone had offed her!'

'No, no, it was Troy Florentine,' wheezed Ethel. 'Can you believe it? He was found drowned in his bathtub this morning. There's quite a circus gathered over at Primrose Lawns. Police are everywhere, and they're taping off the paths.'

Clarissa popped the kettle on, although she had a feeling that, regardless of the early hour of the morning, Ethel would probably prefer a quick snifter of sherry to calm her excitement. 'Who's going to break it to Hilda that her bottle-bronzed hairy god has gone to meet his maker?'

'Who? Tropez, the saint of streaky sun tans?!' Ethel started to laugh, which immediately made her feel a little guilty. The poor man had lost his life and here she was making jokes. She waved her hand dismissively, more to herself than Clarissa. 'They thought it was an accident: too much to drink and he drowned. But I heard that cleaner, you know, the one that looks like Shrek although she's not green. Well, she was telling everyone that the police had called it in as a murder.'

Clarissa handed Ethel an interim glass of water and then leant over her bed, banging the edge of her fist three times on the adjoining wall. 'I would've thought all that silicone in his face would have kept him afloat, I'll tell you for nothing, those cheeks and lips were never his!'

Ethel had barely taken a sip from the glass before their

chalet door burst open throwing Hilda and Millie through the threshold.

'You rang, madam?' Smirking, Hilda held out the small hand-towel she had draped over her arm. 'Is it room service you're after?'

Grabbing two more cups and throwing another teabag into the pot, Clarissa poured the water and gave it a vigorous stir before popping the lid back on. 'It just needs a minute to brew…' She was amused that their means of communication between chalets had actually worked and her three knocks on the wall had brought her friends running. Now she had the unenviable task of telling Hilda about Troy. 'Hilda, dear, sit down and I'll pour you a cuppa. Now I don't really know how to say this, but here goes. Troy Florentine took his final curtain call last night.' She pulled down the corners of her mouth as she side-eyed Ethel, waiting for Hilda's response.

The seconds ticked by as Hilda digested the snippet of information. Clarissa tried to clarify further. 'He's sleeping with the fishes, dear…'

'Not 'arf, he is…' Ethel pinched her nose to stop herself from laughing. 'Along with half a bottle of *Trojan's Tickle* bubble bath and a hairy merkin, if that cleaner is to be believed!'

Hilda was absolutely horrified. 'Jesus wept…' she wailed. 'I had a grip of his merkin last night.' She examined her right hand intently. 'In *this* one here. Look! These fingers have touched it!' She made a show of wiping her palm on the quilted counterpane in an effort to rid herself of some perceived contamination.

Clarrissa shook her head at Ethel. 'Calm down, Hilda, that's just Ethel's sleazy sense of humour; it would have been his wig.' She patted the top of her own head. 'Remember Kitty saying she could see the join when he got sweaty during his tango routine?'

She hoped that explanation would satisfy poor Hilda, who was currently having an attack of the vapours.

'What happened to him?' Tired of waiting and spitting feathers, Millie poured out the tea whilst the others were occupied with Hilda.

'Drowned in his bath, but Ethel overheard them saying it wasn't an accident...' Clarissa gratefully accepted her cuppa. 'If you ask me, there's something very suspicious going on around here. Three murders in less than a week. Now that's not normal, is it?'

'No shit, Sherlock...' Ethel rattled her cup back into the saucer and gave her a bemused look. 'At the risk of sounding like a stuck record, I think it's about time the Four Wrinkled Dears stepped up to the plate, don't you?' She grinned in anticipation.

'Oh no you don't!'

Millie, Clarissa, Ethel and Hilda stopped in their tracks; teacups poised to their lips but not yet making contact, wondering which one of them had uttered those words. They slowly turned to see Pru standing in the doorway, hands on hips in a determined stance. 'How many times have I asked you four troublemakers not to get involved in things that are none of your business? I mean it; you keep out of this. It could be dangerous – very dangerous!'

Ethel bristled. She was not going to be told what to do by anyone. 'I take it that means you and Bree too? Haven't you both got form for er... shall we say "interfering" under the guise of your detective agency? What's sauce for the goose, Prunella, you should know that!' If she could have chalked a No.1 in the air in one-upmanship without seeming to be churlish, she would have done so.

Pru was lost for words at Ethel's unusually tart response. She knew that her own track record for getting into mischief was no better than theirs, and a quick retort was fast evading her. She could hear Bree sniggering behind her, so opted for the best response she could think of. 'That may be, but I've got to look after you; you're my responsibility.' She hoped to play on their sympathy, but she was wrong.

'Right, girls, let's settle the problem this way.' Ethel was on a roll. The idea had only just popped into her head, and it was a delicious one that would allow them a bit of freedom. 'I propose a competition to see who can solve the Harmony Hollows Murder Mysteries first. The Four Wrinkled Dears, that's us, Hilda...' She gave Hilda a warm smile. '...versus The Daft Duo over there.' She pointed accusingly to Pru and Bree. 'What d'you say?'

Bree, who had always loved a challenge since childhood, couldn't contain herself. 'You're on!' She thrust out her hand to shake on the deal. 'But there's a proviso! We'll split them. You four can investigate the 1983 murders; Pru and I will deal with the recent ones.'

Pru glared at her. 'What on *earth* are you doing? You're giving them carte blanche to get up to mischief at the very least, and six feet under at the best.'

'Oh come on! They're going to get involved anyway, regardless of what you say...' Bree hissed from the corner of her mouth in a failed attempt to keep her remark from the Four Wrinkled Dears. 'This way, they're looking for a murderer who is probably long gone and no risk, and as we'll all be poking around together, we can keep an eye on them in the process.'

Pru exhaled loudly, knowing she was on a hiding to nothing.

'In that case...' Hilda jerked her handbag onto her knee, clicked the clasp, and pulled out her trusty notebook. 'I've got something quite interesting that might help you for the recent murders. I think I've figured out how the victims are chosen.'

If five pairs of eyes could have rolled themselves to the

heavens to show their lack of faith in Hilda's offerings without causing her offence, they would have done so.

Clarissa was the first to acknowledge her by patting her hand. 'Not just yet, dear, keep hold of what you've got, and when we get to the right moment we'll call upon your expertise for the occasion.' She hoped that would appease her friend and give them respite from her frequently muddled ramblings that would only serve to confuse the issues at hand.

Disappointed, Hilda sniffed loudly, popped her notebook back into the depths of her handbag, pulled out her handkerchief, and purposefully dabbed at her nose.

'Well don't leave it too long, or we'll have more stiffs around this place than happy campers...'

ROAD TRIP

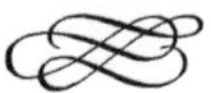

During an investigation, Andy would usually enjoy what the team called a 'road trip'. To have the chance to slip the leash and escape the office was a respite that was always welcomed, but it didn't always live up to the expectation that the name conjured up. This little jaunt to speak to the Mayer-Marshall's agent would only offer them a quick stop at the M6 toll service station for a bacon butty and a coffee in both directions if they were lucky.

He sat in the passenger seat of the Little Kipling CID pool car, waiting for Lucy. Like a child trying to stave off boredom, he began looking through the centre console. After placing on his lap three unused McDonald's sweet curry sauces, a bunch of wooden coffee stirrers, and half a Fisherman's Friend lozenge that was stuck to a paper serviette, he turned his attention to the glovebox. Fishing a wodge of paper napkins, he pulled out the car log book.

'What the...?' He examined his finger and thumb, curling his lip at an unmentionable substance that was stuck to them. His gut reaction was to sniff it to see what it was, but as he expected it would probably be something he wouldn't want to identify, he quickly decided to utilise the paper napkins to rid himself of the sticky gunge.

The driver's door was suddenly yanked open and Lucy slid into the seat, seeing the look on Andy's face and the pile of fast-food accessories on his lap, she smiled. 'What *have* you been up to, Sarge?'

'Just drive, DC Harris...' He laughed as he pointed to the road ahead. 'The sooner we get there, the sooner we get back.'

Lucy turned the key in the ignition and was quite surprised that the engine fired the first time. Pool cars were notorious for being unreliable, as well as being akin to a 1700-kilo skip on wheels. 'I'm hoping we get something useful about Elodie from the agent. Apparently Elodie's parents have given their authorisation for the agent to co-operate with the investigation.' She wasn't optimistic, but considering Elodie had just vanished into thin air, she knew they would be grateful for anything. 'Do you still think she could be a victim?'

Andy shrugged his shoulders. 'I don't know what to think. If she isn't dead, she's been bloody clever at covering her tracks. After leaving Waverley Park Sanitorium, there is absolutely nothing on her. The bank account in her name hasn't been touched since a withdrawal the day after she was discharged, and, more importantly, she hasn't left a digital footprint anywhere. You tell me who in this day and age doesn't leave some sort of trail on social media or the internet?'

'The bank withdrawal was a huge one though, that would tide her over for several months, if not longer. If you've got the financial means and the wherewithal, I don't suppose it would be that difficult to disappear and start a new life somewhere.' Lucy flicked the indicator on and began to merge onto the motorway. 'I've asked for a Zoom call with her parents once they get back from the film location to their hotel. We can base our interview with them on anything we get from the agent.'

Andy sat in silence, watching the trees pass by on the landscaped motorway embankment, their colours alternating between the rich green of downy birch to the swaying fern-like branches of leylandii. He hated not being able to progress an investigation, particularly one as high profile as this. It not only frustrated him but also created sleepless nights when his brain would suddenly decide at 3am that he needed to follow a particular train of thought; regardless of whether or not that train of thought was useful.

The vibration from his phone jolted him from his reverie. He answered on the first ring.

'Ezra! How's it going?'

Lucy listened intently as Andy's conversation with Ezra Maynard went from initial pleasantries to something clearly much more sinister.

'She did *what?*' Andy closed his eyes and exhaled deeply. 'Leave it with me; I'll speak to her. Thanks for letting me know, Ezra, I don't think I've ever known Pru to jog anywhere, not even to the Dog & Gun for a double G&T.' He paused to allow Ezra his turn in the conversation before replying. 'We're not much better this side, either; just on our way to see if we can garner more intelligence on Elodie Marshall.'

They exchanged more pleasantries and a promise to meet up for a beer or two once their respective investigations had concluded, before Andy ended the call.

'That was Ezra. They've had another murder at Harmony Hollows. Jeez, Luce, three in one week. I don't envy him in the slightest!' He blew out his cheeks, allowing the breath he had been holding a chance to escape.

Lucy acknowledged him with a nod of her head. 'I gathered

as much – and I also gather our Loony Librarian is trying her best to get involved too!'

Andy went back to looking out of the window. 'Should we expect any less? She is going to quite literally be the death of me one day.'

A CONFESSION

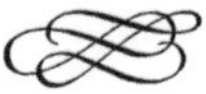

Clarissa, Ethel, Millie and Hilda were, for the first time in their lives, lost for words. They sat huddled together at their regular table in the Marina Lounge, staring at each other.

'Anybody want a mint imperial?' Hilda broke the impasse by offering around the crumpled and torn white paper bag.

'We've just found out that you two are staying in the 1983 murder chalet, and all you can think of is bloody mint imperials!' Ethel sharply admonished.

Silence once again reigned as they mulled over the implications this particular revelation could have on their part of the investigation. Clarissa slugged back the last of her sherry and rummaged in her handbag. Her fingers probed the depths until they came across the prize, a small hip flask. She furtively shoved the empty glass under the table and replenished it with a good shot of Harveys Bristol Cream, quickly returning it to its original place on the table as though it had never moved, the only difference being it was now full instead of empty. A few sips of the liquid of life rapidly brought a healthy glow back to her cheeks. She eyed the resort photographer who had just been the bearer of that priceless snippet of information after they had tipsily regaled her with their plans to solve the historic Harmony Hollows double murder. Her lanyard bore the logo 'HH Official Photographer' and the name 'Sophie'.

'Well, Sophie, is there anything else you can tell us that might help our little investigation, beside poor Millie and Hilda here sharing a couple of single beds with the grisly ghosts of Harmony Hollows?' Clarissa gave her what she hoped was an earnest smile.

Sophie adjusted her carry bag, making a show of it digging into her shoulder. 'Not really, sorry. This is my first season here, so it was just something I overheard in our staff canteen, and then I saw this...' She pointed to the chalet key tab that depicted a colourful marigold flower above the number 13 that was lying on the table. 'It just jogged my memory, and it sort of popped out of my mouth without thinking. Maybe I shouldn't have said anything, but you telling me that you were doing some digging, I just thought it might be interesting and a bit of fun.'

'A bit of fun!? My goodness how *could* you? Two people lost their lives that night...' Kitty squealed from the next table, her face flushed pink, which only served to highlight the intoxicated glaze in her eyes.

Ethel snapped her head around and gave Kitty her best death stare. 'And what's it got to do with you, Kitty Hardcastle?' She tapped the side of her nose. 'Maybe you should keep your big beak out of other people's business and go back to swigging your gin...'

Clarissa jumped in to act as peacemaker, concerned that Ethel's short fuse had suddenly become so much shorter. 'Now, girls, let's not fall out over this. Ethel, do have another sherry, and Kitty, we don't think it's "fun"; we just find it interesting, that's all.'

Kitty, who was still clinging on to the back of her chair and clearly the worse for wear, twisted to face them. Her colour had changed from the previously flushed pink to a pallid grey. 'It wasn't what I would call interesting when it happened, I can tell you!' She hiccupped and fanned her face with a bingo card. 'I knew it was a mistake coming back here, but oh no, you lot know better and, as always, you got your own way!'

Puzzled at her reaction, Clarissa instinctively knew there was more to Kitty's objections than met the eye. She was just about to probe further when the penny dropped. 'Well smack me on the bottom with the *Woman's Weekly*!' she gasped in tribute to one of her favourite comedy sketches. 'You were here when it happened, weren't you, Kitty?'

Once again silence fell over their extended group. The seconds ticked by as they watched Kitty's expression morph between sadness, horror and despair, whilst they were simultaneously experiencing a surge of excitement in the hope that her drunken state might lower her inhibitions and allow her to confess all.

She refused to meet their eyes. Nipping hard on her bottom lip, her chin wobbled as she tried to find the words. 'I wasn't only here – I was also one of Larry Belfont's conquests the week it happened. I knew them both...'

As a collective gasp of surprise breathlessly mushroomed out from the gathered WI ladies, a knowing smile played on Sophie's lips. She cocked her head, a glint of devilment dancing in her eyes.

Oh how absolutely delicious, chair number three would now have a bottom to occupy it!

THE JUDGEMENT

Kitty's confession brought a tsunami of shock that had spread like wildfire amongst the Winterbottom ladies, undulating from table to table as it circled the Marina Lounge.

Bingo cards and big wins were forgotten in favour of another round of drinks so that they could celebrate, as well as relish, Kitty's indiscretion. The fact that it had happened almost forty years ago didn't enter the equation as far as devouring deliciously juicy gossip was concerned. Although Kitty had only provided the basics, it hadn't stopped each and every one of them adding their own little snippet to make the story more exciting and more titillating before they passed it on to the next table. It was the most rapid case of Chinese whispers that Clarissa had ever experienced first-hand. By the time it had reached Miriam and Brenda's ears, Kitty had been romping naked in the flowerbeds at Harmony Hollows indulging in a *ménage à trois* with an Elvis Presley impersonator and Marvo the Magician.

'Well, I'm not spending another night in *there*, that's for sure.' Millie shivered and looked to Hilda for affirmation, and when none was forthcoming, she prodded her arm. 'Surely you must feel the same, Hilda? How can we sleep, knowing a grisly murder was committed in our little chalet... and probably on your bed too!'

Hilda harrumphed. 'How do you know it wasn't on *your* bed? I'm not bothered in the slightest – and it's odds on I'll have forgotten all about it by the time they shout the last bingo number tonight, anyway!' She chortled loudly.

'Where's Kitty now?' said Ethel, guilt starting to gnaw away at her as she tried her best to sound as though she cared.

'Gone back to her chalet. Frank's with her. She's going to have an almighty hangover in the morning,' Clarissa offered.

Ethel lined up her bingo cards and straightened her dobber so it sat in perfect alignment with the edge of the beer mat. 'Yep, but that's not all. Wait until she realises that she's regaled us all with her sordid little liaison from 1983. She'll be too embarrassed to show her face at breakfast for the rest of our stay. I always knew our Kitty was a bit of a loose woman, but she must be slacker than a three-quarter nut on a half-inch thread!'

Pru sat quietly at her table, waiting for Bree to return from the bar, whilst listening to the ladies chattering ten to the dozen. She knew Kitty would never have disclosed tales from her youth if she had been sober, but it did surprise her that she hadn't previously been more vocal in her opposition to their WI trip to Harmony Hollows if it held such a sorry history for her. Then again, maybe too much opposition would have outed her at the time; it had only been an overindulgence on the gin that had forced her hand now.

Although the current murders were very much at the forefront of Pru's inquisitiveness, she also loved the idea of being able to help solve a cold case. She knew no police resources were still allocated to the 1983 murder, so if she were to prod Kitty for more information, she wouldn't be stepping on any toes that would bring her into Andy's bad books. Pru involuntarily jiggled in her seat with anticipation; she had been itching to find out more, and now she would have the opportunity to do so.

'Well, *that's* a turn up for the books, hey?' Bree clumsily banged the drinks tray down onto the table, the fizzy liquid from the gin balloons slopping over the top. 'Oops! Well, that's two less calories for you to add to your waistline!'

'Wasn't it just?' Pru took a sip of her drink and tested the coloured ink in her own dobber by jabbing it down several times on a beer mat. 'I think we might need to treat Kitty to a nice cup of coffee and some sympathy tomorrow, don't you?' She gave a mischievous grin and winked.

Bree was just about to reply when the lighting on the stage changed, and the spotlight beam picked out Maggie Henshaw as she burst through the deep red curtains.

'Ladies and Gentlemen, get your dabbers and dobbers at the ready and let's roll for the £200 bonus ball...' Her cheerful voice filled the Marina Lounge, bringing the WI ladies back on track. She smiled, watching the excited faces caught in the backlight from the stage change to a plethora of coloured hair, greys, blondes and brunettes as they eagerly got their heads down and their cards at the ready. A rolling bonus each night would always guarantee a full audience.

This time Maggie threw a little more into the evening than she normally would. A joke here, a bit of banter with one member of the audience when they got up to go to the ladies' loo for the hundredth time, and she actually warbled a song during the drinks' interval. It was exhilarating, but brought with it a feeling of melancholy. She missed her heady days of entertainment dreadfully, particularly the dancing. She pushed the feelings aside and presented her professional game face. 'And its rolling, rolling folks...' She stood poised, waiting for the drum to stop and for the last bingo ball of the night to be ejected.

'Ladies and gentlemen, it's twenty-nine, rise and shine...'

Amid the excited squealing from the lucky winner and a throng of groans and grumbles from those that missed out, Hilda serenely placed her notebook on the table, licked the end of her pencil and set about making her new entry. She snapped the book shut and popped it back into her handbag. 'Well, I wouldn't want to be the one staying in *that* chalet tonight,' she stated rather matter-of-factly.

Puzzled, Clarissa questioned her. 'In *what* chalet, Hilda? Not the one you're in, surely? Honestly, dear, I've checked and there is nothing, absolutely nothing, in your chalet that was there in 1983. It was all cleared, cleaned and repainted, and lots and lots of people have stayed in it since.' She felt a bit mean lying to her; she hadn't checked to see if anything had remained from that era. In fact, she was pretty sure, judging by the age of the furniture, that every single chalet was still stuck in the 1970s, and that the only things that had been changed were the toilet rolls and bars of soap.

'No, I'm talking about Chalet 29. I've been trying to tell you, but as usual nobody listens to me.' Hilda hooked her handbag over her arm and stood up to leave. 'And as you said before, no doubt when you get to the right moment, you'll call upon my expertise for the occasion.'

Having said her piece, Hilda pulled on her jacket, grabbed Millie's arm, and steered her towards the exit – leaving a very bewildered Clarissa and Ethel in her wake.

A COMING OF AGE

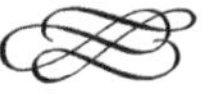

21ST MAY 1983

Kitty sat with her hands in her lap and watched her parents glide across the sprung dance floor of the Marina Lounge at Harmony Hollows. They would fleetingly pass by her before being swallowed up by other couples enjoying the beat of Ronnie Lycett's Big Band Sounds, until, like the colourful horses on a carousel, they would reappear, wave to her and then disappear again.

If truth be known, she had never been more bored in all her short life. She inspected her fingernails, pulled at her skirt and shifted uncomfortably in her chair. The bottle of Pepsi with a straw bobbing from its neck, screamed 'child', which made her cringe. She was so sick of being suffocated and treated as though she were five years old and not the sweet sixteen that Neil Sedaka had so happily sung about. Even the white knee-length socks she had been forced to wear singled her out as a little girl.

A surge of rebellion suddenly ran through her. She kicked off her ballet flats and angrily pulled at the offending socks. She rolled them into a ball, mischievously chucked them under the table, and slipped her bare feet back into her shoes.

She was ready.

To the strains of 'Uptown Girl', Kitty got to her feet and began to dance. She didn't care that she was on her own, she didn't care that she was evoking her parents' disapproval and probably their wrath too. For the first time in forever, she felt free.

She closed her eyes and channelled the beat as her feet skipped and tapped across the room, and suddenly he was behind her, his hand slipped around her waist as he twirled her deeper into the crowded dance floor. A thousand butterflies danced in her tummy.

He had noticed her.

Larry Belfont, the heart-throb and bad boy of Harmony Hollows was dancing with her. After days of giving him coy smiles and ensuring she was always in the right place when he was around, he had made a move. She quickly glanced over to her parents who were deep in conversation with another couple on their table. Finally they had relinquished the imaginary chains that held her.

She knew she was being dramatic and that her parents loved her dearly, but she was ready to spread her wings and fly, and the look in Larry's eyes gave her promise. He nuzzled into her neck, his breath hot against her skin.

'I know a place...' he whispered.

Kitty threw back her head, allowing her hair to tumble across her shoulders. Taking her cue from Billy Joel's lyrics, she teasingly laughed. 'I've never had a backstreet guy...' she seductively whispered. Had she been honest, she would have also told him that she had never had any guy before, let alone a backstreet one, and that her scant knowledge of lust and love had been obtained from her mother's well-thumbed Mills & Boon books.

But honesty was not going to spoil what she hoped was to come.

Before she could object, not that she would have done, Larry had whisked her through the jumble of limbs that were still dancing to the beat, and out through a side door next to the stage.

Hitting the cool evening air, she gasped as the little hairs along her arms stood on end, making her shiver. Larry pushed her against the empty beer barrels, pressing his lips on hers, before leading her through a door into a storeroom. He was gentle, he was attentive and although the hessian sack cloths on the floor were hardly the silk sheets that had been promised in her books, she was taken with the moment.

A moment that she would quickly learn to regret.

CAN'T BUY ME LOVE

Judy Moore, her tiny frame encased in a leather captain's chair, linked her hands together, positioning her index fingers so that they pointed like a church steeple. She tapped her bottom lip with them, deep in thought. 'I'm not really sure what I can do to help you, Detective Barnes.'

Andy sat back in the chair that had been positioned in front of the large desk, Lucy next to him, with her notebook at the ready. He had an overwhelming urge to pick up the brass nameplate in front of Judy that announced she was the Senior Talent Agent for *Middle Cow Creatives*, and give it a good polish. It had more fingerprints on it than a crime scene.

He resisted and kept his mind on the task at hand. 'As we explained in our initial telephone call, the Mayer-Marshalls' daughter, Elodie, is a person of interest in our investigation into a double murder. We are very concerned for her safety and well-being.' He paused, giving her time to take in the seriousness of his presence in her office. He noticed a barely perceptible curl of Judy's top lip accompanied by a look of distaste.

Judy sighed and opened a thick file on her desk. 'I think I

can say without hesitation, and my clients are fully aware of my feelings regarding their daughter, if you are going to worry about Elodie, then you should be more concerned for the welfare of anyone who comes into contact with her – not the other way round. She's a very dangerous woman indeed – regardless of what Waverley Park Sanitorium will tell you.'

Completely taken off guard by such a frank exchange, Andy's mental script suddenly veered off course. He quickly brought himself back on track. 'I believe Mr and Mrs Mayer-Marshall have given you full authorisation to assist?'

'They have, including this…' Judy licked the middle finger of her right hand and quickly flicked through the paperwork in front of her. 'They have already distanced themselves from her over the years, but now they want to sever all links completely, particularly if Elodie is the suspect in your murders, Detective.' She handed him several sheets of A4 paper clipped together attached to a document pouch. 'Which I'm assuming she is…'

Andy took it from her. He had already made the decision to allow her to tell them what she knew without prompt or interruption, as she was evidently eager to give him chapter and verse. 'Why don't you just start at the beginning, Miss Moore? I can leave any questions I have for the end.'

Judy, her lips set in a thin line, cleared her throat. She was grateful to be finally free of what she knew about Elodie Marshall, and, on a business level, to have her most profitable clients at least partly shielded from a scandal that could ruin their respective reputations. She couldn't protect them completely, and their confession to her during a tense telephone call the previous day had sent her scurrying to their contracts to see what impact it might also have on Middle Cow Creatives. This was going to be a difficult damage limitation exercise for all of them.

'As you can see from the documentation, Elodie Marshall is

not their biological daughter.' She paused to allow Andy and Lucy to take in her revelation. 'To put it brutally, Elodie was a PR stunt. Clare and Richard wanted a family, but in the first instance, Clare wasn't prepared to spend nine months "harbouring an alien that would suck the life out of her", as she so succinctly put it...' Judy faked a bored posh accent as she executed air quotes with her fingers. 'Secondly, she knew the effect a pregnancy would have on her figure, and she wouldn't risk the impact it would have on subsequent roles. They knew a baby would enhance their public profile and give them the PR interest they needed for a new film they were working on at the time called *Nine Months' Later*. So arrangements were made and Elodie was brought to them when she was three months old.'

Andy raised an eyebrow in astonishment, something that wasn't lost on Judy.

'It's a cut-throat industry, Detective Barnes, a stretch mark here or a pair of saggy Brad Pitts there, has ruined many a career. Elodie was a difficult child from the off, she spent most of her formative years being cared for by a nanny; there was very little interaction between Clare and the baby. The only exception she made was for photo shoots and magazine articles, and for those the poor child was dragged out, dressed up, photographed with mummy and daddy – and then sent back to the nanny.'

Andy shifted uncomfortably in his chair. 'So there's no love lost, then?'

It was Judy's turn to raise an eyebrow. 'None whatsoever. When she got older and more trouble than she was worth, she was packed off to a private boarding school in the hope she would follow in her adoptive parents' footsteps. She studied dance, drama and vocal coaching, none of which she was particularly good at, much to Clare's disgust, so Cragstone

Manor became more of a hiding place to keep her out of the public eye.'

Lucy was horrified at the matter-of-fact way Elodie's life and subsequent abandonment was being churned out. As though she didn't matter to anyone, least of all the very people who should have loved and cared for her.

Judy continued. 'Then there was the incident with the teacher at Cragstone. Elodie perceived a slight from her and pushed her over the balcony, which almost killed her. The signs had been there for months beforehand, probably years, that her mental health was failing. Other pupils at Cragstone had suffered unexplained accidents whilst Elodie was there, usually after they'd had some interaction with her, but they couldn't prove she was to blame. It took the near death and crippling of that poor teacher to have Elodie put away where she belonged. I still can't believe they released her.' She closed the file in front of her and linked her fingers together again, a sign Andy took to be that as far as Judy was concerned, their meeting was over.

'Do you know which adoption agency they used, Miss Moore, and do you have the paperwork? I take it that the adoption took place in this country?' Andy checked that Lucy still had her pen and notebook at the ready.

'Adoption agency?' Judy let out a long sigh. 'There was no adoption agency, Detective. That's not how the Mayer-Marshalls do things. They paid cold, hard cash for her.'

LOSING ONE'S MARBLES

Hilda lay in her bed, waiting. The sheets and counterpane had been pulled up to her chin, not to ward off the cool night air, but to hide what she was wearing beneath them. She was fully dressed and ready for an adventure. She stared into the darkness and listened to Millie's rhythmic breathing. She knew from experience she would have to wait until her friend passed through the *click-phweep-click* phase of her pattern, before she would begin to emit loud snores that only ever came from a deep sleep.

The clock ticked a tempo that made Hilda's feet tap along to the rhythm under the sheets. A dull *thud, thud* immediately came from the resin edges of her extra-wide T-bar Mary Jane shoes as they clicked together. Millie stirred in her sleep, forcing Hilda to hold her breath.

After what seemed like an eternity, the guttural grunts of Millie's deep slumber filled the room, signalling it was time for Hilda to make her move. She threw back the covers and tiptoed to the doorway, carefully turning the handle. She sneaked through the small gap and quietly shut the door with a gentle click. The outside lamp gave her enough light to find what she was looking for. Her fingers gripped the folded aluminium frame that was propped against the chalet wall. She stood momentarily to get her bearings and, once satisfied with the route she had plotted, she ambled off in the direction of her first port of call: Snowdrop Lawns.

Peeved that her three friends had dismissed the proof she had been gathering on the current murders, she had decided to take the bull by the horns, follow her own scribblings, and intercept the culprit herself. If her calculations were correct, the Harmony Hollows killer would strike again tonight. She would rush to the rescue and then be feted as a hero. Everyone, including her friends, would have to take notice of her then.

'What could possibly go wrong, Hilda?' she chunnered to herself as she ambled along the darkened path, the little Regatta fisherman's stool tucked under her arm.

Twenty minutes later, Snowdrop Lawns had offered her nothing by way of a crazed murderer or a swooning victim. Bitterly disappointed, she folded up her chair and made her way over to Cornflower Lawns. If her assumptions proved correct, Daffodil, Bluebell and Primrose had each been host to a grisly find, so the only two remaining parks that hadn't been blessed with crime scene tape were Snowdrop, which had now been discounted for this evening at least, and Cornflower.

She edged along the walls of the block and carefully angled her head around the corner to peer along the length of chalets on both sides. It was as peaceful as Snowdrop had been; the full moon had bathed its eerie light across the borders of grass before fading out at the edges to meet the orange glow of the chalet lamps. She tiptoed along the path until she came to the storage bin area. She had a good view of the chalet that her suspicions had alerted her to, with the advantage of whilst not being completely hidden, she was at least out of direct line of sight. She opened out the stool, tucked her coat underneath her, and sat down. Still keeping on high alert, she opened the carrier bag she had brought with her and pulled out a flask of tea she had made earlier and her trusty bag of mint imperials.

The minutes ticked by as she relished the warmth from the cup, her keen eyes darting backwards and forwards seeking out any movement. She was beginning to feel it had all been a complete waste of time, when suddenly a shadow caught her attention as it slid silently into Cornflower Lawns. For all her planning and visions of bravado, Hilda involuntarily inhaled deeply and almost choked on the mint imperial she had just popped into her mouth. She visibly stiffened, fearful that the snort she had just emitted would be heard.

With her heart pounding, she watched the well-built figure move silently along the building line towards the chalet she had been keeping under observation. Even though she willed her body to move, it had frozen with fear and completely refused to obey her. Panic had begun to set in.

Oh dear, not good, Hilda, not good at all... she mentally berated herself.

The figure stopped outside the door of Chalet 29 Cornflower Lawns, just as Hilda had predicted in her little notebook, and turned the door handle.

A murder was about to be announced, unless she could stop it...

What if she screamed? Would that scare them away or would it highlight her as a potential victim?

What would Pru or Bree do in a situation like this? Why hadn't she just waited for her friends to acknowledge her suspicions? They would be here with her now if she had.

She didn't want to be just Hilda on her own any more, a hopeful hero; she wanted to be one of the Four Wrinkled Dears who always rode out together on their adventures. She could kick herself for being so stubborn and so stupid.

She had so many questions, but no answers; her brain wasn't

designed to work under pressure these days. The despair Hilda was currently feeling was only matched by the horror of being paralysed with fear. She tried again, the effort burning her muscles – and suddenly, without warning, her trusty fisherman's stool gave way.

The aluminium frame crumpled and flattened out, dropping Hilda down on her bottom with an almighty *thwump* as, legs akimbo, they unnaturally scissored out, going east and west. The flask of tea jerked upwards and sailed through the air before landing with a clatter and a rattle on the paving slabs. Her treasured paper bag holding her mint imperials flew upwards, spilling what seemed to be hundreds of small round white balls. She watched as they scattered across the ground, rolling in every direction. Hilda wished with all her heart that she could close her eyes and it would all be a dream.

But it wasn't.

On hearing the commotion, the figure turned, and although Hilda couldn't make out their features, she was in no doubt that whoever it was, their mere presence had gripped at her heart. It thudded loudly and then missed a beat. She let out a small squeal as the figure lumbered towards her. Scrambling to her feet, she tried to find purchase on the path with her Mary Janes. It was like being on starting blocks as she pushed off, trying to put a distance between herself and whoever was going to be the author of her potential demise. She stumbled forwards, landing on her knees, small stones and gravel biting deep into her skin. She hauled herself up and began to run, her limping gait not ideal for distance or speed, but she kept going, pausing only when she heard a loud 'thud' behind her. She quickly glanced back, half expecting gnarly fingers at the ready to grip her around the throat.

Instead she was gifted a miracle.

If Hilda could have prayed to God for help in her hour of

need, she would never in a million years have envisaged that a bag of Miss Jericho's Sweetest Confectionery would be sent as her saviour. Now no longer chasing her, the figure was lying in a crumpled heap on the ground, quietly groaning and bemoaning half a pound of previously sucked mint imperials and a three-inch concrete kerb.

Still gripped by fear, and with her heart beating as though it would crack her pacemaker and burst through her ribs, Hilda welcomed the surge of adrenaline that gave her an unusual turn of speed back to Marigold Lawns, sanctuary and her friends.

BINGO

'What on earth where you thinking, Hilda?' Pru was beside herself with both concern and annoyance. She used the bowl of warm water to bathe Hilda's knee. 'Clarissa, can you pop the kettle on, a nice cup of sweet tea will help.'

Hilda, more disappointed that she wasn't the heroine she'd hoped she would be, harrumphed loudly. 'After what I've just been through? I think a drop of sherry is more appropriate,' she grumbled.

Chalet 13 was unnaturally crowded with attentive friends, which actually made Hilda glow with happiness. Ethel was busy consoling Millie, who was mortified that she hadn't heard Hilda leave. 'What possessed you to start acting like Roger Bond in the middle of the night? You could have been killed!' Millie wailed.

'Roger Moore or James Bond, dear; it can't be a mix of both…' Ethel corrected.

Hilda took a sip of the sherry that Clarissa had poured for her. 'Nope, I don't think it was Roger Moore. This one was built like a building site hod-carrier.' She widened out her arms to evidence the size of her suspect, carelessly slopping sherry on Millie's nightdress.

Pru, satisfied that she had removed all traces of gravel, soil and goodness knows what else from Hilda's wound, deftly ripped the back from the plaster and stuck it in place. 'What made you go all the way over to Cornflower Lawns in the middle of the night, Hilda?'

Hilda grabbed her notebook from the bedside cabinet and held it aloft. 'Because of this! Not one of you would listen to me, so I decided I'd deal with the problem, and it's a jolly good job I did, or whoever is staying in Chalet 29 would have been another morning stiff, but for me.' She jutted out her chin, proud of what she felt she had achieved. 'It was just lucky I disturbed the murderer!'

'It probably helped that the chalet was empty too!' Ethel added. 'Apparently it was that nice young man from the Marina Lounge, the one that does all the lighting and stage stuff, but he had decided to have a "stopover" at someone else's chalet instead.' She used her fingers as air quotes on the word *stopover* and cheekily winked at her friends.

Millie giggled like a schoolgirl, squeezing her shoulders up to her ears, becoming almost mouselike. 'Ooh, yes he is rather nice, he could definitely light me up anytime!'

'Millie!! Good grief, girl, that's a bit risqué coming from you!' Pru laughed.

Puzzled, Bree decided it was time to get back to the serious stuff. 'I don't understand, Hilda. Why specifically Chalet 29 on Cornflower? Why would you think there was going to be another murder?'

'Because of the bingo. Dearie me, you say I'm losing my marbles; I've seen faster slugs on an iceberg lettuce!' Hilda opened her notebook and began to read out her observations. 'Right, first murder, Daffodil Lawns, Chalet 8: that Mary woman, the one with the boil-in-the-bag tracksuit. Then we had that fat lump in a string vest, Trevor from Chalet 25 on Bluebell Lawns…' She paused to ensure they were following her.

Pru, Bree, Clarissa, Ethel and Millie were suddenly all ears.

Keen to get to the point, Ethel encouraged her to continue. 'Go on…'

Hilda bristled with importance. 'Primrose 27, my Troy Florentine…' She patted her chest and faked grief at his passing. 'And finally tonight, Cornflower Lawns, Chalet 29.'

Five blank faces stared back at her. Pru shook her head. 'Hilda I'm sorry, but I don't know what you're getting at. I don't understand. The only thing in common is Mary and Trevor, because they won the bingo. Troy was a dancer and the one who did win tonight was from Primrose Lawns, not Cornflower. Besides all that, you and the others were supposed to be concentrating on the 1983 murders, not getting yourself almost killed by sniffing around the latest ones!'

'Tssk! The opportunity arose, and I didn't want to forget what I wanted to do, but don't you see? It's the *chalet* numbers. They're the same as the last winning jackpot bingo number called each night that there's been a murder.' Hilda, exasperated, held out her notebook for Pru to read. 'Tonight's winning number was 29, and as each of the lawns has the same set of numbers, I had to assume that it would either be Snowdrop or Cornflower as neither of them have had a murder yet. So I sat and waited outside 29 Cornflower Lawns…'

'To frighten them off?' Bree looked at Hilda's grazed knees, scuffed Mary Jane shoes, and hair that was standing on end. 'I'm not surprised they legged it.' She laughed.

'It was me mint imperials; they came in very handy! Whoever it was looked like a reject from *Dancing on Ice* – a duck on a frozen pond could have done better! So, *now* do you believe me?' Hilda slurped back the last remains of the sherry and waited.

Pru grabbed her mobile phone. 'I can't say I condone what you did, Hilda, which was incredibly dangerous, but I take my hat off to you for your diligence. I can't remember the numbers called, so I'll have to take your word for it if you wrote them down at the time. Which brings me to ask why you started to make notes of them in the beginning.'

Millie quickly piped up. 'She was keeping a book on number patterns, to see if they influenced big bingo wins. I didn't think it would do any harm. I read somewhere that making lists and concentrating on numbers, words and sequences was good for Alzheimer's; it keeps the brain active for longer.'

Pru's heart swelled with affection for Millie. Her concern for Hilda was so touching.

'Right, I think we should all get ourselves back to our respective beds...' Pru checked her watch. 'We might get lucky and grab a few hours' sleep before dawn breaks. Make sure you lock the door securely behind us, Millie, and in the morning I'll speak to Andy and see if he can let his friend Ezra know that we, or should I say Hilda, is possibly on to something.'

Pru wasn't sure what that 'something' could be, but if it did turn out to be a pattern, then maybe it could help the investigation.

PICK YOUR OWN

The familiarity of the gurgling water cooler in the incident room was comforting for Lucy. It made her feel grounded. The road trip to Middle Cow Creatives had unsettled her. The idea of a tiny innocent baby being passed over for money made her feel sick to her stomach. Her mind had thought of nothing else since Judy Moore's revelation. The transaction, for that was what it was, must have been fraught with danger. How was Elodie's grandmother to know what type of parents the Mayer-Marshall's would turn out to be?

'Bad ones...'

Andy broke away from the file he was studying and looked quizzically at Lucy. 'What are?'

'Sorry, Sarge, it was a head thought that came out of my mouth.' Lucy clicked the mouse to open up another screen on the PC. 'The Mayer-Marshalls. How can you pay money for another human being? It's like you've just been to Sainsbury's and plucked something that took your fancy from the shelf. It's obscene.'

'It's been an evasion of UK adoption laws, that's for sure. As far as I can see, there was no social services involvement, and this didn't go through the Courts. It was literally behind closed doors.' Andy studied the document that Judy had given him, baffled that a baby could be sold, given a new identity, and passed off as their own, with not one concerned regulatory body being notified, involved, or in the least bit suspicious.

In the absence of a spoon, Lucy twirled a pen in her mug of tea. 'So what we've got so far is the baby's birth mother died and that it was the grandmother who sold Elodie to the Mayer-Marshall's, no questions asked?'

'Yep, all facilitated through a third party, which was...' He flicked through the file until he found what he was looking for. '...the Mayer-Marshall's personal assistant, who apparently knew the mother before she died. I need you to do some digging on the grandmother, Luce. All we've got from Judy is that her first name was Martha, and she was from the Fallow Falls area. She seemed to think she was living on the Fernlea Estate. We've got to assume she's going to be a minimum of, say, seventy-five by now, and if we're really unlucky, she could be dead. If that's the case, then I need to know if there are any surviving family members. I want the PA traced too; I need the birth mother's name as a priority.'

Lucy scribbled down the bullet points in her notebook. 'There's got to be an original birth certificate in existence though, surely? A birth must be registered within forty-two days, and Elodie wasn't sold to the Mayer-Marshall's until she was three months old.'

'Well, there's no birth records in Elodie's name, so it probably explains the reason why she didn't accompany Clare and Richard on any of their filming locations abroad. No passport, no passage... According to Judy, she always remained in the UK with the nanny.' He offered out his mug to Lucy. 'Don't suppose I could be a pain and ask for an extra strong coffee, Luce?' He gave her one of his winning smiles, hoping she wouldn't think he was being sexist and expecting her to wait on him hand and foot.

'A jammy dodger too?' she teased.

'Oh, only if you insist.' He laughed.

Pru made herself comfortable on the bench in front of the walled gardens, angling herself so the early morning sun provided her with a little warmth. She held her mobile phone out in front of her and waited for Andy to answer. The ring tone echoed from speaker mode. She quickly clicked it off when he answered, preferring to keep his side of the conversation private.

'Hello, my Delectable Detective…' she purred.

She had already run through the scenario that she felt best suited the situation. She would gently lead up to what she wanted to tell him once she had made him feel secure and off guard. 'No, it's good, honestly. It's not as bad as some people make out. You know me, I'll always make the best of it. The ladies are loving it, though.'

She smiled as he regaled her with the dire digs he was staying in with Lucy, complained bitterly about how uncomfortable his bed was, and bemoaned the fact that he was yet to have a piece of toast that had the butter and marmalade spread evenly to all four corners. He then turned his attention to her unexpected phone call.

'No, honestly nothing is wrong. I'm just missing you. Do you think you could sneak a night away? I can always kick Bree out. I'm sure she wouldn't mind sharing a bed with Kitty, she's single occupancy, but has two beds.' Pru listened intently. 'Ah right, I forgot about Frank, maybe not, then…' She giggled.

He promised her he would see what he could do, which lifted her spirits – and then just as quickly flattened them by telling her his investigation was throwing up lots of different leads that would keep him busy with road trips. She utilised the talk of investigations to bring up the subject of Hilda.

'Now don't go off on one, I haven't poked my nose into anything, but...'

She told him about Hilda's antics, her meticulous notes, and what they had led them to believe. 'So, you see if Hilda is right, then someone around here is bumping people off according to the winning number on bingo night. I've just heard talk at reception: people were saying that the guy who works the lighting at the Marina Lounge, Mark something or other, has reported an attempted break-in at his chalet last night. He wasn't there, but apparently there was such a commotion.' She pulled her bottom lip down in contrition, knowing full well that the commotion had been Hilda and her would-be assailant.

She could almost hear his despair through the ensuing silence. He eventually spoke, suggesting over-active imaginations amongst her quartet of Miss Marples were to blame, and that she and Bree were fuelling it by validating their mischief.

'No, no, you're not listening.' Exasperated, Pru huffed loudly. 'This guy's chalet was 29 Cornflower Lawns; Hilda was camped outside it in her fisherman's chair. She saw someone trying to get in, and the winning number that night just happened to be number twenty-nine! It's more than coincidence and over-active imaginations, Andy; you've got to let your friend Ezra know.'

A PROMISE

DS Ezra Maynard gave Hilda a reassuring smile as he took the seat opposite her. 'Now, Miss Jones, have you got the little notebook that your friends have been telling me about? I'm really keen to have a read if I may.'

Hilda, her handbag protectively clutched to her chest, nodded.

'Wonderful, so before you show it to me, is there anything else I can get you?' He indicated to the coffee cup that sat neatly in a saucer in front of her. 'Another drink, maybe?'

Hilda eyed him cautiously. She checked her watch and nodded towards the bar area of the Marina Lounge. 'Is it too early for a sherry?'

Pru, who had agreed to sit with Hilda, put her head in her hands. 'It's not even lunch time, Hilda!'

Nonplussed, Hilda shrugged her shoulders. She had decided that a schooner of sherry would assist her memory and her ability to relate her story, and unless this detective bribed her with either that, or, at the very least, a bag of mint imperials, she was saying nothing. She shifted in her seat, feeling a sudden twinge in her lower back from the tumble she had taken the night before. Even though Pru had cleaned and dressed her wounds, they still stung. 'Don't you offer your suspects a... now what do you call it?' She propped her chin in her hand, still keeping tight hold of her handbag as she narrowed her eyes and stared intently at poor Ezra. 'Ah! That's it, you give them a "sweetener" to make them talk, I've seen it on the telly. So, I would like a sweetener. Can you make mine a large Harveys Bristol Cream, please.' She sat back in triumph and waited.

Pru stood up and indicated to Ezra to continue and that she would get the much-needed sherry for Hilda. If Hilda had asked for a magnum of champagne, Pru would probably have had a whip round and bought it for her, just to get the interview started.

Hilda pushed the notebook towards Ezra. 'It's all in there, timed and dated, just like Millie told me to; I've been very careful.' She tapped the side of her head. 'I might be losing it a bit up here, but I do know when I'm on the right track with something.'

Ezra took the book from her and flicked through the first few pages. He felt a pang of sympathy for her. Old age should be celebrated and respected, but it was a privilege that was denied to so many, and to reach a good age and find your mind was deserting you was such a terrible cruelty. Nevertheless, Hilda was right, her notes were meticulous, albeit her handwriting a little shaky. He checked his own notes and had to concede that if the bingo numbers she had noted were correct, they did match the scenes of the three murders perfectly, and the attempted break-in the previous night. According to Ralph Fairbright, the winning numbers were always logged in case of dispute, so he would confirm with those before he added too much credence to Hilda's theory.

'They're calling the murderer the "Grim Sleeper"; did you know that, Detective Tesla?' Hilda daintily held the stem of the sherry glass that Pru had just placed in front of her and took a sip.

'*Ezra*, my name is Ezra, Miss Jones, and, yes, I've heard that around the resort this morning.'

'Ezra, Tesla, phffft...' Hilda waved her hand dismissively. 'Well, I'll tell you this for nothing, whoever it is went down like a sack of spuds on my mint imperials. They're bound to have hurt themselves, and with a bit of luck they might have broken a leg or two. Just look out for someone that limps, Detective, and then you'll have your killer!' She swigged back the last of the sherry and eased herself up out of the chair. 'Right, I'm off to powder my nose, I'll see you later, Pru...'

Pru and Ezra watched Hilda hobble across the dance floor, dragging one leg behind her, the irony of her amateur sleuth advice not lost on them as they stifled their laughter.

'What do you think?' Pru was keen to know that she hadn't wasted Ezra's time.

'If those numbers are confirmed, I think she's got something.' Ezra took an evidence bag from his pocket and carefully placed Hilda's notebook inside.

Excitement was gnawing at the pit of Pru's stomach. 'You could always set up a sting. You'd have to nobble the bingo night and get a number called for an empty chalet, and then have a team inside waiting.'

Ezra gave her a look similar to one that Andy would give her if she was getting carried away. 'Andy wasn't wrong about you, was he?' He laughed. 'He must miss you when he's away.'

She gave him a mischievous grin. 'He probably thinks he's gone deaf without me wittering away. I do seem to keep him on his toes, though. I miss him too, Ezra, but...' she delved into her handbag, 'I got Sophie the resort photographer to take this. I'm going to send it to him, it's bound to make him smile. She handed her mobile phone to him, enlarging the screen with thumb and middle finger. A rather startling image of Pru, wide-eyed and with her tongue sticking out stared back at him.

'Seriously? I take it you're not a fan of Instagram filters and pouts, preferring to go for the more natural look! I think Sophie has captured the real you perfectly!' Ezra couldn't help but like Pru; she exuded both fun and humility, the consummate match for Andy. 'Right, and I know I shouldn't be saying this, but I know you won't leave this alone if I don't tell you: we think it's a little more than just the three recent deaths. If that's the case, then we could be looking at someone who has been here either on staff or as a guest, for a good many years. Either way, it might be difficult to keep an idea like you've just suggested under wraps, but, yes, it could be something to consider.' He opened his briefcase and popped the evidence bag inside. 'My team are currently going back over reported non-suspicious deaths at Harmony Hollows over the last ten years as a starting point... and *that* is strictly between you and me!'

Pru nodded, feeling a sense of importance to be trusted with such information, information she probably wouldn't have been privy to if it wasn't for the fact she was Andy's wife. 'My lips are sealed, but if I hear anything that could be of use, I'll let you know straight away.'

Ezra gave her the thumbs-up. 'Just remember, *I'm* the detective, not you, Pru. Please don't get up to any mischief. Andy has made me promise to look after you and the Winterbottom ladies, so don't make me break my word.'

Pru grinned and gave him the okay sign with finger and thumb, but deep down she knew it was a promise that she would probably break before the day had come to a close.

'The world is a dangerous place, not because of those who do evil, but because of the people who look on and do nothing.'
– Albert Einstein

THE JURY

Harmony Hollows had stilled. It was like a heart that had given away its last beat.

Even the wind that would usually sweep playfully along the paths or whistle vibrantly around corners, had deserted it. The playground stood empty, the swings hung limply by their chains, and the red rocking horse, head stooped low without riders, added to the melancholy feel that had spread its blanket across the resort.

Clarissa, Ethel, Hilda and Millie sat together, squeezed onto the wooden bench in the gardens opposite the restaurant, their gaily coloured cardigans and dresses giving them an air of a popular comical seaside postcard from the 1950s.

'Lunch is nearly finished, so they'll be tottering outside to enjoy the sunshine and to walk off the jam roly-poly and custard, no doubt.' Ethel dipped into her carrier bag and pulled out a Tupperware box that had seen better days. 'Here you go, no jam roly-poly, but I've got Wagon Wheels and Penguins. Help yourselves.' She passed it along the row.

Clarissa grabbed a Penguin bar and tore at the wrapper. 'If we see anyone who matches our criteria, I'll write them down.

Ethel, you and Millie will follow them to see where they're staying…' She did a test scribble with her pen on the first page of the new notebook to ensure it worked.

'What about me? What am I supposed to be doing?' Hilda was quite put out.

Ethel and Clarissa exchanged glances. 'Well, as you've already hit the sherry this morning, we thought it would be advisable for you to stay with me. The last thing we need is you going arse over tit again and causing yourself more damage!' The look on Clarissa's face ensured this decision wasn't up for discussion.

They carried on sitting in silence, with just the odd crunch from their confectionery accompanying the birdsong coming from a nearby tree.

'Oh my goodness…' Millie spluttered a mouthful of biscuit crumbs all down the front of her polka-dot dress. 'Look!' She frantically pointed at the entrance to the restaurant. 'Over there, he's got a limp,' she shrieked.

Clarissa, pen at the ready, positioned herself for a better look whilst Ethel was up from the bench ready to tail the suspect. She tutted loudly and quickly plonked herself back down again. 'Of course he's got a bloody limp, Millie! It's him from number 12 opposite us. He's only got one ruddy leg, and a cheap false one that's shorter than the other!'

Disappointment took up residence between them and they returned to their previous silence – plus another biscuit each to help them with their mood.

'Oh blimey, here's the camp commandant. It looks like he's coming over, and he's limping. Quick; make out we're busy!' Clarissa shoved her notebook into her pocket, adjusted her sunglasses and nonchalantly lay her arm over the end of the bench, pretending to sunbathe. The last thing she wanted was to alert him to what they were doing if he did happen to be the 'Grim Sleeper'.

'Ladies.' Ralph Fairbright nodded his greeting to them. 'I believe one of you had some sort of involvement in last night's little escapade. I wanted to reassure you that it was just a small misunderstanding. One of our staff got their chalets mixed up. No harm done, though.' He stood grinning inanely, waiting for a response.

'No harm done?! Have you seen my knees? I'll give you no harm done!' Before anyone could react, Hilda had hoisted her skirt up and thrust out both legs to display her injuries. 'I haven't had plasters like these on my knees since I was in kindergarten,' she indignantly spat. She was very aware that Ralph was lying, which added to her pique.

Embarrassed at the brief glimpse of Hilda's purple bloomers, Ralph muttered under his breath and made a bid for a hasty retreat. He turned too quickly and his already sprained ankle gave way. He stumbled sideways, grabbing wildly at Clarissa's arm.

'Dearie me, Mr Fairbright, let me give you a hand...' From nowhere, Nellie Girdlestone appeared. She dropped her plastic bucket and mop and took Ralph's arm. 'Here you go, lean on me, we can hobble off together.' She chortled. 'It's such a shame you abandoned your usual whisky tipple in favour of brandy. Maybe you should take more soda with it; it could be a life saver next time!'

The Four Wrinkled Dears looked on in amazement as both Nellie and Ralph limped off together.

'Excuse me!' Clarissa shouted at the cleaner.

Nellie stopped in her tracks and slowly turned to face the ladies. 'Is there a problem?' she challenged.

Clarissa suddenly had second thoughts about questioning her, but knew if she didn't ask, it was an opportunity wasted. She would just hint rather than question. 'I just wondered, as you've hurt your leg too, would you like one of us to carry your bucket and mop whilst you help Mr Fairbright?'

Nellie's face softened. 'That's considerate of you; it's just a bit of arthritis, but if you leave it there, I'll come back for it later.' Satisfied she had dampened their enthusiasm for her current predicament, Nellie continued on her way with Ralph, leaving Clarissa furtively scribbling in her notebook.

'That's Shrek...' Ethel helpfully offered, so Clarissa would have a name for her notes. 'Well, not really; she's called Nellie, but I think Shrek suits her better, don't you?'

As time passed by, with the assistance of factor 40 suncream on Millie's nose and a quick trip to the ice-cream hut for four cones of vanilla whip topped with strawberry syrup, the ladies continued in their quest to identify the 'Grim Sleeper'.

'Lovely day for it, isn't it, ladies?' Maggie Henshaw unbuttoned her grey blazer and dramatically fanned her face as she walked along the path towards the bench. 'I think we're in for a good couple of days. I hope to see you at the bingo tonight, and we've got a great cabaret beforehand.'

Ethel gave her a warm smile. 'Of course. We're hoping one of us gets a big win before we go home, aren't we, girls?'

Maggie gave them a jovial thumbs-up, reminiscent of the old Butlins-style greeting as three heads nodded their agreement with Ethel's observation. Maggie tapped the side of her nose and hunched her shoulders. 'I've got a bit of a surprise; it's going to be announced today, but until then can I trust you to keep it a secret?'

Hilda was beside herself with excitement. She nodded so hard Maggie thought her head would drop off.

'Apparently there's going to be a Murder Mystery Night in the Marina Lounge, it's still being planned, but it's bound to be fun. Anyway, must dash: things to do; people to see,' Maggie cheerfully added – as she limped off towards the Marina Lounge.

A stunned silence swept over the Four Wrinkled Dears.

'Well, would you credit it? Is there some sort of weird limb anomaly going on around here?' Clarissa tutted as she added Maggie's name to her notebook.

Unbeknown to the four ladies of the Winterbottom Women's Institute, whilst their attention was being directed to limps, lumps and bumps, they had already been singled out by Sophie Hopkins to assist in her grand finale, the likes of which Harmony Hollows would have never seen before. From the steps of the restaurant, she stood watching them interact with each other, noted their camaraderie, their feistiness, their sharp minds and, most importantly, their penchant for snooping and for making mischief.

They were to be her jury of four.

Four women, honest and true...

They would do the job in ignorance, but no doubt very admirably indeed.

WALLY

Stacey slowly pushed open the door to Ralph Fairbright's office, a selection of mail and two files tucked under her arm. She held her breath, hoping he wasn't still in residence. As the gap widened, she was relieved to see that it was as deserted as the Marie Celeste. She had lost count of the number of times she had to quickly sidestep Ralph's roving hand as it came in for a quick slap of her bottom every time she brought in his mail. She now had a planned route around his office that gave her some form of a protective barrier, whether it was a chair, a filing cabinet or, as she had most recently utilised, the floral-patterned tea tray. She knew that it was only a matter of time before she lost her cool and would end up wrapping the colourful metal sheet around the back of his head in self-defence.

Crossing the office floor, her white regulation plimsolls barely leaving a trace of her footsteps on the purple and grey Axminister carpet, she caught sight of the photograph on the wall. She had been dying to get another look at it since her first day at Harmony Hollows when Ralph had pointed himself out to her. He had been keen to set out his history with the resort and his current standing within the company. Now she had the opportunity to give scrutiny. Her finger traced across each row until she found him again.

'Well, well, Mr Fairbright, you were a bit of a looker in your day...' She giggled, very aware that the ensuing years had not been kind to Ralph. She checked out the others in the photograph, but didn't recognise anyone else. She actually wondered if half of them were still alive.

'Sorry, Stacey, is Mr Fairbright available?'

The sudden interruption made her jump. She turned quickly to see Maggie, accompanied by Mark Joynson, standing in the doorway. 'Gosh, I don't know what's got into me; I'm scared of my own shadow these days!' She laughed. 'I'm not sure where he is, he did mention that he was going to pop into town at some point, as he had some business he needed to sort out, so maybe that's where he is. Is there anything I can do to help?'

Mark shrugged. 'I just wondered if there's a chance I could get a change of chalet. After last night, I'm not too chuffed about staying in mine. You know there's been talk around the resort, don't you?'

Stacey was well aware that fingers had been pointing all morning and that poor Mark had been referred to as a 'close shave'. Staff and residents alike had decreed that he should have been the fourth victim of who they had dubbed the 'Grim Sleeper'. If it hadn't been for the exquisite Candy Cane offering him a shared duvet for the night at her chalet, things might have been very different for him. 'I'll put a request on his desk for you, Mark, but in the meantime, I know that Mr Fairbright has sanctioned additional interior locks for all the chalets. I'll mark your place as a priority.' She hastily scribbled a note, ripped it from the pad and placed it on Ralph's blotter. As she turned, she spotted another note that had been wedged between the cards on his Rolodex. She plucked it out and read it. 'Well, it would seem Mr Fairbright has gone into town, but that he won't be back for a day or two.' Stacey was quite put out that he hadn't had the decency to tell her of his change of plans in person.

Maggie wandered over to the wall that was filled with photographs and advertising billboards. She picked along the date order and found the 1982 to 1983 photographs. Her finger touched the exact same one that only moments earlier Stacey had stood in front of. Maggie now did the same, her head tilted as her eyes scanned their faces. She saw them all. Each and every one of them had played a part in her time at Harmony Hollows that year. The young man at the back, the lapel of his leather jacket casually pulled up, stared back at her. She tried to remember his name – it was there, just tickling the edges of her memory. 'I recognise him, but I just can't... oh, wait a minute! That's it! It's Wally Waltzer...' She hadn't meant to shout it out so loudly, but the excitement of having remembered got the better of her.

'Who is?' Stacey joined her and watched as Maggie thumped the image with her finger.

'Him! He was called that when I was here for the Northerns in 1983. He used to work on the waltzers. I was just a teenager, and Wally and Larry Belfont, who was a barman in the Marina Lounge, used to fight for any available female.' Maggie quickly wished she hadn't uttered that last name. Her stomach flipped and her heart thudded as the image she had spent her whole life trying to bury suddenly burst into her head like a flash sequence from a film trailer.

Stacey started to laugh. 'No way, Wally Waltzer! You do know who it is, don't you, Maggie?'

Maggie shook her head.

'It's none other than our very own Mr Ralph Fairbright, camp commandant and resident pervert!'

LAST CHANCE SALOON

Fallow Falls was a picturesque village which boasted a small post office-cum-provisions store, a haberdashery shop, a ladies' salon with an ornate candy pink hanging sign, and a very quaint lopsided pub called The Bell, Book & Candle. An oak plaque above the door bore the date of 1782. Andy and Lucy stood outside, debating if they had the time to grab a bite to eat before hitting the road again.

'That was a supernatural rom com film from the 1950s with Jimmy Stewart and Jack Lemon.' Lucy's stomach took the opportunity to grumble loudly as the aroma of home-cooked food wafted through an open window. 'I loved the film, but what a strange name to call a pub, though; it looks dead creepy.'

'They can be dunking the Pendle witches in the ladies' bogs for all I care; it's not putting me off, I'm starving…' Andy pushed open the blackened wood door, and as his fingertips brushed the coloured lead-light glass he could almost feel the history that charged through the very fabric of the building.

Inside was basic but welcoming, the stone floor stretched out to encompass the bar, an inglenook fireplace, several monks' benches rigid against the walls, and a collection of rickety old tables and chairs. Lucy took a table in the corner whilst Andy ordered two shandies and a beef stew and pickled cabbage for them each from the daily specials board. Lucy found it amusing that they even had a specials board, as according to the laminated menu card on their table, they only did cheese sandwiches, onion sandwiches with cheese, cheese salad sandwiches, tomato sandwiches with cheese and cheese on toast.

Andy sat down and relished the first sip of his cool drink. 'Right, so we're going to get nothing from Elodie's grandmother…' He checked through his notes, underlining the date she had died. 'No relatives that we know of, and the neighbours on the Fernlea Estate knew very little about her. Apparently she moved there mid-1980s, kept herself to herself and when she died, in the absence of family and friends, everything was left to the local cat rescue.'

'That's so sad, I can't believe she didn't acknowledge her own granddaughter in her will.' Lucy rearranged her knife and fork so they sat neatly on the paper serviette.

'I suppose from the day she gave her away, in her mind, she ceased to exist. We need to find out more about the daughter, who she was and how she died. What I can't believe is that nobody knew the grandmother or anything about her. It's as though Martha just appeared one day with her past wiped clean.' Andy acknowledged the steaming bowl of stew that was put down in front of him. 'Thank you…' He gave the barmaid a warm smile.

'Maybe if the grief was too much, she just walked away from everything and started a new life.' Lucy wasn't sure if that was helpful, and she was pretty sure it sugar-coated what was probably a traumatic time for Martha. 'I just hope our meeting tomorrow will yield something for us to work on. Serena Porter is going to be our last hope, she's the one who facilitated the sale of Elodie, and she knew the mother.'

Andy blew on the forkful of hot potato. 'Yep, last chance saloon with this line of enquiry. Even Cragstone Manor couldn't offer anything, but I'm ever hopeful. Serena was the Mayer-Marshalls' PA for over twenty-five years; she's bound to have plenty of dirt to dish – it's just a case of us playing our cards right. I don't want her being obstructive because she fears prosecution.'

THE INVITATION

A shuffling sound from the door of the chalet woke Clarissa. She lifted her head from the pillow, peered into the low light of the room, and listened. The digital bedside clock she had brought with her to Harmony Hollows flashed a muted 06:02 in red.

'Ethel...' she whispered.

Ethel's head, complete with elasticated eye mask pinned firmly in place, bolted upright from her slumber. 'What?'

'Did you hear that?'

'Hear what?'

'That shuffling sound...' Clarissa swung her legs over the bed and allowed her feet to tap across the rug in search of her slippers.

'It'll be those giant cockroaches that wear little wooden clogs on their feet...' Ethel mumbled as she plonked her head back down on her pillow.

'Ethel...'

'What?'

'Are you awake or just talking in your sleep?'

Ethel sat upright again and lifted the mask from her eyes.

'What do you think? Honestly, 'Rissa, it's the middle of the bloody night; go back to sleep!' She snapped the mask back over her eyes, plumped up her pillow and buried her face into it.

Clarissa could have argued with her that it was in fact the dawn of a new day, but instead chose to keep her comments to herself. She knew from experience that Ethel's early morning grumpiness would blossom twofold if she assisted her in getting out of bed on the wrong side.

Once Clarissa's feet were ensconced in her corded slippers, she crept over to the door. 'It's an envelope, we've got mail, Ethel!'

Exasperated, Ethel wrapped the pillow around her ears, trying to block out her friend's chatter. Clarissa cracked open the curtain a smidgeon to enable her to see by the early morning light. She picked up the envelope that had been pushed under the door. It was addressed to all four of them in a flowing handwritten script. She turned it over, examined the back, and gingerly began to peel the adhesive 'V' open. Her fingers carefully probed inside and pulled out an invitation card that was embossed with the Harmony Hollows logo in purple and grey.

'Well, would you look at this, Eth! We've got an exclusive invitation to attend that Murder Night thing they're doing. It's called, "You the Jury". I bet you a pound to a pinch of salt it's based on that American show on TV...' Clarissa was beside herself with excitement as she quickly read through the criteria and instructions.

Ethel lay in bed, the mask now pulled down under her chin, staring at the ceiling. As Clarissa droned on and on, she marvelled at the benefits of having an eye mask that was now acting as a makeshift wattle hammock. She could feel her jawline and neck being drawn up and pushed behind her ears.

'We've been chosen to be the jury, how exciting is that? It'll be like that murder mystery weekend we went on at Montgomery Hall. Remember, Eth? They'll have actors, scenery and lighting.'

Ethel did remember. It was a weekend that was almost the death of them: secret passages, bodies piling up in the industrial freezer in the basement, not to mention the most dire troupe of thespians she had ever had the misfortune to meet who had been hired to entertain them. 'Well, I hope it's a better production than the last one,' she griped. 'I do think it's a bit poor taste, considering what's been going on around here, though.'

Clarissa wasn't the least bit perturbed by Ethel's mood; she was far too excited to care. She turned the invitation over and read the back. 'Well, they're probably using it as a distraction, to turn the real murders into something that's theatrical to take the sting out of it. Now it says here that we've got to keep this between us because our appearance is going to be a surprise for the audience. I think it's going to be what they call an "immersive experience".' She did a little dance on the spot, her slippers tapping a jolly beat. 'It'll all be set up like a proper court, and then they'll bring us in; we listen to the evidence and give our verdict. I bet they chose us because we look like we know what we're doing.'

Eventually finding the energy to sit up, Ethel ripped off her eye mask and groaned as her chin and jowls wobbled, slapped down and returned to their natural position. 'That's debatable. So when is it? What do we have to wear, and are there any free drinks and nibbles included for our participation?'

Knowing full well that Ethel would do the mambo in her underwear, wearing two bananas and a bunch of grapes for a hat in exchange for a pint of shandy and a packet of crisps, Clarissa gave her the invitation. 'It's tomorrow night, 9pm in the Marina Lounge. Oh my! Hilda and Millie will be so excited.'

Ethel wagged a warning finger at Clarissa. 'I wouldn't say anything to Hilda until we're there. Bless her, but you know she can't hold her own water when she gets excited. Our celebrity appearance would be all over Harmony Hollows before a lamb could shake its tail thrice.'

'Twice. The saying is "*two* shakes of a lamb's tail", Eth!'

'Oh feck off, 'Rissa! My lamb's dyscalculic!'

CRY-BABY

Nellie Girdlestone emerged from the resort kitchens and inched her way along the brick wall of the corridor. She checked the coast was clear before hurriedly stripping off her overall. She shoved it into the plastic bag she was carrying and vigorously punched it down. It reluctantly obeyed as it vied for space with a twin pack of quilted toilet rolls and two large jars of coffee she had 'found' in the storeroom of the kitchens. As far as she was concerned, they were not stolen, they were just waiting to be claimed.

Checking her watch, she quickened her pace; she had less than four minutes to make it out through the gates before the change in security guard. With old Bennett on the barriers, she could get away with murder – he was lucky if he could detect his own arse but for the fact he was usually found sitting on it. Once Bennett put his hat and coat on and handed over the mantle to the night guard, Jeff, however, she knew nothing would get past him and out of Harmony Hollows. She clutched the bag just that little bit closer to her chest whilst utilising her jacket to distract from its bulkiness.

'Nellie! Wait a minute, I need a quick word...'

Nellie stopped in her tracks, fearful that she was about to be busted for theft. She turned to see the resort photographer running towards her and cursed under her breath. 'Shit...' That was all she needed! She quickly plastered on a smile and waited.

'Hi, Nellie, I don't know if you remember me, I'm Sophie, the resort photographer, I just wondered if you could help me. I'm doing a collage of Harmony Hollows through the years, and Stacey told me you've been here for over forty years. Is that right?' Sophie pursed her lips and waited.

Puzzled, Nellie didn't want to respond beyond what was absolutely necessary. She needed time to think where this conversation might be leading to. and how much she should divulge. 'Yes, quite some years, why?'

Always good to answer a question with a question, Nellie, keep it tight.

Sophie was under no illusion that she was dealing with someone who was used to ducking and diving. She would have to play this carefully. 'Oh, I just wondered if you would like to get involved, help me to put together some of the old photographs I've found, maybe even give some background on them?'

Nellie's eyes narrowed as she took in the slip of a woman standing in front of her. Nothing out of the ordinary, a slightly prominent nose that acted as a canopy to full lips that boasted a bright red lip stain. But it was Sophie's eyes that made Nellie squirm. She had observed the same cold emptiness that ran deep into those black spheres, hundreds of times before. Every time she looked in a mirror...

Nellie paused, a strange, enigmatic smile playing on her lips. 'I'm sure that can be arranged, dear. It might cost you a drink or two in the Marina Lounge, though.' She gave what she knew was a pathetic attempt at a warm response, not that it bothered her in the slightest whether or not this woman found her endearing.

Nonplussed, Sophie gave her the thumbs-up and excitedly hunched her shoulders. 'You're on...' She pointed to the top of the cigarette packet that had taken the opportunity to escape from the pocket of Nellie's jacket when she'd hugged it in front of her to hide her spoils. 'Actually, I've got a better idea: why don't you come to my studio? I can always bring a bottle, and it would mean you'd be able to puff away to your hearts content; nobody ever bothers me there. I can always tell them I need you for a few hours to help me clean the dark room.' She stared a little too intently at Nellie, but it was her way of willing her to hurry up and make a decision. She still had arrangements to make and her first defendant would probably be waking up – she checked her watch – right about now.

Nellie considered her options: a few hours with her feet up swigging from a nice bottle of Cabernet Sauvignon whilst racking her lungs with half a pack of Embassy ciggies sounded pretty attractive. She nodded her agreement.

'Fantastic! I'll sort that out and let you know when...' Sophie quickly turned heel and skipped across to the reception block, leaving Nellie clutching her carrier bag, wondering if she had enough time to leg it through the gates before Jeff took over.

A sense of unease prickled up Nellie's back before spreading its fingers across her neck, making her shiver. *That's one psycho-bitch, I'm sure...* she thought as she laughed. *Then again, it does take one to know one...*

Cry-baby!

Ralph struggled to open his eyes. The pounding pain in his head was giving rise to a wash of nausea that was slowly creeping up from his gut. His subconscious told him to move his arm so that his hand could check for the damage to his skull, but no matter how much effort he put in, it wouldn't budge. He squinted into the orange-red darkness of his surroundings.

Three Carver-style chairs.

A bench.

A selection of floor lights, and what looked like a TV camera on a tripod.

And one of Harmony Hollows old office wall dividers.

'Ah, I see you're awake, Mr Fairbright...' The disembodied voice filled the room, becoming consumed by the darkness before it echoed back from the walls to surround him.

He frantically turned his head from side to side to seek her out. 'Who are you?' he croaked, his throat raw and dry. 'What are you doing this for?' He was now fully aware that he was bound by rope to a chair so tightly he could feel the blood pulsating in his fingers. His arms had been pulled flat against the wooden arms, the rope wrapped around them, and his legs were taped to the chair. He struggled and writhed, cursing under his breath.

'Come on, woman, don't be bloody ridiculous. Untie me now or you won't know what has hit you when I get myself out of this...' he raged into the darkness.

'There's no point in fighting it, Ralphie; you won't be going anywhere. I've made sure of that.' She was behind him now; he could feel her breath on the back of his neck, chillingly close to his ear. Fear gripped at his heart.

'Please, my hands are hurting...' he begged. 'And I'm bleeding, my head is bleeding.' Ralph, all masculine bravado having deserted him, began to weep.

'Hush, hush, Ralphie, don't be such a cry-baby, how else was I going to get you here? A quick smack over the head with your precious darts trophy and a conveniently abandoned laundry cart worked a treat. Just have patience and all will be revealed – eventually...'

Sophie stepped out from the gloom and stood in front of him.

'Did Debbie Purkiss beg for her life, Ralphie?'

A low moan escaped his lips. 'You've got it all wrong. I loved her...'

'Save it for your trial, Ralphie. I've already chosen my jurors who will decide your fate. It's in their hands now.' She swept her fingers along the three remaining chairs. 'And you'll soon have company to while away the hours. It'll be nice to do a bit of reminiscing together...'

Ralph's heart missed a beat as the colour drained from his face. The reason for his current predicament was becoming clearer and clearer by each chilling minute that passed.

'Yes, Mr Fairbright – 1983 was such a good year, wasn't it?' Sophie sneered.

The thick metal door slammed loudly behind her, leaving Defendant No. 1 to his own bleak thoughts and memories.

The final part of the Perfect Storm had begun.

DO NOT DISTURB

Della Claybourne pulled her dressing gown around her and shivered. This was all she needed halfway through the championships. She tugged on the first sheet of toilet roll and watched it unravel. When she had the desired quantity of 3-ply, she tore it off and set about blowing her nose vigorously.

As a teenager, Della's mum had lectured her on what she could catch at holiday camps during the dance tours she would embark upon. They included, but were not exclusive to, bed bugs, scabies, unmentionable diseases from wayward men that her mum would only silently mouth whilst hoisting her ample bosom up to her chin with her forearms, and, of course, everyone's staple infestation as a kid: the humble nit. She checked her red shiny nose in the mirror and smiled.

'Goodness me, how times have changed! Now all I'm capable of catching is man-flu from good old Terry Tourettes...' She pulled down her bottom eyelid to check for signs of life. Satisfied she hadn't died during the night; she made the decision to update Tom and Macey with the news that she was sicker than first thought, and they would be on their own for the next day or so of the championships. They had qualified through to the quarter finals, which, considering their recent form, had been a surprise and something she was grateful for. She was in no doubt that the Wandering Waltz Dance Studio wouldn't earn any cups, medals or titles this year, so all she could do was dream of other years and opportunities to come. She popped two paracetamol from the blister pack into her hand and gulped them down with a swig of her tea. 'Thanks, Terry!' she spat sarcastically.

Terry 'Tourettes' Chapman had been a great ballroom dancer in his heyday, but the fact that his mother had probably never washed his mouth out with a bar of carbolic soap had contributed to his foul-mouthed rants, his subsequent nickname, and people's reluctance to send their kids to his dance school. She had lost count of how many parents hadn't cottoned on to the fact that the 'foxtrot oscars' he frequently shouted out wasn't actually a dance routine that they had willingly forked out six-shillings per class for him to teach their offspring.

She quickly tapped out a WhatsApp message to Tom and Macey, telling them she would be taking to her bed for a day or two longer and not to bother her. She had a good book she had been promising herself to binge-read for ages, and a bottle of Lucozade that had been kindly left for her on the bedside cabinet. She poured a glass of the orange fizz and took a sip. She was surprised at how quickly her childhood memories rushed at her with one taste; it had been her mum's go-to every time she had been ill.

She checked the fridge for supplies. Plenty of milk, half a loaf of wholemeal bread, margarine and enough boxes of Cup a Soup in the wardrobe to feed the five thousand and two bags of cheesy Wotsits. Years of dieting had conditioned her body to expect and accept less. Satisfied she would survive the next forty-eight hours, she plumped up the pillows on her bed and arranged her book and nibbles on the bedside cabinet before pouring herself another glass of Lucozade.

As she turned to lock the chalet door, she became light-headed, her vision suddenly blurred and her body heavy and ungainly. She slumped down onto the bed and touched her forehead. The rapid onset confused her. 'I must be worse than I thought...' She took a deep breath, hoping that would balance her, but a buzzing sound began to ring in her ears, bringing with it a weird brain fog and pins and needles to the tips of her fingers. Della shook her head to rid herself of the feeling of detachment, but only succeeded in making herself dizzier.

She tried to stand up, but instead slid from the bed onto the floor as the darkness began to descend over her just like a curtain slowly coming down on a performance.

Within seconds, Della was out cold.

The large metal laundry cage squeaked and rattled its way along the paths of Daffodil Lawns, occasionally drifting to one side when the wheels flattened an unlucky flower or two. Sophie, wearing a borrowed cleaner's tabard and a baseball cap, confidently strode through Harmony Hollows, her precious cargo neatly ensconced in a canvas drawstring bed linen bag positioned at the bottom.

It couldn't be a more perfect cover to move a body. Who would ever suspect a lowly cleaner and a pile of dirty laundry? She wanted to giggle, but had to settle for a slight smirk of satisfaction lest she should be spotted 'enjoying' her work – which around this place would be a definite giveaway.

She had left a rather convincing outline in Della Claybourne's bed created from a couple of pillows, and a 'Do

Not Disturb' sign on her chalet door. That would give her plenty of time to deposit Della in the chair next to Ralph, bring her round from the fast-acting concoction she had cleverly added to the Lucozade she had left for her after overhearing from Della's protégés that she was confined to barracks with flu, and then finally give her the same welcoming speech she had given him.

It was all so perfect and was coming together nicely, just as she had planned. Apart from Maggie Henshaw. Sophie had dropped the idea of making Maggie her number four. She didn't have anything to go on, so maybe Maggie didn't have a story after all, she'd just simply been in the wrong place at the wrong time and consequently didn't deserve a role in her production. There was also something that wasn't quite right about her, not in the sense that she could be a danger to her, but as though there should be an affinity between them. It unsettled her. It made her feel like a child again, the fake warmth and then the betrayal. Back then she had been a commodity, one that had been brutally discarded when no longer required.

The hurt and the anger bubbled up beneath her calm exterior. She savagely pushed them down, buried them as deep as she could. She would need those emotions later and didn't want to waste them on a memory.

'Now is not the time, Sophie...' she whispered as she veered the laundry cage behind the chalets that led to Marigold Lawns. She would worry about Maggie later, for now, she had another fish to fry.

An overheard conversation had provided a new and previously unknown player into the game that had taken precedent over Ms Henshaw. Knowing what she had in store for the occupants of her four chairs, Sophie was pretty confident that under the circumstances, Maggie would not be in the least bit perturbed to have lost her seat to another.

FINAL DESTINATION

Kitty dropped her glasses to the end of her nose and closed the book she had been reading. The library edition of *Little Women* had done nothing to cheer her mood. Each time she thought of her tipsy outburst in the Marina Lounge, her cheeks burned with embarrassment.

Kitty Hardcastle never, ever let her guard down. She had always upheld an air of elegance and superiority, until that fateful evening when she had indulged in one gin too many, and with one slip of the tongue had publicly aired her dirty laundry – and in the process, had tarnished her long-held reputation. A reputation she wanted to believe was chaste – just so long as everyone else didn't count Frank as a saucy blemish on her moral character.

She padded over to the kettle that was sitting forlornly on the melamine table with a single mug holding a teabag, her bare feet making no sound. She flicked the switch and stood admiring the brilliant red of the 'Thrill of Brazil' OPI varnish on her toenails. She had envisaged her feet, encased in her gold sandals, gracing the dance floor of Harmony Hollows with Frank's arm held tightly around her waist. Instead she was now holed up in her chalet with only Louisa May Alcott, two stale digestive biscuits, and a packet of paracetamol for company, too ashamed to face anyone, let alone Frank.

The fact that her many years of indiscretion with Frank was common knowledge amongst her WI friends was beside the point, Kitty was now a social piranha. That thought made her laugh; it was something Hilda would say. She mentally corrected herself to being a pariah instead, not that it made her feel any better about herself.

The kettle had failed to make even the slightest hint that it was boiling. She tested the side of the metal with her finger, pulled out the lead, pushed it back in again, flicked the switch off and then on again.

Nothing.

Irritated, she yanked the plug out of the wall socket. If she couldn't have a cup of tea, she would have something a little more enjoyable instead. She grabbed the Hendrick's gin bottle from her wardrobe and shook it. The liquid sloshed invitingly inside. She unscrewed the top and sniffed, taking in the earthy, citrus-sweet odour. Decision made; she grabbed the already opened bottle of tonic from the mini fridge. The hiss as she turned the metal cap told her that it still had enough fizz to make a decent G&T. She made good measures of each in the glass beaker, adjusted her pillow, slipped between the sheets and embraced Louisa May once again.

As far as Kitty was concerned, she was being held up as an example of debauchery and licentious behaviour by her friends, so she might as well go the full hog and give them something else to talk about by taking to her bed with a large tumbler of mother's ruin in the middle of the afternoon.

Barely two chapters in, Kitty's eyes had become heavier and heavier, the lines on each page wavering in and out of focus. She edged herself up from her pillow and gulped down the last of the gin, setting the glass back with a rattle onto her bedside cabinet. She lay back on her pillow and closed her eyes, not relishing the bout of 'the spins' she was now experiencing. She tried to measure her breathing, but the nausea still swept over her.

Sleep. That was what she needed, a little nap.

It wasn't long before she had slipped into a deep, unnatural slumber. A slumber that was not facilitated by tiredness or gin, but by a special mix that had been added to the tonic water by unseen hands.

'Housekeeping...' the voice announced as Kitty's chalet door was suddenly opened. The baseball capped figure crept into the room and looked down on the comatose Kitty, just as a mother would on a sleeping child. 'Sweet dreams, Miss Hardcastle,' Sophie muttered under her breath.

She popped her head out of the doorway and checked the coast was clear. She pulled on the handle of the laundry cage, positioning it over the threshold ready to accept its latest cargo. She dragged Kitty from her bed and threw her onto the edge of the drop down side of the cage, leaving her slumped and folded in half like a rag doll, her head dangling in the mass of sheets and towels. She momentarily admired her uncomfortable position, before grabbing her legs and tossing her over into the depths of Harmony Hollows dirty laundry to accompany Della Claybourne.

'How ironic that you should air yours before ending up in mine...' Sophie giggled as she quickly covered her up with a blanket. Shutting the door to Chalet 19 behind her, she navigated the twists and turns of Marigold Lawns, the squeak and rattle of the laundry cage once again eerily echoing along the paths as it transported her two victims to their final destination.

IT'S A MYSTERY

'I take it this was Ralph's idea, then?' Mark adjusted the large pull-down screen on the stage and checked it was clipped safely into place with no movement.

Maggie shrugged. 'No idea, I'm assuming so, as nobody else here has admitted to having anything to do with it; we were just given the briefing sheets with what needs doing before tonight.' She pulled the bingo drum to one side and slipped the cover over the top. She was grateful that she wouldn't have to spin the bloody thing and juggle balls, if only for one night.

'Is he back from his jaunt, yet? It's a bloody cheek arranging something huge like this, and then expecting us to pull our fingers out and do it all when he's buggered off somewhere nice.' Mark jogged across the dance floor to his tech booth to set up the live-stream and audio.

'Nope. Nobody has seen sight nor sign of him. When you've finished that, can you give me a hand with this? Apparently, we have a real-life jury of four that needs a sort of *Britain's Got Talent* judge's desk.' Maggie rolled her eyes and grinned as she pushed two tables together on the dance floor.

'What's the format, then?' Up until now, Mark had been

concerned only in setting up his side of the job, but this had piqued his interest.

Maggie held out her hands. 'I've just got the basic details. It's a sort of murder mystery; they've got suspects for a murder, who I think are played by actors. It's being filmed somewhere else and live-streamed. Four people will act as jury here. They'll be given the background on each suspect, and from that they have to decide who is guilty of the crime with a bit of audience participation.'

'Couldn't they have just done it here on the stage? Surely that would have been more fun, like a proper play. I've seen it being done at those mystery weekend dinners – lots of hotels do them.' Mark angled the mic. 'Testing, testing, one, two, three...'

'Maybe it's not just us it's being streamed to; it could be in all the Clampitt & Shoehorn resorts. To have them appear individually at all the camps would probably be too expensive, but that's just a guess.' Maggie knew how careful the directors of C&S could be, and she couldn't see them forking out more than they needed to if they could help it.

She wasn't entirely convinced it had been one of Ralph's better ideas, particularly in light of recent events at Harmony Hollows, but who was she to argue the toss? She delved into the large black bin bag that had been left for her and pulled out little notepads with tiny pencils attached. 'Nellie, can you give us a hand with this, please?' She glanced over to the bar area where she had last spotted Nellie Girdlestone replacing the drip mats and giving the floor a last once over with the mop. There was no sign of her. 'Blimey, that ruddy woman could give Lord Lucan a run for his money; she's forever disappearing at the drop of a hat.' Miffed that yet another task was being left to her, she began to chuck the notebooks randomly on the tables.

'Right, I'm done. If there's nothing more you need, Mags, I'll see you tonight at 8pm...' Mark gave her a friendly pat on the back before disappearing through the stage exit door.

Left alone with her bin bag and instruction sheet, Maggie shivered, a feeling of being watched had crept over her. She quickly looked around the lounge, taking in dark corners, curved booths and the stage, searching for anyone who might still be in the room with her, but knew it was a pointless exercise. There were far too many hiding places for her to be able to see someone if he or she chose to dip out of sight and hide. She quickly finished throwing the notebooks on the tables, pushed four chairs in front of her makeshift BGT desk, and as fast as her bad leg would carry her, disappeared through the same door that Mark had left.

FOUR DAYS…

Harmony Hollows was a hive of excitement as the 'Murder Mystery – Trial by Jury' posters, sporting a silhouetted outline of Sherlock Holmes, began appearing around the resort. Some took the opportunity to have a moan about the bingo being cancelled, but all in all the majority of holidaymakers couldn't wait for something a little different.

Pru and Bree watched the Winterbottom WI members chattering and gossiping outside the Marina Lounge, planning their early attendance that evening to ensure they got the best seats.

'I think they've all had enough of bingo and ballroom, judging by the anticipation for tonight, don't you?' Bree carefully licked around the bottom of her ice-cream cone, the double choc chip threatening to drip onto her jeans.

Pru nodded. 'From what I can gather, the tippy-toes lot are having a day off, so no doubt they'll be there tonight too. I do feel a bit uncomfortable with Harmony Hollows staging this after what's happened, and I must admit I've been wondering what Ezra thinks, particularly if they ran it past him first.'

With a mouthful of ice cream, Bree could only offer a grunt of acknowledgement.

'I tell you what has surprised me, though: the girls! I saw Clarissa and the gang this morning, and even though they knew about tonight, they seemed to be very cool about it.' Pru licked the strawberry syrup from the side of her hand. 'You know what they're like. I'd have thought they would have been bouncing all over the place, with at least Hilda prepping for some note-taking.' She giggled, and then felt a little mean.

They both sat in silence enjoying the sunshine and the remnants of their cones, watching the comings and goings of their fellow holidaymakers.

'We haven't done very well this time, have we?' Pru mused.

Bree adjusted her sunglasses and angled her face to the sky, a wry smile playing on her lips. 'With what? Winning the knobbly-knees competition?'

'Our murder investigations! In fact, we've been pretty shit at it. I've been thinking about it. We're none the wiser on the 1983 murders, apart from the fact we now know that Kitty was there at the time getting up to mischief, and potentially could have been involved somehow...' Pru popped the tiny end of the cone into her mouth. 'And on the recent ones, all we've got are bingo numbers in the notebook of a woman who has ruddy Alzheimer's!'

'Aww, she's not that bad!'

'Who? Surely you don't mean Kitty?!' Surprised that Bree would defend her, Pru playfully punched her on the arm. 'Traitor!'

'No, I meant Hilda. Let's face it, Pru, we've either lost our touch, or old age is making us more sensible and less likely to put ourselves in the firing line.'

Pru was inclined to agree. Each time a burst of inquisitiveness had come over her, her sensible head had advised otherwise, and she had a feeling Bree felt pretty much the same. She supposed that was why tonight seemed odd because of the circumstances, whilst at the same time being exciting too, as it was right up their street. On the other hand, was she really ready to give up so easily?

'Right, tell you what. Why don't we go and find Kitty, see if we can probe her for any info on the double murder. I know I said we'd leave that one for Clarissa and the girls, but I'm inclined to swerve the recent ones, not least because Ezra knows Andy, and I really don't need earache from him.' Before Bree could agree, she was up on her feet, striding out towards Marigold Lawns and Chalet 19.

They still had another four days at Harmony Hollows, four days in which any one of them could become the next victim.

Like a clock counting down the seconds, the heart of Harmony Hollows began to beat a steady rhythm once again, as the winds of chance and misfortune changed direction.

Time was running out – but for whom...?

How do I look?' Ethel twirled around the chalet in her Sunday best. The hem of the emerald green ditsy floral print dress undulated as she spun.

Clarissa, her eyes twinkling with delight, adjusted the shoulder pads on her cream jacket. 'Gorgeous, absolutely gorgeous. Now, what have you decided to wear, Hilda?' She held up a navy-blue shift dress that she had chosen from her own wardrobe, and tenderly tucked it under Hilda's chin. 'I think this would look lovely on you; it really brings out the colour of your eyes.'

Ethel started to laugh. 'They're pink 'Rissa, from the sherry she's been knocking back the last two days!'

Her gentle teasing was taken as it was intended, in good fun. The Four Wrinkled Dears giggled together, drank a little more sherry than they ought to, and dressed and undressed themselves in various outfits, giving marks out of ten, ready for their star appearance.

'This takes me back. It's just like when we were teenagers and we needed to get ready together for the disco nights at the village hall.' Ethel refilled their glasses from a very special bottle of 19 Crimes Cabernet Sauvignon she had brought with her from home. It had been a bottle that Albert had purchased for her from the Guilty Grape off-licence, and after he had gone she had promised herself not to drink it alone. Now had seemed the perfect time to share it with her friends. Her eyes suddenly pricked with tears at his memory. She held her glass up. 'To my Albie...' she whispered.

Her friends held their glasses high to toast the love of Ethel's life. 'To Albie!' they chorused in unison. Millie placed her arm around Ethel's shoulders and hugged her tight.

Clarissa could only imagine the heartbreak Ethel was feeling. The saying that it was better to have loved and lost than not loved at all, didn't really sit well with her. She had never been in love; she had never shared her life with anyone; and therefore would be incapable of feeling loss and heartbreak. And that was just the way she liked it. She sat down on the bed and looked at her friends laughing together, supporting each other, and just simply being there, as Millie gently wiped the tears from Ethel's cheek with a tissue.

Then she suddenly understood.

Oh what a fool I have been... she thought and sighed. *I have loved and shared my life, and I've done so without even realising it.*

LIGHTS, CAMERA...

The promise of a nice bottle of red, a place to puff away on her ciggies to her hearts content without getting caught, and the chance to put her feet up and sift through old photos had been the clincher for Nellie. She had slopped her mop around the floor behind the bar in the Marina Lounge a couple of times to make it look like she had actually done the job she was paid to do, before ditching the mop, bucket and her overall behind the beer pumps.

When she had received Sophie's call to arms, she had been a little undecided at first. She had planned a little excitement for herself that evening, but the news that the Bingo Bonanza Night had been cancelled, which meant she could no longer indulge in her favourite pastime, had given her the opportunity to take Sophie up on her invite. She'd grant her an hour or two of her expertise and then make her way back to the Marina Lounge in time for the Murder Mystery Night. Wild horses wouldn't keep her away from something as deliciously dark as a murder trial.

She ambled along the paths on Bluebell Lawns, into Cornflower and finally through the little entry that led to the old disused fairground. She cut through the 'Keep Out' fence that had been bent back, no doubt by curious kids who belonged to holidaymakers who spent more time playing bingo than keeping tabs on their little ankle-biters. Nellie paused by the waltzers; the once colourful sign of reds, yellows and blues that announced *Dante's Whirling Waltzers* was now more muted shades of brown and orange from the rust that had eaten into the metal. The cars, long since abandoned, displayed their torn and ravaged seats that were home to flora and fauna. The young carefree Nell Collins of yesteryear would no doubt have held in awe Dante's whirligig and its memories, but the Nellie Girdlestone of today wouldn't entertain such ridiculous sentimental hogwash.

Life was neither considerate nor kind as far as she was concerned. It didn't gift love and contentment, and it certainly didn't grant wishes. Nellie had learnt that the hard way.

Shaking off a sudden wash of melancholy, she skirted the Roll-a-Derby and edged her way through the gate that had been torn from its top hinges by elements that had battered it relentlessly over the years. It hung lopsidedly, granting a gap wide enough for her to squeeze through.

She wondered if Sophie was as much an outcast as she was, considering where management had put her. There were so many other available spaces she could have been housed in rather than a dilapidated building on the outskirts of the resort in an area that nobody ever went to any more. Well, not since the old fairground had been condemned and a new one constructed next to the lido.

'Ah there you are. I was beginning to think you'd changed your mind.' Sophie was relieved to see Nellie. Her attendance was paramount to her plans. 'Here you go, this way...' She held open the door to her lair.

Totally oblivious to the danger she was in, Nellie duly followed her through the threshold. 'I hope you've got something decent to drink, I don't like white wine, by the way, I did make it clear it had to be red,' she grumbled. 'And I haven't got long; I want to see this murder mystery thing at the Marina Lounge…'

Sophie ushered Nellie ahead of her. 'Oh don't worry, Nellie, you won't miss a thing. In fact, you're going to be the star of the show…'

Nellie didn't know what had hit her. It was so sudden. A searing pain at the back of her head followed by a blinding flash of light behind her eyes knocked her sideways. She slumped against the brick wall, her right shoulder taking the brunt of the fall. She slid to the floor, her cheek crushed against the concrete, the smell of engine oil and damp permeating her nostrils as her consciousness deserted her.

Sophie leant in and clicked her fingers in front of Nellie to gauge her awareness. Knowing what Nellie was capable of, she certainly didn't want to take any chances. She'd seen daintier tighthead props than Nellie in a game of rugby. Satisfied she would offer no resistance; she grabbed her ankles and began to drag her down the long corridor. Nellie's jumper rucked at the back with the momentum, so her bare skin scraped on the rough floor as her head rolled and swept from side to side. Flinging open the second door, she pulled Nellie into the room and slammed the door behind her.

Three of her four chairs were already occupied.

Ralph Fairbright, Della Claybourne and Kitty Hardcastle sat confused, scared and restrained. They watched Sophie haul Nellie onto the fourth chair and with a strength and dexterity that evidenced her familiarity with the routine, she tied and gagged Nellie too.

'Well, isn't this nice! All of you back together again. How many years has it been?' Sophie tapped her chin with her index finger, pretending to ponder the decades. 'Oh yes, it's exactly forty years ago tonight. 23rd May 1983, to be exact. Now, how spooky is that?'

She relished the look of horror on the faces of her captive audience. Their eyes darting backwards and forwards, seeking each other out. Nellie gave a low moan as she began to regain consciousness, a bit earlier than Sophie had planned, but other than giving her another smack across the back of her head with the shiny red aluminium baseball bat she had purchased specifically for the occasion, she would just have to go with the flow.

Sophie held up a document and one by one they were made to read it. 'Is the penny dropping now?' She waited. 'No? In that case I won't spoil the surprise...' She checked her watch and adjusted the camera angle. 'Right, are we ready, folks? Lights...' She flicked a switch. The harsh white that flashed from the LED's was savage on their eyes. She laughed as they attempted to shy away. 'Give it a few minutes; you'll get used to it.

'Camera...'

Sophie steadied herself and took a deep breath.

A LETHAL COMBINATION

Lucy got out of the car and brushed the crumbs deposited on her trousers by a bag of crisps and a packet of cookies. Pushed for time and not wanting to stop for refreshments, she and Andy had devoured the snacks during the journey to Serena Porter's home in Shevington Bush.

Andy pointed to a row of neat cottages, each one displaying a vibrant show of nasturtiums in Paintbox Mixed, hanging from baskets and window boxes. He wondered if it was coincidence and the neighbours just liked the same colours and flowers, or if it was a village rule they adhered to. Either way, it was very 'chocolate box' pretty. Lucy seemed to be less impressed, paying more attention to a splodge of melted chocolate on the inside of her trouser leg.

'Here we go, *Daisy Dell...*' Andy pointed to the white gate that bore a wooden nameplate. He carefully made his way up the short path, taking care not to tread on any of the flowers that softened the edges and draped over the crazy paving, Lucy followed, mimicking his dainty steps. The black rustic fox-head door knocker thudded under his touch, striking the receiver plate three times. The door was quickly answered by an elegant woman dressed in black leggings and a white hooded sweatshirt; her auburn hair tied loosely in a pony tail.

'Ms Porter? I'm DS Andrew Barnes, seconded to Little Kipling CID.' He held up his warrant card. 'This is my colleague, DC Lucy Harris. I'm hoping you will be able to help us with an ongoing murder investigation. We are urgently trying to locate Elodie Marshall, the daughter of Clare and Richard Mayer-Marshall, who we believe you know something about.' The look on Serena Porter's face as the colour slowly drained from her skin, leaving a waxy pallor, gave Andy hope that she wouldn't be an obstructive witness.

She swallowed hard and instinctively chewed at her bottom lip to the point of drawing blood. Her tongue darted out and quickly licked it away as she drew in a deep intake of breath.

'I know what you're here for; you'd better come in.'

They sat down at the dining table with Serena, her hands visibly shaking as her fingers plucked at the drawstring to her hoodie. Andy indicated for Lucy, her file spread out in front of her, to take the lead.

'Serena, we've spoken to Judy Moore at Middle Cow Creatives...' Lucy paused, waiting for a reaction. Serena's sharp intake of breath was enough. 'We know, Serena. Judy has told us what happened, but it would be so much better in your own words.'

They sat in silence, the *tick-tock-tick-tock* from an antique Fusee mantel clock was strangely hypnotic. A solitary tear trickled down Serena's cheek, which she made no effort to acknowledge. 'She was my friend, I just wanted to help. There was nothing in it for me. When Debs died, I just liaised between her mum, Martha, and the Meyer-Marshalls. I swear to God I didn't take a penny – that was their arrangement. I just did the introduction when Martha asked me to find someone.' The tears fell more freely as she allowed her secret to unfold. 'I just thought the baby would be so much better off with them. They had money, status, everything that the baby could possibly have wanted or needed.' She buried her face in her hands and wept.

'I was so, so wrong...'

Andy and Lucy exchanged glances. Andy gave a barely perceptible nod, indicating he wanted her to continue, she had made a connection with Serena. Lucy reached across the table and placed a reassuring hand on her arm. 'We need to know Elodie's real name, Serena. It might have a bearing on our investigation and how we can find her – and her mum too, your friend Debs. We need to know about her, how she died. Was it an accident or illness?'

Serena's sad eyes met Lucy's. Her bottom lip quivered as she fought to find the words. 'That's the thing, you see, she was murdered – and her killer was never caught...'

Andy flung his file onto the desk and began to bark out orders to his team. Lucy followed in his wake.

'I want everything you can get me on the 1983 double murder at Harmony Hollows Resort. The victims were a Deborah Anne Purkiss and Lawrence Peter Belfont...' He beckoned Lucy to take a seat. 'Luce, can you do the searches on the aliases that Serena thought Elodie might use and see if anything comes back. Don't forget to mix and match them too; it's not a given that she would automatically use a first name and surname in that combination. See if anything comes back, and let me know immediately if you get a hit.'

Lucy's fingers began to tap over the keyboard. 'I'll update the DI and ensure this is kept in-house for the moment; the last thing we need is the press getting a whiff.' Her index finger tapped the mouse, opening another screen. 'Do you think she's still alive, Sarge?'

Andy, his lips set thin in concentration, nodded. 'I have no doubt whatsoever that she is, and after Serena's insight into her troubled mind, she is definitely our number one suspect for Gertrude and Agatha Timpson, too.'

Things were starting to move in what Andy hoped was the right direction. A good feeling of tension began to form in his chest, the type that combined excitement, anticipation and a sense of relief that this investigation was beginning to get a break. He inhaled deeply and exhaled in a slow, long measured breath, a feeling of dread washing over him.

Harmony Hollows, a double murder and Pru with her 1983 press clipping in the Dog & Gun. And now he had two Agatha Raisins and a quartet of Miss Marples currently doing a knees-up at Nettleton Shrub's budget version of Butlins – the scene of the original crime.

He closed his eyes and sighed.

What a bloody lethal combination.

SURPRISE, SURPRISE

'Come on, budge up a bit...' Brenda used her ample curves that had expanded by at least another two inches since indulging in Harmony Hollows' all-you-can-eat breakfasts, to push Miriam along the velour-covered booth seat in the Marina Lounge.

Miriam swung her handbag and caught a glancing blow to the side of Florrie Patterson's head. 'Sorry, dear, that was meant for Brenda...' She chuckled. Florrie made an exaggerated show of rearranging her carefully coiffured hairdo whilst giving Brenda a headmistress-style glare.

'You can glower at me all you want, Florrie Patterson; I need more than ten centimetres on the end of the seat to park my arse. This booth is supposed to accommodate six, not just you and fatso here...' She animatedly pointed at Miriam.

Pru, hearing the commotion, rushed over from her table. She was aghast at the change in Brenda who had always been so cuddly, warm and inoffensive. She didn't know if it was the atmosphere at Harmony Hollows that was bringing out the worst in some of her ladies, or that they had been holed up for too long together in the same place. 'Come on, girls, we're on holiday; let's be happy,' she gushed, and then just as quickly wished she hadn't sounded like an extra from *Hi-De-Hi*. 'This isn't like you, Brenda, and it's not nice to comment on someone else's appearance; it can come across as mean.'

Suitably chastised, Brenda turned up her nose in an air of superiority and settled herself comfortably into the booth with her Campari and soda.

The Marina Lounge was full to bursting. Every single available seat was taken, every booth filled to capacity, and some extra chairs had been brought in from the restaurant. The heavy stage curtains were pulled back to reveal a large screen and two floor-to-ceiling speakers had been placed either side of it in front of the wings.

Bree moved her jacket from the seat so that Pru could sit next to her. They had arrived early and had bagged one of the best tables at the front. 'I haven't seen Clarissa and the gang yet, have you?'

Pru did a meerkat impression, stretching her neck to check the tables that the WI ladies had used every night since they had arrived. 'No, not yet. They'd better be quick, though; I don't think there are many places left to sit.' She took a sip of her drink and grabbed a handful of crisps from the open bag on the table. 'I suppose there's one good thing to come out of tonight; at least there won't be a last bingo number called, so we can all sleep soundly in our beds...'

She actually thought it was quite ironic to hope for anything that remotely resembled a 'sound sleep', considering they were all about to watch a murder mystery which, even poorly acted like the one they had endured at the Montgomery Hall Hotel, would still give everyone the heebie-jeebies. She had visions of Millie and Hilda nipping into Clarissa and Ethel's beds for the night as a means of reassurance and protection should the need arise. Pru was still amazed she had managed to cajole Millie into remaining in Chalet 13. Hilda wasn't bothered in the slightest, but Millie was another kettle of fish.

'Still no show for Kitty either. I know she's taken it badly, but I am getting a bit worried about her to be honest.' Pru shook the crisp bag, disappointed it was empty. 'I just can't understand why she didn't answer the door to us, and don't say she might not have heard us over the radio, I knocked really loud three times – and she's ignoring calls and texts, too.'

Keen not to worry Pru any more than she already was, Bree gave her a reassuring hug. 'We'll knock again in the morning, and if we don't get a reply, maybe we should speak to housekeeping; they're bound to have a master key. We'll just say she's ill and it's an emergency.'

They sat quietly for a few moments.

'Oh God, what if she's been another victim of the murderer and she's lying dead in there?' Pru felt sick.

'Don't be daft. Look, Brenda swore she saw her looking out of her chalet window this morning. She's just embarrassed; she'll get over it – eventually.'

A slow handclap that began to quicken its pace, interrupted them. Maggie was making her way through the tables towards the dance floor, and it seemed that the applause being offered was for whoever was walking behind her. Pru stood up to have a better look.

'It must be the jury...' Bree nodded towards a table draped in a black cloth. Four glasses and two jugs of water had been laid out, along with a set of cards placed face down.

The applause grew louder the closer Maggie got to the stage. 'Ladies and gentlemen, may I present to you our jury for the night...' She held out her arm to encompass the room before sweeping her hand towards the four figures that jauntily stepped out into the spotlight.

'Oh God, kill me now...' Pru exclaimed loudly. 'How the hell did we miss this?' She turned to Bree for confirmation of their ignorance.

Bree tried to stifle her laughter. 'Jeez, I wouldn't let those four loose to give a verdict on Brenda's bunions!'

The Four Wrinkled Dears stood in line and took a bow to the audience, clearly relishing their moment of stardom. Maggie, microphone in hand, moved in to do a brief introduction. 'How are we feeling, ladies? Are you ready to take up your roles as our jury panel?' Excited chatter filled the Marina Lounge, the audience keen for the proceedings to start. Maggie tipped the microphone towards Hilda, making her bristle with importance.

'We're very excited, me especially, I loved Bendabit Crumblebatch in Sherlock Holmes. Do you think he'll give me his autograph on this?' Hilda rummaged around in her handbag, looking for the Holmes poster she had sneakily purloined from reception.

Clarissa quickly intervened. 'He'll have a hard job, Hilda my dear. He's currently in Australia filming.'

'How very dare he, I do hope he's taking good care of his didgeridoo whilst he's there!' Hilda, in a moment of sharp wit, played up to the audience, their laughter filling the room. 'Well, there's no time to waste, then. The game is afoot!'

Maggie looked to the lighting and tech box, waiting for Mark's thumbs-up, as she quickly ushered them to their chairs. 'Ladies, if you'd like to take your seats at the jury table, I think we're about to go to the live link.'

The show was about to begin...

THE TRIAL

The red recording light flashed its sequence, giving Sophie time for her countdown. She had dressed well for the occasion, returning to her natural look. Gone was the over-the-top vibrant make-up, to be replaced with just a touch of peach sherbet blusher and a slick of lip-gloss. Her hair loosely tumbled over her shoulders and the navy-blue suit she had chosen for the occasion fitted her to perfection.

She wanted them to know who she really was.

'Right, no last-minute nerves I hope?' She menacingly addressed her captives. 'Just remember, this is your chance to shine, your opportunity to tell the truth.' She focused her attention on the camera for a second or two, and then quickly rounded on them. 'This has been forty years in the making – you *owe* me this!' She checked her notes. They had taken her years to compile, so many questions asked, some answered, but many left without resolution. She had built a picture for each and every one of them from newspaper cuttings, people who had known them in the day, her secret acquisition, and her own gut feeling. She had a script for each of them.

The red camera light became static.

Sophie inhaled deeply.

'Action...'

Her darkly menacing demeanour immediately changed: it lightened. Her voice became softer, almost lyrical in a strange sing-song way.

'Ladies and gentlemen of Harmony Hollows, and my ladies of the jury, I am Sophie Hopkins. You may know me as the resort photographer, but I am also a cold-case researcher. Exactly forty years ago tonight, May 23rd 1983, the most heinous of crimes took place here.' She leant into the camera, pausing for dramatic effect, her eyes popped and her lips pursed in anticipation.

'Murder!'

Sophie pointed to the wall divider that had become a makeshift murder board, strategically positioned behind her, so that it was masking her captives from the audience. Two grainy photographs had been pinned dead centre. 'Debbie Purkiss and Larry Belfont had their young lives savagely taken from them in Chalet 13 Marigold Lawns by an unknown assailant...' She looked directly into the camera again. 'And tonight, we are going to solve the crime that baffled a nation. One, or maybe all of them, are responsible. It is up to you, the jury, after hearing the evidence, to decide...' Sophie slid back the wall divider. 'Ladies and gentlemen, I give you the suspects in the Purkiss-Belfont murder trial. Let justice begin...'

An audible gasp of anticipation came from the audience in the Marina Lounge as the camera angle projected images of Ralph, Nellie, Della and Kitty onto the big screen, trussed to their chairs by thick rope, each with a gag tightly tied around their mouths.

Clarissa, Millie, Hilda and Ethel had their pencils and

notepads at the ready, totally oblivious to the audience's excited reaction. Hilda stuck her tongue out from the corner of her mouth in concentration. 'How clever, they've got people from here to act in it. They must have invited Kitty like they did with us.' She licked the end of her pencil and wrote *'one or more murderers'* as a crib note.

Pru gripped Bree's arm. 'It's Kitty...' She sat puzzled, aware that Clarissa and the girls had fooled her by turning up as the jury, so would it be so off the wall to think that Kitty had done the same? Were they all in on it?

'Bloody cheapskates! They've roped in half of our WI to star in it!' Bree was not impressed. 'This is going to pan out worse than Montgomery Hall. I mean come on, Kitty to acting is like Hilda would be to *Mastermind*!'

Pru frowned, deep in thought. 'After what she confessed to the other day, there's no way in the world she would have volunteered for this –and why are they tied up and gagged? That doesn't make sense. If it's supposed to be a trial, they'd just be normal, sitting in a pretend dock or something.' Pru studied Kitty's eyes as the camera lingered on her. They were bloodshot and teary; her pupils were huge, almost masking their true colour, a clear sign of fear, something that couldn't be faked as they darted from side to side. The uneasy feeling she had in her stomach suddenly became a bubbling turmoil of impending doom that made her feel sick as the realisation hit her. Kitty's eyes were begging her to do something.

Grabbing her bag, Pru stood up quickly, knocking her drink over. 'This isn't bloody acting, this is real...'

THE KNOWING

Let justice begin...

Maggie's heart missed a beat. She stood rigid to the spot staring at the screen as Sophie Marshall, the resort photographer, gave a simpering smile to the audience. Her face, now huge as the camera zoomed in, beaming her out across the room.

Let justice begin...

The tendrils were there, just floating and plucking at her mind, little fingers tapping into her memory. She had the most awful feeling in the pit of her stomach, a feeling she hadn't experienced for many years. It was fear, not just for herself, but for Ralph, Nellie, Della and the other woman too. There was something very, very wrong with what was going on at Harmony Hollows. The chilling tale that was being depicted on screen was clearly still being viewed by the audience as harmless entertainment. She listened to them laughing and chattering away, already making notes on who they thought would be guilty, based just on their appearances alone.

Let justice begin...

Since the day they had first chatted to each other at Bluebell

Lawns, she had felt there was something very familiar about Sophie, something she couldn't quite put her finger on. She studied the screen as the camera focused on each of the alleged suspects in turn. She knew Ralph had been at Harmony in 1983, and she'd heard talk that Nellie had worked the bar in the very lounge she was now standing in, during that season. She studied Della Claybourne. She was part of the dance gang in 1983, not that she had much to do with her at the time, but she knew she had been one of Larry's conquests. Kitty she knew very little about, apart from being one of the Women's Institute ladies.

Let justice begin...

She mouthed the three words that were invading her thoughts, worming their way into her memories. 'Let justice begin...' she whispered. The intonation, the accent that Sophie had used, it was all so familiar, as was the feeling of dread. She saw Pru suddenly startle and jump up from her table knocking a drink over. The glass rolled across the table, momentarily stilled at the edge and then dropped down, smashing loudly on the floor.

And at that moment, Maggie knew.

DEFENDANT NUMBER 1

RALPH

'Welcome back, ladies and gentlemen. Are you all sitting comfortably? Shall we begin?' Sophie tipped her head and held her hand to her ear, pretending to listen for their response as the camera once again brought her face into focus. 'Excellent...' She made herself comfortable in a chair next to Ralph.

'Ladies of the jury, I give you Ralph Desmond Fairbright. Now our Ralphie here worked the waltzers in 1983, and this is his story...' She began to read from her prepared statement.

'Ralph Fairbright didn't just jump the cars on Dante's Whirling Waltzers in 1983; Ralph Fairbright also liked to jump the young ladies who spent their summer holidays at Harmony Hollows.'

Sophie utilised her fingers as air quotes, turned, and with a look of disgust, smacked Ralph over the back of his head with the palm of her hand. Ralph's head snapped forward and quickly jerked back again. The ultimate in humiliation.

'Sadly he wasn't always successful, losing out to another camp Lothario – our very own Larry Belfont.'

She wagged a finger at him, pleased to see that her little

game was having an impact on him and he was beginning to cry. 'There, there, Ralphie, don't be such a cry-baby...

'During that season, Ralph became infatuated with one of the dancers, Debbie Purkiss. Debbie was at Harmony Hollows to have fun, to be carefree for just a very short time. She wasn't looking for love, or commitment, she just wanted to be free of responsibility. Not too much to ask, really. But poor Debbie was preyed upon by Ralph and Larry with their lustful intentions, although Ralphie here will have you, the jury, believe he was in love with her.'

She leant in close to Ralph; she could smell the fear on him. 'Did you really love her, or is that another one of your lies?'

Ralph frantically nodded as though his life depended on the right answer. Sweat slowly trickled down his face, to be absorbed by the cotton gag that pulled at his cheeks.

'Hard to answer with your mouth full, isn't it?' She cackled, the madness within her getting stronger.

'On that fateful night Ralph made advances to Debbie and was rejected. After the fairground had closed, and after downing a few snifters of whisky, his favourite tipple, he followed Debbie back to her chalet, but she was not alone. She was accompanied by Larry – he had won the prize. Can you imagine, as a woman, being referred to as a prize? *Well that's what she was to these two. She was Larry's prize, and Ralph here was most put out. So, with jealousy eating away at him, Ralph desperately tried to think of a way to stop their liaison – and the only way he could do that was by...'*

Sophie's face again became the focus of the camera; her eyes became as big as saucers.

'Murder!'

I KNOW WHO YOU ARE

Pru was frantic; she had paused by the doors to the Marina Lounge to listen to the first part of the alleged Murder Mystery Night, and once Sophie had finished, she was under no illusion that this whole set up was real. It wasn't a play, it wasn't entertainment, and it most certainly wasn't make-believe.

The script was real, the players were real, and she had a strong feeling that the outcome would be horrific.

She pushed the doors open, the laughter and chatter of the audience briefly following her out before it was scooped back and held in by the doors as they closed behind her. Holding her phone to her ear she ran outside, the sudden coolness of the night and the dim lighting making her wish she had company. She had left Bree behind in her haste to get outside.

'Pru!'

She turned to see Maggie, closely followed by Bree, running after her. Relief washed over her as she waved the phone at them. 'I've got to phone Andy, let him know what's going on.'

Maggie stepped in front of her. 'I know who she is, and I

think I might know where she is, but we don't have much time. Come on! This way... We need the old site map from Ralph's office. I remember seeing a framed edition on his wall...'

They began to run towards reception, Pru still trying to contact Andy. His voicemail answered on what seemed like the hundredth ring. She waited for his message to finish and for the beep to tell her she could speak. 'Andy, there's something happening here, there's something not right. It's to do with the old murders, and maybe the new ones too...' she blurted out, her voice going up several octaves as the words tumbled over each other. 'You need to get here, and let Ezra know too. There's a crazy woman with four hostages pretending it's a game, but it isn't a game, it's really happening, I think she's the "Grim Sleeper". Her name's Sophie. Andy, please get here quickly.'

Lucy looked at her watch, yawned and rubbed her eyes. They stung from far too much screen time. She had been keeping her fingers crossed that her team would finish on time, but Andy had sanctioned overtime with the DI for her and two DCs. It was now nearly 9pm, with no sign of a wind down. The combination of names they had been given for Elodie by Serena Porter had yielded nothing of value, apart from a copy of the original birth certificate. Running that name through the system had also been depressingly negative.

'Luce, what have you got on Giselle Moreau from the original attempted murder job at Cragstone Manor? Once we trace her, she's going to be worth speaking to.' Andy chucked a file on his desk and rubbed the back of his neck; the beginnings of a headache had kicked in with a vice-like grip on the muscles.

Lucy swivelled her chair around to face him. 'I was just

about to give you a shout on that. Giselle Moreau was an alias, her real name was Margaret Henshaw, born in 1968 in Liverpool...'

Andy dragged a spare chair over to sit next to her, just as his phone began to vibrate in his pocket. He checked the caller screen. It was rare that he wouldn't answer to Pru, but his nightly call with her to say how much he missed her and for several air kisses would have to wait; this was important. He let it ring, waiting for his voicemail to kick in. 'Right, so any reason for an alias?'

She shook her head. 'Nothing nefarious, just to simply reinvent herself. She was apparently ashamed of her roots and found it difficult to be accepted in the world of classical dance as a less privileged teenager. She was clever, great with accents and languages, so it was pretty seamless for her to become Giselle.' Lucy scrolled the screen. 'After the fall, she spent years in rehabilitation with injuries to her pelvis, back, legs and some facial reconstruction. She gave up teaching, reverted back to her real name and never danced again.'

Andy tapped his pen on the edge of the desk. 'So, where is she now?'

'You're going to have kittens when I tell you, I've just done a search on her given name, and this promo photo popped up.' Lucy pointed to the screen. 'She's at Harmony Hollows on the entertainment team.'

Knowing his appearance at Harmony Hollows to interview Maggie would fill Pru with delight, he remembered she had called. He picked up his phone, clicked on voicemail and listened. Lucy watched his expression change, and his body language become tense. He finished the call and tried to ring Pru without success. Three calls went unanswered.

'Lucy, get me DS Ezra Maynard at Nettleton Shrub CID on the phone.' He fumbled with his mobile phone and keyed 'Ez' into his contacts list. Ezra's personal number popped up. 'Second thoughts, give him a ring on that.' He threw his phone at Lucy.

'Come on! Do it on the hoof, we're needed at Harmony Hollows urgently, and tell Ezra to get there too.'

DEFENDANT NUMBER 2

DELLA

Having given her audience time to digest Ralph's story, Sophie readied herself to present Della's story. The short hiatus she had given them to make notes and to pop to the bar for another drink or two had also allowed her time to throw a mental leash around the 'other her'. She was afraid that if she allowed it to emerge too early, like a butterfly, its wings would perish in the wrong season.

The staccato pulse of the red light once again became static. She was on.

'Welcome back, ladies, gentlemen, and members of the jury. I now give you Delphine "Della" Claybourne.

'Della was just sweet sixteen and never been kissed when she was at Harmony Hollows during May 1983, taking part in the dance championships. She was just one of so many young girls that fell under the spell of Larry Belfont...'

Sophie positioned her chair so that she could sit next to Della. Taking in her current demeanour, it was hard to believe that Della had ever been young or pretty. Her hair was knotted and stuck to her forehead with perspiration. Her eyes, haunted but haggard in equal measure, the terror she was feeling being played out upon the deep wrinkles that creased her temples.

'On the promise of love, and that she was so very special, Larry seduced poor young Della and then, just as quickly, broke that promise. Della, used, abandoned and humiliated, was forced to watch Larry ride the waltzers with another potential conquest – Debbie Purkiss.'

A small tic began to manifest itself at the corner of Sophie's mouth, it spasmed across her cheek and was quickly followed by an uncontrollable jerk of her right shoulder. Her head twitched and tilted. She pulled the mental leash tighter; she didn't need the 'other' her just yet.

'Della followed Larry and Debbie back to Chalet 13, the rage building so freely in one so young. She heard Larry make the same promise to Debbie that he had made to her, before taking Debbie in his arms. Rage has to be expressed, it has to be released, it has to be appeased, so Della did the only thing she could to stop the pain of rejection...'

Sophie stood behind Della and grabbed a handful of her hair, yanking her head so that it faced towards the camera.

'Murder!'

ABANDON SHIP

Ethel put her pencil down and took a slurp of the sweet sherry that Clarissa had brought to the table. 'I don't like this at all, it's quite scary.' She looked around the Marina Lounge at the tables and chairs that had become vacant during the interval.

The once jovial atmosphere had morphed into a chilling and dark undercurrent. The majority of the audience had purchased their drinks, complained bitterly to the Marina Lounge team on the inappropriateness of the entertainment, and had chosen to take their beverages into the Blue Studio where poor Pinky Perkins had been hastily called upon to do a musical set to appease the guests.

Hilda grabbed her handbag and stood up. 'I'm not doing this anymore; it's not fun, it's horrible, and if I'm not mistaken, I think you'll find this is really happening. It's not a murder mystery trial at all.'

Her astuteness was not lost on Clarissa, who had had also noticed that Pru and Bree had disappeared, which set alarm bells ringing. If those two had scarpered somewhere together, there was definitely something afoot. 'Come on, ladies,' she said as she slugged back the remnants of her brandy. 'I know we've all been dying for a bit of excitement; I think this may be it...'

The four figures hurriedly ambled across the dance floor and disappeared through the door at the side of the stage, leaving Sophie Hopkins addressing a room that was rapidly beginning to resemble the Marie Celeste.

DEFENDANT NUMBER 3

KITTY

'Have we all powdered our noses and replenished our drinks?' Sophie pretended to wait for a response. 'Oh good, so are we all ready for the next part of the story? Excellent.'

She positioned her chair at the side of Kitty. Sophie was a little concerned that this one might expire through fright before she had the chance to do the deed herself. She hoped not, as that would take all the pleasure away from what so far, had been a truly exhilarating evening. All those years of planning, research and resolve had come to this moment, so to lose one to natural causes rather than by her own fair hand, would be such a blow.

'It's okay, Kitty, I'll be as gentle as I can with you...' Sophie insincerely simpered.

'I now present to you Kathleen Norma Hardcastle, better known to her friends as Kitty. Now Kitty is a bit of a latecomer to this trial. She was one that hadn't appeared in any documents, newspaper clippings or searches, so I must apologise if her story seems a little scant.'

Kitty, her eyes wide in horror, trembling from head to foot, began to fight against her restraints, her chair wobbled and teetered, forcing Sophie to intervene. She gripped her by the shoulders and forced Kitty and the chair back onto four legs. She tutted and wagged her finger. 'Now, now, Kitty, don't be a silly girl, you'll only make things worse.

'Kitty is a stalwart member of the Winterbottom Women's Institute, but what her lovely friends have only just discovered, is that Kitty was also a bit of a jezebel in her day.'

Sophie dramatically lifted her hand to her mouth to give an aside, as though she was sharing a secret with just the audience and not her captives. 'Still is, from what I've been hearing, just ask Frankie boy from Rubber Springs and Gaskets coach tours! Anway, I digress from our story...

'Kitty was another of Larry's conquests, another sweet sixteen. I think we're seeing a bit of a pattern here. He took her innocence the evening before his own life was taken. Kitty didn't take too kindly to being passed over, did you, Kitty? Was it revenge for taking something that was so precious from you, your virginity? Or maybe fear when he threatened to tell your parents about your little rough and tumble on the sacking in the beer shed if you didn't stop fawning over him, cramping his style? Or was it your insatiable jealousy of Debbie Purkiss, who you believed took him from you?'

Kitty's terror was now mixed with shame and shock.

'Surprised are we, Kitty? I know what you're thinking. How on earth did I know that?' Sophie had an arrogant triumph about her. 'Because of this...'

She held up a small brown book. 'Larry had a journal; you were all just ticks and crosses on his pages with marks out of ten!' She quickly rounded on Nellie. 'I found your hidey hole, Nellie; thieving magpies just love to hoard things, don't they?

'So, struck with shame, fear and jealousy, Kitty did the only thing

she could under the circumstances, whether it was to stop Larry from snitching to mummy and daddy, or to exact revenge on Debbie...'

Sophie smirked as she approached the camera.

'Murder!'

DEFENDANT NUMBER 4

NELLIE

Sophie, completely oblivious to the furore her broadcast was causing back at the Marina Lounge and around Harmony Hollows itself, was gearing up for her final story. She had left this one until last as it was the most delicious of the four. She had no concerns that she would be interrupted by anyone, least of all the extra security patrols that had been brought in, until after she had relieved each one of them of their lives, just as Debbie Purkiss had been relieved of hers. She was confident that the only two people who knew of the existence of her dark room beside herself, and the whereabouts of her victims, were both currently hog-tied and gagged, sitting on chairs in front of her.

Ralph and Nellie.

She composed herself, allowing the mental leash to gain some slack. Now was the time for the 'other' her to be released; she needed her for what she was about to do. She had thought long and hard over her ending, and it was perfect.

The red light on the camera once again became static, Sophie fixed a welcoming smile on her face, but it was a smile that failed to reach her eyes.

'Well, I hope you all have enjoyed the evening so far. What a murder mystery event this has been, ladies and gentlemen! But before I forget, I must offer my thanks to Ralph, Della, Kitty and Nellie, as without their assistance, tonight would not have been possible. Volunteers are so hard to find, but they certainly stepped up to the plate, wouldn't you agree?' The laughter that followed wasn't hers anymore – it was the other her. Its echo was distant. She closed her eyes, trying to decide if it was approaching her or drifting away. As she slowly began to lose herself, the thoughts of Sophie that was the 'here and now' began to fade in and out like a waning heartbeat. 'Not yet, it's too soon...' she hissed. 'I haven't finished.

'And last but not least, we have Nellie Girdlestone, better known as Nell Collins in her heyday at Harmony Hollows. Our Nellie, whom you will recognise as the one that cleans your chalets, used to be a drinks host and table girl at the Marina Lounge. By all accounts, according to Larry's journal, she was a bit of a stunner in her day, and no doubt you will have guessed it, she was another one of his floozies.'

Sophie looked disparagingly at Nellie and tutted. 'Not that you'd know that by looking at her now...' She snorted.

'Nellie was Larry's "go-to" when there was a dearth of attractive young ladies at Harmony. If it was a poor season for pickings, Larry would crawl back to the ever-willing Nellie and jump into her bed, but as soon as the coaches arrived and the young cuties piled off, Nellie was dropped like a hot potato, leaving only cold rumpled sheets to comfort her.'

Sophie stopped reading from her script and gave Nellie a look of false sympathy. 'Oh boy, that must have stung, Nell. What was it like to feel second best? Turned you into a bit of a stalker, didn't it? Larry couldn't get rid of you: every corner he turned; you were there.'

If hate and a desire to do something violent to someone could be portrayed with just one look, Nellie had perfected it.

She was nothing like Ralph, Della and Kitty. There was no fear in her eyes, no trembling, no frantic attempts to escape, no tears. Nellie was solid, she was calm. Her eyes held such savagery and cruelty, it was now Sophie's turn to feel a little uneasy. But she continued with her task.

'Now our Nellie has a bit of a sideline at Harmony Hollows. Nellie is like a tubby little magpie. She collects things – your things! All from your chalets under the guise of carrying out her daily cleaning chores. Jewellery, money, trinkets; in fact, anything she can sell without attracting suspicion. She also favoured a little bit of blackmail here and there, didn't you, Nellie?'

Sophie waved Larry Belfont's journal at her. 'It's all here, Nell, and oh what a bad girl you were!

'Ladies of the jury, it's here in black and white! Larry Belfont caught Nellie with her hand in the till snaffling the bar takings, and threatened to report her unless she packed up and left Harmony Hollows. He had no further use for her and she was becoming a thorn in his side.'

This time Sophie chose not to sit too close to Nellie; she remained out of arm's reach. She wasn't taking any chances. 'You didn't want to leave, did you, Nell? Harmony Hollows was your home, the only home you had ever known. Nor did you relish the prospect of being arrested...' For the final time, Sophie approached the camera, ensuring it focused only on her face before she spoke.

'So Nellie did the only thing she could do under the circumstances...'

She allowed her tongue to moisten her lips, her breath, shallow but sharp, eliciting her special word.

Murder!'

Sophie had thought long and hard about her ending. Everything had been for show. There was to be no trial by jury, no verdicts given, no meaningless sentences to be carried out.

This was all smoke and mirrors; it had just been a delicious game.

They were all guilty.

She flicked a switch and turned off the camera. It had done its duty, now their crimes and scandals had been publicly revealed.

All their deadly sins.

She rearranged the four lengths of rope she had cut to size and tested one. Sophie relished the pull as she yanked the ends apart. She had contemplated cutting their throats with the large butcher's knife she had reverently laid out on the table, but on reflection, that would have been far too messy. She would strangle them, one by one, a fitting death that would mirror the murder of poor Debbie Purkiss.

Ralph Fairbright: lust, jealousy and objectification – GUILTY.

Della Claybourne: Shame, jealousy and rage – GUILTY.

Kitty Hardcastle: Fear and jealousy – GUILTY.

Nellie Girdlestone: The murder of Debbie Purkiss and Larry Belfont – GUILTY.

Sophie had known all along that it had been Nell's hands that had wrapped themselves around Debbie's neck. She had known all along that it had been Nell's arm that had ferociously pounded down on Larry's head wielding a metal doorstop, until his skull was crushed and he was unrecognisable.

She had always known.

A fellow inmate at Waverley Park Sanatorium had unburdened herself before death, and Sophie had been her bedside confidant. Annie Bloom had been sworn to secrecy by the one person who had known the truth about the Harmony Hollows murders. Her sister...

Nellie Girdlestone.

It had been pure fate that Annie had chosen Sophie to

confess her all, and that sobering confession had set Sophie on the road to self-discovery.

But they had all been complicit in their own way. They had all been at Chalet 13 after the deed was done on that fateful night, and they had each failed to intervene. Debbie Purkiss might have lived if just one of them had raised the alarm, but instead they chose to leave her to die, more fearful for their own reputations. Three chances to save a life.

Ralph, Della and Kitty.

They had it coming,

They only had themselves to blame...

THE NAUGHTY SQUAD

Maggie used her shoulder and hip to push against the door to Ralph's office. The lock popped easily, leaving Pru and Bree astonished at her breaking and entering skills. She clicked the desk lamp on and pulled a large, framed print from the wall and placed it on the desk.

'Here you go, Harmony Hollows in its heyday, 1968...' Her finger traced the plan through the glass. 'There!' She stabbed at the far corner of the resort map. 'That's the old fairground site; it's been abandoned for donkey's years.'

Pru and Bree leant over her shoulder, taking in the black lines, pathways and little squares that represented the chalets dotted around the camp. It had changed quite considerably over the years. 'What's that?' Pru pointed to a block of lines that were heavily shaded either side.

'That's the old underground inspection tunnels. They lead to a bunker system, which used to house all the workings for the fairground. Mark once showed me an old photo of the generator room, and that's when I recognised the distinctive caged lighting behind Sophie on the live feed.' As she was talking, Maggie was rummaging around in Ralph's store cupboard. 'Here, take these.' She handed two torches to Bree, whilst Pru frantically tried to phone Andy again. It was engaged. With no time to spare she tapped out a text telling him where they would be, and took a photograph of the site plan.

Within minutes, they were running along the path that led to the camp backlot. It was well hidden from view by trees and hedges and was surrounded by a large chain-linked fence. Maggie found a gap and squeezed through, closely followed by Pru and Bree.

'Hey, girls, wait for us...'

Pru stopped in her tracks and side-eyed Bree, the familiar voice making her heart sink. She turned to face her caller. 'Ethel! What on earth are you doing here?' She looked behind Ethel and groaned. 'And Clarissa, Hilda, and Millie too! You shouldn't be here. Please go back to the Marina Lounge; we'll see you there later.' But the full complement of her Naughty Squad stood their ground, chins jutted out with a determination that she knew only too well.

'We're here to help... Many hands make light work, Pru. We're in this together – and besides which, we've got to deliver our verdict to Sophie!' Ethel was adamant in her stance.

Exasperated and fraught, Maggie rounded them up. 'Look, we haven't got time to stand here arguing. This is going to be dangerous, so you've either got two seconds to go back to your chalets, and put your winceyettes on, or face the consequences with us!'

Hilda was most put out. 'For all you know, dear, I might sleep in my birthday suit!' she snapped back.

'Dear God, woman...' Ethel sniggered. 'They wouldn't know what to iron: you or the ruddy bedsheets!'

The Four Wrinkled Dears, fuelled by a few too many sherries, giggled uncontrollably, forcing Pru to hush them. 'If you're coming with us, keep the noise down and do as we tell you...'

Maggie ushered them together and led the way. The seven silhouettes bobbed in and out of shrubs and bushes; their shadows cast from eerie lighting, elongated and then just as quickly shrunk back against broken billboards and cracked walls. They passed the haunting outline of the old waltzers, the hook-a-duck stand, and what was left of the big wheel, its warped metal standing like a disjointed skeleton against the night sky.

'Ooh look, girls, a merry-go-round!' Hilda, suddenly sidetracked, ambled over to the carousel, and climbed onto the decking, her fingers stroking the faded and peeling paint of a once white horse, its galloping legs paused and frozen in time. She clung on to its mane, jammed one foot onto the stand, and cocked her leg up, landing heavily in the saddle. 'And they're off...' She whooped, slapping the haunch of her long-abandoned steed.

'Bloody hell, Hilda, we're on a mission! What on earth are you playing at? Get down right now!' Clarissa hissed.

Suitably chastised, Hilda pouted and did as she was told. 'I must be getting old, I think that dismount has just put me hip out...' she grumbled, as the now aptly named 'Magnificent Seven' continued on in their quest.

Eventually Maggie stopped by a crumbling brick wall covered with ivy and pulled a section of greenery to one side to reveal a door.

Pushing it quietly open, one by one, they all disappeared inside.

~

'Ezra is going to meet us there; he's bringing an Operational Support team with him.' Lucy's hand shot up and grabbed what they fondly called the 'Jesus handle', particularly when Andy was driving. She clung on for dear life as he rounded a bend.

'My phone has just pinged; what does it say?' He dropped down a gear to take the next bend before accelerating out of it. His eye caught the road sign that told him Nettleton Shrub was another six miles away.

She clicked it open and quickly scanned the text. 'Oh dear, Pru's doing her usual and has gone off on a murder hunt. She's sent directions as to where they'll be; it's some sort of generator bunker on a disused fairground. She's sent a screen shot of a site plan.'

Andy's jaw clenched painfully. The already tense knot that had gnawed at his gut since her voicemail message had now grown tenfold. 'Forward that to Ezra, tell him we'll meet him there.'

The headlights picked out trees and hedges as he raced along the lanes towards Harmony Hollows. He just hoped he wouldn't be too late.

WHY NELLIE, WHY?

Sophie opened the celebration bottle of wine and poured herself a glass. She relished the burn of the red liquid as it slid down her throat. She tipped her head and admired her four captives, wondering which one she would despatch first.

'Eeny meeny miny moe...' Her finger bounced from one head to the next until she stopped at Nellie. She could almost feel the palpable relief that emanated from Ralph, Della and Kitty. 'As you are the actual murderer of Debbie and Larry, I think that honour should go to you.'

Nellie sat rigid in her chair with not an ounce of fear or remorse showing in her eyes. It rankled Sophie. This was supposed to make her feel better, for her bloody awful life to have some reason for how things had turned out. She needed to hear it from Nellie's own lips. She ripped off her gag. 'Why, Nellie?' she rasped. 'Come on, it takes a psycho to know one, we all like to have our moment of glory. Tell me yours.'

Nellie's steel blue eyes didn't leave their target. They followed Sophie as she flitted around the room. Finally, she spoke.

'You haven't got a bloody clue. You're a beginner, Sophie, a pathetic little wannabe...' Spittle flew from Nellie's mouth as the rage that had been held in check began to surface.

'Aww, have I touched a nerve? Just two little murders and you think you're Hannibal Lecter! Don't make me laugh.' Sophie wound the piece of rope she had selected for Nellie around her hand. She stood behind her, ready.

Nellie slowly turned her head. 'I'm double figures. Sophie – double figures, my dear. Thieving trinkets just wasn't enough, it soon lost the excitement, but a game of bloodbath bingo every now and then, well, that was the icing on the cake...' She licked her lips. 'Mary, Trevor and Troy, all mine, and so many more over the years. I'm invisible, Sophie, nobody notices the old hag of a domestic, do they? If you pick the right victim, they think it's just natural causes, a heart attack here, a stroke there; doctored drinks and little gifts are so easy when you play to their wants and greed.' Nellie cackled loudly as she winked at Ralph. 'It's all about that last breath, it's quite delicious, and such a privilege to see and share it, and an honour to know that I have facilitated it. That's what Debbie and Larry gave me: they gave me purpose.'

Sophie stared long and hard at Nellie. They really weren't that different from each other, only it was Nellie who had inadvertently created Sophie by her murderous ways; she had made her who she was.

'Never underestimate your enemy...' Nellie hissed.

'Oh believe me, I won't...' Sophie grinned as she placed the rope around Nellie's neck. She pulled the ends together at the nape and began to twist and tighten it. As she watched Nellie's skin pucker under the hemp, she called upon the 'other' her to come forward, to take up the mantle, Sophie needed her strength. She leant in close to Nellie's ear. 'Au revoir, bitch...'

A sudden commotion from behind the door momentarily distracted Sophie and gave Nellie time to act. She jerked her head backwards and forcefully butted Sophie in the face. Sophie released her grip on the rope and automatically threw her hands up. A shooting pain sparked behind her eyes as a warm, sticky wetness flowed through her fingers from her nose. She slumped to the floor.

The force she had used to take out Sophie made Nellie topple over backwards, still attached to the chair. She landed on the concrete floor, her head taking a sharp blow as she landed. Stunned, she lay there as the door to the bunker burst open, throwing Maggie Henshaw through its threshold, followed by a ragtag band of women who spilled in after her adding to the chaos.

Nellie's guttural laugh bounced from the walls of their makeshift prison as she eyed their assembly. 'Bloody hell, hold on to your hats, boys and girls, the Bloomer Brigade have arrived...'

TALLY HO!

Maggie had been the first through the door, closely followed by Pru and Bree, and bringing up the rear, the Four Wrinkled Dears. Hilda's war cry of 'To infinity and beyond' as she tripped over the threshold, throwing her full weight into Ralph's lap, made Clarissa wince.

'We really must stop meeting like this...' Hilda chuckled, in an attempt to lighten the fraught mood. Ralph looked decidedly uncomfortable as Hilda dug her elbow into his groin to ease herself up.

'Pru, get a grip of Sophie, see if she's okay, but keep her down...' Maggie took control directing each one of them to a task.

Bree and Clarissa helped pull Nellie's chair upright, with Millie untying the rope that had bound her hands to the wooden arms. Nellie gave a furtive glance towards Sophie as Millie moved to untie her legs. Sophie was still lying on the floor, with Pru fussing around her. Nellie's eyes darted around the room and, seeing the open door, her decision was made. Before anyone could react or suspect her, she was up on her feet, barging Hilda out of the way. For the second time in as many minutes, she ended up in Ralph's lap.

Nellie took to her toes at a pace that belied her size and age; she was down the tunnel and out through the main door before the others could point their fingers at her guilt.

'What the hell...?' Pru was suddenly pushed backwards by Sophie, her level of consciousness now giving her the ability to react. Sophie was quick, too quick. Pru made a grab for her, but her fingers barely clutched at Sophie's jacket before she pulled away from her. She stumbled forwards, grabbed the knife from the table and disappeared through the door in pursuit of Nellie.

Maggie's reaction was instantaneous. 'You take care of this lot; I'll go after her...' She didn't wait for a response before she too had gone.

Blue lights from several police vehicles reflected and bounced from the twisted metal of the roller coaster, their strobing effect adding an eerie touch to the abandoned fairground. Andy, Lucy and Ezra stood at the chain link fence.

'Right, the OS Team have formed a cordon. We need...' A sudden movement near to the fence line distracted Ezra. 'Hey, stop...'

The heavy-set figure that lumbered out of the darkness veered away from them, and then just as quickly disappeared behind one of the few remaining fairground kiosks. Ezra alerted his team before squeezing through the gap in the fence. 'What's on that far side, Andy?'

Andy checked the site map again. 'A covered arcade. It's extensive, and stretches right to the boundary line of Harmony Hollows.' He peered into the darkness, desperate for a glimpse of Pru to know she was safe. 'This way...'

'Right, let the team search it, we need to find this bunker.' Ezra took the lead, tracking his way through the bushes and dilapidated hot-dog and ice-cream stands, with Lucy and Andy trailing behind.

THE STUFF OF NIGHTMARES

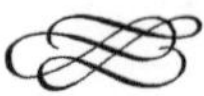

Emerging out into the chill air, Sophie stopped and listened. She could hear shouting coming from the break in the fence, the only route out of the fairground, and then suddenly Nellie's lumbering silhouette broke out from behind the waltzers. Sophie tracked Nellie's progress, assisted by the bright full moon. She was making for the indoor section of the fairground.

At any other time, Sophie would have called it quits. The most dangerous part of the derelict fairground was the arcade, but her desire to see Nellie dead was stronger than her desire to ensure her own safety.

She gripped the knife to her chest, and throwing caution to the wind followed her.

~

Nellie stopped and listened.

The arcade had been the last place she had wanted to find herself, but with all escape routes cut off, she had been forced to come here. The huge building, with its twisted metal girders holding rotted floorboards above her head, was oppressive. Almost everything had been stripped from inside, leaving a smashed fruit machine that had been tipped on its side and empty kiosks lined up against the walls. The children's teacup ride would not have been amiss in a horror movie. The one-eared white rabbit in the centre, his top hat held up by a clawed paw, displayed a crack that ran the length of his face, distorting his eyes and nose.

It was the stuff of nightmares, and, true to form, this was her nightmare.

Nellie had nowhere to go but up.

She closed her eyes, trying to imagine any other escape route, but the only one available was upstairs to the next level, into the old offices and through the fire-escape door. From there she could drop down onto the flat roof and then over the perimeter wall of Harmony Hollows.

Crack!

Nellie's head jerked around as the sound of glass crunching underfoot alerted her to the fact that she was not alone.

'Come on, Nellie, I know you're here.' Sophie's voice echoed around the void. 'I won't let this go; I won't rest until you are dead. You do know that, don't you?'

Nellie toyed with the idea of flight or fight. If she had been less woozy from the blow to her head she would have stood her ground, but now was not the time to stay and play. She quickly edged her way around the walls until she found the staircase. Slowly and silently, she made her way upstairs, using the metal railing to steady herself.

She crept carefully across the expanse of floor, the door to the office in her sights.

'Boo!'

Nellie nearly had kittens. Her heart pounded so savagely she thought it would burst through her blouse. Standing in front of her was Sophie, a strange, malevolent smile picked out by the moonlight, greeting her. 'Hello, Nellie, we meet again.'

This time there was no flight; Nellie was going to have to fight. She lunged at Sophie, her weight and size taking the slight frame of her adversary with her. They coupled together, grappling and rolling across the floor, forcing plumes of dust and debris to rise and dance in the shaft of moonlight that shone through the hole in the roof.

Nellie had not anticipated Sophie to be as strong as she was; it was taking more effort to contain her than she would have liked. Sophie pulled away, crawling on her hands and knees across the floor. Nellie grabbed her by the ankles and dragged her back, her nails raking her skin.

For one brief moment, tangled on the damp musty floorboards together, they paused to face each other. Nellie looked deep into Sophie's eyes and for the first time in her life, saw an evil that equalled her own. Without warning, a sharp, intense pain suddenly punched her gut, as Sophie's arm jerked upwards. Nellie fell to one side, a warm wetness seeping through her clothes. She looked down at the handle of a knife that was embedded in her belly.

Nellie laughed, the sudden shock of her predicament confusing her as she caressed the smooth black enamel with her fingers. 'Touché, Sophie, touché...' she whispered as she held her hand up and marvelled at the blood glistening on her skin.

If time had been an option for Sophie, she would have celebrated her triumph and revealed her true self to Nellie, but fate had other ideas. A loud cracking noise assailed their ears as the floor beneath them shuddered, dropped and then opened up. They both frantically clawed out at the splintered wood, and then at each other, as they desperately tried to save themselves.

Falling,

Down,

Down,

Down.

Nellie and Sophie, limbs bent and broken, landed heavily, still entangled together, on the concrete floor twenty-five feet below, amongst an avalanche of debris.

In the eerie silence, they both lay embraced together, a falsehood of position that made them appear friends rather than sworn enemies. Nellie's life force was rapidly leaving her as she rasped loudly, struggling for breath. 'Why? Why should you care?'

Sophie's eyes narrowed with pure, unadulterated hate. She had never despised anyone as much as Nellie. 'Because you just didn't take away Debbie's life when you murdered her – you took away mine as well...' she spat.

A look of confusion spread across Nellie's face, but with no time to understand, she began to rattle and gurgle. She spasmed once, twice and then finally fell silent. Her head lolled to one side, her eyes, glassy and still, holding no regret, no apology, and no peace.

Sophie lay motionless. She felt no pain, just a surreal sense of tranquillity. She had finally found her release: she was free.

Nellie had been so right; it *was* all about the last breath.

ABSOLUTION

Maggie stood over the two bodies, twisted together in a macabre embrace. She cleared a space of glass and debris and knelt down next to Sophie. Pulling her away from Nellie, she took her in her arms and comforted her, stroking her hair and wiping her tears, the rusted shard of metal protruding from her chest catching the moonlight. 'Oh, my little Elodie, where did it all go so terribly wrong...?' Maggie soothed.

Sophie blinked to clear her eyes, taking in the woman who had seemed so familiar to her, a woman that, given different circumstances, would have been gifted chair number four and almost certain death. 'Who *are* you?' she whispered.

'Ah mon enfant, tu ne me reconnais pas?' Maggie gave her a wistful smile.

Sophie's face softened as she remembered. 'Miss Giselle! Is it really you?'

Maggie nodded, cradling her like a mother would a child. She knew Sophie's life was slowly ebbing away. For all that had happened between them, her heart broke for the young girl she had once been, the child that had tried so hard to please.

Sophie slowly lifted her hand and touched Maggie gently on the cheek, her finger tracing the deep scar. 'I'm so sorry, will you ever forgive me?'

Knowing she had the power to absolve Sophie of her guilt and anguish, to give her a peaceful passing, Maggie gave a wistful smile. 'I already have...' she said as she held Sophie's hand tightly. 'It was so long ago, we're different people now. But why the others, Sophie? Why Nellie?'

Acceptance settled upon Sophie's face as she looked up through the fractured floorboards, her pale blue eyes taking her higher and higher through the hole in the roof to where the dark indigo sky held dancing stars and moonbeams of light.

'It was for my mum.' Sophie wept, an eerie, almost profound moment where the tears fell, but she made no sound. 'Debbie was my mum...'

Maggie stroked her face, trying to bring a peacefulness to her final moments by giving tenderness to the little girl that had never known love.

'I am the clouds that gather. I am the winds that destroy. I am the lightning that strikes...' Sophie coughed, her breath becoming more laboured.

'I *was* the perfect storm...'

In the silence that hung between them, Sophie May Hopkins closed her eyes for the last time, carrying with her the knowledge that she, and she alone, was the only person in her life that had been present for both her first breath, as well as her last.

'Death is not the greatest loss in life.
The greatest loss is what dies inside us while we live...'
— Norman Cousins (1915–1990)

IT'S A WRAP

Ezra and his team stood back, a reluctant audience to the grotesque tableau of death in front of them. Broken glass glittered on the floor; the fractured boards of the arcade, snapped and splintered, lay around them. For all his years in the job, the poignancy of Maggie weeping as she cradled the broken body of Sophie, with the spreadeagled corpse of Nellie lying next to them, still pulled at his heart.

He sighed deeply, allowing a moment of reverence for them both. 'Can you call it up, Andy? Hostages released, no serious injuries, and two dead...'

By the time they had found the bunker entrance, Pru and Bree had already released Ralph, Kitty and Della, and were leading them out through the tunnel with the help of the ladies that Andy so fondly referred to as the four Miss Marples. Their Ealing Comedy gait as the old dears crossed the desolate lot had given a strange feeling of light entertainment alongside the harsh reality of death.

'Lucy, can you deal with Maggie? We need to secure the scene and bring SOCO in.' Ezra handed her a small pack of travel tissues. 'Here, you might need these.'

Lucy gratefully accepted them. She could see how distraught Maggie was. 'Will do, Sarge. The trembling trio have been taken by ambulance to Nettleton Shrub A&E. I've arranged a patrol to follow up and get first account statements from them.' She looked to see how Andy was faring with Pru and Bree. She had decided to give them space as she really didn't fancy being privy to Andy giving the pair of them down the banks for once again poking their noses into an investigation.

She totted up on her fingers. This night would culminate in five current murders and two historic ones being stamped and filed as solved, not to mention any others that had come to light from Ezra's ongoing enquiries at Harmony Hollows.

She huffed loudly. They had certainly been on the right track when they'd nicknamed this place 'Harmony Horrors'. She felt a little sad that the original detective inspector on the Purkiss-Belfont murder enquiry, old Dennis Skelhorn, hadn't lived long enough to see the result.

'Well...' Hilda huffed loudly as she clinked her sherry glass down on the bedside cabinet in Chalet 13, Marigold Lawns.

Ethel rolled her eyes. 'Well, what? Well, that was a nice holiday, or well, I didn't think much of the entertainment – or how about, "Well, that was a bit of a buttock-clenching moment"?'

Clarissa laughed. 'Probably all three, with more thrown in, as and when we think of them. I must say, I never liked that Nellie, but can you imagine someone of her age being responsible for all those murders?' She eagerly replenished everyone's glass with a top up of Harveys.

The Four Wrinkled Dears sat in silence as they savoured

their drinks and thought long and hard on what the evening had held for them.

'What's wrong with being that age? We still have fun, don't we? We can still kick ass when needed. We're the Fearsome Foursome...' Ethel chuckled.

'More like the Farcical Foursome! Honestly, girls, when will you ever learn? I can't believe you actually thought it was a good idea to go creeping around Harmony Hollows, knowing full well we had a psycho running amok!' Pru stood in the doorway, hands on hips, trying her best to look annoyed at them whilst secretly admiring their tenacity and zest for adventure. She hoped that when she and Bree arrived at the age they were, they would still have the WI ladies' passion and enthusiasm for life and, dare she say it, their attraction to danger. She gave Bree a complicit smile.

'Two psychos, we had two psychos and how bloody exciting it was too!' Ethel corrected her. 'I'd been feeling so down since losing my Albie, but this has given a bit of colour to my cheeks. Anyway, you can talk. You two weren't exactly backwards at coming forwards!'

'But it could just as easily have got you killed too, Ethel!' Bree added her tuppence worth. 'We're just so relieved everyone is safe, but sadly we've decided to pack up and leave early tomorrow – whilst we still can! So enjoy your last night, behave in a manner that won't get you into any more trouble, and we'll see you at reception 10am sharp.'

As the chalet door clicked shut behind Pru and Bree, Clarissa, Ethel, Millie and Hilda sat on the two beds, subdued and disappointed.

Ethel slugged back her sherry and held her glass out for more in an act of rebellion. 'I shall behave in any manner I wish, Bree Richards: with mischief, audacity, outright naughtiness and a bloody good story to tell. I'll be damned if I'll meet my Albie at those pearly gates one day with a ruddy slipped halo around me neck instead of a purple pashmina from Frugal Finds!'

To laughter and warm hugs, the ladies of the Winterbottom Women's Institute, toasted their quirky ways, their firm friendships and almost ten days of alcohol poisoning accompanied by yet another near-death experience...

And to their next big adventure!

AN ANNOUNCEMENT

For the first time since their adventures at Harmony Hollows and the thankfully uneventful trip back to Winterbottom, Pru felt she could breathe a sigh of relief. She had once again managed to get all her ladies back home safely, and with stories to tell their children and grandchildren for months to come.

'It didn't go quite as planned, did it?' She placed the tea tray on the coffee table and handed Andy the plate of biscuits. 'Life can be so cheap sometimes.' Her bottom lip wobbled slightly as the image of Maggie cradling Sophie invaded her thoughts again.

Andy popped the bookmark between the pages of his current read, ready to give her his undivided attention, and raised an eyebrow at her choice of evening beverage. 'It can, but the important thing is to remember there is more good in this world than bad. Sometimes circumstances influence people and cause further harm to an emotional state that is already fragile, and then we see the results. Harmony Hollows was just the catalyst.'

'I know, but for a child to be so affected by what happened to her that she kills others for pleasure... it's just awful.' Pru took a sip of her tea.

'Sophie was damaged from the beginning, Pru; it was events that compounded that damage. As soon as Sophie discovered who she really was and that she was sold to the Mayer-Marshalls, in her mind Elodie ceased to exist. Then to discover her real mother had been murdered, well, it set her on a road she had no chance of turning back from. Meeting Nellie's sister in Waverley Park was pure chance and sheer bloody bad luck.'

'So she really *did* kill those elderly sisters in Little Kipling then?'

Andy nodded and kissed the top of her head, inhaling the scent from her freshly washed hair. 'She did, and she killed Nellie too. If you and Maggie hadn't intervened when you did, she would no doubt have murdered Ralph, Della and Kitty.'

Pru nibbled on the biscuit to quash the nausea that had suddenly swished around her tummy. 'And Nellie? Did she kill people just for pleasure too?'

'Yep, it was like living in a confectionery shop for her working at Harmony Hollows. She could pick and choose whatever victim took her fancy, according to the winning bingo numbers that dictated the chalet. Nellie used that method as a bit of added excitement. She wouldn't know who the victim would be until the number was called, so it kept her on her toes.' He grabbed a bourbon and bit into it, using the other half as a pointer to continue his explanation. 'She murdered Debbie and Larry through sheer jealousy, but discovered she actually enjoyed it. God knows how many she did away with over the years.' Andy felt some sympathy for Ezra, who would probably be running on that side of the investigation for months to come.

Pru shifted the cushions around to support her back and to keep her surprise for Andy out of sight. 'And Ralph, Kitty and

Della just happened to be in the right place at the wrong time, but they could have saved Debbie if they'd raised the alarm?'

'No, according to the 1983 report, death was instantaneous, I think that was just something Sophie got into her head; she had to blame someone. Anyway, what's done is done. It's sad so many people were affected and that some died as a result.'

They sat cuddled together, a calm, comforting silence between them. Pru watched the minutes tick by on the wall clock.

'Andy...'

'Yes, my little turnip...'

'Remember that night you nipped home from Nether Wallop to comfort me after Albert passed away?'

'I certainly do...'

'Well, my little stud muffin, you must have been on top form...' She laughed as she quickly whipped out the little pair of white crochet booties from behind her back and held them up for him to see.

'It would appear we're now cultivating a little swede in the vegetable patch that's due for harvesting in a little over seven months!'

EPILOGUE

The corridor was long and dimly lit. He tentatively took small steps, unsure if he should go further into the dark or turn back. His feet, clad in blue Vans Classics, wavered over the plush carpet runner. He held his arms out to the side and touched the walls, his fingers tracing along the wood panelling. He stopped at the first painting encased in an ornate gold frame.

She was so beautiful; he was in awe. He moved forward to be closer to her, only to step back suddenly, horrified at the deep welt around her neck, stark against her alabaster skin. He wanted to stay, to avenge her, but he was urged to move on. Although his heart wished to remain, his feet reluctantly carried him forward.

'Look at me, look at me...' the voice rasped from the darkness.

He tried to shy away from the demon of his dreams, eerily silhouetted against the window at the end of the corridor, but he was waiting for him, just as he did every single night. A night he was compelled to relive over and over again. But this time it would be different. The rage built within him as he continued on, finally reaching his destination. He flexed his muscles, feeling the power behind the weapon that was now gripped in his hand as he stood before him. He pulled back from the first strike losing the momentum, but the second blow was complete, its ferocity a pleasure.

One.

Two.

Three.

He continued to strike down, again and again, until his nemesis was crushed and unrecognisable. Sated, he dropped to his knees and cried out like a feral animal...

~

Ralph woke with a start, perspiration dripping from him as he peered into the darkness. The shouting and screaming that had assaulted his ears had come from his own lips. He pressed his face into his hands and wept.

'I didn't mean to, Larry, I thought you'd taken her from me,' he moaned. 'I thought you'd killed her.' Ralph savagely wiped the wetness from his face with the back of his hand and rose from his bed. Stumbling to the window, he pulled back the curtains and looked out to the ink-black sky, searching for answers from the ghosts of his past.

But he already knew the truth.

Larry had been innocent; it had been Nellie Girdlestone who had taken her from him. The only thing he had ever loved.

His little dancer.

And in her desire for a twisted and sadistic notoriety, Nellie had also confessed to one murder too many, something he now knew he had to rectify.

Ralph slowly made his way to his office, padded softly across the room and sat down at his desk. Taking a pen, a sheet of paper and a swig of Dutch courage from a whisky miniature that had been a work's Secret Santa gift, he fervently expunged his guilt onto the pale blue lines. Forty years of knowledge, forty years of pain and forty years of sin. He knew he would never find peace in this life, but perhaps his actions now would bestow him with an easier rest when his time eventually came. He licked his lips, relishing the spiced woody mixture.

I, Ralph Desmond Fairbright, wish to confess to the murder of Larry Belfont on the 23rd May 1983...

His story was brief, his remorse lingering. Every line held his grief, pain and regret. He carefully folded the paper, addressed the envelope, and slipped it inside. He moistened the flap and pressed down, sealing his confession. Draining the small bottle, he silently toasted the festive kindness of an unknown colleague, grateful for even the tiniest tipple in his hour of need.

Tick-tock, tick-tock...

As the minutes passed, counted down by the old wall clock, he suddenly succumbed to an intense pain that gripped at his heart, tearing his breath away. Ralph clutched his arm and gasped, his throat burning and a cold sweat covering him as he fell into the savage agony that coursed through his veins and seared his belly.

He slumped forward, the envelope still clutched in his hand. His eyes, hauntingly sad, rested upon the sepia-faded photograph in a gilt frame marked, *'Harmony Hollows Staff 1983'*. The small bottle, now empty of its lethal amber contents rolled across his desk, stopping as it touched a silver pendant engraved with a little dancer. How ironic that his confession would prove to be so timely.

Squeeze.

He stroked Debbie's hair away from her face, a rage building within him as she lay lifeless on the bathroom floor of Chalet 13, with Larry spreadeagled on the bed in a drunken stupor.

Throb.

He had to avenge her murder; he would make him pay.

The bloodied head of Larry Belfont played like an old movie behind his eyes. The deep scarlet slowly spreading out like a halo, unsure if it was a memory, or his own now tainted blood, pulsing through his veins.

An error of judgement, clouded by jealousy...

Beat.

One night...

Squeeze.

Two victims...

Crush.

Two killers...

Tick-tock.

Two identical miniature bottles and a sleight of hand...

Then silence.

And just like that, Ralph Desmond Fairbright, Harmony Hollows Greycoat, lusty Lothario, liar and murderer, was gone.

Nellie's final victim from beyond the grave.

'Life and death are one thread,
the same line viewed from different sides...'
— Lao Tzu

THE END

ALSO BY GINA KIRKHAM

PRUNELLA PEARCE MYSTERIES

Murders at the Winterbottom Women's Institute (Book 1)

Murders at the Montgomery Hall Hotel (Book 2)

Murders at the Rookery Grange Retreat (Book 3)

THE CONSTABLE MAVIS UPTON ADVENTURES

Handcuffs, Truncheon and a Polyester Thong (Book 1)

Whiskey Tango Foxtrot (Book 2)

Blues, Twos and Baby Shoes (Book 3)

ACKNOWLEDGEMENTS

I usually start with '*I never quite know where to start with acknowledgements*' and then rattle on for eternity – and to be honest, after several previous attempts on my other books, there's sadly still no sign of improvement!

I am always so very grateful for the smallest of things as much as the biggest of things in my life.

To the wonderful ladies of The Women's Institute. Without you there would be no Kitty, Ethel or Clarissa and no tales to tell. Your kindness, generosity and fabulous sense of humour became the inspiration for my characters. I loved your excitement and enthusiasm to be included, and hopefully I have created them just as you asked, like you, full of mischief, a little bit naughty and so much larger than life. Thank you for inviting me to speak at your meetings and thank you for all you selflessly do for others.

For Loulou Brown my brilliant editor. It has been a pleasure to work with you again and to get another chapter of *Murders* into shape, you made the whole process so simple, straightforward and stress free and best of all, you 'get' me, my humour and my style of writing. Here's to being together again in the future.

This is a very special thank you to Tara Lyons at Bloodhound Books. Tara you are an absolute dream to work with, not only did I gain a fabulous Senior Editorial & Production Manager when I signed with Bloodhound, I also gained a beautiful friend. Thank you just doesn't seem enough.

To Abbie Rutherford, who had the unenviable task of proof-reading *Harmony Hollows.* Thank you so much. I actually think vodka sounds so much better than Diamond White, and any bloopers you found were definitely down to predictive text and not me – honest!

I was over the moon this year to hear that Hannah Deuce was back with the team. I really appreciate all you do for me, Mavis and the Winterbottom Ladies. Massive thanks also go to Betsy and Fred the founders of Bloodhound Books for once again taking a chance on this quirky old trout!

I was honoured to be asked to participate in the **Children in Read** charity book auction again last year. Paddy Heron and his team from CiR do an amazing job and work so hard, they have raised a staggering £117,000.00 from their auctions. The winning bid for a dedicated, signed copy of *Murders at the Rookery Grange Retreat* and to have a character named after them in book four of the series, *Murders at The Harmony Hollows Resort,* was Mark Joynson. So, say hello to 'Mighty Marko'- Harmony Hollows sound engineer, lifeguard and imagined superhero!

On 29th November 2023, the world lost a truly lovely man, Dean Sullivan. He was a teacher, actor, writer, director and all-round beautiful person. Dean was such a rock to me in my early days of writing and gave me a wonderful piece of advice:

'Grab the passion to entertain and shake it hard darling, it'll either fall to pieces or burst into fruition...'.

I am so glad I listened to his wise words. I miss his laughter and kindness, his messages at daft hours and his fabulous selection of hats but most of all I miss his friendship. You are always in my thoughts, Dean.

Huge hugs and a thank you to Josephine Bilton and Maggie Rawet. Jo is my go-to for a first draft read through to make sure I'm on the right track with a storyline. She's been a superstar and gives great constructive feedback. Maggie is my friendly face in the audience and good luck charm when I do author events and appearances, she has been such a huge support over the years and as soon as I see her (usually front row isn't it, Maggie?) I know everything is going to be okay.

Special thanks to Lisa Cutts and Graham Thomas, without their expert advice and experience of major crime scenes and chain of command, I would probably still be scrabbling to get out of Mr Google's black hole of despair that I'd fallen in to whilst researching!

A big thank you and mention to Heidi and Chris Sharpe, hosts of The Old Coach House in Harrogate.

Their beautiful Airbnb cottage was my sanctuary for the final editing process of *Murders at The Harmony Hollows Resort* whilst in Harrogate for the Theakstons Old Peculier Crime Writing Festival in July. I don't want to praise it too highly or it'll get booked up and I'll miss out on staying there again – but it was absolutely fabulous, and they are the most perfect hosts!

I very quickly discovered how amazing readers and book bloggers are. There are too many to mention individually, and I would hate to miss someone out, so this is a collective thank you. A bit like a group hug. As writers, where would we be without them? Our words wouldn't be heard, our stories wouldn't be told. They would lie dormant on paper or screen, meaningless. They only come to life because people read them, enjoy them and spread their love of our books.

Once again (I have to mention him as I truly am the doting elder sister), to my very handsome, debonair brother, Andy Dawson – for no other reason than him being handsome, debonair and of course, my brother, and to his gorgeously funny wife, my new sister-in-law, Anne-Marie (aka Mrs Dawson). What a fabulous addition she is to our madcap family.

To my sister Claire, so far away but you will always be in my heart.

To my beautiful daughter, Emma and my gorgeous grandchildren, Olivia, Annie and Arthur. You are my sunshine, you make me smile every day, I'm so very blessed to have you in my life and to be part of yours.

And last but definitely not least, to my handsome and very funny hubby, John. The love of my life, my bodyguard, chauffeur and human SatNav. The man who makes me laugh every single day (and frequently think of murder too). He has endured hours of torment as my muse and 'go to' for ideas for this book and my previous ones. He rolls his eyes and groans but still continues to reluctantly participate in the most bizarre acts all in the name of research – well, at least that's what I tell him it's for! Without his love and support there would be no stories to tell – and I'd still be driving around various parts of the UK, panic struck and lost.

I hope I haven't missed anyone out, but knowing me and my scatterbrained head-thoughts, I probably have. I'm so sorry if you haven't appeared here because of my forgetfulness, but please know there is a humongous 'thank you' in my heart for you. You will always be so very much appreciated.

Gina x

A NOTE FROM THE PUBLISHER

Thank you for reading this book. If you enjoyed it please do consider leaving a review on Amazon to help others find it too.

We hate typos. All of our books have been rigorously edited and proofread, but sometimes mistakes do slip through. If you have spotted a typo, please do let us know and we can get it amended within hours.

info@bloodhoundbooks.com

Milton Keynes UK
Ingram Content Group UK Ltd.
UKHW031521230924
448673UK00004B/51

9 781917 214759